TO DAVID, NOA, MAYA, MAYA, AND IZZI—

MY EVERYTHING.

*And in loving memory of my beloved Grandma
Rachel—Survivor, Fighter, Mama Bear, and Executive
Chef in Heaven's Kitchen—the voice in my head.*

Good artists copy, great artists steal.

—PABLO PICASSO

You can look at a picture for a week and never think of it again. You can also look at a picture for a second and think of it all your life.

—JOAN MIRÓ

WOMAN ON FIRE

PROLOGUE

ART BASEL, MIAMI

FROM THE CORNER of her eye, Jules catches the woman's piercing anthracite stare, those distinct dark brows locked and loaded, observing her intensely as though she were a painting. Her pulse races as she pivots slightly, purposefully giving the woman a better view. *Careful*, she reminds herself. Every move counts.

Jules has prepped hard for this moment. She studied Margaux de Laurent's predilections, knows the woman's style and taste as though it were her own. She carefully assembled her look tonight. Gone is the bookish journalist, and in her place emerged this other being—elegant, sexy, and suggestive. Jules's unruly chestnut curls are blown out into beachy waves. She has shed her studious tortoiseshell glasses for contacts and is wearing a one-shoulder crimson Hervé Léger bandage dress that is glued to her body—curves that she's spent her whole life camouflaging beneath baggy sweatshirts. The dress was sent to her with one message: *This is what you're wearing*. The *or else* was implied. The sender doesn't know that Jules is already one step ahead of her.

The ensemble also came with shoes—four-inch-high Anika Baum stilettos—no surprise. Because Art Basel is not about the art; it's about the shoes. Shoes tell the whole story—who you are, what you can afford, if you are an impostor or the real deal. Either you are a fifty-dollar-day-pass patron (a nobody) or a VIP pass carrier (a somebody who knows somebody) or, as in Jules's case, a proprietor of the much-sought-after magenta "First Choice" V-VIP pass (a contender). "Details are the deal breaker," she was told months ago when the investigation first began. "Margaux de Laurent is considered the most important gallerist in the world. You ignore the details, you're out of the game."

Margaux's garnet-glossed lips curl seductively in her direction. But Jules knows better. That look is not lust; it's about control. The woman then places her half-finished champagne flute on a passing waiter's tray and grabs two newly replenished glasses. She raises one flute at Jules, intimating that there is more at stake here than meets the eye. It is *her* party, after all, the most coveted see-and-be-seen event at Basel, and she expects Jules to act the part she assigned her.

The De Laurent Gallery soiree, sponsored jointly by UBS and LVMH, is an exclusive, hand-delivered-invitation-only affair, a lavish showcase of the gallery's emerging and established artists. The gathering includes A-list celebs and models, drug dealers and politicians, influencers and socialites, critics and collectors, all cross-pollinating in the courtyard of the Versace Mansion, now known as Villa Casa Casuarina, and who probably won't leave until sunrise. Margaux's goal is not just to sell her artists' work but, more importantly, to elevate her brand and eclipse her competitors.

Sleek in a Tom Ford androgynous-meets-porn shirtless tuxedo dress, Margaux relishes her belle of the ball status. And it makes Jules sick just to look at her. The twin mounds of her bronzed breasts are perched high and visible, her deep cleavage immobile—*a still life*—untouchable and fake, like the woman herself.

Goose bumps rise along the nape of Jules's neck as Margaux makes a beeline toward her. *Stay calm, look confident*, she warns herself. There are no second chances. Everything is riding on this. Glancing quickly across the courtyard, past the partiers, Jules spots Adam, encircled by a group of journalists, discussing his paintings. He doesn't see her yet; doesn't even know she is here. It is safer that way. God, he looks good. Ruggedly handsome with shaggy, soccer star hair, Adam sports a fashionable blazer, which Jules knows he hates. He's way more comfortable in ripped jeans and one of his many rock concert T-shirts.

Squeezing her eyes shut briefly, she tries not to think about what was. She needs to stay focused and protect him—all of them—from Margaux. Fear ripples through her, and she fights it off. *Is anyone safe from that bitch?*

Balling her hands into tight fists, Jules knows that it's going to take a hell of a lot to trap Margaux and get the real story out. Not the one being published in the paper tomorrow, but the truth. *The story behind the story.*

Sashaying through the decked-out crowd, Margaux appears oblivious to the sycophants angling for her attention as she moves with pantherlike precision toward Jules. The fawning guests, intersected in Venn diagram circles, separate, allowing her passage. Jules holds her breath as Margaux's silky jacket lightly grazes her exposed skin. This close, she can't help but inhale the woman's overpowering scent—Tahitian vanilla with hints of rose: Clive Christian No. 1 Imperial Majesty—one of the world's most expensive perfumes. She read a British *Vogue* article months ago detailing Margaux de Laurent's "must-haves."

"Dress fits like a glove," Margaux whispers in Jules's ear. "Take notes and be ready." She shuts down any follow-up questions with a hard press of her lips against Jules's unexpectant mouth. It requires all of Jules's willpower not to spit away the taste of champagne and cigarettes. "And stay in your lane," Margaux warns her as she hands Jules the flute of Ruinart champagne, then sluices past her toward the other side of the courtyard.

When Jules looks up, she meets Adam's stunned gaze. He spotted her, saw the kiss. His mouth is dropped open. *What the fuck, Jules?*

It's not what you think, her eyes transmit back. She quickly looks away, tries to blend in with nearby guests. She can't deal with him right now. She must get through this without interference. Her heart pounds as she turns to watch Margaux step up to the podium next to the ornate fountain topped with Poseidon's head in the center of the courtyard. The celebrity deejay stops the music midmix, and everything else around her screeches to a halt.

Margaux commands the room, her battlefield. Soaking up the adulation, she clears her throat and waits until the collective silence feels uncomfortable. She likes it that way. The game of it, the power play. Everybody knows Margaux de Laurent thrives on attention. Jules scans the room filled with hundreds of mesmerized faces and yearns to shout, *You idiots, she's playing you!*

Everything is staged flawlessly, like a movie set. The extravagantly decorated courtyard and pool deck are filled with paintings carefully placed among giant ice sculptures and hundreds of gilded candles. The waiters, all young, muscular men wearing tight black jeans and sleeveless white tanks, are chiseled and glossy, like Chippendales dancers. Even the weather cooperates. Unseasonably warm for a winter's night, with a made-to-order breeze. *Too* perfect. Jules exhales deeply. Something's got to give.

"Good evening, and welcome," Margaux begins. "I'm Margaux de Laurent, and I'm thrilled to be here with you tonight." She doesn't need a microphone. Her rich voice resonates, her British accent posh and well-heeled, reflecting her privileged upbringing. "This is DLG's eighteenth year presenting at Art Basel. Tonight's showcase is particularly important to me because it's more than just an exhibit—it's personal." She gestures toward the large covered canvas perched behind her, and everyone's gaze follows. She has her audience in the palm of her hand. "This painting has been missing from our family collection for eight decades. Until now . . ." There is a pregnant pause as Margaux makes a panoramic sweep of the packed house, then turns to her assistant standing near her dressed in head-to-toe black. "Unveil it."

The drape comes off in one dramatic swoop and Jules gazes up in awe at the enormous canvas, and then a shock wave hits her as though she walked into a restaurant and a surprise party were waiting for her on the other side of the door. She may be imagining it, but Margaux smiles directly at her from the podium, a mercurial grin that quickly dissolves into a sneer. Jules's blood thumps; her anger mounts. That painting does not belong to her.

"*Liar!*" Jules screams at the top of her lungs, but no actual sound emerges. Her voice is hollow. Perspiration slides down the back of her designer dress. *This can't be happening.*

But it is.

The clapping is random at first, and then a resounding ovation breaks out, deafening, like the winning goal in a World Cup game. Jules's face burns, yet her hands are cold, as though her body temperature is malfunctioning, realizing that *she* is the one who has been played.

Margaux revels in the applause. Her hard gaze finds Jules once again. Her iced smile is no longer a mere victory lap—it's a *You're fucked* with a cherry on top.

Jules sees Adam trying to push through the packed house and make his way toward her. Before she can react, she feels a hard rap on her shoulder and follows the finger. A sharp-faced young woman stands before her in a white leather minidress so tight that it would take a scraper to get it off. Jules recognizes her as the Door Girl, who stood at the mansion's entrance marking off the guest list—which clearly isn't her day job.

"Follow me," the woman commands under her breath. *As in now.* Jules's legs no longer seem to hold her up. Her gaze shoots to the other side of the room, searching for Adam, but he is gone. *Where?* Her head is spinning. *Think, think.*

Her gut warns her to run like hell, but the bigger part of her knows that she'd better do as she is told. The *or else* looms over her head like a black cloud. Jules follows the woman out of the courtyard, through a discreet side door, down a short narrow staircase, and into the unknown. Before she can see what's happening or revise her decision, Jules's purse is snatched, and she is pushed roughly into the back seat of a waiting vehicle by a firm, meaty hand.

She turns briefly, and through the car's tinted rear window she spots the Door Girl standing in the zigzag shadows of a lit-up palm tree in the distance. Suddenly, without warning, a hood is placed tightly over Jules's head and her hands are tied. The air leaves her lungs, and it feels like her head is departing from her body as the car accelerates. She braces herself against the sticky leather seat. Why didn't she leave or run or scream when she had the chance? Is the damn painting worth her life and those of the people she loves?

EIGHTEEN MONTHS EARLIER

ONE

CHICAGO

JULES IS DRESSED for her interview—black slacks, white blouse, red flats. Never mind that her new boss doesn't even know that she exists or that she's going to crash his office.

"Do you really think this is a good idea?" Her mother sits down next to her at the kitchen table, having brought them both coffees and sprinkled donuts that she'd picked up from Stan's on her way home from work. "To be honest, if someone turned up at my office without an appointment asking for a job, they'd most likely be shown the door."

Her mother looks exhausted from a long day in court. They both grab a donut—their appetizer before dinner. "Well, I tried to reach him through normal channels and got nowhere," Jules explains. "Weren't you the one who taught me that 'sometimes it takes balls to be a woman'?"

Her mother laughs, and her smile, though tired, still manages to light up the kitchen. "I'm sure I did." She takes a bite of the donut, then removes her suit jacket, which seems to be sticking to her. "But this is Dan Mansfield. You can't just barge in. Besides, I've heard he's an asshole."

"Really? From who?"

"Steve. Dan interviewed him a few times in connection with some of our bigger cases. And—"

"Umm, Steve the Asshole Boss calling Dan Mansfield an asshole. Now there's a twist." Jules practically inhales the Nutella-stuffed donut as she shoves it into her mouth.

"Exactly." Her mother laughs. "Takes one to know one. Why don't we just order pizza later, curl up on the couch, watch *The Bachelor*. I could use some mindless guilty pleasure. It's been a day." She unknots the silk bow of her ivory blouse. "I'm spent."

Her mother works too hard. "Tape it. We'll watch it when I get back, I promise." Jules rises, hugs her mother, then rinses out her coffee mug in the sink. Her mother eyes her in the way that means she's looking at her but thinking of something else. Maybe it's about a case. She really needs a life outside of the courtroom— Jules tells her that all the time. Her mother yeah-yeahs her, but it's just the two of them against the world. There's no dad in the picture. No one else to share the financial burden. He took off long before Jules was born. Jules knows that she was the outcome of an accidental pregnancy during law school, but her mother has always told her, *He was the mistake, not you.*

Putting the rest of the dishes in the dishwasher, she kisses her mother lightly on the cheek and grabs her car keys off the hook. "Don't worry, okay? What's the worst thing that could happen— Dan Mansfield tells me to leave? Meet you on the couch later. Love you."

As Jules walks briskly down the narrow corridor of the *Chicago Chronicle*, she hears the roar of a man's voice in the distance.

". . . and do you really think I give a crap what the mayor ate for dinner? Give me a goddamn story I can print!"

It's him. She's sure of it. Jules recognizes the baritone with a tinge of smoker's rasp, having seen Dan Mansfield countless times on television, reporting live from exotic locations. She wasn't nervous before, but now she feels slightly terrified to meet her personal hero, whose bestselling memoir on investigative reporting is perched on her nightstand like a Bible. She glances again at her watch. Her timing is good. Nathan, a friend from graduate school, who interned at the *Chronicle*, told Jules that the optimal time to catch Dan was after seven p.m. She spots a brown stain on the lower left side of her shirt. The Nutella. How did she miss that? The problem is—her mother was right—Dan is not expecting her. This could get tricky.

As she passes one closed door after the next, Jules is surprised by how quiet the building is for a newsroom, even at this hour. Like a ghost town. And the interior could use some major attention. The peeling beige stucco ceiling and the brown paneled walls appear as if they hadn't seen an update since the seventies. *Where is everyone?* Even her college newsroom was bustling at this hour. Journalism is not a nine-to-five gig. The good stuff always happens later.

Following the echo of the voice, Jules stops in her tracks when she sees a light seeping surreptitiously through the closed door of the corner office just up ahead. *That's got to be his.* She's left messages and has sent her résumé to Dan Mansfield twice. But nothing. Zero. No response. What's the worst thing that can happen now?

Standing at the door, she reads the small, engraved black sign: DANIEL MANSFIELD, MANAGING EDITOR. *Bingo.* Exhaling deeply, she covers the chocolaty stain with her résumé folder and knocks.

"Who is it?" a woman calls out gruffly.

"Jules Roth."

"Do you have an appointment?" She sounds irritated.

"I'm . . . his niece."

Jules shifts her weight from one foot to the other. *Please let me in.* The woman answers, scowling. She is either forty or sixty depending on the angle, plain faced and bulky in a shapeless beige potato sack sweater rolled up at the elbows. Her saving grace is a smattering of cute freckles bridging her nose. "Dan doesn't have a niece." The woman's keen dark eyes narrow in, her forehead scrunching up like an accordion. "Who are you and why are you here?"

Clearly the gatekeeper, but in between the sliver of doorway space and the woman's arm, Jules sees Dan, his back facing her, head bent, typing away inside his office. She waits a few seconds and then goes for it, pushing past the woman and taking her by surprise.

Dan stops typing and looks up with a slight smirk, as if a young female intruder is a daily occurrence.

"I tried stopping her," the woman tells him, hands on sturdy hips, her eyes launching bullets at Jules.

"And you are?" Dan asks calmly, folding his arms.

Jules holds her breath longer than intended. *It's really him.* The thick, wavy, gray-black hair, the rumpled blue work shirt with an army of pens lining the pocket, the black eye patch over his left eye—just like on TV. She speaks rapidly. "I'm Jules Roth. I just graduated from the Medill School of Journalism. I want to work for you." She gnaws her bottom lip, a nervous habit she hasn't been able to shake since middle school. Aloud, she sounds disappointingly juvenile; this is not at all like the powerful speech she'd rehearsed in her head on the way over.

"Impressive entrance. Well, you made it past the prison warden." He gestures to the doorway, where his assistant is still standing, cross-armed and red-faced. "Many have tried, none have survived. Thanks, Louise. I'm fine. I'll take care of this. You can go home now."

Heaving a sigh of relief, Jules doesn't waste a minute. She whips out her résumé from the folder, leans over Dan's desk, and plunks it down. Dan eyes the document, then scrunches it up into a ball, chucks it into the trash basketball style, and scores.

"For starters, I don't give a shit what's on paper." He pushes a stack of files out of his way and nods toward the chair in front of his desk. A good sign. Jules eagerly takes a seat. "But I am curious"—his left brow arches—"how did you get past the security guard? Not that he would have noticed. That guy is too busy flirting with the interns."

Jules feels the heat prickling up her neck. "I flirted with him and told him I was your niece and came here to meet you. All true except for the niece part."

Dan laughs hard, and his whole cranky face lights up to reveal the existence of a younger, perhaps once-joyful man. "Not bad." Just as quickly, his darker expression returns. He leans back, studying her. "Let me save you time and energy. I already have an assistant. And more importantly, I didn't set up this meeting, and I have neither interest nor time to train you—or anyone else, for that matter."

As he speaks Jules notices the deep scarring lining his hands, like raised spiderwebs. *Burns.* And his left hand . . . missing the index finger. And, of course, the patched eye. The injuries are a result of an explosion at a meth lab facility that he and his team were investigating a few years back in El Paso. Dan paid a hefty price. The undercover operation went bad. The cartel got wind of the investigation and blew it up with him inside. She read about it. It made national news. Dan survived the explosion, but the other reporter from his team did not.

She looks away from the burns and focuses on his face. She knows he is not waiting for her response—he is challenging her. She clears her throat. "Here's the deal, Mr. Mansfield."

"First strike." Dan raises the index finger on his good hand, like a referee. "Mr. Mansfield is my father, and I couldn't stand him. But I do like deals, so keep going."

Jules eyes the myriad awards lining the three shelves behind him and the action photographs of Dan as a young reporter in war zones hanging on the far wall, and on the console behind his desk she sees a small, framed photograph of a little girl in a gymnastics outfit who must be his daughter. "The deal is, Dan,"—she emphasizes his name—"my classmates are all vying to work for various magazines, newspapers, and online media. I graduated with one plan only, and that is to work for you and your investigative team. And here I am."

He stares at her like she's just escaped the asylum. She quickly changes tactics and starts ticking off stats. "I was the editor in chief of my high school newspaper, editor in chief of my college newspaper, editor in chief of my grad school newspaper . . ." She waits for a reaction—and gets nothing, not even a blink. "And . . . I worked summers all through high school at our community newspaper, and they hired me as a front-page reporter." Rambling, Jules can't stop, having crossed the line from being interesting to going up in flames. "I also had three internships during college, and I . . ." *Did he just roll his eyes? That's it. Pull yourself together now.*

Jules stands. Bold, but necessary. "Look, I'm not here to waste your time or mine. I will do anything to get the story."

"I'm no longer with the investigative team. I'm the managing editor now." Dan flips over the papers on his desk aggressively, which tells Jules two things: He's not happy about it, and he's not being completely transparent. There's no way that Dan Mansfield has stopped investigating—that's like the Barefoot Contessa announcing she's given up cooking to become a maître d'.

Jules knows she's blown it, so she pulls out her lone, last card. "Do you remember Porn Gate?" she blurts out. "Six years ago?"

Dan's brows knit together as he clasps his hands and leans forward. There, she got his attention. "Of course, who doesn't? But it wasn't my story. It was our competitor's paper . . . a high school girl was used as bait to break the biggest porn ring ever of young girls being trafficked—a story that landed one governor, four state senators, and a truckload of other sick fucks in jail."

Jules heaves a deep sigh, making space to air out her deepest secret. But it's go big or go home, and she is sure as hell not leaving. "Well, you're looking at her—Anonymous Girl. That was *my* story. In high school. I brought it to the paper."

His chin pops up as though yanked by a marionette's string. "And why the heck didn't you bring it to me?"

She meets his one-eyed gaze evenly. "I tried. You ignored my calls." She goes for it. "But I'm here now. You can make it up to me."

Dan gulps an unexpected chuckle. "Gutsy. I like it. So you're the one, huh."

"I'm the one."

"They won a Pulitzer."

"Yes . . . they did."

She detects the near-invisible but faintly impressed smile, so she keeps going. "You ignored me once. Do you really want to make that mistake twice, Dan? I've wanted to work for you since I was a teenager. I have followed your career since you were a war reporter."

"You were in diapers," he asserts correctly.

"I'm exaggerating to make a point," she counters. "Look, you take on the stories that no one else can break and you break them. I will work for free for the first three months, though I prefer to be paid." She squares her shoulders and waits.

And that's when Dan laughs—actually cackles in her face. She feels the red splotches spreading across her cheeks, but she does not budge. She waits out the laughter. Eventually, he stops, cocks his head, and assesses her, only this time with genuine interest. She sees her reflection in his gaze: a serious young woman who doesn't wear makeup because she has more important things on her mind. She can tell by the pursed lips and the folded arms that she was not wrong to ambush him. She knows people, reads expressions and body language. Her delivery started off shaky, but the wrap-up clearly caught his attention.

Dan's phone rings, suspending the moment. "What?" he shouts into the receiver. "When? How many? Jesus Christ. Yes, I'm on it. We'll send our people over."

Jules freezes. Dan hangs up the phone, moves past her as though she were furniture, leaving her in his office. But she follows him as he enters the newsroom, where only a few stragglers are still working at their desks. "Where is everyone?" he yells. "There's a shoot-out going on right now in Englewood. Four people are dead. A coked-up sniper with an AR-15 is holding the building's residents hostage—threatening to shoot more of them. I need reporters. Where the hell are Barb and Alan?"

Someone responds—an invisible voice from a random carrel. "They went home."

Dan throws up his arms. "Home? Are you kidding me! Am I the only one who works past five o'clock in this amateur shithole?" He pivots angrily on his heel and sees Jules standing in the corner with a pen and a pad that she grabbed from his assistant's desk just in case. "You—Anonymous. Make yourself useful. Come to my office now. I'm going to give you a list of names and you're going to make calls and get me what I need. Can you do that?"

He doesn't wait for an answer. Jules follows him back into his office, feeling the rush of adrenaline, the internal ticktock heat of pumping out a story.

Dan doesn't waste a beat. He's pacing while on the phone, shouting at her like a short-order cook. Three televisions are blaring at once like a dysfunctional Greek chorus, simultaneously telling the same breaking story three different ways.

"Get a list from the police department," he barks at her. "Tell them it's for me. Find out who is alive and who is dead. Contact the families. Find out who lives in that damn building. I need re-actions. It's the worst part of the job, believe me. Lesson one: It's not about the attack—it's about the people. Readers don't want stats; they want faces. They want to know who died, who was left behind—the autistic child who just lost his mother. Find out whatever you can. I'm going to look into the shooter and who's behind all this." Dan begins to cough but talks through it. "Can you do that, Jules? And why aren't you writing this down?" He stares at her yellow pad, which she hasn't touched.

"I got it all." She taps the pen to her head, as though she has a microchip implanted inside.

"How's your typing?"

She saw Dan typing when she walked in earlier. Her fingers could outrun his pace by a mile.

"Good enough," she says.

"I want fifteen inches on my desk in two hours."

"Done." Their eyes meet. No further conversation is needed. The job is hers.

TWO

MUNICH, GERMANY

MARGAUX PULLS BACK the faded gingham drapes, glances out the slightly opened kitchen window at the shining streetlights below, then grabs her binoculars. The Old Man has been sitting in the exact same position in his bedroom for nearly an hour, barely blinking, like a propped-up corpse.

She has been surveilling him for nearly three days, and it feels like a jail sentence. From her vantage point on the fifth floor of the building, Margaux can see straight into the man's tiny apartment, one of a dozen shabby units in the bland, nondescript white stucco building in Munich's Schwabing neighborhood, which was once known for its Bohemian charm but now looks run-down, like an attractive woman who let herself go. It had been easy securing this prime positioning from the elderly tenant, another relic from the past. Margaux had offered the old woman 20,000 euros and a weeklong stay in a luxury hotel nearby in exchange for a no-questions-asked usage of her home. Not bad for someone who barely scrapes by on that amount a year. She should have thrown an air conditioner into the deal—Margaux can barely breathe in this stuffy hotbox reeking of mothballs and grease.

Each day the Old Man, known as Carl Geisler, becomes even more pathetic than the previous one. Watching him execute all his OCD behaviors is unbearable, like hitting the replay button repeatedly. *But this will all be worth it*, Margaux assures herself as she grabs a pack of Gitanes off the chipped white Formica table next to her, lights up a cigarette, and waits ten minutes for the grandfather clock in the corner of the small dining area to strike eight p.m.

Here we go again.

On cue, the clock chimes. Margaux puts out the cigarette, retrieves the binoculars, and watches the Old Man rise from the worn-in chesterfield club chair in the corner of his bedroom, right foot inside his slipper first, then the left one. He then removes both feet and puts the shoes back on in the exact same manner. He does this repetition three times, then walks over to his bed, reaches under it, and pulls out a tired-looking black leather suitcase. He places it carefully onto the bed in the exact same spot as always, not one centimeter off. Margaux knows this because he uses a ruler to measure it, the wooden kind from generations past. She isn't concerned that Geisler will catch her spying on him. He never looks outside; hasn't peered out a single window even once. Apparently, that's not an activity on his regimented daily schedule.

Rolling up her sleeves, she opens the window a tad more to let some fresh air inside and quickly checks her phone. A slew of emails and texts has poured in that she'll deal with later. It's just after lunch, New York time. She told her office that she was heading to Paris on business, which she did for two days, using her private plane, before booking a separate connection to Munich. She flew coach, incognito, using a fake passport. After receiving that classified report last week, Margaux knew she had to act swiftly, alone, and most importantly, not leave any footprints.

Her personal hacker, an ex–Silicon Valley game designer with an Adderall addiction—the guy never sleeps—learned that a junior reporter at the German news-magazine *Spotlight* was allegedly sitting on what might be the hottest art exposé since the end of World War II. He believed Margaux would be interested in the details that he'd plucked from the woman's computer. *Interested? What a joke.* If the information proves true, this little trip will be priceless and save her galleries from financial ruin.

She checks inside the taupe Birkin bag at her side once again: there are the pills and a gun with a silencer—if needed. *If I have to watch the Old Man measure out precisely four centimeters around that suitcase one more time, I may just shoot myself instead.*

As she observes Geisler and his never-ending eccentricities, Margaux contemplates the man's wretched life, from growing up in a Gothic castle on a hill overlooking the Elbe River in Meissen to ending up in that decrepit cardboard box apartment. *What a waste.* She shakes her head, recalling her own pathetic childhood in Oxford, raised in a somber fifty-six-room estate—the loneliest place on the planet—an only child reared by a revolving door of dour-faced nannies who hated her even more than her two parents hated each other. She'd exhausted five spinsters by the time she was thirteen. Never mind that the last nanny left abruptly because she claimed to have been poisoned. Margaux smiles fondly at the memory of slipping rat poison into that tight-lipped bitch's afternoon tea and watching her suffer. That was one of her better pranks.

Geisler begins counting to ten. She sees him mouthing the words as usual. *Now comes the interesting part . . .* He flings open the suitcase in a grand, Houdini-esque gesture, then slowly, tenderly, unpacks the drawings as though undressing a woman for the very first time. Or ever—judging by his depraved looks. Removing each of the works on paper, he holds them to the light, then traces them delicately with his fingertips and begins to talk to them. Margaux watches his thin lips move and knows enough German to understand that he is whispering words of endearment: *Liebling, liebling.* She waits it out. The fondling, the sparks of joy in his eyes as he gently caresses each paper filled with graphite and charcoal images. And not just any drawings or scribbles or etchings, but *stolen* renderings by Renoir, Monet, Cézanne, and Gauguin. Margaux grinds out the fourth cigarette in tonight's chain-smoking lineup, puts on her gloves, and straps the large bag over her shoulder. Three days is more than enough. *It's time.*

TWENTY MINUTES LATER, Margaux easily picks the flimsy lock of the Old Man's front door—so cheap that she could have done it with a hangnail. She knows he is sleeping. He took his two pills, got into his nightshirt, turned off the light, and, according to his pattern, will be snoring by 8:47. The guy is programmed like a Swiss train.

She tiptoes through the short, musty foyer, past the bedroom and toward the kitchen, which is bare-bones and sterile, with just a rusty-looking teakettle and a cheap aluminum pot on the stove. Glancing around, she eyes the old wooden cabinets and one lone oversized pantry. She goes for the pantry first, opens it, and stands back in shock.

Christ.

Resting on homemade floor-to-ceiling shelves are countless rolled canvases stuffed and stacked like sardines between juice boxes and tinned food. She estimates at least one hundred rolls of varying sizes jammed on each shelf. Her heart palpitates as she carefully squeezes out the first roll from the shelf that is at eye level and unrolls the tattered canvas. A vibrant oil—rabbis dancing with Torahs overhead, surrounded by women and children and flying acrobats—*Chagall.* She pulls out another. Nude bathers congregated like fairies in a forest—*Cézanne.* The third, ballet dancers anxiously huddled together preperformance—*Degas.* Wheat fields filled with cypresses—*Van Gogh.*

Roll after roll, masterpiece after masterpiece—Margaux can barely breathe. It's as if she's been given the keys to the Louvre and told to take anything she wants. She quickly seizes as many canvases off the shelves as she can and finds a few large garbage bags under the kitchen sink and fills them to the brim. The hacked report she read is a lie—it doesn't even begin to tally the treasure trove hidden here in this grimy apartment. As she opens the kitchen cabinets, she is shocked to find enough canvases to fill a small U-Haul. Geisler's stash must be worth at least a billion dollars, perhaps more. Old Masters. Fauves. Impressionists. Cubists. Expressionists . . . *How did he get away with this?* Rage begins to scorch through her. *Him?* Not that agoraphobic deadbeat but his father—Helmuth Geisler, Hitler's chief art dealer, the infamous art thief.

Digging her boots angrily into the floor, Margaux hears her grandfather's voice striking in her ears like cymbals: *Focus, then file pertinent information, Margaux. Don't make it personal. It's not about you, but about the art, the history.* Squaring her shoulders, she hungrily eyes the masterpieces. *It's not about you, but about the money.* Her words—not her grandfather's.

She identifies each painting, each famous artist inside her head, until the mental Rolodex verges on kaleidoscopic explosion. Roll after roll, it just doesn't stop: Pissarro, Matisse, Kandinsky, Klee, Beckmann, Munch, Derain, Braque, Nolde, Dix . . .

She glances around the dilapidated room, which looks like a model unit from Bellevue. Bare, rotted walls, a sweaty ceiling, moldy and devoid of color—not a single painting hanging up. *Who is this freak?* She walks toward the closest window, pulls back the broken blinds, thick with dust, and spots that same black Volkswagen with tinted windows driving by the building that she saw three times yesterday. Coincidence? Margaux shakes her head. No such thing. Someone else must have gotten wind of the *Spotlight* article. She makes a mental note to check into it. Hurriedly, she moves toward the bedroom, leans against the door, and hears the Old Man snoring loudly, a death rattle. *Soon—very soon.*

Margaux pauses, thinking again of her beloved grandfather, Charles de Laurent, who died when she was twelve. If only he could see her now . . . art dealer turned burglar. She'd argue that this was not a robbery but self-defense. Stealing from someone who stole the art is not a crime but payback. Helmuth Geisler and his Nazi cohorts confiscated many of her grandfather's paintings back in Paris during the war. *But not everything.* Her brilliant grandfather, always one step ahead, saw the writing on the wall. He heard the stories from his colleagues and clients in Berlin and Munich whose collections had been confiscated or destroyed. He was determined to protect the vast De Laurent collection well before the Nazis banged down his gallery door.

And when they did, he was prepared when they stormed his gallery on the rue La Boétie nearly a year prior to the Nazi invasion of Paris, demanding he hand over his massive trove. He told Margaux that he was forced to give those criminals three hundred major works of art but had already saved more than two thousand masterworks from the family collection. He'd sent them first to the South of France for protection, and from there, the paintings were smuggled to Lisbon, London, and New York for safekeeping. Except for one painting—the one that his beloved but sick young wife, Sylvie, had treasured the most. He'd mistakenly hung on to it too long and was too late when he tried to save it from that bloodthirsty Helmuth Geisler. Her grandfather never got over that loss.

Suddenly, Margaux doesn't care about being quiet or careful. She starts opening drawers and cabinets, slamming them shut. *It's here . . . That painting has got to be here.* Her heart bangs in sync with each crashing sound.

"Who's there? Who's there?" the Old Man cries out in German from the bedroom. Margaux freezes, picturing him getting in and out of those threadbare slippers three times. He enters the room in a faded white nightshirt, carrying a weak flashlight, and looks like the Ghost of Christmas Past with his veiny, transparent skin and that ridiculous fringe of snow-white hair enveloping his balding, mottled scalp. He sees Margaux and the garbage bags bursting with canvases, the pantry door wide open and all his meticulously stuffed rolls snatched off the shelves.

"No. No. No!" His piercing cobalt blue eyes widen demonically.

"Yes. Yes. Yes!" Margaux can't help herself. She has zero empathy for this wretched Nazi heir.

"My father's children—" he starts spitting out, his voice quaking.

"Where is *Woman on Fire*?" she demands, moving toward him with clenched fists. He backs away into the wall, his hands pressed against it, paralyzed.

"No, please," he begs, his glow-in-the-dark eyes terrorized. "I don't have it. It's not here . . . just the others that I protect from the thieves. I have responsibilities."

"Fucking liar!" It takes everything inside Margaux not to beat him to a pulp. "You are a thief. I want it now."

"Please, whoever you are, leave me be. I'm just a quiet man who lives with beautiful art."

"Art stolen by your father." Her face burns. "Confiscated from museums, collectors, galleries, artists. Taken from *my* grandfather. Your father got away with his crimes"—she points at him—"but not you."

The Old Man's shriveled body diminishes before her eyes. "My father was a hero." His voice is weak, but his fists are balled. "He saved paintings that the Nazis would have destroyed. A hero—do you hear me—a hero, not a villain. We have proof, evidence, paperwork, signed deals—"

"Ahh, the paperwork," Margaux snickers, eyeing the paltry fists. She could blow on him and he'd fall over. "Signed deals. You mean *forced* deals. All your evidence has been forged."

"Lies, lies," he sniffles. "My grandmother was half Jewish."

She dissolves into laughter. "I know. The grandmother. The half Jew. I read all about it. Helmuth Geisler used that lie to get back all of the artwork he'd stolen—and the Allies, those damn fools, believed him." She shakes her head in disgust. "How many paintings are in this apartment?"

Geisler is silent. He cups his hands over his mouth like a small child preventing the truth from tumbling out.

Her voice softens, becoming smooth like clotted cream, a fail-safe tone she utilizes whenever she needs to manipulate someone. "You're right, Carl. You *have* done such a good job protecting all your father's artwork from bad people. Now, how many paintings are you guarding in here?"

His body straightens. His crazy eyes gleam with pride. "Fifteen hundred and twenty-seven, plus twenty-three drawings."

She then sees him eyeing the stove. Tiny beads of sweat begin to bubble across his forehead.

"What's in there?" she demands, walking toward it. "Is it in there? Is it?"

"Nothing. Please go. Leave me and my paintings alone."

Keeping both eyes fastened on Geisler, Margaux flings opens the stove, looks inside, and gasps. More canvases. At least another hundred. But these works are not rolled like the others. No, these are layered like lasagna, as though he is about to bake them. She sees the Matisse first. *This imbecile is stashing a Matisse in the stove.* She's heard about this stolen Matisse. Easily worth over $30 million. *Oh well. Mine now.* She places it gently on the kitchen counter, then spots an oil by Max Beckmann, the German Expressionist, and beneath that, folded in half, a Picasso . . . She stands back, her eyes blazing at Geisler, who hasn't moved an inch from that wall. "A Picasso folded in half? Were you planning to make a sandwich out of it, you sick fuck?" she shouts.

"No, no. You don't understand . . ." Geisler shakes his head, again childlike, as though insisting that he did not take the cookies from the cookie jar despite the crumbs outlining his lips. "I'm innocent. I protected them," he whimpers.

"Innocent. Just following orders, right?"

"Yes, yes, right." His head stops shaking; his body stops trembling. "Exactly right."

"Where is the damn painting?" Margaux knows she is running out of time. She walks over again to the window and glances out at the street. That Volkswagen is still circling. She must get out of here, with or without the painting. She now hovers over Geisler and pulls the gun out of her bag.

"*Woman on Fire*," she demands.

"Don't hurt me," he begs, cupping his heart. "My sister has it."

"Your sister? She died three years ago." She shoves the gun to his temple.

"No, Beatrice is gardening. In Salzburg. The painting is there with her," he cries, looking bewildered. "Please, please, my pills. I need my pills."

"Yes, I thought you might." Margaux forces her voice to care. She needs to put an end to this travesty. The painting isn't here. "In the bathroom?"

"Yes, but don't touch the pills. Don't move them out of order. They are laid out exactly right, exactly as they should be."

This part is going to be so easy. "I won't move a thing, Carl, I promise. I will bring you the pills and water, but only if you tell me, and I'm asking you one last time . . . where's that pretty painting?"

"Yes, two pills . . . the first and the third one. Not the second or the fourth. I swear . . ." he pleads, "I don't have it. The last I saw it was at the house in Salzburg. My mother . . ."

His mother died ten years ago. The guy is clearly confused. Margaux checks her watch again. She should have been out of here fifteen minutes ago. She has no worries that the Old Man will scream, nor does he have time to run away or anywhere to go. His life stopped in November 1972, when his father died in a car crash and he was named guardian of the Tainted Treasure Trove; the Least Likely having won the Game of Thrones. He has no friends, no acquaintances, no neighbors, no one watching out for him. No one will miss him. This will be clean and fast.

She walks into Geisler's bathroom, removes the two cyanide pills from her bag that she had reshaped to look like his blood pressure pills. She makes a mental note to send an extra ten thousand to the hacker for being so precise with his information. She fills a cup of water from the bathroom sink and returns to Geisler, now hunched over the stove as though praying. She hands him the pills, and he actually thanks her as he takes them.

"I will put all the paintings back just as you had them, if you go back to bed," Margaux bargains with him.

"These pills taste different." He smacks his lips. "Like bitter almonds from the garden in Salzburg."

"Yes, just like the ones in the garden." Ignoring his mumblings, she leads him back to his bed. Disoriented, he allows her to. She waits while he does his slipper song and dance and then gets into the bed. She pulls the covers over him, tucking him in tightly.

"*Gute Nacht, Liebling,*" Margaux whispers, closing the bedroom door behind her just as he begins to choke.

Margaux feels nothing. She gives him one last look from the doorway, bolts down the hallway for the bags of paintings, and then stops in her tracks. Her grandfather once mentioned that the painting was bigger than he was. It couldn't possibly fit inside that cabinet or the stove. She glances backward. There is only one spot in the apartment big enough for that painting. Her heart beating rapidly, she sprints back into the bedroom, pushes Geisler off the bed, ignoring the hard thud to the floor, and lifts the mattress. And voilà. The burnt orange color peeks out from the box spring slats, as though imprisoned. A woman trapped behind bars.

"It's you." Margaux's voice is barely a sound, and her feet remain planted. *Woman on Fire.* Not gardening in Salzburg but being held captive by this madman. *My grandfather's favorite. If only he could see me now.* Margaux can't help it. Her eyes, which never shed a single tear, turn glassy as she carefully peels the canvas out from under the bed.

Standing next to the dead man at her feet, she quickly pulls out her phone, which she'd stuck inside the waistband of her jeans, and sends an all-caps text to the hacker:

NEED BACKUP NOW

Rolling up the masterpiece and placing it protectively under her arm, Margaux closes the bedroom door behind her, grabs the garbage bags stuffed with paintings from the kitchen and the bag with the gun, then slips quietly, triumphantly, out the door.

THREE

MANHATTAN

M R. BAUM, YOUR ten a.m. is here. It's that reporter from *Vogue*."

Ellis looks up from his desk. His assistant waits patiently in the doorway for his response. He smiles fondly at her and mentally pats himself on the back. Alexandra is one of his best hires. Smart, organized, patient, and knows not to bother him about trivial things.

"Bring her coffee and have her wait in the conference room." He glances down at the newspaper splayed in front of him. "I need a few minutes here. Something came up."

"Of course. No problem." Alexandra lurks as though she has more to say, then changes her mind and pivots out the door. Ellis listens to the familiar clackety-clack of the stilettos down the corridor. One of the many perks of working for Anika Baum, Inc. is that Ellis makes sure each employee receives a custom-made pair of shoes from him personally on her fifth-year anniversary. His company comprises over 90 percent women, and he keeps it that way. Reverse sexism? He couldn't care less. "I celebrate women," he tells any reporter who asks—because they always do. "I have a day care facility in my building, a manicurist, and a masseuse. The job is high pressure, with long hours, and I demand excellence. They deserve it. So, sue me."

He likes to make a production out of the gifting of the shoes. Whether it's a secretary or a vice president, Ellis has his chef prepare a special lunch for him and the employee, and then he presents her with a pair of personalized Anika Baums. He asks for only one thing in return: absolute loyalty. Each AB employee is handpicked and undergoes a rigorous internship process before she is hired. He knew the second he laid eyes on Alexandra that she was the one to mind his private affairs. Classy, cool under pressure, non-gossipy, a workhorse with solid midwestern values, who always puts his needs first.

The truth is it makes Ellis feel good to see his shoes worn by those who could never afford them. The most modest pair of ABs costs over three thousand dollars, and the top-of-the-line pump goes for fourteen thousand dollars a pair. They say that owning a pair of Anika Baums is like having Picassos wrapped around your feet.

Ellis swivels around on his cushy leather chair and takes in the panoramic view outside his spacious Midtown headquarters, a historical landmark overlooking Central Park. The sun shines bright, and the motionless sky is a perfect shade of robin's-egg blue—the ideal backdrop for the skyline, which fits seamlessly inside his floor-to-ceiling windows. That was his chief demand to the architect. *I'm claustrophobic. I need to breathe.*

Turning away from the window, he stares at his beloved shoe wall—a vast mural showcasing the best of his luxury line, each pair illuminated inside individual squares. Every shoe has its own name and personal meaning to him. *She would have loved them.*

Returning to the papers on his desk, Ellis rereads the front-page news article for the sixth time in the past hour: An old man found dead in his Munich apartment. Cyanide. A man who happens to be the reclusive son of Helmuth Geisler, the Third Reich's art thief.

Ellis doesn't cry, doesn't own tears anymore, and yet an unfamiliar wetness fills his eyes. In his mind, he sees the one face that he has tried to forget all these years but that haunts him anyway in his sleep—Helmuth Geisler. That man wasn't just a thief, but also a murderer. He stood there in their apartment foyer on November 16, 1941, and ordered his mother's death. And young Ellis, just shy of eight years old, was made to watch.

"Do you know what happens, young man, when an Aryan woman falls in love with a Jew? When Miss Germany 1927 chooses a kike over one of her own?" Geisler asked Ellis, whose mouth was gagged with a dish towel, the silent tears streaming down his tiny face. "She falls."

Ellis will never shed the memory of that man, that face—those small, round glasses shielding beady eyes and bland features, the tight, compact stature, the thin black hair greased back and parted down the center. He squeezes his eyes tightly, desperately trying to ward off the next image. That smug satisfaction on Geisler's face—a sly grin creeping across slippery lips—when his mother finally collapsed while wearing high heels—the very same shoes Ellis had secretly worn inside her bedroom earlier that day.

His mother was merely the appetizer. It was all about the painting for Geisler.

Ellis recalls another day a few years earlier when that famous painter came to their apartment. *Ernst Engel*. He sat with his mother over tea and described what was burning in his mind. A woman, a tempest, consumed with passion, fire, torment, sensuality—part Medusa, part Aphrodite, part Mother Nature. A woman who wasn't just a woman—rather a force—a cyclone of color. Engel said he envisioned her—Anika—as that woman. *Would she do it?* Would she remove her clothes and let him paint her? It would have to be their secret, she whispered. Her husband could never know. Engel could only come and paint her when Arno was away. A deal was struck, a silent conspiracy signed between the two of them. *Three* of them, if you counted young Ellis leaning against the door, listening in . . .

"Mr. Baum. I'm sorry to interrupt once again. It's been nearly twenty-five minutes . . ."

"Cancel the interview," Ellis says firmly, barely looking up.

Alexandra pauses. "Do you think that's a good idea?" she prods carefully. "You are their main profile piece. You can't just—"

"Alexandra." Ellis holds up his palm. "I can and I will. Apologize on my behalf. Blame my health. Reschedule. Do whatever you have to do. I need to be alone right now."

Her eyes smart as she pulls back her shoulders and slowly retreats out the door in his personal favorite Anikas from the 2016 collection. Simple, black, with his signature wraparound leather strap that goes up the calf, with sleek high heels that are studded with tiny diamonds so discreet that they are barely visible.

His heart hammering, Ellis unlocks the middle drawer of his desk, shuffles past the important papers and the one document he wishes he could ignore—the death sentence he received from the oncologist—and removes the secret burner phone lodged in the back, the kind that drug dealers use. He keeps it on hand for private matters. Taking a deep breath, he makes the call.

"Yes, hello . . . I know it's a surprise. It has been a while. I am fine, thank you," Ellis lies. *Not fine.* No one knows the true story of his childhood, the origin of Anika Baum. No one knows that he came to this country a thirteen-year-old refugee, an orphan, starving and half dead from having lived inside sewers and basements to survive the war. Not even his wife, their three children, or his five grandchildren know the truth. Nor Henri, his secret lover of twenty years. After seventy-plus years of living in America, the truth even for Ellis is grainy—a melding of colors, scattered points, like a Seurat painting. He has nothing left of his childhood as evidence of what was. Helmuth Geisler made sure all remnants of his past were decimated.

Except for one thing.

Ellis clears his throat, struggling to maintain his composure. "Remember that favor you once promised me? It's time, Dan. I'm calling it in."

FOUR

CHICAGO

JULES IS NERVOUS as she walks across the editorial floor toward Dan Mansfield's office. She passes at least five rows of cubicles filled with reporters and copy editors. No one even looks up from their work. There are no hellos, no "Welcome to the *Chronicle*," no sprinkled donuts. In fact, no one utters a single word or gives a hint of acknowledgment, even though Jules can clearly see that everyone is watching her from the corners of their eyes. The problem is, and no one needs to tell her, that she is Dan Mansfield's girl—*his* personal pick. She didn't rise through the ranks, pay her dues as an entry-level journalist doing grunt work. She will be reporting directly to Dan, leapfrogging over a dozen heads to get this prized position. She heaves a deep, worried sigh. Journalist Envy is a disease. *I'm going to pay for this.*

It was the Englewood hostage piece, the day she barged into Dan's office, that put her on everyone's radar. She worked all night, got Dan everything he needed. On her own initiative, she drove out to Englewood, considered one of the most dangerous areas in Chicago, and interviewed several residents who lived in the same building where the shooter was holding their neighbors hostage. Her golden ticket was finding and interviewing the shooter's mother, who works at the Chicago Public Library. It was an emotionally charged piece and landed her a front-page sidebar to the main story and bought her a permanent job. Dan saw to it personally. She swallows hard. *But it won't buy me friends.*

Holding her head high, ignoring the din of whispers behind her, Jules knocks lightly on Dan's door. Louise answers and eyes her critically. "The niece has arrived," she announces. But instead of telling Jules to go away, she ushers her inside. "He's expecting you. I see you brushed your hair this time." Louise smiles, her reddish freckles expanding across her nose. "Dan's wrapping up a meeting. Wait here, grab a coffee." She points to the half-full pot of coffee in the corner of the office.

Jules sits, downs her third cup before nine a.m., and reads the morning paper laid out on the Lucite coffee table. She hears Dan and another man speaking harshly inside his office and wonders what it's about. Eventually, Dan pops his head out, acknowledging her. He doesn't look happy, and neither does the publisher who storms out of the office and strides right past her.

"Come on in," Dan calls out to her. Jules nods at Louise and then heads into the office.

"Hi, Mr. Mansfi—Hi, Dan," she corrects herself as she sits on the chair in front of his desk.

As Dan puts on his reading glasses, he eyes the door, clearly still annoyed by his interaction with the publisher. "How do you feel about homework?"

"Homework?" Jules hasn't even been here five minutes. "If it's necessary, of course I'm fine with it."

He removes his glasses and tepees his hands. "Good, because it *is* necessary. I know it's your first day, but don't expect an orientation. I don't have time for that." He indicates the newsroom on the other side of the wall. "And I'm sure you didn't receive a welcoming committee out there. I've already heard all the complaints."

Jules's face turns red.

"Don't let it get to you. The first thing I learned when I was out in the field is that it's not a popularity contest. Just do your job, but watch out for the backstabbers. Look, I'm going to hire whoever the hell I want. I've been here over twenty years—they're never going to fire me. Every Pulitzer on their top shelf comes from my investigative team." He shakes his head in dismay and points to the door. "The team *they* disbanded . . ." His eyes glaze over, and Jules doesn't know how to respond. It must be because of that explosion in El Paso and his dead colleague. But how could they do that to Dan? He's one of the best investigative reporters in the country.

"Like I said, don't worry about those assholes," he continues. "They're just jealous that they didn't think outside of the box and try to interview the shooter's mother and get a real story." He stands, walks over to his door, nods at Louise, and then gently closes it. "I've got something much more interesting for you to work on." He scribbles something on a notepad and hands it to her. "Here's an address. Meet me there in an hour. Take a cab. Save the receipt." He lowers his voice conspiratorially. "The thing is, Jules—you're not actually going to work for the paper . . . officially, at least."

"I'm not?" She raises a brow.

"No, you're not."

FIVE

EVANSTON, ILLINOIS

SITTING WITH HER back against the wall in the small café on Sherman Avenue, Jules is in prime position to view everything around her at once: the homey interior, the giant blackboard with colorfully chalked items, the large windows, the coffee counter, and the barista. Scanning the wooden tables filled with students and academic types, she wonders why Dan had insisted they meet at a café outside of the city—*not* near his office. She is already halfway through her soy cappuccino when she sees him through the window hurriedly crossing the street.

Entering with his briefcase pressed at his side, Dan wears retro Ray-Bans and a black Members Only jacket, a relic from the eighties. He waves to her, orders coffee for himself, and sits across from her. He plops the briefcase down on the table, then adds three packets of sugar to his coffee with one rip. "Just so you know, I'm never early."

"Just so *you* know, *on time* is late for me," Jules retorts, smiling. She watches Dan toss back the sugar-loaded mug. Up close, his face is drawn and his heavily hooded good eye is bloodshot. "Is everything okay?"

"Yeah, fine." Wasting no time, he snaps open his briefcase and hands her a large file. "This is for you. Read it tonight. And Jules . . . it's for your eyes only. Put it somewhere safe."

He notices her beat-up backpack hanging over the chair and raises a brow, and she hears the echo of her mother's voice: *You're not a student anymore. Get rid of that old backpack—you've had it since high school. You need a proper tote to show you're serious.* Jules suddenly feels self-conscious. "I'm getting a new bag."

Dan flicks his wrist. "I don't give a damn about your bag. Just keep the file under wraps. Discuss it with only me." He leans toward her. "But no cowboy antics this time—got it?"

Pursing her lips, Jules knows he's referring to the Englewood piece. No one told her to go out on her own. But she got the story—that's all that mattered.

She squirms in her chair. "Okay, I hear you . . . but truthfully, I'm confused as to why we're here. You said earlier I'm not *officially* working for the paper—can you define that specifically? Are you paying me directly? Sorry to be blunt, but some basic answers would be great."

Dan swigs his coffee. "Yes and no."

"Well, that clarifies things."

They both laugh. "Look, as I said in the office, this is going to be interesting but complicated . . ." He folds his arms across his chest. "You strike me as someone who craves that. Lots of moving parts. To be totally transparent, it's also personal. I can't tell you all the details right now, for various reasons, but what I've given you in that folder is deep background to help you understand the magnitude of this." He plants his elbows on the table, leans forward. "What do you know about stolen art? Nazi stolen art."

Jules squints slightly. "You mean like *Monuments Men* art?" she asks, referring to the George Clooney movie based on a true story that took place during World War II, in which a special unit was set up to save masterpieces stolen by the Third Reich before they were destroyed.

"Yeah, exactly that kind of art."

"I know a bit. Years ago, I went to an exhibit at the Art Institute on the Third Reich and art. My mother thought it was a good idea to see it just before my bat mitzvah. Anyway, my recollection is vague, but I do remember that there were dozens of paintings on display that had been confiscated by the Nazis, artwork they called 'degenerate'—labeled immoral and forbidden by the Reich. I also recall being surprised to learn that Hitler and several members of his inner circle were artists in their younger years. I found that really shocking." By the encouraging look in Dan's eyes, it's obvious he wants her to keep going. "I also know from recent news stories that Holocaust survivors and their heirs are trying to reclaim their stolen artwork. Many have been trying for years. Lots of legal roadblocks." She tilts her head. "How am I doing?"

"Better than I expected," he admits. "You have a base. That's good. Here's the deal. Someone has approached me to find an extremely valuable painting that means a lot to him. I guess you'd call it the *Mona Lisa* of modern art—worth millions. For him, it's not about the money; it's personal. But to be honest, every single stolen artwork still out there is fucking personal. After some initial digging, it's clear we are dealing with a much bigger story." Dan finishes his coffee and signals the barista for a refill. "There was a murder in Germany recently and a major robbery of art.

Over a thousand masterpieces that have been lost for generations are rumored to have been part of the dead guy's collection. And from my understanding, this particular painting may be among the stolen art."

"So . . . stolen art was stolen from the robber?" Jules feels her heart skip, followed by the familiar tingle spreading through her body. She loves beginnings, the anticipation and infinite possibility of an unsolved story. "Any leads?"

He presses his lips tightly together. "Low-level leads. Not much, but a start. Like I said, this case is somewhat personal . . ." His gaze drifts elsewhere.

Jules waits. One important trick she's learned is that silence moves the needle. When there is silence, people tend to talk—blab—to fill in the uncomfortable space. Some of her best quotes and information have been a result of waiting, listening, and organically getting the goods.

"He's a celebrity in the fashion industry and . . ." Dan's voice catches. "The ol' 'silence is golden' trick. Journalism 101. Well played. Here's the deal, Jules. This is going to be Porn Gate, *the Sequel*—an investigation that appears small but will have huge ramifications, high stakes. Can you handle that?"

Handle it? She swallows hard. Dan has no idea what she had to handle with Porn Gate, the Original. A barrage of questions fight for space in her mind. "I just need to know exactly what I'm handling."

"Read the damn file and we will talk more tonight," he says.

"Can I ask what, exactly, the publisher thinks I'm doing for you?"

Dan's lips curl. "The usual for newbies. That you're organiz-

ing my files, finding sources, getting quotes, checking facts, doing scut work, helping Louise."

Jules inhales the aroma of warm coffee, then sighs. Louise
must hate her already for invading her turf. "And what does Louise think about all this?"

"Good one." Dan throws his head back and laughs, as though
appreciating an inside joke that only he gets. "Louise doesn't need
to think. She is beyond that. She has been by my side since day
one. Whatever I do, she knows about it. *She* told me to hire you.
She was impressed that you quarterback-rushed her and charged
into the office. Everyone at the paper is terrified of her. She told
me, and I quote, 'That girl has guts. She's one of us.'" Dan spreads
his arms wide. "Welcome to the investigative team. Disbanded,
off the books, but still highly operational. Can I trust you, Jules?"
He doesn't wait for her response. She's made it past Louise,
collected two hundred dollars, and is ready to go—that's all he
needs to know.

SIX

CHICAGO

LATER THAT NIGHT, Jules sits on her bed surrounded by a sea of papers. She barely has room for her legs. She glances at the clock on her nightstand. Nearly midnight, and it feels as though she's only just begun to dive in. So much to comprehend. She's organized all of Dan's documents, numbered them, divided them into sections by date and country. What he handed her was a history lesson, a semester's course load to digest in a single sitting.

Downing more coffee to stay awake, she eyes the tall pile marked 1939 near the corner of the bed. Even though she saw that degenerate art exhibit at thirteen years old with her mother, she now fully comprehends the sheer magnitude of the Nazis' relentless mission to destroy the avant-garde, particularly painters. Hitler and his henchmen went after the German Expressionists with a vengeance never seen before.

As Jules flips through page after page and studies the myriad black-and-white photographs, she learns that between 1933 and 1945 the Nazis seized more than 600,000 works of art from private collections, museums, galleries, and schools, as well as from the artists themselves. Hundreds of thousands of paintings and sculptures were destroyed. And yet, while the Reich went on a rampage of destruction throughout Europe, they also "saved" the most valuable works for themselves—auctioning off huge quantities of so-called forbidden art, particularly with the help of Switzerland, to fund the Nazi war machine and line their own pockets. Was *Woman on Fire* one of those "lucky" paintings that survived Hitler's cultural cleansing?

The phone rings, interrupting her thoughts. Jules glances at it: Unknown Caller. *As in Dan.*

"Hi, Dan."

"And?"

"It's disturbing. Phenomenal, actually. I'm still plowing through mounds of material." She hesitates. "What's the end game here besides a heavy-duty art history lesson?"

There's an awkward pause and she hears him sparking up a cigarette. "No one knows you, Jules."

"Thanks . . . I guess?"

"What I mean is, I'm recognizable. Everyone knows that if I'm on a story they sure as hell better dot their i's and cross their t's. But you . . . We can get you inside all this, and I can pull the reins from behind the scenes." Jules hears cars honking in the background and Dan exhaling. He must be smoking outside. "I have some ideas. I'm just waiting for approval."

Approval. Who's calling the shots here? she wonders. "From who?"

"From whom." He corrects her grammar.

"Seriously?"

"Keep reading. I will see you in the morning." He hangs up.

Jules leans back against her headboard. There's no way in

hell she is going to sleep now. She's about to become Anonymous Girl once again. Bringing her legs to her chest, she hugs them tightly. No one, not even her mother or her closest friends, knows the truth of what transpired after that story broke, the hard lesson that came with that Pulitzer Prize–winning piece.

RICK JANUS, LEAD reporter on the Porn Gate exposé, had called Jules the morning after the prize was announced asking her to join his team celebrating that evening at the Hyatt Hotel with the rest of the newspaper staff. She begged her mother to please let her go. Just for a little bit, she promised. Her mother was ridiculously overprotective. But at seventeen, Jules was at least a good decade younger than everyone else on the investigative team—and probably everyone at the entire newspaper. She promised she'd be back by curfew. And no, she would not be drinking, even if everyone else was.

She lied.

She also lied about what she was wearing. She left her house in the navy-blue belted sheath dress that she wore to her sweet sixteen. But in the hotel bathroom, she quickly changed into a formfitting black off-the-shoulder jersey dress that she secretly bought at Forever 21—the kind of dress her mother disdained. But this was her big moment to be with the team and celebrate. She wanted to look sophisticated. Admittedly, she wanted to look good for Rick. They'd been working closely together on the story for the past six months, and she couldn't help it—she had a crush on him. I mean, who wouldn't? He was the paper's brilliant, handsome lead investigative reporter, and he kept telling her that the story could never have happened without her—that *he* couldn't have done it without her. He kept complimenting her reporting skills, meticulous documentation, and research. He kept saying she was as good, if not better, than any member of his team.

Three glasses of champagne and two shots later, Jules found herself alone in a hotel room with him. She'd followed a small group back to his room for an after-party and waited until everyone left but her. Rick was leaning against the dresser, eyeing her from across the room, and her whole body tingled. He must be feeling it too. This couldn't be just in her head. But Rick was in his early thirties, recently separated, and, she knew, way too old for her. But she was mature. High school boys were so dumb and childish, and they didn't interest her. Her mother always called her an old soul. She smiled back at him, and he held her gaze. It was obvious he wanted to be with her too.

"Great night," she said, feeling nervous but also light-headed and loose.

"It sure was." She noticed him shuffling his feet against the carpet. "Couldn't have gotten the prize without you, Jules. And this story is just the beginning. You're going to do big things one day." He cocked his head slightly, giving her the once-over, and she was glad she bought the dress. Normally, whenever she'd meet him and the team at the paper, she'd come straight from school, wearing jeans, sneakers, and oversized sweatshirts. He was looking at her differently now, blowing air out of his cheeks as though trying to cool down.

"I'm a bit drunk here. I think it's best if . . ." he stammered, gesturing toward the door.

But he didn't finish the sentence, and whenever Jules replayed the scene in her head—she knew the truth: *She didn't let him.* Instead of leaving, she stepped toward him, drunk and high on the success of their award-winning piece and her own desire.

She kissed him first, and he didn't stop her. He wrapped his arms around her, pressed her tightly against him, his breath heavy with champagne and kamikazes, then pulled her down to the bed with him.

Rick's hands roamed all over her, moving too fast, and Jules realized she wasn't quite ready for this. In her mind she had been, but the reality was much different. She wanted to tell him to slow down, but the room was spinning, her head was on fire, and she felt sick to her stomach. Before she knew it, her dress was off, her strapless bra was unsnapped, and her panties had been tossed aside. And before she could formulate a coherent sentence, he was inside her. She screamed, and he immediately pulled out.

"Jules—are you okay?" He sat bolt upright, staring down at the trickle of blood between her thighs. "Oh my God. You're a virgin?"

"Yes," she managed.

His face went pale as he slapped his palm against his forehead. "I'm a fucking idiot—what was I even thinking? This was wrong on every level." He popped off the bed as though he were catapulted into the air and searched frantically for his jeans. Finding them on the other side of the bed, he quickly put them on and sat back down next to her. Shaking his head, he began breathing heavily as though he'd just run ten miles. "I drank too much, but I know better. No excuses." He touched her arm gently, but his fingertips felt scalding against her hot skin. "I'm so sorry."

No words emerged. Jules pulled the sheets up to her chin, to cover her body, her shame. This wasn't his fault; it was hers. She followed him up to the hotel room. She knew right from wrong. And yet, she'd felt something powerful between them, and age didn't seem to matter. *She* kissed him first.

He was no longer looking at her with that remorseful gaze but now staring at the opposite wall as he spoke, as though there were a third person in the room. "Sometimes you end up working closely with someone and become so passionate about a project together that those feelings get confused. They shouldn't, but they do. Not your fault, Jules—it's mine. I wish I could take it back, but I can't."

And the way he was looking at her, his wavy, dark brown hair bobbing ever so slightly with pity, like she were one of the sex-trafficked girls in their investigation, hurt more than anything else. Jules had planned to ask him for a summer internship with his investigative team, hoping it would eventually lead to a permanent job one day—but now she never would or could. What had she been thinking? That they would run off together into the sunset, recorders in hand?

He picked up her black dress from the floor near his feet and extended it to her as though it were an olive branch. "Please keep this between us, and I will too. Just let it go, okay?" He then reached for the phone on the nightstand and began checking his texts. She was dismissed.

I ruined everything.

Rick got up and went into the bathroom with his phone. As soon as the door closed, Jules quickly slipped on the dress, which she would dump later that night. She felt cheap, discarded—but mostly, disappointed with herself for misreading the situation. Gathering her things, she hurried out of the hotel room door without saying goodbye.

As she got into a waiting cab, Jules knew that her first time would always feel like her last. She also knew that her first big journalism prize would forever be tarnished. She vowed to never let anyone or anything get in the way of a story again. But she did exactly as Rick Janus had asked. *She told no one and let it go.* And yet, it never really went away. It cleaved and clawed at her, until it became a new layer of skin: thicker, tougher, and impenetrable.

SEVEN

MISSOULA, MONTANA

E LLIS HAS NEVER been to Montana. Everywhere else in the world, but not here. He doesn't do nature. He prefers the indoors—air-conditioning, immaculate five-star hotels—contained, pristine spaces where he feels in control. But this trip was long overdue.

He glances out the tinted glass window of the SUV. Despite his misgivings, Missoula, with its sapphire sky, jagged mountain range, and the glittery river beneath it, is breathtaking, like something out of his friend Ralph Lauren's *Survival Guide* campaign. *My shoes would never survive here.* He can't help but chuckle to himself, picturing his sleek stilettos getting caught in cow manure and mud. He then checks his watch for the umpteenth time that morning: 6:55 a.m. *Perfect. My grandson should still be sleeping. The element of surprise is key.*

"Must be that road up ahead," Ellis tells his driver. "The unmarked one to your left."

"Yes, that's it." Paul, his driver of over a decade, who travels with him and takes him wherever he needs to be, eyes Ellis reassuringly from the rearview mirror.

No one in Ellis's family knows that he flew his private plane out here to see Adam—especially not his wife or their eldest daughter, Hannah, Adam's mother. Too many questions; he just couldn't risk it. Only Alexandra knows the details. He needed her to do the legwork for him: get the directions to his grandson's secluded hideaway and go over all the instructions with Paul.

As they turn onto the dirt road, Ellis sees the small cabin in the distance where Adam—admittedly, his favorite grandchild—lives alone. He shakes his head in dismay. *The boy was raised in luxury and is now living like the Unabomber.*

Swallowing the lump forming in his throat, Ellis recalls that horrific day four years ago, probably one of the worst days of his life, when he and Vivienne got that middle-of-the-night call that Adam had overdosed on heroin. Their beautiful, talented grandson, who at the young age of twenty-five had taken New York's art scene by storm, was hanging on by a thread. Miraculously, he survived, and after spending two weeks recuperating in the hospital, he entered rehab for nearly three months. Once he was released, Adam left his family, his lowlife friends, and his meteoric career behind him in the dust, opting for total seclusion and anonymity—and for getting as far away from the Baum family name as he could go. That total shutout has saddened Ellis deeply, but at least Adam is alive.

As they pull up the gravel driveway, Ellis's chest tightens and he feels a sharp, stabbing pain. It has been happening too often lately and is getting worse. He will call his doctor when he returns to New York. *Perhaps coming here was a mistake, a rash decision.* He stares at the back of Paul's neatly trimmed salt-and-pepper head of hair—the man who keeps his secrets.

"Paul."

His driver eyes him again through the rearview mirror. "Yes, Mr. Baum . . . Are you okay?"

"I'm fine, thank you." Suddenly, Ellis feels constricted, needs air. He rolls down the window, sticks his head out slightly, and gathers his breath. "I will call you when I'm ready to leave. This could take awhile. The town we passed through earlier looks lovely. Go relax, have breakfast."

Paul parks and turns around, eyeing Ellis skeptically. "Maybe I should just wait here for you."

Before he can respond, Ellis sees a light turn on in the house, and then a window shade pulls back and the outline of his grandson's profile appears.

"I've got this," Ellis says uneasily. But does he? He never second-guesses himself. "You can go now."

"Why don't I stay in case you—"

"Paul, please, just go." Ellis cuts him off and opens the car door.

As the car reverses down the driveway, the front door flings open and Adam stands at the threshold, barefoot and shirtless in flannel bottoms surrounded by a trio of dogs. He is much more muscular than Ellis remembers. His hair is longer, shaggy, and he's grown a beard too—a Mountain Man in dire need of a good shave. But there's color in his face. He looks healthy. Stronger. Walking toward him, Ellis takes a deep, grateful breath. *God knows I've missed you.*

"Grandfather." Adam's eyes are wide with disbelief. "What are you doing here? Did Mom send you?"

"No one knows I'm here. Not your mom, not your grandmother. It's been far too long. You look well . . ." Ellis, who isn't a hugger or one for public displays of affection, reaches for the young man and pulls him in close. He smells like morning—teeth not yet brushed, slightly musky, remnants of paint. Something about Adam brings out the warmth in him. When Adam was a little boy, he was always off painting or sketching in a corner by himself while the other grandkids rabble-roused or played on the swing set in the backyard at the house in Bedford. Adam was a loner, reminding Ellis of himself. But that all changed drastically as the boy grew up, especially after college—Adam became unrecognizable. He was the life of every party, always surrounded by a bevy of scantily dressed young women and heavily tattooed artsy and drug dealer types. His life became fast-paced, full of gallery showings, after-parties, and after-after-parties—a constantly in motion, sleepless, toxic, drug-induced existence that he attempted to hide. Even during family holiday dinners, Adam couldn't sit still for five minutes. It was the cocaine, Ellis was certain, and he was deeply worried about him. Adam had become Chelsea's flavor of the month, and everyone wanted a piece of him. The boy had nothing left of himself. The onslaught of attention and ceaseless demand swallowed him up whole.

Ellis gestures toward the screened door. "Can I come in?"

"Of course." Adam steps aside, holds back the excited dogs, and ushers his grandfather into his home.

Wiping the dust off his shoes on the floor mat, Ellis enters the room and stops cold. The exterior may look like a dump, but this . . . *It's incredible.* Each wall is a painted canvas filled with life and bold color—even the ceiling is covered with vibrant brushstrokes, varying textures, and roiling hues of gold, burgundy, orange, green, lavender, and turquoise—*happy colors*. Ellis slowly absorbs each image: lovers embracing, friends toasting one another in a café, children frolicking in a park, naked women by the sea, nature in every format—mountains, water, trees, sky, flora. The brilliance of the art is overwhelming and takes Ellis's breath away. Unlike Adam's celebrated technique of the past, which was ominous and abstract, this room conveys joy and light— therapeutic imagery. Except for that one image over there. Ellis's gaze is drawn to the farthest wall, by the kitchen.

Walking tentatively toward it, he feels the weight of his grandson's eyes on him as he stops just inches away and takes in the composition of an older man in a well-fitted suit with a shock of thick, silvery hair, his head dipped pensively. He stands alone, hands clasped behind his back like a butler, surrounded by an avalanche of shoes coming at him from all directions, a fuselage of bullets with spikes. Stilettos. *Me. My grandson painted me.* Ellis can't help himself. He turns to Adam, speechless. His eyes become misty.

"Adam." His voice chokes: his grandson's name emerges not as a word but as a breath.

Adam smiles broadly, and Ellis can see the endearing dimples of a boy etched on the recovered face of a man who nearly took his own precious life. He knows right then he's made a mistake.

Ellis starts coughing, then muzzles the harsh sound with his pocket handkerchief. "Please forgive me. I'm afraid I've made a grave error of judgment. I came here to ask you something—a favor. But now I see that it was impulsive and unworthy." He steadies himself. That damn chest pain again. He sits down on the nearest chair, an old, worn-in La-Z-Boy. His entire body sinks like an anchor into the soft, inviting cushion.

Adam hovers over him. "Let me get you something to drink."

But Ellis grabs Adam tightly by the arm and stops him. "I tried you know . . . to see you. But you never took my calls, so I stopped bothering you. I should have fought harder to be there for you. I've thought about you every single day." Tears fill Ellis's eyes again, and he doesn't bother wiping them away this time. All this emotion—is it the cancer? Seeing Adam again? That image on the wall? Ellis's mind and body begin to wrestle like adversaries. "I felt that perhaps I was the root of your problems. That my company and all the attention that comes with it hurt you somehow. Too much pressure. All that paparazzi. You hated that kind of attention when you were a boy. Maybe it was *my* doing that lent to the burden of it all . . ."

Adam squeezes his grandfather's clinging hand. "None of it was your fault. *I* was the problem. I was living too hard, too destructively. All I ever wanted was to paint and be left alone. I went against who I was and became this other person, trying to live up to the hype surrounding me. My system crashed. I got your calls, the messages from you and Grandma. But I needed time alone, to figure myself out and work through my problems sober." Adam releases the hand and lightly pats Ellis's hunched shoulder. "But I'm glad you're here." He gestures toward the kitchen with a slight smile. "I wish I could offer you a Bloody Mary. I know how much you enjoy those. But I only have juice."

"Juice is fine. No drinks for me, Adam . . . That's another reason why I've come. I wanted to tell you a few things." Ellis's breath thickens, but he pushes through it. "I drank too much. It was a problem and a secret . . . one of many." *Too many.* He leans back, and the chair recliner pops up, surprising him. Both he and Adam laugh, and then Ellis's face turns serious. "While you were in treatment, so was I. I thought if you could do it, then I damn well better get help too. I checked into a private program for six weeks, outside of Chicago. Only your grandmother knew about it. I was attending meetings there with other prominent men—celebrity addicts, I suppose you could call us." He smiles faintly. "I'm just over three years sober."

Adam stares at his grandfather, openly surprised by the confession. "Thank you for sharing that. I know how hard that is for you." He then walks to the kitchen, pours them both fresh-squeezed orange juice, and sits on the couch across from his grandfather. They both remain quiet, contemplating each other. "But that's not why you're really here, is it?"

"No, it's not." Ellis shakes his head. "Do you remember when you were around ten and painted a picture for me? You loved nature so much even back then. Anyway, you painted a tornado. You were obsessed with them. Only this particular tornado had a woman's face embedded inside it."

Adam grins. "Yes . . . I remember."

"Well, I still have it. I treasure it. It reminds me of something in my past." Ellis begins coughing again.

"You're not well. What's really going on?"

Ellis brushes it off. "I'm old. You see, I have these nightmares . . . They used to come once every few months or so, but now they occur every time I fall sleep." Ellis's mind drifts. His thoughts become fragmented. There's so much he wants to say right now, to share with his grandson. "Perhaps I'm not so well . . . nearing the end. But I've had an interesting life, wonderful in many aspects. Your grandmother, your mother, all my kids, the grandkids." *And Henri*, which Ellis doesn't say. "Anika Baum is my legacy."

Adam places the juice down on the table. "Let me stop you right there. I'm not your guy. I can't take over the company. Please don't ask that of me."

Ellis smiles. "That's not why I'm here. Your sisters will take over the company one day. They are already an integral part of the business. It's for them, not you." He glances out the large window near them and sees the lovely mountain range through it. "I've never told anyone this . . ." He thinks about the conversation he had with Dan Mansfield last week. "That is, until very recently. I was not born here, you know."

Adam leans back against the couch. "Yes, I know. Belgium. Your family came from diamonds."

"Lies." Ellis begins to feel feverish. *So many lies.* "Not Belgium. Not diamonds. No family. That was all made up for media consumption, until I, too, believed it. The truth is, I came from nothing. From Germany, not Belgium. I grew up—if you could call it that—during the war. I lived underground for most of it—sewers, basements, even inside a large chimney—from the time I was eight years old until I was thirteen. I'm half Jewish, you know. I arrived in this country alone, was raised in foster homes until I was old enough to support myself. But I was smart, quick, and creative, and most importantly, I had nothing to lose. In America it was so easy to rise, to conquer . . . to become. This dark past that I've hidden . . ."

Adam quirks his brows, reminding Ellis of his daughter Hannah, who makes that same inquisitive expression. Over Adam's shoulder, he sees the image of the lovers—so young and carefree, everything ahead of them. *If only life were that.* He emits a deep, pain-filled sigh. "My mother was a great beauty. She came from a small town outside of Munich and moved to Berlin in her teens.

She won beauty pageants, modeled, and fell in love with my father. His name was Arno Baum. He was a Jewish banker, married with children of his own. She was Catholic, carefree, Bohemian. They fell in love, but never married, though she called him husband, took his name, and gave it to me . . ." *And his family hated me.*

Ellis's mind flashes back to that young blond girl with golden braids who still makes cameo appearances in his nightmares. She approached him while he was playing ball in a small park near his apartment: "He is not *your* father, you little bastard—he's mine!" Her pretty face scrunched with rage as she spat at both him and his mother and then ran away. "Don't ever listen to her or anyone else," his mother reassured him as he cried. "Arno Baum is your father. Will always be your father."

"Are you okay?" Adam asks gently.

Ellis's voice takes on a tremor as the various memories fight for space in his mind. "You see, Adam, I was around five when an artist first came by our apartment to paint my mother. The artist was Ernst Engel."

"*The* Ernst Engel?"

"Yes, the very same."

"And what happened?" Adam's bright green eyes—*Hannah's eyes*—sparkle with curiosity.

Too much happened. Ellis looks away, past his grandson, no longer seeing the lovers or the mountains, or anything tangible. He is back there again . . . in the dim foyer of his mother's spacious apartment, on his knees, his mouth bound, and he is surrounded by soldiers with guns pointed at his mother. But it was that man—Helmuth Geisler—that he saw, Geisler's sharp voice that he heard, yelling at his mother, and Ellis couldn't make it stop.

"You modeled for that pig—that degenerate artist—Ernst Engel, didn't you? I now possess that painting as evidence," Geisler shouted. His tiny, pointy teeth reminded Ellis of a squirrel. "You fuck a Jew, give birth to his bastard, and then model for an artist who was a known enemy of the state. *Was*—Ernst Engel is dead. And you know what that makes you, Miss Germany . . . *dead*." He turned to Ellis and bent over. "Stop the crying, you little shit. Your mother is a whore, and she is getting what she deserves."

His mother dropped to her knees and begged Geisler to spare Ellis, lying that he was not Arno Baum's biological son—that his blood was Aryan, like hers. Ellis began shouting that he wanted to die with his mother, to take him too—but no one could hear his muffled pleas. And Geisler agreed with his mother. He, too, wanted Ellis to live, to bear witness to the show of shows—the one runway that burned like wildfire through Ellis's young brain and still consumes his cobwebbed mind. They stripped his mother down to her undergarments and made her dress up in high heels and in her fancy red dress—the color of blood, Geisler said, the color of the painting.

Wasting no time, the Nazis hung a placard around her neck that read: "I fucked a kike. I am a whore" and pushed his mother out the front door, leaving Ellis all alone in the apartment. Glued to the window and still gagged, he saw the men parading her down the street. They made her walk around in circles in those high heels for hours, round and round, until she could no longer stand. And when she finally collapsed, they dragged her away and Ellis couldn't see anything. But he heard the shots, five of them, and then nothing. And in that nothing, that murky deadening silence . . . he imagined everything.

"And your father . . ." Adam whispers.

Ellis pauses, his breath is shallow. "I never saw him again either. I tried searching for information on his family years ago through the Holocaust museum in Washington, but there was nothing, so I stopped. I do remember a few things . . . a neighbor back then, a widow living next door to us who adored my mother, came for me. I barely recall what happened, except that she fed me and put me into a bed in her guest room. And then a few days later in the middle of the night, she brought me to someone in the back of the local bakery—a man dressed in all black. No one knew his real name. But that man saved my life."

"Who was he?"

Ellis closes his eyes briefly. "I'll never know. But it wasn't just me. There were other orphaned kids he saved. He snuck us out of town through the forest, through sewers, farms . . . dirt, scum. Everything I remember from then on was black, filthy, smelly, and cold. I was always hungry. But the grime and rot were the worst part." He looks away. "I survived."

When Ellis finishes his story—a story for him that never really finishes—he peers up at his grandson, whose face is wet with silent tears. "You see, Adam, every shoe I have ever created is to honor the memory of my mother, Anika. To never forget *that* walk. She held her head high as they laughed at her. And people, neighbors, and others in town who I thought were her friends, threw things at her—tomatoes, garbage, even shoes. She saw me up in the window. Or maybe it was just a figment of my imagination, I don't know . . . but in my mind, we had one moment, one last exchange. She saw my face pressed to the glass and smiled courageously. That smile told me to be brave no matter what. And then she was gone as if she never existed. I couldn't save her . . ." Ellis glances down at his trembling hands.

Hands that were once slim and smooth but are now stippled with age spots.

Adam gets up off the couch and stands before his grandfather. "What is it you need from me?"

Ellis slowly reaches into his jacket pocket and hands Adam the article on Carl Geisler's death and the details surrounding the stolen treasure trove. "It's Geisler's son," he explains. "Murdered and robbed. I believe the painting of my mother may have been hidden in his apartment. Rumors are now circulating that Geisler was harboring paintings by Picasso, Chagall, Matisse, Cézanne, and an Engel, among many other masterworks." His voice breaks. "I know in my heart *Woman on Fire*—that's what Engel called it—was there. Helmuth Geisler told my mother that he had the painting in his hands—I heard it with my own ears. It's the only image I will ever have of her, the only connection to my past. I'm determined to find it and bring it back home where it belongs, with our family."

"Do you have any proof, hard evidence of the painting's history?" Adam asks. "Did you ever hire someone to help you?"

Ellis searches his grandson's eyes. "I'm ashamed to admit that I was too busy hiding my past. So I did my own search and was able to obtain a few important documents. One is a brochure announcing works of modern art sold at an auction in Lucerne, Switzerland, in 1939. *Woman on Fire* was on that list. All the works sold there were Nazi-looted art. Most of the paintings were purchased anonymously, and the money supported the Nazi war machine. Despicable." Ellis takes a deep breath. "I don't know who bought *Woman on Fire*, or what happened to it from there, or how it ultimately ended up in Geisler's hands. But I do know the painting also made a pit stop in Paris several months prior to the

Lucerne auction, and Helmuth Geisler was somehow involved in that as well." He leans forward. "And that's why I'm here. I possess a document signed by Geisler to a courier transporting the painting from a gallery in Paris to Lucerne." Ellis feels his cheeks quiver, his pulse racing. "And the gallery . . . De Laurent."

Adam stares wide-eyed at his grandfather, a red flush sidling up his neck and face.

Ellis purses his lips tightly. "Exactly."

"Margaux de Laurent." Adam's tone is stilted.

"Yes, *Woman on Fire* was once in the hands of her grandfather, Charles de Laurent. His signature is on the courier's document, beneath Helmuth Geisler's. Did the painting belong to de Laurent? Did he represent Ernst Engel in Paris? Was the man *forced* to sell that painting to Geisler? Is there a bill of sale out there? So many questions. Not to mention that Ernst Engel was murdered in 1939 and *Woman on Fire* may have been the artist's very last painting—and, if so, extremely valuable." Ellis feels weak. "If I believe the painting was there among the stolen artwork in Geisler's possession, then you can be sure Margaux does too. And I don't need to tell you what that ruthless woman is capable of . . ."

Adam's face dims, and Ellis immediately regrets bringing that up. Did he really think that Adam, a recovered heroin addict, could somehow help him find his long-lost painting before Margaux de Laurent's dirty hands get there first? . . . *Shame on him.*

Ellis stands; his legs are wobbly. "I'm sorry for putting this on you. I had this crazy plan concocted in my head. But seeing you so settled here in this beautiful home you've created—I've changed my mind. It was an emotional ask. And wrong. I will handle this alone."

Adam also stands, his voice so subdued that Ellis barely hears him. "The thing is . . . and the memory is so vague, but Margaux may have mentioned that painting to me. Five years ago, when I was with her at the family's château in the South of France, I remember her showing me several paintings her grandfather had saved during the war, and she talked about one that her grandfather couldn't save but had meant everything to him. Something about a woman in flames—that's all I remember. But I was so high then that I can't be sure if it's true or something I only imagined."

Ellis begins coughing uncontrollably and struggles to gather his breath.

"You're sick, aren't you? Tell me the truth."

There's no sense in hiding anything from the boy now. "Yes, but no one in the family knows," Ellis confesses, thinking about the death sentence the oncologist handed him a few weeks ago tucked away in his office drawer. "One year, tops. Eighteen months if I'm lucky."

He picks up the newspaper clipping lying on the coffee table and waves it. "The Geisler heist has pushed me over the edge, dredging up so many painful memories that I've tried to let go. But that's the irony—it won't let *me* go. Because for the first time in nearly eight decades, I know the painting is out there waiting for me to save her. I can feel it, smell it, Adam, in the same way that I can sniff the leather on any pair of shoes and know just by its scent its quality and its maker." Ellis gently tucks the article back inside his breast pocket, removes his handkerchief, and dabs his perspiring forehead. "I may have a real chance at seeing my mother once again . . . perhaps for the very last time. I just need to find her before Margaux de Laurent gets there first."

Turning away from his grandfather, Adam walks toward the window and peers out at the majestic landscape he calls his backyard. He stares into the glass for what feels like an eternity, then spins around slowly, purposefully, like Ellis did when he was a small boy twirling in the armoire mirror in his mother's high heels. "Whatever you need . . . I will do it."

EIGHT

CORRENS, FRANCE

MARGAUX INHALES THE crisp country air, and in one voracious breath all the familiar scents come rushing in—the outlying aromatic hills, the vineyard up ahead, the olive grove to the left, even the cool, hidden Neolithic caves on the outskirts of the château that she explored countless times as a kid. *I missed this place.*

It's been months since she's been back to Correns. The small Provençal village just north of Brignoles is where her family has owned a 2,500-acre château for more than a century and where she spent precious summers with her grandfather. Her fondest childhood memories took place here. But that all ended abruptly just after her twelfth birthday, when her grandfather died. And now Château de Laurent in all its rustic glory is no longer for pleasure, just business. *Except for the walks.* Out here, in the open air, Margaux still feels her grandfather's immense presence, hears his booming voice, as though he were still walking alongside her.

Wearing tall boots, skinny jeans, and her favorite fluffy old white cardigan, which still hangs in her closet from when she was a teenager, Margaux moves briskly along the trail from the château to the *Maison*—the House—a 10,000-square-foot bunker hidden beneath the vineyard's grapevines and the lush woodlands surrounding it. Built as protection by her great-grandfather just after World War I, the Maison is where the family safeguards its legendary art library—a comprehensive *catalogue raisonné*. It's also home to the most significant top-secret art world intelligence—blackmail material, her father used to brag. *And now . . . the Geisler collection.*

As she approaches the Maison, Margaux can practically hear the echo of Grand-papa Charles's deep voice: "You certainly have the eye, *ma chérie*. But what truly separates good art dealers from great ones is the *ear*. Listen and learn . . . know your history. Be a sponge, a *scholar-dealer*, an expert of authenticity and true talent. People will choose you not for your magnificent galleries and collection—*that too*—but for your knowledge. Know what your clients want. Study your artists, your competitors, your competitors' clients—everyone's preferences. And most importantly, learn their secrets." His thick, silvery brows would narrow lovingly as he gave his only grandchild pearls of wisdom that went way over her head, though she absorbed them anyway. "But," he warned with a wagging finger, "if you get sloppy or stumble, people remember, and you will pay the price. Always remain one step ahead of the competition, and sometimes, I'm afraid, the means to get there can often be"—he looked away as though seeing a wild animal in the distance—"questionable."

Questionable indeed. Margaux moves faster. She recalls every single word gifted by her grandfather. In contrast, her father,

Sébastien, who took over the galleries after her grandfather died, was sloppy, careless, with nothing to offer her. A clown, stumbling more times than she could count. And he paid the price.

Stopping briefly at the familiar large boulder on her path, Margaux climbs it just as she did as a young girl. She sits at its crown, knees to chest, imbibing the stunning panoramic view. In the distance, she sees the mouth of the Gorges du Verdon, the magnificent river canyon where she has spent countless hours hiking. After her grandfather's death, no one gave her any boundaries or rules or spoke of dangers. No one seemed to care about anything she did. Her parents were too absorbed in their own lives and lovers to notice her long absences. So Margaux did whatever she pleased. By the time she was fourteen, she learned to depend solely on herself, until her parents' existence meant nothing to her; they were merely roadblocks to her one day taking over the family business right out from under them—which, of course, she did.

For a moment, she contemplates skipping her business dealings at the Maison today and heading out to the Argens River at the mouth of the canyon. It was always her favorite part of hiking, the very end, when she'd cap off a grueling climb with a naked swim. It was pure bliss, frolicking alone in the turquoise water beneath the sun's scorching rays . . . just her and nature. It felt like the whole world belonged to her. *Except for once when she decided to share her slice of paradise.* She would never make that mistake again.

Jumping off the rock, Margaux resumes her walk and shakes off the invasive memory of what happened that ill-fated night of her father's death. What matters is that she got away with it. But if she closes her eyes right now, she can still picture the pompous bastard, hear his menacing, drunken laughter. That bombastic sound never seems to go away.

Her father squandered nearly everything her grandfather spent his entire life building and nurturing, *her* legacy. No one in the art world knew just how bad financially things were at DLG when her father died, leaving her sideswiped by his massive debt. Upon learning that the galleries were nearly bankrupt, Margaux did everything she could to cover up the truth from her investors, her artists, the media, and most important, her collectors. She began secretly selling off De Laurent properties around the globe to keep the more important galleries afloat in Paris, New York, Hong Kong, Basel, and London. This château—her grandfather's Garden of Eden—would have been next on the hit list if she had no other options. But she held off because the château's grapes— the "jewels," as her grandfather had lovingly called them—are still profitable. Their award-winning rosé is what pays her employees' salaries, but just barely.

Two month ago, after a long, hard meeting with DLG's accountants, Margaux was told that she would be forced to declare bankruptcy by year's end—the ultimate humiliation. They suggested that she seriously consider selling off the family's famed art collection. *Unacceptable!* she shouted at the accountants. *Never.* The gossip would be fierce and unforgivable. *And her grandfather . . .* this would kill his memory. She was determined to find another option, and she put her personal hacker to work. Once she learned of the tainted Geisler treasure trove, she knew it was the answer to her problems. *The* option.

Eyeing the rows of lush vines around her, Margaux is amazed by the grapes—ripe and plentiful, especially at the beginning of the *vendange*—harvest season. Her mother would always complain that it smelled like garbage. She should know—coming from trailer trash—but Margaux has always loved the aroma, a potent mix of honey and kerosene. It makes her feel alive.

Continuing down the serpentine path, she relishes the welcoming crunch of the twigs beneath her boots, like a drum roll announcing her arrival. When she reaches the Maison, she types in the security code and enters the cozy three-bedroom residence and looks around. The television is blaring, and there are remnants of a half-eaten croissant with jelly sticking to a plate and a coffee mug left behind on the kitchen table.

"Wyatt," she calls out to no response. He's clearly here. He must already be down in the cellar.

She walks inside the master bedroom, Wyatt's room. The windows are open, the bed unmade, and his clothes are scattered across the floor. A slob. She circumvents the mess and enters the extra-large walk-in closet the size of a small bedroom. She kneels and lifts the discreetly placed lever sticking up from the floor, which opens to a makeshift staircase leading down to a mammoth Gothic-style wine cellar.

As she descends, Margaux takes in the cellar's skeletal stone and pointed ogive-shaped arches lining the cavernous stone walls. It twins the château's cellar, only this one is a fake—a perfect cover in case it is discovered.

Moving vigorously down the long, cold tunnel, she passes a dozen decorative wooden antique doors embedded into the wall. Another trick of the eye. None of the doors open except for the very last one. She presses another code and enters. While the cellar looks like a pop-out from the Middle Ages, what lurks beyond the fortified door is a hi-tech fantasy, replete with a state-of-the-art library and a cutting-edge computer system that would make the Pentagon jealous.

The music is blaring Nirvana when she enters, and Margaux sees Wyatt Ross finger-tapping his large desk, encircled by multiple screens and lit-up electronics like a celebrity deejay playing Ibiza. A former Silicon Valley hotshot, Wyatt found his true calling as a hacker and a thief. She pays him an obscene amount of money for his exclusive services, his loyalty, his secrecy, his cunning, and, most of all, his disdain of humanity. He thrives in the underworld of technology, a snake in cyber grass, and doesn't make mistakes. *Not yet at least.*

"Margaux." He looks up, feigning surprise, when he sees her face reflected in his computer screen. She knows better. Surely he saw her approach the house and walk through the cellar. Their surveillance system covers the entire château. He is expecting her. She plays along.

"It's been awhile." She smiles coolly.

"You look great," he says.

"And you look like you." She grins, assessing him. He has that affected hipster appearance—a two-days-late-for-a-shave scruff, a worn-in black T-shirt, ratty jeans, and, of course, the requisite scuffed-up Doc Martens. He also has an ornate wrist tattoo, a Sanskrit-looking quote. She can't be bothered to ask him what it means; she doesn't care.

"Coffee, or wine? It's early, but hey, why not. A fine vintage courtesy of the winery." He stands. Wyatt is tall, lanky, and thin, like someone who smokes constantly and eats only when he must. She can tell by his uneasy demeanor that he feels the weight of her fixed gaze upon him. She likes that she makes him nervous.

"Wine. And it's never too early." Margaux sits on the leather couch, stretches out her legs, lights up a cigarette, and offers him one, and he takes it on his way to the bar in the corner of the large office.

"I'm thrilled the paintings arrived safely," she begins. "Your people certainly knew what they were doing. They were waiting for me the second I came out of the building with two stuffed garbage bags like Santa Claus. And they cleaned up nicely . . . no fingerprints, no footprints. A spotless sweep, from my understanding. The German authorities still don't have a single clue."

"Oh, they have a clue all right, but not about you—about Geisler," Wyatt remarks. "I dug deeper into that *Spotlight* reporter's files while you were away. There was classified information revealing that a small group of German government officials knew about Geisler's secret stash at least a year ago and left that demented old man alone with all those paintings while they tried to figure out what to do with him. They were probably terrified of causing the publicity nightmare that's happening right now." He laughs. "Hitler's very own art thief's heir living free and easy with over a billion dollars' worth of stolen masterpieces stockpiled in his kitchen. You'd think somebody would have gotten on top of that train wreck long ago."

He returns to the couch with two glasses of the family's reserve rosé, Margaux's favorite of all the wines produced at the château, and sits down across from her. She looks briefly into the glass and can practically see the parting of the grapes, the perfect blend of Cinsault, Syrah, Grenache, and her favorite, the light-skinned white Vermentino variety with its dark green, pentagonal leaves. Her grandfather took great pleasure in explaining the differences among the grapes during their long walks. She often wondered back then if he loved his precious vineyard even more than his paintings. She looks up and eyes Wyatt's dirty boots kicked up on the coffee table in front of her. She gives him a death stare. "Do I want to know what happened to the woman whose apartment I used in Munich?"

He quickly removes the boots from the table. "My men *are* the best. Discreet. And no . . . you don't." Wyatt's voice has a faint Southern twang, a remnant of some blue-collar Podunk town in Kentucky where he was born, then ran away from and never looked back. He also has a permanent twitch in his right eye, and Margaux focuses on that.

"And the reporter of the story?"

"Silenced."

"And how, may I ask?"

"Better that you don't." His gaze suddenly turns dark and flat.

"I see . . . And that car?"

"I'm still trying to track down that Volkswagen you saw circling Geisler's apartment building," he tells her. "I traced the plate you gave us. It was rented. Name was fake. But don't worry, I'm on it. My bigger concern now that we have the paintings is how to get the ball rolling fast enough so we can maximize our profits. I don't have to tell you that stolen art is a tricky beast. Once a painting is reported stolen, it immediately loses value. Rumors are now circulating, guessing which paintings may have been in Geisler's collection. No one knows for sure . . . but they will. We need to move ASAP."

Wyatt gestures to the thick glass window leading to the archives, where three mammoth-sized vaults are located, and the Geisler paintings are stashed. Each vault has its own purpose: one stores artwork for safekeeping for DLG clients, another is designated for paintings that are for sale, and the third contains the family's permanent collection—those works that are never to be sold. Her grandfather did not miss a beat.

"Here's how it's going to go," Margaux instructs him. "No more than two paintings to any one collector or museum. Sell the paintings under the radar, using the dark web or whatever black magic you have at your fingertips." Her voice rises. "No matter what, we must remain completely anonymous. Be sure to tap into only those museum curators who can be bought and those clients who can be blackmailed if need be. I suggest hitting up the Latin American drug dealers first. Then Russian mafia. And, of course, that sleazy cadre of Chinese politicians who are buying up major works in droves." Her eyes bore into his. "Anyone with a conscience is off our playlist. Not a single painting is to be released aboveboard. Even if there is a demand, it could be a trap. Am I clear?"

"Perfectly." He sucks in a deep breath, then lets it out slowly with an irritating hiss like a balloon that's been punctured.

"I don't want anyone connecting the dots to me," she stresses. "And as far as laundering the money goes, follow all protocols so that by the time it gets to my bank account the money is washed. For each painting you place, you will receive a large bonus. That should be incentive enough." Her eyes skid slowly across his as if to remind him that he is dispensable. "One thing . . . the painting by Ernst Engel—*Woman on Fire*—remains here. That one is not for sale ever, period."

Wyatt raises a brow, but she ignores it, owing him no further explanation. He finishes his wine and pours them both another glass. "There's also the delicate matter of those Jewish families fighting to get their stolen art back," he says.

"I don't do delicate."

"Hear me out. This isn't just a heist—this is Holocaust history we're dealing with. It's going to be a restitution circus, especially after the world gets a glimpse of the big-ticket items Geisler had in his collection—and believe me, they will." He points to the vaults behind them, on the other side of the wall. "I'm referring specifically to the Matisse, the Chagall, the Cézanne, those two Picassos, the Klimt, and that Rembrandt. Those works are all by A-listers, and you can be damn sure they will have their people searching, spying, breaking firewalls, waiting for slippage. We're talking over a billion dollars in inventory. I can do a lot to camouflage us, but I can't prevent leaks or hackers."

"Are you finished with your little soapbox lecture?" Margaux's face clouds over. "You can and you *will* do whatever it takes, which is why I'm paying you through the roof." She leans in. "You are personally responsible for any leaks, and you'd better out-hack the hackers. You"—she wags her cigarette between Wyatt's eyes—"are going to plug up any holes. Pay whoever you have to in crypto. And no fucking slippage."

Wyatt meets her venomous gaze, knowing better than to show Margaux any sign of weakness. But she sees the tiny drops of sweat accumulating at his temples anyway. She leans back against the couch, smoking quietly, contemplating him. Wyatt likes to be bossed around, and she likes making him grovel. But enough of this. Grinding out the last of her cigarette, Margaux checks her watch and stands. "Let's go see the paintings."

He leads her out of the computer complex toward the first vault, which contains not only Geisler's collection but also precious art that her family has safeguarded under lock and key for three generations. Among them, works by Rembrandt, Titian,

Velázquez, Rubens, Monet, and a Picasso from his Surrealist period that the artist painted specifically for her grandfather.

"Exactly how many paintings did we acquire from Geisler?" she asks, testing Wyatt as she does everyone who works for her. She already knows the answer.

"All of them," he replies, pleased with himself. "Fifteen hundred and twenty-seven, plus a suitcase full of drawings."

Good answer: the right one. "Where is *Woman on Fire*?"

"In the last vault—with the untouchables—along with several other paintings from Geisler that were seized from your grandfather's gallery in Paris: Picasso's guitarist, Cézanne's card players, Van Gogh's irises, and a Modigliani muse. I also added two Salvador Dalís that belonged to your father into that vault. I assume you don't want any of those sold?"

He assumed correctly. "Not until I give further notice. Tomorrow morning, I will go through all of Geisler's paintings and assess them for you and pick which are to be sold first." She tilts her head at him. "Excellent work."

Wyatt smiles like a boy who just won the spelling bee. "Is that an actual compliment from you?"

She laughs lightly. Seizing the moment as an invitation, he moves in closer. "Tomorrow we are working, but what are you doing right now?" Wyatt's voice is husky as his body curves slightly. His breath is a combo of cigarettes, wine, and weed.

This wouldn't be her first time with him, nor her last. Despite his disheveled appearance, Wyatt knows what he's doing in bed. *Hmm, why not celebrate?* She reaches out and slowly runs the back of her hand along his facial scruff, which is surprisingly silkier than it looks. And that eye twitch thankfully seems to have stopped doing double time.

Greenlighted, Wyatt pulls Margaux toward him, and she wraps her arms loosely around his neck, kissing him hard on the mouth, and then aggressively inserts her tongue. He moans loudly as she presses her taut breasts against his chest and feels the desire growing between his legs. He pushes her roughly up against the nearest wall, hard, the way she likes it, then yanks off her sweater and the shirt beneath it. She doesn't wear a bra; never has. He removes the phone from her hand and pitches it onto the pile of her clothes next to them. She sees the ample bulge straining against his jeans and reaches for it, deftly unzipping his jeans. She pulls them off, quickly tossing them aside with his T-shirt, and then slowly makes her way down his torso. Wyatt leans against the cold wall to brace himself as Margaux takes him fully into her mouth. He moans above her, and she anticipates getting him off in less than thirty seconds. But he stops her in midaction.

Margaux looks up and wipes her lips, surprised. "Is there a problem?"

"You're going to join me here," he demands, asserting his manhood. Feeling generous, Margaux lets him. Nor does she stop him when he pulls her up toward him and proceeds to unbutton her jeans and remove the boots and the panties until she, too, is fully naked.

Wyatt holds her at arm's length to really look at her. Margaux knows what he sees: the flawless skin, the firm breasts tipped with sharp rose-colored nipples, the manicured narrow path of dark pubic hair.

"You're so goddamn beautiful," he murmurs.

"I've been told," she replies, unaffected.

"And it means nothing to you." He runs his fingers from her breasts down along the trail of her flat, toned abdomen.

"Exactly."

She also knows what Wyatt is thinking. What they all think of her. *Woman or monster?* She prefers monster. It keeps everyone at a necessary distance and on their toes. Wyatt brings her down to the floor with him, spreading his clothes beneath them for cushion before he lowers his head and buries his face between her thighs. Margaux is about to take in the pleasure when she notices her cell phone, lying faceup near her head, light up. As Wyatt goes at it, she reads the text:

It's Adam—call me.

Adam . . . Her whole body ignites, and Wyatt grins from below, thinking it's him. Suddenly, Margaux is overwhelmed by the tsunamic sensation, the loss of control overtaking her body— but not her mind, which is clear and already calculating. Sinking her nails deep into her hacker's busy shoulders, she orgasms hard and fast. Sated, she stares up at the vaulted ceiling and smiles. *Adam Chase is finally back from the dead.*

NINE

J ULES REACHES INSIDE her new Kate Spade tote bag, pulls out the translated article surrounding the details of Carl Geisler's murder from the German news-magazine *Spotlight*, and slaps it down on the café table. "What do you see?"

Dan puts on his reading glasses that are hanging on a flimsy string chain around his neck, takes the article, and examines it. "Well, there's the story, of course. Pull quotes and photos of stolen art. A picture of Carl Geisler looking like he's had one tranquilizer too many. Another of his father goose-stepping through the Louvre with Hitler . . ." He looks up. "Is this a trick question?"

Jules stabs the article with her pen. "It's what you don't see here that matters. Tell me, who wrote the story?"

He brings the article closer to his face. "Holy shit." His good eye twinkles at her with admiration.

She acknowledges the compliment with a knowing smile. "That's right. 'The Spotlight Staff.' The cover story—their biggest scoop in more than thirty years of the magazine's existence—

I know because I checked—and what, no byline? How is that even possible?"

Dan shakes his head and swigs his sugar-loaded coffee. "It's not. There's not a single reporter on the planet who wouldn't demand their name on that story. Even if it was a group effort, all names would be given credit. Unless . . ."

Jules eyes him closely, waits for it. The third cup of coffee is the charm. Dan is suddenly animated, ten years younger.

"The reporter is being protected or quashed . . . the question is, why? Who got to him?"

"Or her," Jules corrects him.

"Or her," Dan grumbles.

"I think we need to find out exactly who was reporting the story and the chain of events before and after."

"I can do that." Dan writes himself a note inside his phone.

Jules waits for him to finish typing, and it is excruciating to watch. He uses one finger. "And the other thing . . . You gave me hundreds of pages of stolen art background. I read it all. I've got notes and questions for you." She clasps her hands together. "We are going after a painting, and I'm missing the one key fact here. You know as well as I do that I can't possibly search for lost artwork—a family heirloom—without knowing who wants it and why." She leans across the table. "Whose painting is it?"

Dan's lips curl into a hybrid smirk and smile. "The golden question."

"I'm serious."

His jaw clenches. "So am I. My source asked to remain anonymous."

"And I respect that more than anything," she argues. "But

unless I know who it's for, I'm driving blind. You said time was of the essence." Her gaze bores into his; she's hoping he will bend.

Dan folds his arms. No budge in sight.

Jules chews the inside of her cheek. "I get it. You don't trust me yet. I know I've been working with you for all of five minutes, but *you* brought me in on this team. A team of two," she emphasizes. "I can't work my A-game without knowing basic details."

Dan shifts uncomfortably in the chair, knowing she's right but clearly deciding whether he can really trust her. He begins hitting the pink sugar packet back and forth as though it were a hockey puck. It's irritating. She reaches across the table and stops the packet in midpass.

He stares back at her as though she were a referee who just made a bad call. *Fine*, Jules thinks, releasing the packet. She will wait it out. She pretends to look at her phone but sees nothing. An inspirational meme from her mother. A text from a college friend wanting dinner plans. The answer is coming. She knows it by the painstaking intake of Dan's breath.

"Tell me something about you that no one knows," he says instead.

"What?" Her voice snags. "We're playing that game—really?"

But Dan isn't laughing this time. He is struggling with revealing a source who's asked for anonymity. She sees it in his eyes. This isn't a game to him.

She pauses, tilts her head. "I already told you about Anonymous Girl."

"No . . . that's not enough. That was so you'd get the job." He points his finger at her. "Tell me something about *you*."

"And then you'll reveal the source?" She's not above barter, but this is ridiculous. Childish. "I don't work like that. What you see is what you get."

"No, Jules, it never is. There's the story. And there's the story behind the story. Every good reporter knows that's the one that matters." He lets out a long sigh. "Fine, I'll go first. I'm a recovering alcoholic. I put work before my family's needs, and because of it I lost the two people I love more than anything." He glances down at the floor. "There's always a price tag. That's the story behind my story. Your turn."

"I'm very sorry about that. That must be really hard." Dan an alcoholic? She recalls the picture of his daughter in a gymnastics outfit on the console behind his desk. Does she talk to him? Jules suddenly feels twitchy. What does he really want from her? There are only two choices to give him. Rick Janus—there's no way she's going there. Fine, the other one. She clears her throat. "Okay . . . I'm a mistake—the product of a law school dropout and the girl who graduated number one in her law school class. He took off before I was born. A coward. How's that?" Jules purses her lips. "But my mom is amazing—smart, on top of her game, works too hard, and worries too much."

"Clearly, the apple doesn't fall far from the tree." Dan grins.

Jules laughs. "Exactly."

"Sounds like you got the mom you needed and you're probably the best mistake she's ever made." Dan's face softens. "Did you ever try to find the dropout?"

Jules nods. "Yep. Married. No kids. Lives in San Diego. Real estate. Looks like an asshole. Decided he wasn't worth my time." She exhales deeply. "If that guy could run away from someone like my mother, then I figured he didn't merit running after."

Dan looks out the window briefly, then circles back to her. "I only wished my piece of shit father took off. It would have saved us piles of hospital bills we couldn't afford. My mother's right arm never worked properly again after he got through with her. Did you know that my first Pulitzer Prize–winning piece was on domestic abuse, how rampant it is, and how the courts let those scumbags get off too easy?"

They stare at each other across the table, feeling a new sense of camaraderie. Dan places the sugar packet neatly back into the black plastic container near his elbow. "You know what I always say: 'What doesn't kill you—'"

"Makes you write about it." Jules finishes his sentence.

"Damn straight." With a heavy breath, he leans forward, clasps the edge of the table, and whispers, *"Woman on Fire* belongs to Ellis Baum."

Jules can't help it. Her mouth drops. This, she wasn't expecting.

"Yeah, *that* Ellis Baum. The model was his mother, who was murdered during the Holocaust by Helmuth Geisler. I'm sure that name popped up multiple times in the documents I gave you. Anyway, Ellis hid his past from everyone—including me. But he's dying—nobody knows that either, by the way. He reached out, asking for my help. And I plan on giving it everything I've got. He's a close friend, and I don't have many of those." Dan smiles wanly at her. "It must be my sparkling personality."

"There's that," Jules says, still trying to mask her surprise that the source is Ellis Baum, fashion icon. And he's dying . . .

"How do you know each other?" she asks. "I would never put the two of you together. You're not exactly a fashion statement." She points to his Members Only jacket.

He laughs. "Ellis would wholeheartedly agree with that assessment. I don't think anyone would put us together. But that's a whole different story. I think we've hit our quota for the day." Dan starts to gather his things. "We need to move quickly. Most importantly . . ."

"You don't want to disappoint him." Jules finishes his sentence again. Dan nods slightly and now *she's* a bit concerned. Every journalist knows that working a story on behalf of a close friend or family member puts blinders on any investigation. Emotion is a Stage IV Blocker, one of her professors once told her class. You must be detached and dispassionate to find the clues and navigate the inevitable forks in the road. Rule of thumb: The closer you are to a story, the further away you will be from the truth.

"We will get Ellis Baum's painting back," she assures Dan. He knows the Rule; has probably used the Stage IV Blocker line himself on more than a few occasions. "Now that I know the source, I would like to interview him myself."

"Gutsy." Dan says as he snap-shuts his briefcase. "Cancel your plans for the next month. You're going to do a hell of a lot more than that."

TEN

NEW YORK

THE FRONT DOOR bursts open down the hall. Without fail, every time Henri enters the apartment, Ellis feels a flutter in his chest. He pictures Henri standing in the foyer, tossing his green flak jacket onto the wooden antique piece they found at Sotheby's, his dusty camera bag dropping to the floor in front of it. His shoes are probably caked with mud. No matter. He's just glad Henri is home safe. Hearing a pause in the footsteps, Ellis imagines Henri catching a glimpse of himself in the large seventeenth-century gilt-wood Spanish mirror and raking his hand through that mop of sandy brown hair laced with gray. Ellis sighs deeply. More than twenty years spent in secret with a man almost half his age. Why Henri stays, Ellis will never know—nor does he ask anymore.

"El—it's me," Henri calls out brightly.

"Yes, I know. I'm in here."

Broad smile with teeth like Chiclets against bronzed skin stands in the doorway of the study. "How's my Shoe Guy?"

Ellis absorbs the most beautiful face he's ever seen, and it just keeps getting better with age; a face that on too many occasions he was unable to separate from Vivienne's, especially in bed. When Vivienne's body writhed beneath him, Henri was always in his head. To be fair, Vivienne's loveliness materializes often when he's with Henri. Ellis has been fiercely loyal to both his wife of nearly fifty-two years and his lover. They know of each other and accept what is clearly unacceptable. He keeps them separate. Henri stays in the city, and Vivienne alternates between the houses in Bedford, Montecito, and the Hamptons. His life with her is out in the open, and Henri remains an open secret.

"Welcome back. How was it?" Ellis asks as Henri enters the room. He's spent the past three weeks photographing Nigeria for *National Geographic*.

"Well, it's definitely not Bali." Henri laughs, and as usual, the rich sound warms Ellis as though it were a throw blanket. "A mess, a death trap—but God knows, the people are beautiful. The photos, El, are unbelievable."

He met Henri Lamonte twenty-two years ago when he was still a fashion photographer and was hired to shoot an Anika Baum ad. If Ellis closes his eyes long enough, he can still recall with vivid detail the night after the shoot, when Henri, just shy of thirty years old, seduced Ellis in the confines of his office. He remembers every look, nuance, touch, and scent of that precious memory and calls it up whenever he needs to ground himself. Despite Ellis's wife and close-knit family, Henri somehow knew exactly who Ellis really was, what he'd been hiding. Ellis has always known yet chose to live the life his mother would have wanted him to lead. *But is that even true?* he asked himself repeatedly over the years. From what little he remembers of her, Anika

Baum was artsy, nonjudgmental, ahead of her time. She relished him prancing around their large apartment in her high heels and clothes. He could still hear that joyful laugh wafting through the air, like a bouquet of fresh flowers if blossoms had sound. No—it wasn't his mother prohibiting his lifestyle; it was him alone denying his own desires, perhaps as punishment for surviving the war when she didn't. A boy without a family, without a mother, was determined to build a family with a mother as its centerpiece. And while Vivienne was perfect, he was not. The way he'd compartmentalized his life didn't make sense, just like Henri's devotion to him didn't make sense. *And yet here we are,* Ellis thinks as Henri leans over and kisses him hard on the mouth, then stands back, assessing him.

"What did the oncologist say?"

"Stable. Nothing's changed," Ellis lies, as Henri walks to the bar to make himself a dirty martini and pour Ellis a club soda.

He looks up from the bar. "You're lying."

Eyes like X-rays. "Yes, that too," Ellis concedes. "Things aren't improving. Let's leave it, shall we."

Henri sits on the couch next to Ellis, and his hand presses firmly against his thigh, lightly stroking it. Ellis knows Henri sleeps with other men on occasion or when he is traveling—one-nighters, sometimes lasting a little longer—but only once throughout their years together was it too long and unbearable. What defense does he have? He is way too old for Henri, and he'd never leave Vivienne. And Henri has never demanded that of him. Nor has Henri ever insisted over the years that Ellis come out, not even in the fashion world, where everyone is out. Henri respects that Ellis comes from a different place in time and never demands anything of him—*except this.* Stolen moments together in their spacious Tribeca apartment that Ellis pays for and where Henri lives when he's in town and not traveling to some far-flung assignment. Their time, their sacred space, is precious to them both.

"I went to see Adam," Ellis tells him.

The roving hand stops. "Adam? How is he? Wait—you traveled to Montana?" Henri freezes dramatically, then shakes his head in disbelief. "You know there's nature there, right?"

"Yes, I know." Ellis grins. "Believe me, I was surprised by how lovely it is. Adam is doing wonderfully. Henri, there's something . . ." He stops speaking, collects his thoughts. "Something I've wanted to share for a very long time."

"Sounds serious." Henri leans back against the plush chocolate brown leather couch and listens as Ellis slowly spills it all: his mother, the war, the painting, the lies, his suspicions of Margaux de Laurent, unraveling and releasing all the corked truths of his past.

"Why didn't you tell me any of this before?" he says quietly when Ellis finishes. "Why all the Belgium fibs? Your family dealing diamonds? You know I don't care about that stuff. It would have explained so much. Why you don't cry. Why you stare off for hours. Why you push me away as if you don't deserve the pleasure, *us*. See that image over there . . . ?" Ellis glances in the direction of Henri's accusatory finger, at Henri's favorite picture of Ellis, an enlarged black-and-white photo framed in cherrywood that he took when they first got together, when Ellis wasn't aware that he was being photographed. Ellis wears a bulky cable-knit sweater, staring out the snow-lined window of their apartment. His face is resolute, his gaze distant, his jaw clamped. "That's the face I have never been able to reach." Henri sighs. "This explains everything. I only wish that I'd known sooner . . . that you trusted me."

Ellis gathers Henri's hands inside his own and gazes lovingly at the long, nimble fingers, the streaks of veins like marble that he knows so well. "I didn't trust myself. The truth is that *I* couldn't accept my own past. But lately it has begun to feel more real than the present. I'm sorry."

Henri searches Ellis's pained face for more clues. "What can I do to help? I can tell, there is something, isn't there?"

Ellis contemplates his lover, inhales the air around him. Long plane ride, musky scent, dried perspiration. *Him.* It's intoxicating.

"Griffin Freund," he says finally.

Henri yanks his hand away and his face falls briefly, then he looks up, confused. "What about him?"

An elongated silence wedges between them. The only time they nearly broke up for good was over Griffin Freund, the former chief curator at the Museum of Modern Art. A publicity hound with his flamboyant and risqué acquisitions and, in Ellis's mind, a grandstanding manipulator and opportunist. Eight years ago, Henri was hired to do a photo shoot for MoMA and fell hard for that man. It was more than a one-night stand; more than an affair. It had begun to evolve, and Henri for the first time slipped away, snake-charmed by Freund. It was seven months of pure hell, and then, miraculously, Henri fell out of love. He returned to their apartment, no apologies, no excuses, no explanations, but back. That's all that mattered.

Henri is going to hate this. "I need you to contact Freund once again."

Henri's eyes widen suspiciously. "Contact? Where are you going with this?"

How does he even begin to explain . . . Ellis clears his throat and swigs the club soda. "All I think about twenty-four-seven is how

I am going to find the painting. Everyone knows Griffin Freund left MoMA on bad terms. It's been rumored that he's been earning millions on his own as an art consultant, advising some bad eggs—drug dealers, sleazy Wall Street types, and other power-mongering criminals—on their art collections. I've been racking my brain about the stolen paintings from the Geisler collection—we're talking the caliber of Picasso, Chagall, and Matisse. Major works. There's no way those paintings will be sold through normal channels . . ." Ellis wipes his damp forehead with the back of his hand. He looks around for his pocket hankie, but it's in his coat hanging in the foyer. "Mark my words, if those paintings do surface, Freund will be first in line snapping up whatever he can for his sleazy clientele. And it's no secret that he works hand in hand with Margaux de Laurent."

Henri's face tightens. He's angry, and rightfully so. "So let me get this straight. You're bringing this up because . . ."

"Yes, Henri." Ellis swallows hard, and it feels like a sharp rock ramming down his throat. "Because I need you to be there, in Freund's bed, in his ear, if my painting lands in his hands or if you hear anything of its whereabouts."

Henri glares at him. "Just to be clear, you are willing to pimp me out to help find your painting?"

Ellis eyes the enemy—the martini in Henri's hand. His heart palpitates; his voice lowers. "Yes, that's exactly what I want." *It's the very last thing I want—poisonous Griffin Freund back in our lives.* He looks deep into Henri's soft brown eyes. But the warmth has evaporated. "I know this is"—Ellis searches for a civilized word for despicable, loathsome, deplorable—"not optimal. It would require you to play pretend for a while, for me."

"'Pretend'? 'Not optimal'? What the hell, Ellis." Henri slams down the glass, and the liquid spills on the coffee table. Neither moves to wipe it up. "This is the man who got between us." His voice rises, and his teeth clench like someone just pulled in the reins. "Think of what you're asking. Really, can you handle that?"

Ellis bites down on his lip. *Eighteen months if I'm lucky, the doctor said. That's it. That's all I've got.* "Yes, for the painting, I can handle anything." He watches Henri guzzle the last of the martini and feels the intensity of his lover's emotion in that one swig: anger, hurt, frustration, confusion, and betrayal.

"I know this is a lot to take in," Ellis says gently.

"A lot to take in. Jesus, Ellis, I don't know who you are right now."

"Neither do I."

Another unwelcome silence suspends in the air, and this time it seems to expand. Ellis feels the daggers piercing his chest and welcomes the pain, deserves it. "This is beyond difficult for me, but I need you to do it. I need to know that I covered all my bases," he says. "Henri, please. I know exactly what I'm asking . . . I don't have a lot of time."

Henri stands, paces the Oriental carpet, stops in front of Ellis, and stares at him for what feels like an eternity. "Big mistake. But fine, I will do this for you."

ELEVEN

CORRENS, FRANCE

*T*HE WORLD IS *looking for you,* Margaux tells the exquisite painting that she brought into her bedroom last night. *And yet here you are, lovely, safe with me.* She tacked *Woman on Fire* up on the yellow paisley hand-painted wall next to her bed, as though the masterpiece were a boy band poster. If her grandfather knew that she used thumbtacks to view the painting . . .

"Presentation is an art form," he would tell her during their long walks. "Framing, lighting, and installation are everything. But be careful. If a client notices the frame *before* the picture, you've erred—you've lost the sale. And the frame, Margaux, must never overshadow, must always *serve* the artwork. The lighting sets the tone but must never cast a glare over the image, and where you display the painting tells the whole story. Remember that."

She remembers it all—everything her grandfather told her, the only person in her life who mattered, whose words were worth remembering. She stares at the painting as though seeing it through his wise eyes once again . . .

"What was your favorite painting, Grand-papa?" she asked him one day while visiting him at the Paris gallery when she was ten. He was in his eighties, sharp as ever, insisting on being at the gallery every single day. "Tell me the story again."

Smiling, he ruffled Margaux's long, dark, wavy hair as they observed a Monet together. She caught sight of her reflection in the framed painting on the gallery wall.

"Well, do you like this one?" her grandfather asked.

Crossing her arms and eyeing the lilies, she angled her head, mimicking her grandfather's pose. "No. It's too dreamy. Too pretty. Too predictable."

He belted out a hearty laugh. "What have I done to you, *ma chérie*? But if Claude were alive to hear that, I guarantee he would have loved it. He couldn't stand the flatterers surrounding him. You know, I met him here at the gallery back in my early twenties. My father was a major collector of his works. You are a strange child. Brilliant and highly opinionated." He pointed to another painting. "That one. *Tightrope Walk* by my old friend Ernst Ludwig Kirchner."

Her grandfather liked to play this game, testing her reactions to important canvases. Her face split into a wide grin. The shocking colors, the figures in motion, the broad, abstract brushstrokes. Harsh and electrifying. Not prissy like Monet. And the tightrope walker's expression appeared angry and determined. She related to it, could feel the woman's intense emotions as if they were coming from her own face. "Yes, that one I like . . . I feel it here." She pointed to her gut. "That's how I know what I like."

Her grandfather looked pleased. "What about in your heart?"

Margaux paused. She never felt anything in her heart. It's like it was dead, no beat, lifeless. "Yes, there too," she lied.

Her grandfather's eyes were shining. His approval mattered to her. She also knew that even though her father was now overseeing all the galleries, her grandfather didn't trust him. She'd hear him yelling at her father, calling him an imbecile, chiding him for his poor work ethic and lecherous personal life. Gently lifting Margaux's chin up with his bony forefinger, her grandfather said, "You are my favorite, and you know why? Because 'instinct' is not something that can be bought or sold or trained. The very best dealers are born with it. And like me, you have it."

She straightened her small shoulders. "And you are my favorite too, Grand-papa. You know why? Because you never lie to me."

Not like her father, who always lied. Or her deceitful mother. Her grandfather followed Margaux's gaze to the gallery door, to where her father was supposed to have picked her up two hours ago. His mouth tightened apologetically. "Your father has always been this way, petulant and selfish. And your mother . . ." He shook his head. *My mother,* she thought, *is even worse.* "I'm sorry. It's hard for you, isn't it?" She nodded, and he squeezed her to him tightly. "When it hurts, Margaux, I find that the right painting always makes things better. Remember this: Art never leaves, even when people do."

She leaned into his fleshy belly. "Don't leave me, okay?"

"I will do my very best to stick around."

That was the only time her grandfather ever lied to her. She looked up at him with dark, trusting eyes. "Tell me the painting story again. The first time you saw *her* . . . your other favorite."

❧

That day was like any other day, only it wasn't. It was *the* day. Charles de Laurent kept checking his watch, anticipating the top secret delivery. This was the twelfth masterwork that had been smuggled to him from Germany, sent once again by the artist Max Kruger, now serving as a double agent, pretending to work for the Nazis while secretly doing everything he could to help save Germany's modern art, particularly the targeted abstract works of the Expressionists—Hitler's nemeses. The Expressionists conveyed everything the Third Reich hated: paintings that distorted subjects for emotional effect to evoke moods, sensations, and new ideas. Charles was determined to do whatever he could to protect important paintings that the Nazis labeled "degenerate" and those artists being persecuted as enemies of the state.

Today's delivery was deeply upsetting and personal. It was the last known painting by his close friend Ernst Engel, one of the founders of *Die Brücke*, the modernist movement of Expressionist artists. The Nazis had arrested Engel nearly a month ago, and Max Kruger, who aided the Nazis in the arrest, secretly returned to Engel's studio in Berlin to save his best friend's works. He sent Charles this painting to protect—Engel's last and, apparently, his favorite.

Kruger wrote him a coded message. *They will come for this. Hide it at all costs.*

Charles sat in his large fan-backed leather chair, nervously tapping his pen against his Biedermeier desk as he waited. He'd closed the gallery for the entire day in anticipation of a morning arrival; the painting was allegedly very large and difficult to smuggle. The knock finally came at half past four: three knocks, pause, then two, pause, then three—as instructed. Charles felt the adrenaline rush as he jumped up to answer the door to a rough-hewn-looking man dressed in wrinkled head-to-toe black, standing there empty-handed.

"M. de Laurent." His washed-out blue eyes stared vacantly. "Looks like it's going to rain."

"Yes, yes. The rain." Charles acknowledged the cryptic password as he glanced both ways down the rue La Boétie. Late-afternoon pedestrian traffic. Nothing unusual. He whispered, "Through the alley, directly in back. I will meet you there."

Twenty-five minutes later, after the handoff, Charles locked himself in the basement of his gallery inside his art supply closet with the large crate—two other paintings had been sent to him by Kruger, plus the Engel canvas. Pressure pounded at his temples as he cut through the thick wrapping. There was no chance that Ernst Engel would make it out of the Nazis' hands alive. As the leader of the "enemy" art movement, most likely he was already dead.

Charles's stomach churned. So many brilliant artists' lives had been destroyed in the past few years since the Nazis went on a modern-art purge. Forbidden to paint. Forbidden to buy supplies. Forbidden to sell their work. Forbidden to meet with other artists. Forbidden to leave the country. No one needed to tell Charles de Laurent, the top dealer in Paris, that once an artist's hands are bound, he is as good as dead. Truth is that those bastards killed Ernst Engel long before they captured him.

Breathing heavily and sweating profusely, Charles unbuttoned his shirt and flung his jacket to the floor, kicking it aside, as he carefully unrolled the prized canvas and then stood back to take it in. Drawing in a deep breath, he slowly absorbed the magnificent composition. Those weren't mere colors before him, but rather brilliant hues of light shooting at him from all directions: the dazzling golden highlights in the woman's resplendent hair, the apricot glaze blushing her skin, the azure filling her penetrating eyes, the passionate plum entwined with cobalt fanning the flames that engulfed her. He could practically taste it, this lush fruit bowl of pigment. But he knew nothing of the painting's origins. *Who was the model? Where did Engel find her?*

Usually Charles sat with his artist, wined and dined him or her, until the inspiration for the work was revealed. Because he *had* to know, had to feel exactly what the artist was feeling. But now, he would never know the story behind this woman, this goddess of fire. He lightly touched her face with his fingertip, feeling the complicated dichotomy of its smooth and coarse texture. *This is a woman you never let go*, he whispered aloud between the concrete walls.

"You see, Margaux, that painting left me breathless," Charles explained to his granddaughter. "The very day it arrived in the gallery, I decided not to sell it but to keep it for myself. I took her home, removed my favorite Cézanne hanging over the bedroom fireplace—"

"*The Bathers?*" she interrupted.

"Yes, *mon cœur.*" He smiled at this precocious girl whose mind worked so fast he could barely keep up. "*The Bathers.* And in its place, I hung *Woman on Fire.*"

"And Grand-maman . . . tell me again, please." Margaux pushed, as usual. Nothing was ever enough.

Charles's thoughts drifted to his beautiful young wife, Sylvie. The only woman he ever truly loved. He wasn't unlike his rogue of a son, who cheated on his wife at every opportunity. He, too, had his indiscretions in his early days as a young art dealer overseeing Paris's most talked-about gallery. Nubile models and opportunistic artists came through those magical doors, threw themselves at him. Such fervor. But love—*real love?* For him, there was only one woman. "Your grandmother was very sick. She was only thirty-three when she passed. But when I brought that painting home, I swear it gave her life, a renewed sense of strength and purpose. And when she finally left me, Margaux, she ended her days smiling. It was that painting. Truly a gift. I believe your grand-maman lived longer just to look at it every morning." His eyelids fell. He squeezed Margaux's hand.

"And then . . ." she prodded. It was exasperating sometimes, he thought. This girl never knew when to stop.

"There is no then." He cut her off abruptly. "*Fini*—it ended there. *Woman on Fire* was taken from me—stolen—by a bad man named Helmuth Geisler, who made it his life's mission to make art and artists suffer." He quickly turned away from her; the light in his eyes had extinguished.

Margaux had many more questions for her grandfather, but the pained look on his face told her for once to hold her tongue. She knew then, without really understanding why, the story of the painting was not *La Fin*—the end—but rather just the beginning.

PUNCHING UP THE pillow behind her head, Margaux takes a long drag on her cigarette, feeling a sadness, a familiar loss, rise within her as she thinks about her grandfather. She pushes the melancholy away.

Look at you, she tells *Woman on Fire* with her eyes, *so powerful and defiant. And yet. Men have cherished you, coveted you, but they didn't protect you as they should, did they? Not even my grandfather. Somehow, he let you go, allowing his favorite painting to fall into the smarmy hands of Helmuth Geisler and then, ultimately, to that worthless son. They couldn't protect you. But I will.*

She slips in AirPods and blasts Coldplay. As the music begins, she hears a faint knock and sits up, angry at being interrupted once again.

"Go away," she shouts at the door, sick of the pestering staff asking ad nauseam if she needs anything. "Yes, privacy!" she snarled earlier at that young woman Elyse or Elize, whatever her name is. Margaux just wants time to think, to be alone with the painting for a little longer before returning her to the vault.

"It's me," Wyatt Ross calls out. "We need to talk."

"Give me a second." Margaux likes to sleep naked. It doesn't matter that they've had sex all week at the Maison. This is her sanctuary, her private space. She grabs her robe from the floor, puts it on, opens the door, and Wyatt walks in. As usual, he's wearing a black tee and jeans and a half-smoked cigarette dangles from his mouth.

He eyes *Woman on Fire* on the wall. "And there she is."

Margaux sits cross-armed on the edge of her bed. "So?"

Wyatt stands before her, then reaches past her and uses the ashtray on her desk. "I was up all night working out a plan. I'm building a fake account targeting two specific groups on the dark web for our paintings—one, the Italian mafia, an offshoot of the Camorra ring, and the other, a neo-Nazi branch based in Chemnitz."

"Why them?" Margaux asks, becoming irritated when he starts snooping around, inspecting her personal items. This is the first time he's ever been inside her bedroom, and the last.

"A few years ago, the Italian police discovered that the Camorra had a cache of stolen paintings, including two Van Goghs stolen from the Van Gogh Museum in Amsterdam in 2002—remember that heist?"

"Of course. Everyone remembers that."

He waves his cigarette. "From my understanding, the Camorra don't simply steal precious art—rather, they *acquire* it when someone owes them money or when they think they can 'artnap' it and, in return, get a major ransom from a private owner or a museum. This group is a perfect fit for our needs. They know art, they use the dark web to sell off their stolen works, and they are silent and loyal to the cause. And the neos . . . well, it's obvious why I've chosen them. They want to keep Nazi-stolen art in the hands of Nazis. An easy play. I want to 'frame' them, so to speak, with possessing paintings from the Geisler collection. I'm working out the details."

He sits down next to Margaux on the bed, and she can tell he's freshly showered by the still-wet ends of his hair. "I came by to ask you to choose four paintings to steer their way. My plan is twofold—place those paintings with the mafia and the neos and take a small cut at first, and once they see we are legit and that they stand to earn a large profit by fronting the works—we will send more works their way and take a much bigger cut. Like I told you, if a painting is declared stolen, its value immediately nosedives. So we need to move on this quickly, carefully, and not get caught."

"Four paintings? What are my guarantees that I'm not just throwing away multimillion-dollar works? You trust these thieves?" She pops up off the bed and hovers over him.

"I trust myself. There's only one reason for doing it precisely this way. *Diversion.*" Wyatt's lopsided grin is slow and sexy; he is clearly pleased with himself. Margaux wants to smack it right off. She also feels his eyes landing on her cleavage. She tightens her velour belt. *Not here. No way.*

"Diversion," he explains as though she were his student, "is necessary to keep everyone looking to the left while we move paintings to the right. Let people believe that the Geisler murder and robbery was a mob hit. Four major paintings landing on the dark web buys us real time. It will keep everyone off our trail while I work my magic."

"And what if your scheme backfires?" Margaux demands. "What if it puts the authorities right on our trail?"

"Backfires?" He looks offended. "It won't. The Geisler robbery is the biggest story to hit the art world in decades. Lots of people have a vested interest in those works, and everybody is busy gathering evidence as to which paintings were in the collection." Wyatt points to *Woman on Fire*. "But we have a very short window here, Margaux. Our advantage is that *we* know exactly what's in the treasure trove and can drop the paintings and earn out before the authorities get their lazy asses in gear and assemble the puzzle pieces." He stretches out his long legs, making himself a little too comfortable on her custom-made Hermès duvet while smoking. "Your call."

"Didn't anyone ever teach you any fucking manners?" Her brows draw together. "Your big foolproof plan is to hand over my paintings on a silver platter to the dependable mafia and reliable Nazis?" She laughs mockingly. "And how exactly do you plan to do this? Leave the paintings on a church stoop wrapped in a blanket? Drop them off at a skinhead convention? There are people watching every move of these groups." She pushes Wyatt's legs off the duvet. "I think your plan is flimsy and you're fucking crazy."

His eye twitch takes off, ticcing in fifth gear, but he doesn't back down. "Let me put this another way. We have at least one point five billion dollars' worth of stolen art in our vaults. The Geisler heist is on everyone's radar. Not to mention that heads are spinning right now at the Bundestag. Reporters are demanding to know exactly when the German government knew of the Geisler collection. Everyone is digging like moles through Helmuth Geisler's wartime documents as well. The mob and the neos buy us *time* to get in and get out. It's the best plan we've got. Trust me." He reaches over and presses his hand on Margaux's exposed thigh. "For the record, I *am* crazy, but I'm also setting the rules of engagement to our advantage. Yes, millions will be lost initially. But it's the price tag for hundreds of millions gained. You do the math."

She peels his hot hand off her leg and glares at him. She stands, tightens her robe, walks toward the window, and stares out at the manicured grounds two floors below. Pivoting slowly, she says, "Fine. I will come by the Maison later."

"That's all I wanted to hear." Wyatt stands and scratches his head, lingering.

Margaux gestures to *Woman on Fire*. "In the meantime, find out details about the painting. Who was the model? What's the story behind it? What was the painting's history, particularly during the war? There must have been contracts along the way, a trail. I want to know *everything* there is to know about her."

"Why does that matter now? She's ours. Her history stops here."

"'Ours'? You mean *mine*. It matters," she snaps. "Because *I* want to set the rules of engagement. I want to know exactly who else will be looking for her and get them out of my way." She eyes the door, indicating that it is now time for Wyatt to get out of her way.

He drags his boots in the carpet, giving Margaux a few seconds longer to change her mind and invite him to stay. When the invitation doesn't come, he stomps out without a goodbye. She laughs to herself. Predictable.

She pads around her bedroom filled with teenage décor.

Nothing's changed, and she prefers to keep it that way. The same cream-and-butter-trimmed French desk and matching armoire, the floor-to-ceiling bookshelves filled with dog-eared first editions, myriad equestrian awards, scattered rocks that she pilfered from the canyon, a glass bong on her desk shelf perched next to a framed photo of her with her grandfather out at the vineyard. No photographs with friends—*what friends?*—or other family members. Who cares about them? Her room remains unchanged and untouched by others. *Just once.* Once it was violated and brutally trespassed. Her chest constricts at the memory. But never again.

Margaux glances up at *Woman on Fire*, judging her from across her room. She challenges the omnipotent painted gaze right back. At 170 centimeters, the life-sized blond goddess is nearly her height. Her perfectly oval face is set with large, penetrating, almond-shaped aquamarine eyes. Her high-priestess cheekbones appear sharp as blades, and that body—full breasts to be devoured, sensual curves swirling in a blaze of color. *Yes, she definitely knows what happened here.*

The betrayal. Margaux feels the familiar burning sensation scorch through her body and seize her by the throat, as if it were happening again in real time. *You see, they thought they could get away with it,* she tells *Woman on Fire* with her eyes. But they thought wrong.

Margaux walks slowly toward the painting. *Who are you? Were you good? Or were you like me? Were you real? Or merely a figment of the artist's imagination?*

She gently removes *Woman on Fire* from the wall and tacks her up again at eye level. Standing before her—woman to woman, eye to eye—Margaux takes in all that beauty, all that color. *No one can get to you now,* she vows. *Just me.*

TWELVE

MISSOULA, MONTANA

THE CABIN NESTLED in the backwoods is camouflaged by towering pine trees standing guard like staunch soldiers. Jules is convinced that whoever Adam Chase is, he clearly doesn't want to be found. She inhales the cool, citrusy air from the opened back seat window as the driver pauses at a makeshift mailbox sticking out of a thick tree like an ax to a target.

"Yep. Number 18. That's it. Must be up the road," Dan tells the driver as Jules strains to see the mysterious cabin through the narrow opening between the trees.

As they pull up the dirt driveway and park, she grabs her tote bag and carry-on from the trunk while Dan pays the driver. Her heart skips a beat. After three weeks of straight-up research, this is finally happening. Fashion powerhouse Ellis Baum and his grandson, the artist, are about to jump off her stack of documents and come to life.

As she clutches her stuffed tote to her chest, butterflies begin to swarm in her stomach. Oddly, she's more nervous to meet

Adam than Ellis. Especially after everything she's read about him. The instant fame, the hard drugs, the bad boy rep, the arrests, the overdose, the rehab, and then, of course, the mysterious four-year disappearance. She even had to sign a nondisclosure agreement from Ellis before she came here.

"Jules, you with me?" Dan calls out from the other side of the cab.

"Coming." She lifts her sunglasses, feeling the warmth of the early-afternoon sun on her face, and walks toward the cabin, which is surprisingly small and bland, devoid of any domestic touches. There are no bright flowerpots, shrubs, or plants, no welcome mat, no colorful rocking chairs on the porch, nothing personal— just an "I exist" vibe. From her vantage point, Jules sees the sky-spearing mountain range and the sparkling river enveloping the back of the cabin, and she guesses that's where all the action is.

The front door flings open and three overly friendly golden retrievers lunge forward. Jules kneels and pets the dogs, laughing as they slobber all over her. She hears Dan introducing himself to Adam. As she slowly stands, she meets Adam's piercing emerald gaze, and the impact is sudden and unexpected, like she's just been sucker-punched.

Google did not do him justice. Not even close. Jules tries to keep her breath even as she drinks him in. Framed in the open doorway wearing torn jeans and a faded Guns N' Roses concert T-shirt, Adam looks like a model for an outdoors magazine. His hair is shaggy, his full mouth is chapped, and his chiseled face is shadowed with a beard, but perfectly, as though he charcoaled it in himself. And those eyes—at first glance they are bright green but this close they are a deep jade rimmed with yellow. *Are those even human?* Jules doesn't even notice that Dan has already gone inside, or that she hasn't budged an inch. Her feet are rooted to the porch like they've grown out of the wooden slats.

"Hi, I'm Adam." His hands are tucked inside his jeans.

Pull it together. "Hi . . . Jules Roth." She extends her hand and tries to sound professional. When Adam takes her hand with a slight grin, she notices the small raised scar slicing into his top lip, a lone imperfection that somehow adds another ten points to his looks, and wonders how he got it.

Adam ushers her inside the cabin and asks if he can take her bag. As he reaches for her carry-on, Jules smells his cool, clean scent, piney like the outdoors, as if he's just rolled around in the grass. She knows from Dan that he's been living out here alone, secluded and cut off from society like a fugitive. He must have a girlfriend. An unexpected flush spreads across her cheeks as he peels the bag from her clenched hands and closes the door behind them.

Jules lingers at the door, not sure what to do with herself. Dan is already across the room, immersed in conversation with Ellis, whose arm is draped around Dan's shoulder. She can't put the two of them together. They just don't fit. Her gaze wanders around the large room itself and her mouth instantly drops open. It's not a room at all, but an art gallery with painted images everywhere. Entering slowly, she suddenly feels dazed by the onslaught of color and detail. Such a sharp contrast to the anemic exterior of the cabin. She turns to Adam, who is watching her reaction. "This is incredible. Mesmerizing. I feel like I'm inside a kaleidoscope."

Inside a kaleidoscope. Did she just say that aloud? Jules is keenly aware that Adam is throwing her off her game. He's ridiculously attractive—but so what? What the hell is wrong with her?

Adam shrugs and gestures to the walls. "I know it's a bit much. My mother came here to visit once and was so overwhelmed that she got an immediate headache. Now whenever she comes, I meet her at the hotel in town. She calls this place the Migraine Museum." He laughs.

Jules laughs back, but only vaguely hears him. She is too entranced by the walls and yearns to examine each lifelike image closely. Forcing herself to snap out of it, she walks toward Ellis and Dan, who is waiting to introduce her.

Do not act like a groupie, she warns herself. *Do not mention how you and your mother love the "Walk of Fame" red carpet segment of the Oscars, in which celebrities display their custom-made Anika Baum stilettos for the camera . . . Seriously, "kaleidoscope"?* She extends her hand and maintains eye contact. "Mr. Baum, it's an honor to meet you. I'm Jules Roth. I've been working with Dan—research." *Good, solid.*

"Delighted." He gives her a slight bow and brushes his lips across her hand, as though greeting royalty. She smiles at his chivalry and elegant attire. Never mind that they are in the middle of the woods, Ellis Baum is wearing a suit and tie, and Jules is suddenly self-conscious of her baggy boyfriend jeans and simple black sweater—her working staple. Her long, unruly hair is wound into a tight topknot, and she opted for her glasses over her contacts. As usual, she downplays her looks. But this is Ellis Baum . . . she should have upped the ante.

"Dan told me all about you, Miss Roth. You're young," he observes.

"Call me Jules. Yes, young . . . but an old soul," she counters lightly. His blue eyes gleam, and Jules mentally pats herself on the back.

"Please have a seat." He gestures to the couch and then sits on one of the two uncomfortable-looking wooden chairs across the coffee table. Dan takes the other one. Jules wonders once again how exactly they know each other. She has no doubt that she will soon find out.

Ellis glances at his fancy-looking watch. "My grandson made lunch, and I'd like to get down to business as soon as possible. We have a lot to cover," he explains. Jules pictures him at the helm of a board meeting, with his commanding voice carrying just a hint of an accent. "My flight is at six o'clock tonight. I had planned to spend the night here, but unfortunately, I have another obligation that came up tomorrow morning. I'm sorry."

Adam heads to the kitchen and returns with a tray of sandwiches, fruit, and cut veggies, placing it on the coffee table. Jules notes that there is no kitchen table or dining room area—just this. The main room takes up most of the cabin. There's a kitchen with a closed door next to it—must be his bedroom.

Dan, not surprisingly, takes over, breaking the ice with a few journalism jokes and then switching gears to more interesting war stories from when he was a young reporter covering the Middle East. Jules laughs at the right moments and throws in a clever comment or two but is acutely aware of Adam's right knee—the one with the hole in the jeans where tiny, light brown hairs are peeking through—touching hers accidentally at various points in the conversation. She tries to ignore the knee grazes and focus on Dan and Ellis, who eats his sandwich with a fork and knife.

When they finish lunch, Adam swipes off the crumbs from his jeans, stands, and begins to clear the dishes.

"Let me help." Jules follows him to the kitchen while Dan and Ellis chat about the current political situation. She checks out the small but tidy kitchen. No dishwasher or any modern amenities—

except for a high-end cappuccino maker. *Even a recluse needs good coffee*, she thinks while looking at Adam. "I'll wash, you dry?"

He smiles and nods. As she scrubs the dishes, she looks out the window over the sink and sees the mountains in the distance. Trees and wildflowers blanket the sprawling backyard, and the gorgeous river shimmers behind it as far as the eye can see. Is this land all his? To the far right, she spots what looks like another cabin. "Is that your neighbor?"

"No. That's my studio," he tells her. "I don't have neighbors. Or at least none that I know."

No connection with neighbors. His mother meets him in town. *Who is this guy?* "How long have you lived out here?" she asks, even though she already knows the answer.

"Almost four years."

"And you don't know your neighbors?" she prods. *He's a recovering addict who ran away from fame and fortune—of course he keeps to himself. Stop the interrogation.*

"I prefer it this way. I like the quiet."

"Well, it's certainly not the hustle and bustle of New York." *OMG. Hustle and bustle?* Adam makes her nervous. He eyes her with a raised brow. He knows that she knows everything that everyone else knows: the fame, the drugs, the parties, the overdose, the seclusion.

"Yep."

A one-word answer means he doesn't want to talk about himself. Not to her, at least. Jules washes the dishes quickly, and she tries to think of a subject changer, but nothing comes to mind. Nor does he try to correct the uncomfortable silence. Clearly, he prefers it.

"Why are you even here?" Adam asks, turning to face her as he dries a plate.

Why am I even here? Her face turns red. "I'm working on this investigation with Dan. I thought that part was pretty clear." She closes the faucet and meets his inquisitive gaze directly. "You're staring. Is it my hair, or the fact that my glasses are steaming up?"

His turn to blush. "Touché. I'm sorry, that was totally rude. It's been a while since I've been around people. I'm feeling a bit claustrophobic, I suppose. How about if we cut the superficial bullshit. You know exactly who I am, where I've been, how long I've been here. You strike me as someone who does her research."

"I've been told I resemble a librarian." She smiles slightly, hoping to lighten up the weird tension. Some guy she went on one date with told her that she resembled a *hot* librarian that he'd seen on one of his porn sites. She was insulted, even though he meant it as a compliment.

"I bet you researched me," he teases, clearly trying now.

This I can do, she thinks. She tilts her head and gives it back. "Guilty as charged. I not only researched you, but I also printed out articles on your paintings, your career path, your favorite video store as a kid . . ." All true, but she tries masking it as a joke. She grabs a dry dish towel off the counter and wipes off her wet hands. "And apparently, there is strong evidence that you are a super slow dish drier." She points to the wet stack next to the sink as proof.

His eyes sparkle as the sunlight from the kitchen window hits them. "Really? And where did you get that top secret info?"

"I never reveal my sources." Back in control, Jules spins on the worn-in heel of her boot. Best to get out on a high note. "Let's not keep your grandfather waiting."

He blocks her slightly as she walks past him and leans in with an airy whisper. "Did you catch the fork and knife with the sandwich?"

"First thing I noticed." She chuckles, and they both walk back into the other room. There, much better. Dan's briefcase is wide open, and papers are already stacked on the coffee table in thick, typical Dan-sized piles, ready to roll.

Dan looks up when they enter. "Okay, perfect. Everybody, sit down and let's begin . . ." He points to the stack closest to him. "There are lots of loose ends here, and we're shooting from the hip at this point, which is normal. Whenever I begin any investigation, I give everyone a part, a role. It keeps things organized and focused."

"Like actors in a play," Adam interjects.

"Exactly that." Dan nods. "Except I'm not playing around, and there are rules to this. Rules to every investigation. Rules to teamwork. Rules to our success. First, there is only one leader calling the shots, and that's me, or it gets confusing, and we lose control." He gives Jules a hard side glance. "Second: No cowboy antics. No jumping off the path because you think you know something that I don't. There's an order to this. No undue risks without my approval. Rules, got that? If followed correctly, the rules will get us the painting." He pauses for a swig of water. "And if you don't follow the rules, if you take matters into your own hands, keep secrets, or think something is a little bit bendable, well then . . ."

Why does he keep looking at me? Jules wonders as they all turn to her. What rules have I broken? Running to Englewood on my own and getting a front-page story? You would think he'd celebrate that. *Why am I the wild card here?*

NEARLY AN HOUR passes spent listening to Dan's sleep-inducing history lesson on stolen art, investigations that went right, those that went wrong because rules were broken, and on and on. It takes all of Jules's inner restraint not to scream, *We get it—follow the fucking rules! Move on!*

When the sermon is finally over, Dan reaches inside his brief-case and pulls out three mini yellow pads, then removes three identical Bic pens from his shirt pocket lineup and hands them out. "Take notes. You too, Ellis. Most importantly, no one is to know anything about this meeting outside of this room, unless I say so. Are we clear?" Dan eyes each of them slowly.

Jules notices that Ellis purses his lips tightly and blinks four or five times in rapid succession—indicators of lying. Did he already tell someone about this? Should she mention this to Dan, or was that only in her head? Although Ellis appears a good twenty years younger than his actual age, he is old. The blinking thing might be an age thing. But then again, the pressed lips . . .

Dan continues in drill sergeant mode. "Ellis, there's someone we should meet as soon as possible to get things in motion. The downside is the meeting would be in Amsterdam. Is that doable?"

"Amsterdam?" Ellis leans forward, loosens his tie, clears his throat. "Why there?"

"Because *there* is home to Bram Bakker. Do you know who he is?"

Ellis nods. They all do. "Of course. He's that famous art de-tective," Ellis says. "Don't they call him the Sherlock Holmes of international art theft? He's the one who found that Rembrandt that was stolen from the Louvre in a cave in Slovenia, right?"

"That's him," Dan says, scratching his eyebrow with his pen cap. "Bakker specializes in exposing forgeries. He also has a very discreet side gig tracking down Nazi-looted art, and he's been highly successful. I spoke to him briefly a few days ago—introduced myself, gave him a few minor details about the painting. He told me one thing that is necessary: no posting anywhere that the painting is missing or alerting any authorities, because it will also tip off whoever has the painting that we are officially searching for it. Got it?"

"When you say 'posting,' are you referring to the Art Loss Register?" Jules asks, having recently come across the world's largest database of stolen art and antiquities in her research.

"Exactly the ALR, as well as lesser-known lost art sites," Dan explains. "For now, we stay off everyone's radar while we get our ducks in a row. Apparently, Bakker also has close connections with the police and the underworld—both sides trust him. It's well worth our while to meet him." He nudges Ellis lightly with his elbow. "So . . . Amsterdam?"

Ellis glances at Jules and gestures toward the kitchen. "Would you mind grabbing my bag over there in the corner? I need to check something on my calendar."

Jules jumps off the couch, retrieves the handsome leather bag in the corner, noting the designer, Brunello Cucinelli—nothing but the best, of course—and hands it to Ellis, who pulls out a matching calfskin portfolio engraved with a gold EB emblem.

"Just as I thought." Ellis points to the calendar. "Next month is Amsterdam Fashion Week. It takes place every year in February and September. I haven't gone there in years. I only attend the Paris, Milan, and Tokyo shows. But this makes it a much easier arrangement." He pens a note to himself, then winks at Adam.

"The best part is I won't have to explain myself to your grand-mother. And we will fly private, of course."

"Excellent." Dan checks off the first item on his list. "From there, you'll return to New York, and I hope to meet up with a source in Germany, poke around Munich for a few days." He nods at Jules. "You may be joining us. I haven't decided yet."

Amsterdam *and* Munich—would she really be joining him? *But what do I tell my mother?* Last week, Jules evaded her mother's probing questions about traveling to Missoula. She couldn't reveal that it was for Ellis Baum, because then the barrage of questions wouldn't stop.

It began with demanding to know why Jules needed to fly to Montana and exactly what kind of story she was involved in and with whom. *I know you're twenty-four. But it's about safety, not snooping.* Her mother was relentless. *It is totally about snooping,* Jules countered. *You know I can't talk about it. Besides, I don't interrogate you about your cases or clients.* She really needs to get her own apartment soon, but it's just so convenient living with her mother, not to mention the money she's saving. She eyes Dan with a mix of surprise and curiosity. This is the first time he's mentioned the Munich leg of the trip.

"Are you planning on going to *Spotlight?*" she probes. He shoots her a look to be quiet, then shrugs as if to remind himself that he is not operating as a lone wolf anymore and must trust everyone in this group.

"Yes," he says. "I'm hoping to meet up with the editor there to get a better grip on the exposé surrounding the Geisler fiasco. It's worth a shot." And *yes,* his good eye transmits to Jules, he will be looking into why there wasn't a byline on that huge scoop, but no one else here needs to know that.

Dan turns to Adam. "From my understanding, you're planning to return to the art world—make a comeback. Your role in this investigation, of course, will be as an artist, as yourself. Not too difficult, right? You left at the pinnacle of your career. My sense is that you will be received back in New York with open arms." His jaw clenches slightly. "But are you sure about all this? If I can be frank here—it's hard as hell to return to the 'scene of the crime' after recovery. Lots of challenges."

Jules wonders if Dan is talking about himself.

Adam narrows his gaze. "I'm aware of the challenges. I don't see this so-called comeback as a long-term commitment. It's temporary," he explains, gently rubbing his scruffy jaw, and Jules has an inexplicable urge to reach out and touch it. She also notices that he is perspiring slightly at the temples. Nerves. Does Dan see that too?

"Once we find the painting, I'll return here and pick up where I left off." Adam glances at his grandfather. "For our purposes, I've already gotten the ball rolling and contacted Margaux de Laurent." He eyes Dan squarely. "I'm sure she is next up on your agenda."

"You bet she is." Dan shows Adam his notes as proof. "Nicely done on contacting her—I was going to suggest it. So, let's start there. What do we know about Margaux de Laurent?" He hitches a brow. "From my preliminary research, she has a reputation for being ruthless and underhanded and stops at nothing to land the biggest and best artists. But as of now, there is no hard evidence about any actual wrongdoing relating to this painting, just . . . hunches." He eyes Ellis, who looks like he's about to burst. "And yet, there is one crucial detail here that matters: Margaux may be the *only* person other than Ellis who has a strong connection to the painting. We know this from Ellis's document showing that the painting made a stop in Paris, specifically at her grandfather's gallery in 1939, and that he signed the document, which leads one to believe that de Laurent's signature—his permission—was required." Dan riffles through his files and pulls out exhibit A, a copy of Ellis's document confirming the painting was sent via courier from the De Laurent Gallery in Paris to Lucerne. "It's worth looking into deeper—the question is, did de Laurent *own* the painting?"

"Plus, there are the financial issues to discuss," Jules chimes in.

"Getting to that next." Dan slips the document back into the file folder and takes out another one. "From what Jules discovered during her initial research, DLG—as Margaux's twenty-two galleries around the world are known—has had a major financial setback these past few years, perhaps nearing bankruptcy. For one, there's been a stop order on the construction of what was to be their largest gallery, in Chelsea." He waves a copy of that document. "It's a fifty-million-dollar project, initiated by Margaux's late father, Sébastien de Laurent, before he died."

Jules notices Adam's face changing colors. *Interesting.*

Dan glances at his papers. "There are bounced checks everywhere, from what I'm gathering. Anyway, the painting, *Woman on Fire*, according to estimates—and I'm lowballing here—could easily be worth upwards of a hundred million dollars, given it's the artist's last known work. And from what I'm learning about Ms. de Laurent herself, it would be more than tempting for her to get her hands on that painting. In fact, it would be *optimal*, given her dire financial situation. But again, just a working theory; no hard facts here." He clasps his hands tightly together. "Adam, I appreciate you trying to get close to her again to see what you can find out, but like I said—going back, there's risk, and—"

"I can handle this, okay?" Adam looks slightly embarrassed, and Jules feels bad for him. "Let's move on."

Dan pours himself another glass of water and refills everyone else's glass. He turns to Jules. "Which brings me to you . . . But first, let's backtrack a bit to what we know about the painting itself and its journey. Let's not skip steps. Jules, you're on."

Nodding, she reaches inside her tote and pulls out a few files. "Okay . . . so after the painting left the De Laurent Gallery in Paris, the next sighting of *Woman on Fire* was at a special auction of Nazi-looted art in Lucerne in 1939, as we all know, led by the Swiss auctioneer Theodor Fischer, whose auction house dominated the Swiss art market at the time." She glances at Ellis. "I saw your document about the auction, and I also found a copy of the actual auction brochure announcing the sale of one hundred and twenty-six paintings and seventeen sculptures—all stolen artwork of the highest caliber. We're talking the likes of Gauguin, Chagall, Matisse, Kokoschka, Kirchner, and Picasso. The important thing is we can confirm by the two documents that *Woman on Fire* was on that list. Look here." She points to the faded brochure. "Listed and sold. But to whom is still a mystery. After that, there is a big void—seventy-nine years, to be exact. We believe that the painting somehow ended up with Carl Geisler. Again, rumor, not fact." She notices Ellis's hands are clasped beneath his chin, as though in prayer. "I plan to leave no stone unturned, Mr. Baum. The Nazis, to their own detriment, created an impeccable paper trail, documenting everything they did." She eyes Dan. "Our work begins."

Adam, who has been quietly listening, says, "Back to Margaux for a minute. There are a few pertinent details to add here. She is not merely ruthless or reckless, as you say, Dan. That's much too simplistic. She is complicated, brilliant, speaks four languages fluently, and shouldn't be underestimated for a second. She is a master manipulator. She spies on her clients and her competition. She employs a former FBI detective to do her dirty work and a former Silicon Valley exec to do everything else. I don't know them personally—just that they do exist. The key thing to note is that Margaux is not about the get, but the *game* . . . There's a difference. I've seen her in action hundreds of times. She ultimately gets what she wants, but *how* it goes down is the thrill for her. If Margaux is our target and she is somehow involved in this Geisler heist—and my gut tells me that she is—you need to understand that rules"—he eyes Dan intently—"simply don't apply."

Nodding, Dan jots down some notes. Adam glances briefly at the floor, then raises his lids. "There's something else—and my grandfather already knows this. Margaux once alluded to the painting when we stayed at her château in the South of France. I vaguely remember her telling me about her grandfather's favorite artwork—a woman engulfed in flames—which had been stolen from him by the Nazis." He sinks back into the cushion of the couch. "To be honest, the memory is fuzzy. I was high as a kite, but I thought it was worth mentioning."

Dan's pen lifts in the air and there is a long pause, then he makes another note. "This is all good stuff. What else do we know about her? Little things can be big things. Anyone?"

Ellis begins to enumerate. "Let's see, she sits on the board of the Met and is part of the gala planning committee—as am I, of course. She also sits on the boards of the Guggenheim and MoMA—as do I. We run in similar circles, fashion and society events, but I avoid her. Always have." He glances at Adam. "And not just because of what she did to you. I never liked her even before that. She has many acquaintances, but no real friends, from my understanding. My clients talk. As they say in the fashion world, 'You are where you sit.' And Margaux always makes sure she is photographed sitting center stage among A-list celebrities, particularly during Fashion Week. I hear that she pitches them left and right on her newest acquisitions." He slowly combs his hand through his thick, silvery mane. "For me, it all comes down to Adam and what happened between them. What she did to him . . ." He peers at his grandson, as though concerned that perhaps he is revealing too much.

Jules wonders what exactly happened between them. The way Dan is looking at Ellis, it's clear he already knows. She wants to ask but holds back. She will find her moment.

Dan claps, signaling a new direction. He turns to Jules. "Back to you . . ."

"Back to me." She does a lame version of jazz hands, and both Ellis and Adam laugh.

Dan's mouth presses into a firm line. "There is one role that I have in mind for you. Art reporter. You're going to write an in-depth piece on stolen art for the *Chronicle*. That will be your cover. This way, you can interview curators, collectors, government officials, art dealers—all the players—and be able to approach Margaux directly, if necessary. Basically, this will allow you to do your investigative research out in the open and give us some flexibility. There may be other avenues to explore that have nothing to do with Ms. de Laurent. Your role might be the most significant of all here," he tells her. "I can't do any of it because I'm the managing editor of the paper and my hands are tied. But as discussed, I will be working behind the scenes."

Anonymous Girl, Jules thinks. *No one knows me. Everyone*

knows you. I'm free, you're not. Dan nods back, as though hearing her thoughts.

"Be careful," Adam warns Jules. "Margaux is smarter than all of us. And . . . you're her type."

"Her type?" Jules's face turns pink.

"Yes. She goes for straitlaced, serious women, preferably heterosexuals. She likes a challenge. Her sexuality is not about sex; it's about control. She has seduced many of her gallerinas." He glances at Dan. "That's slang for the young women who work at art galleries. Anyway, Margaux plays them against one another. It's a sport."

"I can take care of myself," Jules counters. She knows she sounds defensive.

"See, that's the thing." Adam leans forward, and Jules can see down the stretched mouth of his T-shirt. "If you plan on taking on this role and getting real information, then you can't play pretend. You can't just *assume* a role. The art world is its own kind of unforgiving animal," he says. "You need to know what you're talking about. Speak the lingo—whether it's Margaux you're dealing with or anyone else. Otherwise your cover is going to fall apart."

"Makes sense," Dan concurs.

Jules lets out the air filling her cheeks. "I'm a very quick learner, but not an art expert by any means. And I certainly don't want to be the weak link here."

Adam nudges her with his exposed knee. "You're here through Wednesday, right? That gives me forty-eight hours to give you a quick tutorial. You'll need to understand New York's art scene, the players, how to speak Margaux-ese. How to talk about art. I can help you prepare. If you're okay with that." He searches her face.

Am I okay with that? Jules orders every facial muscle she owns not to move.

"And I bet with a little effort you can look the part too," Ellis chimes in, assessing Jules as he would one of his models, and she wants to crawl under the coffee table. "A few minor tweaks and a good hairdresser. You're lovely. It won't be too hard."

A tingling sweeps up Jules's back and across her face as she feels all eyes on her, dissecting her. She prays that she doesn't look as embarrassed as she feels. She prefers her nose in a book or at the computer, researching. She hates being the center of attention. "Good plan," she manages.

Ellis glances at his watch. "My driver is picking me up soon. I'd like to take a little walk with Dan before I leave." He eyes Adam and Jules, then stands. "This is an excellent start." He places his hand on Dan's shoulder in the same chummy manner as when Jules first arrived. She notes Dan's wistful expression, like a young boy getting his father's approval. "Shall we, Danny?"

Danny. Jules can't help but smile. Ellis is probably the only human in the world who could get away with that.

Dan averts his gaze from the others, pretending to search for something in his briefcase, but Jules sees it anyway—the wetness shimmering in the corner of his eye. It debuts briefly, glistening like a tiny pearl unveiling itself from a protective shell, and then, just as quickly, he reverts from vulnerable *Danny* back to hardcore Dan. *There are a lot of unfinished stories going on in this room,* she thinks. Adam's eyes lock onto hers. He feels it too.

THIRTEEN

S HE'S SMART, THAT one. I like her," Ellis tells Dan as they walk along the heavily timbered bank of the Blackfoot River behind Adam's cabin. Ellis has removed his jacket and tie, unbuttoned his shirt, and rolled up his sleeves. Never mind that he's walking along the stretch of river in two-thousand-dollar loafers.

"Jules is quick on her feet and gutsy as hell. And that's my greatest compliment, but it's also my biggest concern when it comes to her. She's the type who will take any risk for a story. I've got to keep an eye on that." Dan picks up a rock and skips it three times across the river. In the far distance, he makes out two fly fishermen. "And don't be misled by her youth—she's tough. When I first met her, she stormed my office, wormed her way in, and wouldn't leave until I gave her a job. A real pain in the ass." He laughs to himself. "And then that very same night she took it upon herself to head out to the toughest neighborhood in Chicago, where a shoot-out was taking place, find the shooter's mother, and land her exclusive interview on the front page—all in less than six hours."

"She reminds me of you." Ellis laughs.

"That's what I'm worried about." Dan points to his patched eye.

Ellis clears his throat and lingers next to a cluster of evergreens.

"There's something else . . . I wasn't totally straightforward earlier. I *did* tell someone about the painting and the investigation, but I trust him completely."

"Okay . . ." Dan crosses his arms, plants his feet in the dirt, and waits for it.

"His name is Henri Lamonte, a photographer. He's a close friend and . . ." Ellis's voice trails off. "No, not exactly a friend. Henri has been my lover for more than twenty years. I'm not ashamed of him or us. It's just not how I've chosen to live my life. Out of respect for Vivienne, and our family, I've kept that part of my life very discreet. Vivienne knows, but Adam doesn't."

Ellis watches as Dan processes the information. He can see it clicking inside the good eye, itemizing the details like a grocery store cash register.

"I'm sorry I never shared this with you before." Ellis's heart is thumping.

"Seems like you've skipped over a lot of significant things." Dan is now giving him that non-trusting look that he saw when they first met in rehab. Ellis recalls that encounter vividly, when Dan walked into the introductory session late, looking like hell.

It was a blustery, snowy night. They were housed in a large cabin in the middle of nowhere in Galena, Illinois, when Dan stormed in, covered in snow, disheveled, and clearly drunk. He seemed to be trying hard to keep it together while assessing the room full of men—who was trustworthy, who was an asshole. Ellis knew that feeling all too well. There were six of them already seated on worn-in leather couches. Two A-list actors, two musicians—one young and popular, the other a has-been—a Silicon Valley CEO who invented a loathsome video game that became a cultlike obsession among teen boys, and him. Ellis knew he'd passed some sort of litmus test when Dan chose the spot next to him to sit.

But right now, Ellis knows he's just been relocated, landing in the non-trustworthy pile in Dan's mind, with the assholes. And that look hurts more than anything.

Dan's good eye smolders. "What I don't understand is why you didn't tell me any of this when we were at rehab? All those nature walks, endless hours of talks. Me spilling my guts about my drunk-ass father who used my head as a punching bag, and all you talked about was your damn work pressures. And yet your mother was murdered in front of your face by Nazis and you're gay, Ellis—what the fuck?"

"Danny, listen to me . . . You're right, okay?" Ellis's chest tightens. "Yes, I'm a gay man who chose to live my life as a hetero-sexual, until I couldn't. I wasn't forthcoming with you because I didn't accept anything about myself. I buried my past—but to be fair, my past buried me first. When I came to this country, I was just a boy on the run. I invented a fake background so that I could survive. In America, you could be anything. Belgium and diamonds—I created a fairy-tale persona that seemed to fit, that allowed me to rise to the top of my field as a designer. I rejected my real past, but now all I do is relive it, and it's literally killing me."

They hold each other's gaze, the tension between them pal-pable. They both glance up to watch an incoming flock of birds soaring over the water. "Okay," Dan cedes finally. "Tell me why you told Henri. There's a reason, right?"

Ellis breathes a heavy sigh of relief, kicks a sharp stone out of his way, and scratches the tip off the tobacco-colored shoe leather. "Henri had a lover several years ago while we were together—it broke us up for a while. It was very tough for me. The man—his name is Griffin Freund—at the time happened to be a top curator at MoMA. He was booted out of his job for impropriety, allegedly dealing with black-market paintings on the side. No surprise, he's one of Margaux's closest associates and part of the group of art scum who contributed to my grandson's downfall. Henri eventually broke off the relationship with Freund, and we managed to work through it." Ellis pauses, scanning the rolling hills beyond the river. *God, it's gorgeous here.* "I told Henri about the painting because I guarantee if *Woman on Fire* or any of the stolen artwork from Geisler's collection somehow surfaces, Freund will be right there with his clients' checkbooks wide open. He still works closely with Margaux. From what I hear, he advises the clients, she supplies the artwork." Perspiring, Ellis wipes his forehead with his tie. "Because of this, I asked Henri to reacquaint himself with Freund to see what he can find out on that front."

Dan searches Ellis's pained face. "Just to clarify, by 'reacquaint,' you mean . . ."

Ellis stares at the rush of water crashing against a large boulder near them. "Yes, by 'reacquaint' I mean sleep with if it comes to that. And yes, I offered up the only man I have ever loved on a silver platter to one of the most despicable humans alive to find this painting. Henri is angry but doing it for me anyway. This dying business pushes one to do things one would never do." He eyes his scuffed loafer and digs it harder into the ground as punishment. "You can see I've hit rock bottom here."

Dan wraps his arm around Ellis's stooped shoulder. "No, I can see this painting means everything to you."

"Every last thing." Ellis's eyes become watery, and he chokes up. Too many tears—eight decades' worth. "About the lying . . . forgive me, Danny."

FOURTEEN

JULES TRAILS A few steps behind Adam, who is carrying a pillow, sheets, and warm blankets for her bed. The temperature dropped dramatically, and her sweater is too thin. Wrapping her arms around herself, she inhales the crisp mountain air and lets it fill her. *This place is stunning*, she thinks, taking in the vast mountain range in front of her, a bumpy silhouette against the inky sky. And the stars are so huge and luminous, as though someone tripped and thousands of diamonds fell out of a black velvet bag, scattering everywhere.

"I've never seen so many stars in my life," she calls out. Adam stops midstride and turns.

"It's the best part about living here," he says. "Here. Take this blanket and put it over you. You look cold." His teeth gleam against the night, making him look slightly eerie, like a jack-o'-lantern. "By the way, there's a telescope in the studio. I can bring it outside for you if you're into that sort of thing."

"I'd love that. Thanks."

They continue walking past a bistro table and chair for one. *For one.* He's so alone out here and nothing at all like the articles that have been written about him. In fact, Adam is the opposite.

Shy, nice, polite, quiet. And so attractive, but modest, as if he never knew that about himself. If her friends could see her now . . . they'd never shut up. Jules tries to shake off the thought. *Rules.* The "unwritten" one that she'd learned the hard way—that Dan didn't mention in his soapbox lecture earlier: Never sleep with your editor, coworker, or anyone involved in your story; it's a recipe for disaster. And never sleep with a source. As Jules thinks this, her gaze is drawn to Adam's broad shoulders and V-shaped torso in front of her. And his hands—she noticed them earlier when he was drying the dishes. Elegant, veiny, and refined, like branches. Ellis has those same hands. And the way Adam's eyes twinkle boyishly whenever he smiles. *Just stop*, she chides herself. *You've been down that road before—one that you vowed never to take again.*

They enter the studio, and Adam flicks on the light. "Let me know if the smell bothers you. I'm used to it, but it can be potent. If it does, I will sleep out here and you can stay in my room." He laughs lightly and points over his shoulder as if the cabin were right behind him. "Dan's back is going to kill him tomorrow on that couch. He passed out before I could open it up for him."

"And with his shoes on too." Jules giggles. "Thanks—but all is fine, really. The truth is, I feel like we've invaded your space."

Adam has a glint in his eye as though he's enjoying a personal joke. "I guess I've officially become a hermit—my mother's words. It's me, not you. Don't worry about space invading." He drops the sleep supplies onto the cot in the corner of the studio and turns to face her. "Dan's intense."

"You think?" She raises a brow. "I know he comes off abrasive and controlling, but I have learned more in the past month working with him than in all of my college and grad school years combined. And he seems to really care about your grandfather. What's their connection?"

"Danny," they both say simultaneously and laugh, and Jules feels an electrical current between them.

Adam shuffles his feet against the dusty wood floor. "They met in rehab. My grandfather said Dan was the only guy there he could count on."

Rehab? Jules's eyes pop. Ellis too? Throw in Adam, and she's pretty much working with a team of recovering addicts. Her thoughts quickly shift from rehab to Adam standing so close. *Too close.* She takes a cautious step backward and turns her attention to the wall on the opposite side of the room, where dozens of paintings are hanging. "Wow—do you mind if I check those out?"

He gestures to go right ahead. Again, just like Adam in real life is the opposite of how the media portrayed him, these paintings are a stark contrast to the images he created inside the cabin. Abstract and ominous, these canvases seem to be wildly, tauntingly in motion. Filled with chaotic slashes of grays, muddied browns, jungle greens, and blacks, the volatile brushstrokes and roiling textures depict darkness, violence, death, and destruction. Jules's head begins to spin. A line of sweat trickles down her back. It's a horror show. How is she ever going to sleep in here? A part of her yearns to run out the door to a safe place, but instead she moves in closer to what feels like encroaching danger, as though knowingly about to touch a hot stove.

Adam stands back, leaning against a thin wood column, gauging Jules's reaction. But she no longer sees him. He begins to fade into the background, a pale figure against the sheer force of his work. Now she gets it, all the articles written about him.

This is Adam Chase on heroin. Adam the bad boy artist. Adam partying with half-dressed women tucked drunkenly into each armpit. Adam cliff-hanging over hell.

Suddenly chilled, she sees him anew. *This* is art . . . his expression of pain and suffering. The happy-go-lucky images back in the cabin now feel like impostors—lightweight wannabes—not who Adam really is deep down. Slowly, painstakingly, she turns to him, trying to find the right words. "Tormented. So very different from—"

"Yes," he cuts her off, sidling up to her. "These works are what put me on the map—and nearly destroyed me. I was in a very dark place when I created them. Margaux understood this like no one else and exploited it. I've suffered from depression since I was a boy. Now I manage it. I'm on the right meds. But back then . . ." His voice turns breathy. "She capitalized on my mental health, but I let her. She knew I was at my very best and most profitable when I was bottoming out and did everything to ensure I stayed down there. The heroin addiction was her insurance. Destruction sells, Jules—and self-destruction—well, just ask Van Gogh. It makes everyone feel better about their own inner demons." Adam squints hard, as though warding away the approaching Dementors.

Watching him, hearing his sinister words, Jules gets goose bumps. Perhaps Dan was right. Maybe Adam returning to the "scene of the crime," to the dark side also known as Margaux de Laurent, may not be the best idea. Will it drag him back down? Is finding his grandfather's painting worth Adam even taking that chance? He turns away from her, as though realizing he revealed too much.

"I may be out of line here," she begins, "but is it a good idea for you to go back—"

Adam's hardened gaze stops her cold. "I have to do it. At first, it was just for my grandfather. But if I'm being totally straight up, after four years of self-imposed hibernation, it's time to confront the fear, to know that I can *be* okay in the real world, the art world. My old world. So yeah . . . I'm doing this."

He turns to his paintings. "Come this way." He leads her toward a large canvas in the far corner of the studio. She takes a step closer to it. An enormous skyscraper is angled sideways. Along the building's edge, as though it were a promenade, a pack of well-dressed, bejeweled women wrapped in furs and capes are walking poodles. Noses in the air, they are surrounded by beggars, the homeless, and prostitutes whose faces are plagued with anguish and despair. Random bystanders, cars, taxis, and bicycles are piled high around the building in sardine-like clusters. But the women just keep walking. Misery meets indifference. The canvas screams claustrophobic, urban hell.

"Tell me about this painting," she whispers. *But do I really want to know?*

"Every painting has a story. This one I called *Nightmare on Fifth Avenue*." Adam laughs, then stops abruptly. "But I never explain why I painted something because that doesn't matter. Look at it. Don't tell me what you see. Tell me what you *feel*."

I feel your arm grazing my shoulder, and I can't concentrate. The turpentine is burning the insides of my nose, but I would rather die than complain. Jules starts to say something, but no words emerge, and he is no longer looking at her; rather, he is staring at the canvas. A morose veneer consumes his face, as though he is reliving its gory details, feeling it once again through her interpretation.

"Before I came here," Jules begins softly, "I spent weeks studying art from the Holocaust era. German Expressionists, and in particular Ernst Engel—his paintings before *Woman on Fire*. Your technique reminds me of his—turbulent, angry, passionate, and magnetic. He also captured urban angst in a changing Berlin." Her hands clasp tightly at her hips. "I don't quite understand what I'm seeing here. But it feels like a volcano just erupted inside me and hot lava is moving beneath my skin, and I can't make it stop." She meets his watchful gaze squarely. "Nor do I want to. It's provocative and sinister, but extraordinary."

Adam's hardened expression changes, like the sun peeking through rain clouds. The way he is looking at her, the air seems to be thickening around them. *The Rules. Remember the Rules.*

"Too many people have blown smoke up my ass because I'm Ellis Baum's grandson." He scrapes his shoe against the floor; his tone waxes bitter. "For some reason, your words feel genuine. No bullshit. That's what I like about you." Adam buries his hands deep inside his pockets, twisting the material as though searching for coins, then looks away. "There's water in the fridge and a small bathroom in the far corner. I get up early with the dogs, so don't get worried if you hear loud footsteps outside the cabin in the morning. It's just me." He steps away from the paintings, and from her.

Her voice catches in her throat as Adam heads toward the door. "Sleep well," he calls out. "We'll get started on the art stuff after breakfast." And then, without another word, he picks up the telescope to bring outside for her. Before she can respond *Thank you* or *Good night*, he is gone.

Staring at the closed door, Jules waits a few seconds, then locks it. It's so quiet in the studio that she hears his boots stomping back to the cabin, the amplified crunch in the distance. There's a long pause midway, and she wonders if he stopped at the Table for One. The only other distinctive sound is the loud drumroll of her heart. She presses her back against the wall and slides down it slowly.

Something inexplicable just happened, she thinks. She sits there for a long while, just breathing, eyeing the complex, disturbing paintings surrounding her that embody Adam Chase.

Her eyes meet a medium-sized unframed canvas across from her that's not hanging on the wall but stacked against it among other unframed, half-finished canvases. She gets up, walks toward the painting, picks it up, and aims it directly under the light. It's an oil, an abstract, a woman. Ebony hair, coal-fired eyes, naked, yet wearing high heels with wraparound straps up her long legs like a Roman gladiator—*Anika Baums?* The woman's breasts are round globes perched high, her rose-tinted nipples are erect and mighty. She stands atop what looks like a planet—a fiery ball of lime green and cobalt swirls—*Earth, perhaps?* Her stilettos dig into the planet like twin jackhammers intent on breaking it apart. Jules feels the light hair on her arms rise. *It's her. Margaux de Laurent.*

FIFTEEN

MANHATTAN

IT'S BEEN FOUR years since Margaux has seen Adam Chase. Four years since she breathed his air. Four years since he overdosed on the heroin that she provided. And no one has ever known that it wasn't the first time he nearly died from drugs, but it was their last time together. Margaux regrets that night deeply, and she regrets nothing.

If ever she felt a semblance of emotion for a man other than her grandfather, it was for Adam. His talent, his body, his taste, the way he looked—so concentrated and radiant when his brush met the canvas. She will never forget seeing his brushstroke that very first time in that dingy studio in Hell's Kitchen nine years ago. She could feel the blood pumping beneath her skin. Within seconds of viewing his work, she knew she would not leave without locking him down as her artist, her lover—*hers*.

Adam was barely twenty-one, raw and innocent. But he had that rare quality her grandfather used to say only a handful of artists possess: *longevity*—the gifted ability to transcend time and trend. He was an old-school Expressionist with New Age ideas, and the combo was killer. A few years later, when he painted high and naked, Margaux had never seen anything like it. A human tempest. He'd throw things—paints, canvases, brushes, chairs—ahh, the rages. They were glorious. When he finally calmed, the infantile antics subsided and the true artiste would emerge. He'd sit on his tiny wooden stool—Mozart at his piano, Einstein at his blackboard, Curie in her lab—and genius would ooze from his fingertips. Adam took her breath away, and the fucking—*they were always fucking*—was epic, all-consuming. He was in a league of his own and belonged to her. She controlled him with her mind and her body, and later, when she felt him slipping away, the syringes did the work for her, until it went too far.

Margaux shakes off the memory and studies her no-makeup reflection in the bathroom mirror. Every lover she's ever had has told her that she is most beautiful in the morning, when she is natural. That's why she prefers nights. That's why she transforms by applying her ever-present bold red lipstick whenever she goes out—it hardens her, makes others stop in their tracks and wonder if she is pretty or terrifying. She likes that, the uncertainty.

But not tonight. Tonight, she will go soft. Just for him.

THEY PLANNED TO meet at Buddakan in the Meatpacking District at nine. Asian food was always Adam's favorite. He arrives first, though Margaux was already there twenty minutes earlier, watching him through a tinted window from a car parked discreetly across the street. She'd recognize that hands-in-jeans-pockets strut anywhere, and he's wearing the same distressed brown leather bomber jacket, his favorite. His close-cropped hair has grown out. It now hangs in relaxed, shaggy layers, and he has a beard. He appears broader, stronger than she remembers. She sees him pause at the entrance, as if deciding whether to stay or to bolt. Her heart races. *Stay*, she commands silently. *Fucking stay*.

As Margaux watches him, there's a part of her that feels something akin to maternal. *He's alive. Standing.* This time, she can't stop herself from reliving that night when she nearly lost him. He was lying flat on his face in his Tribeca apartment, the blood oozing from his mouth and nose. So much blood. It all happened so quickly after she injected him in his neck, after he begged her for more when he'd already had way too much. She can still hear the snap-back of Adam's neck, that hard thud to the floor and his top lip splitting open, his beautiful bone-thin body seizing and contorting until he went completely rigid. *Live*, she begged him. *Just live.* But he wasn't moving.

She had to get out of there. Grabbing her purse, her coat, Margaux wiped off her fingerprints after placing both the heroin packet and syringe inside Adam's limp hand. She then tore out of the apartment building and ran. Barely breathing and still shaking, but far enough away, she called Wyatt Ross to handle it. The ambulance arrived just in time. She returned to Adam's building when she heard the sirens and stood on the sidewalk with the other bystanders, watching as they carried him out on a stretcher. The media got wind of it, of course—Ellis Baum's grandson—and they were circling like sharks to blood. "It's the artist Adam Chase . . . brilliant but an addict . . . Overdose . . . Dead . . . No, I think he's still breathing." No one knew that Margaux was the culprit. Her drugs, her dealer, her handiwork.

The police interviewed her a few days later. She lied, claiming to have been at a business dinner with her tech support—a man named Wyatt Ross. Her alibi checked out (of course), and

Wyatt, after she called him, managed to quickly hack then destroy the video recording from the building's security cameras before the authorities could review it. Most importantly, Adam was so far gone at that point that he didn't even remember that Margaux was there with him that night. Like everything else in her life, she got away with it.

But she lost Adam. He left her, the gallery, the art scene, their friends, the drugs, her bed. He refused her calls, deleted her from his life—and she's never felt abandonment so profoundly. She told herself repeatedly that it was just a matter of time. A junkie always returns to his dealer, and so does an artist. And now, she thinks as she watches him enter the restaurant . . . both have come knocking.

She tells her driver to wait an additional ten minutes. An excruciating but necessary wait. Margaux is never early. Never on time. Entrances are everything. That, and only that, she learned from her mother, a society whore, whose entire life centered around practiced entrances. *Never arrive anywhere early. Early means eager, Margaux. Eager means desperate. The kiss of death. Late means you had more important things to do. That's power. That's presence.* Margaux checks her watch, waits an extra three minutes, and gets out of the car.

Adam's back faces her as she approaches him, seated in a private booth in the large, trendy restaurant, its décor a flamboyant fusion of the Far East meets Versailles. He looks up when she stands before him. He does not reach out to hug her nor make any physical contact.

"Margaux."

"Long time."

"Yes." He gestures to the seat across from him and she slowly sits. They silently observe each other for a few awkward moments.

"Not in black?" Adam asks.

"I thought white . . . to show you how much I've changed." She is pleased that he noticed.

"Change is for amateurs—didn't you once say that?" Adam says with a laugh.

Smiling with pursed lips, Margaux studies him closely, face-to-face after so long. She maintains blankness. Her greatest skill in business and in life is her ability to sustain a poker face, revealing nothing. Yet inside, she feels everything. *Look at him. Clean. Sober. Alive.* His eyes are clear and bright, no longer clouded over, bloodred with broken vessels, or hooded by lack of sleep, drugs, and depression. And the beard works—no longer a boy but a man. She crosses her legs and presses her thighs tightly together. She still wants him. Right here, right now. In the old days, they would not have wasted a minute. One look from her and they would have done it in the bathroom stall. Or she would have gotten him off under the table. The riskier, the better. *That's the difference,* she thinks as she studies him. It's in his eyes: He now plays it safe.

They are both uncomfortable in the silence. Adam folds his arms, glances over at the ten-foot-high kitschy golden Buddha statue across the room. Margaux follows his gaze. An eyesore if ever she saw one. The waitress thankfully arrives and asks if they want drinks. *There.* That's when Margaux really sees it. The pause, the hesitant breath, followed by a well-rehearsed, *No thank you. Club soda, please.* He's committed but not fully confident. *Noted.*

"Make that two," she says. *See, I can play pretend too.*

As she studies him, Adam leans forward and says, "I'm painting again."

She stares at him. A million questions paddle through her head. But most importantly, and most suspect: He can go to any art dealer and they would jump at an Adam Chase comeback. With their turbulent history, why her, and why now?

"I see . . ." Her tone is wooden. Make him say it, make him beg.

He clears his throat. "I left when I was in a very bad place . . . We both know how bad. I'm making my amends. I left you, left us. Took all the paintings, ripped them right off your gallery wall. I ruined the exhibition we had planned at the Guggenheim. I know what I did to you, to us, your reputation . . . Margaux, I'm sorry."

I'm sorry. No one says "I'm sorry" to her because apologies are unacceptable. If you screw her over even once, if you slip up, there are no second chances. Everyone knows that. But this is Adam. Brilliant, broken, pretending-he's-got-it-together Adam. Her former lover who could make her cum just by looking at her. There's no denying the chemistry. *Adam is painting.*

"Tell me about the work," Margaux says coolly, concealing the excitement stirring inside her.

"It's a series of women. Abstracts, of course." He cups his hands over his water glass. "I'm calling it *Tunnel Vision*, because the images evolve from dark to light."

"I'm bored already." She fake yawns.

"Yes, I suppose you would be." He pushes away the small plates in front of him and leans forward. His eyes sparkle like jewels in a treasure chest, and she can barely contain herself. "It's like nothing I've ever done before. The women are not portrayed as sexual objects but rather as *mood*. It begins dark, morose— the way you like it. But it builds to light and uplifting, a newer, fluid, more evolved generation of women." A broad smile spreads across the horizon of his handsome face. "Very millennial-esque."

"Don't make me vomit."

But he is animated, and Margaux can't help it—she must know, must see the work, feel the canvases. More importantly, she needs to get there before anyone else does.

She eyes him demurely. "What makes you an expert on women?"

"You," he says, his voice richer than she remembers it. "The series starts with you. It is the very first image . . ."

"The darkest one, I presume."

"Yes," he says simply.

She says nothing, afraid her words may betray the moment.

"I want to come back." He reaches over and touches Margaux's hand, the one gripping the edge of the table. "No one understands my work like you. We both know I could go to Pace, Zwirner, Gagosian. They would sign me in a heartbeat. But I want you. That is, if you'll still have me."

Have you . . . I could devour you. His penetrating gaze explodes through her like a detonated grenade. "Let me see the paintings first, and then I will decide." She stands. "Enjoy your meal. I will be in touch."

She walks slowly toward the door, head held high, shoulders aligned—her runway walk. She feels the weight of his gaze at her back, taking in her body, the sleekness of her short yet elegant A-line dress. She exits, ignoring her driver, who is waiting for her out front. Margaux keeps walking, seeing no one or nothing around her. Her adrenaline is surging, and she can practically feel the percussive pounding through her chest like a tribal call to war. She clenches her teeth to prevent any emotion from seeping out. Adam Chase has come home.

SIXTEEN

AMSTERDAM

ONE MONTH AFTER the meeting in Missoula, Ellis and Dan are standing on a street corner near the Prinsengracht canal when it begins to rain. Ellis tightens the belt of his trench coat as he and Dan duck under the closest awning, belonging to a small café. Dan checks the GPS once again.

"Bram Bakker said the apartment was very close to the Rijksmuseum. Must be that way." He points to the narrow cobblestone street up ahead, then takes a deep whiff. "God knows it smells like Amsterdam. Damp. Sausages. Marijuana. Day-old fish. Or better yet, like my gym bag when I forget to take out my wet bathing suit."

Ellis laughs. "I remember the first time I came here, years ago. I was invited by the cultural ministry to kick off Fashion Week. It was February and freezing. A beautiful gala was held at the Hague for us. But there was this torrential downpour as we were arriving, and Vivienne just had her hair done. We got into one of our worst fights ever that night. She took a cab home without me." Ellis sighs. The part he doesn't mention is that Henri was also in Amsterdam at the time, doing a photo shoot for *Vanity Fair*—it was the only time when his wife and his lover's paths crossed. It was a mess. "Don't ask. But the museums, the youth, the energy make up for the crappy winter weather."

Dan glances sideways at him. "How are you feeling? That cap looks dapper, by the way."

Ellis tips his newsboy cap. The truth is his chest hurts. Must be nerves. And the long flight certainly wiped him out. "I feel fine. Thought you'd like the hat. I was going for Sean Connery in *The Untouchables*."

"Your hat and my eye patch—we make quite the pair." Dan chuckles as he leads Ellis down the street toward Bakker's third-floor walk-up with large picture windows and a prime view of the canal. Apparently, Bakker uses this apartment away from his office to meet high-profile clients.

"I hope Jules wasn't offended that I told her not to come," Ellis mentions as they make their way up to the second floor. "I felt it best that the initial meeting be just us."

"She understands," Dan says. "Jules is not one to get her feelings hurt easily. How can she, working with me? She's spending the morning at the Anne Frank House. We'll meet up with her later."

Bakker answers the door wearing a navy sport jacket with a pale blue button-down and khakis. Midforties; dark, slicked-back hair; stylish glasses; attractive in a meet-your-friendly-banker sort of way; a gentlemanly façade. Ellis learned from Dan that Bakker is the most feared and respected art detective in the world, having recouped more than two hundred stolen works of art—Rembrandts, Picassos, Van Goghs, Klimts, the list goes on.

He takes their coats, ushers Ellis and Dan toward the dining room table, and places breakfast before them. It's a king-sized feast, a smorgasbord of fresh bread with local delicacies: cheeses, cold meats, jams, honey, and a rich-looking chocolate spread. "I'm sure you're hungry."

Ellis admires the presentation. "Lovely, thank you."

"Be careful or we might just move in," Dan jests.

Bakker sits, gestures for them to eat. "By the way, Mr. Baum, my wife is a huge fan of your shoes."

Ellis smiles appreciatively, then spots a Van Gogh drawing hanging on the wall over Bakker's shoulder. Bakker turns slightly, following Ellis's gaze.

"Van Gogh drew that when he was locked up in an asylum in Provence in the late eighteen hundreds," he explains. "That drawing is the reason I do what I do."

Not one to miss a good story or good coffee, Dan adds three heaping spoonfuls of sugar to his cup and leans in. "Tell us."

Bakker turns back to the drawing. "My grandparents hid a Jewish family in their home after the Nazis invaded Amsterdam. The Wertheims were among their close circle of friends. Sadly, someone—a neighbor, we believe—outed them in the summer of 1943, and the Nazis sent the entire family to Auschwitz. All except one daughter perished." He looks at his guests. "This Van Gogh belonged to the family, and it's the very first piece I ever recovered—*for her*. It took me three years, but I found it hanging in a small museum just outside of Florence."

"Italy." Dan whistles. "Surprising."

Bakker gives a lopsided grin. "Actually, not surprising at all. The five countries that have the most looted art and have done the worst job of righting the wrongs of history are Italy, Spain,

Russia, Hungary, and Poland." He makes a panoramic sweep of the room. "Eighty percent of my business is advising collectors on the provenance of art and antiquities to prevent them from buying forgeries. But finding Nazi-stolen art—the other twenty percent of my business—is what lets me sleep at night. I do a lot of work in Italy." He points to the table. "More tea, coffee?"

Ellis, bracing himself against the chair, feels the color drain from his face. He downs a full glass of water.

"Are you all right?" Dan asks.

"Yes, yes. Must be the jet lag," Ellis manages. *No, not all right at all.*

Bakker locks eyes with Dan. "This is very tough, I know . . . Let's begin, shall we, Mr. Baum? Please tell me your story. Everything you know about the painting. And then, perhaps, I can help formulate a plan."

Ellis shares the details of *Woman on Fire*, and Dan fills in for him when it becomes too difficult. Anika Baum. Ernst Engel. Helmuth Geisler. His mother's murder. The auction in Lucerne. Charles de Laurent. Ellis and Dan tell Bakker everything they know except for their suspicions of Margaux de Laurent. They decided earlier that it's best to hold off that piece until they know for sure that Bakker can be trusted.

Bakker takes voracious notes, and Ellis wonders how much of his story resonates. Who does Bakker know, what does he know, what is he writing? All that scribbling is so disconcerting that Ellis finally looks away, focusing instead on the minimalist décor of the apartment—the crisp ivory walls, the state-of-the-art appliances, the sleek wood, and clean lines. Stark but expensive, with no personal touches except for the Van Gogh.

Bakker stares at his notes quietly, flips through pages, and finally speaks. "If my calculation is correct, *Woman on Fire* was sold at the Lucerne auction in 1939, the same year Ernst Engel died—rather, was murdered. Most likely the painting was his final canvas, which in turn makes it his most valuable, most sought-after piece, worth multimillions, I'm guessing."

"This is not about the money." Ellis's voice rises.

"Not for you, it isn't," Bakker counters. "But for others, it's *only* about the money. The illicit art market is considered the third-highest-grossing criminal trade in the world after drugs and arms—a value of nearly nine billion a year. That is my personal estimate because it's nearly impossible to put an exact figure on what's being traded on the dark web." He sits back, lights a cigarette, then, seeing the grimace on Ellis's face, he quickly puts it out. "First, we do the obvious. Start from the very beginning and follow the trail. I'm going to investigate who bought the painting anonymously at the Lucerne auction. I have a close contact in Switzerland who comes from a long line of auctioneers. Perhaps he can assist us."

"We believe that the Geisler treasure trove is key to finding *Woman on Fire*," Dan emphasizes. "There are rumors of an Engel masterpiece in that collection—we believe it's this one."

Bakker agrees. "Definitely worth looking into that angle. But the one thing I've learned in this business is that nothing is as it seems. Also, I'm going to check immediately with my sources on whether any major artwork has recently hit the black market, because the paintings will turn up, no doubt. In my experience, criminals in possession of stolen art want to get rid of the works as soon as possible. For them, art is used as payment and security. But it's like the game of hot potato—moving from hand to hand—no one wants to get caught holding the stolen artwork.

As you probably know, the minute a painting is presumed stolen or listed on any important art sites, it instantly loses value." He takes a long sip of his coffee. "Given that, these people move at lightning speed—make their money and get out. The key here is timing. Getting ahead of it."

"Are we late in the game?" Dan asks.

Bakker circles something. "The heist was nearly two months ago. So, yes and no. I have contacts who would know . . . who keep tabs for me. Also, I will discreetly check with certain museum curators who are known to take payoffs if they've either seen or heard anything. It's a large art world, but a very tiny art world *elite*." He looks from Ellis to Dan. "Information can be bought."

"Whatever it takes. Money is no object here," Ellis says quietly.

"Is it true that some of the most prominent museums have been the most difficult about coughing up stolen art?" Dan asks.

"Sadly, yes." Bakker taps his pen against his notes. "They tend to look the other way or feign innocence. But everybody—I mean *everybody* in the business—knows that if a provenance is missing on a major work between 1933 and 1945, chances are very good that it was stolen or its history compromised."

Ellis thinks about Griffin Freund and Henri. Perhaps with Bakker on the case, he doesn't need to involve his lover in this after all. Dan was right. This meeting was well worth it. Maybe they *should* mention their suspicions of Margaux de Laurent. They don't have time to mess around here, and Bakker seems honorable.

Bakker continues, "Certain countries and museums cling to their stolen art by using the very same tactics the Nazis themselves used to steal the artwork in the first place. For example, in Nazi Germany, if families were put in concentration camps, their archives and provenance records were destroyed and replaced with fake documents and forced bills of sale. Other times, the Nazis fabricated tax debts that were marked 'paid' by the acquisition of the Jewish family's art. The Nazis were meticulous about creating a fake 'legal' paper trail to support their illegal activities." He takes a slice of bread and adds the chocolate spread to it, clearly aware of Dan and Ellis watching his every move. "Many museums fighting to keep the art in question sling those old Nazi records as proof that the Jewish families actually *sold* their art to the Nazis, and boom—the provenance is suddenly legit, which means they don't have to give up a beloved painting. The portrait of Adele Bloch-Bauer by Klimt is a perfect example. This, my friends, is what we are up against. The so-called good guys are using the bad guys' ammo to serve their own purposes."

"A shit show," Dan says.

"Yes." Bakker points to the Van Gogh behind him. "Lotte Wertheim, the only member of the family to survive, died two years ago and bequeathed that drawing to me as a thank-you. You can't begin to imagine my surprise when it arrived at my door." His eyes well up. "She and I had flown together to Italy to retrieve the drawing and bring it back to Amsterdam. It was all she had left of her family, her life before the war. And I will never forget this . . . when the museum curator reluctantly handed over the painting to her, his last words were: 'Isn't it enough that you survived? And now you want the painting too?'"

Ellis's face burned beneath his skin. Dan shakes his head.

"Mr. Bakker, this painting means everything to me," Ellis says finally.

Bakker's features mollify. "I know, and it would truly be my honor to deliver *Woman on Fire* back to you. But what you need to understand is that even if we are successful, it won't erase the past. I wish it could. These paintings are what many in my field call 'the last prisoners of the war.' Getting the painting back will be bittersweet. You will feel at first a great sense of triumph, but the trauma remains." His forehead tightens. "Mr. Baum, it won't bring your mother back."

Ellis feels the emotion rising, gripping his throat. "See, that's the thing—for me, it will. This is not just a family heirloom. It's not a famous fruit bowl or ballet dancers or a dreamy garden in Giverny. This is my mother. She *is* the painting. And she is Ernst Engel's very last image before those bastards murdered him, murdered her. This painting is both my history and history's history. It is the only image I will ever have of her, the only connection to my past that I can gift my family to express who I really am, where I've been."

Ellis stands because he can no longer sit, no longer contain himself. His legs are unsteady, his joints ache, his chest hurts. He paces around the table. No one dares say a word. And then he stops moving, his eyes unblinking. "Talk to your shady characters—to your mafia, your crooked curators, your Swiss bankers with their vaults filled with secrets and lies. I am a very wealthy man. I'm willing to pay for information—anything or anyone connected to this painting. Time is the only precious commodity left here." He stands beneath the Van Gogh, a self-portrait of a man standing alone by a barred window, and he can relate. "I don't have time to ponder the bittersweet memories or get therapy for my loss. That ship has long sailed. I'm dying, Mr. Bakker. Just bring her back to me."

SEVENTEEN

JULES DOES NOT go to the Anne Frank House. Instead, she walks right past it and the long line of visitors snaking around it. *They should have taken me to that meeting.* Her face feels flush. She's the one who did all the research, compiling all the history, all the legwork around *Woman on Fire*. She handed all of it—*well, most of it, at least*—to Dan. And what did he do in return? He cast her out like an intern who was told to go get coffee while the Big Boys did the real work. *Fuck that.*

She glances over her shoulder as though someone were following her and then makes a split-second decision to hop in a cab and, yes, break a Dan Rule. Well, not exactly break it, but bend it a tiny bit. Just a little recon . . . She's here. She has the entire morning to herself, and there's no way in hell that she's going to waste it touring the city.

Eight minutes later, Jules finds herself on Bloemstraat in the Jordaan area, the art gallery district. She glances at the notes in her phone and at the building in front of her. *Is this it?* Galerie Van der Pol? She shakes her head. Can't be. This place looks like a car repair shop with its windowless avocado green aluminum accordion façade and a simple door. No nameplate or sign alluding to Amsterdam's most cutting-edge contemporary art gallery. Unless it's like one of those trendy underground clubs striving to be undetectable to elevate its desirability. She searches for a clue, but there's nothing. Just a simple gold-painted number 91 in the center of the door and an unlocked yellow bicycle with a basket parked next to it.

She spots a small intercom, presses it, and waits. The street is active with young people, artsy types; everyone is on their phones. Suddenly, a woman's voice calls out something in Dutch from the intercom. Jules has no idea what she is saying but replies with a fake name and *journalist*. The door buzzes open, and Jules enters. Her mouth feels parched, and her stomach begins to unsettle. *Dan is going to kill her.*

But her legs push forward anyway, even though her good sense tells her to turn around. She walks down the long, narrow corridor lined with abstract paintings, then looks back briefly and eyes the exit. She should be at the Anne Frank House, not here . . . The corridor opens to a large, sprawling gallery filled with giant sculptures and at least a half dozen installations. Jules waits in the middle of the room, her heart pounding. Feeling heated, she opens the top two buttons of her blouse. No one is here. Where is that voice on the intercom?

"Hello," Jules calls out. "Hello?"

A door creaks opens in the distance and a well-dressed woman walks toward her. Jules's breath skips a beat. It's *her.* She was not expecting the woman to be on-site. Her plan was to leave a message with an assistant—whoever was manning the gallery—and to have a look around. A good old-fashioned snoop. But now she'd have to act.

Carice van der Pol is sleek and elegant in a slim black pencil skirt, cream turtleneck, and black suede boots. Her honey-blond hair is pulled back into a tight chignon. No jewelry, no makeup except for highly glossed nude lips. Her eyes are a startling bright china-blue. As the woman crosses the room toward her, Jules recites the details in her head: Carice van der Pol, thirty-one years old, born in Maarheeze, a southern town of the Netherlands. Her parents are musicians. She studied art history at the Sorbonne. But the only fact in the Wikipedia biography that matters to Jules is that Carice worked for three years at the De Laurent Gallery, Paris.

And, of course, the other thing. The thing she hasn't told Dan just yet.

"How can I help you?" The woman's voice is low, curt, and her English is heavily accented.

Jules responds with the same fake name she used as Anonymous Girl. "I am Mia Clark, a reporter from Chicago. I write about art and culture. I am doing an in-depth travel/art piece on prominent international art galleries. And—"

"I see," the woman interrupts, her brow rises. "And what other galleries from Amsterdam are you interviewing for this article?"

Be careful, Jules reminds herself. She skirts the question. "You are my first, top of my list. I will be here for a few days and then off to Berlin, Paris . . . and Barcelona is the final stop."

"Quite the journey." Carice crosses her arms suspiciously. There are two chairs near them, but she doesn't ask Jules to sit down. Jules knows she didn't plan this out properly. In fact, she has no real plan at all—which is inexcusable.

"Yes." Jules nods. "It's a lot of travel."

"What can I do for you, Miss Clark?" Carice's voice is icy, guarded. "I'm very busy."

Jules glances around the empty gallery. *Clearly not busy at all.* She points to the tote at her side. "This will be quick. Can I tape you?"

"I prefer not." Carice checks her watch with an exaggerated sigh, as though she is late for a meeting. "Five minutes."

Nodding appreciatively, Jules grabs her pad and pen out of her bag, and Carice gestures her toward the chair. She sits down too. Good sign. Sitting means Jules can easily turn five minutes into ten.

"How did you get into the art business?" Jules asks. *Dan is going to murder me.*

Carice slowly crosses her long, slim legs. "This gallery belonged to my aunt. She has been in business over fifty years. I have recently taken it over." She gestures to the room filled with art. "We represent both emerging and established artists. Exclusively Dutch talent."

"And how did you get your start?"

"My aunt, of course."

"I mean, did you work at any other galleries?" *Like De Laurent Gallery?*

"Why is that important?"

Because you were on the yacht the night Margaux de Laurent's father died, that's why.

Think fast, or this woman will end the interview. "Our readers love knowing how someone got her start. The journey, that sort of thing," Jules explains.

Carice presses her shiny lips together. "Yes, well . . . I studied in Paris at the Sorbonne and then worked at the De Laurent Gallery for a period as a . . ." She pauses as though searching for the right English word. "First in sales, then as a curator. After that, I returned to Amsterdam to take over my aunt's gallery."

"I see . . . De Laurent. Margaux de Laurent is fascinating in her own right." Jules goes for it.

Carice's porcelain cheeks splotch to a light pink. "Yes, fascinating."

Wait it out. She will talk. *They all do.*

But she's wrong. Carice swipes her skirt and stands. "Time's up. Good luck with your story."

Jules remains seated. Their eyes meet. *C'mon, Carice.*

"I don't know who you are." The woman's eyes blaze. "But I would recommend you stay far away from Margaux de Laurent."

Because I'm her type. Jules reads it, feels it. "And why is that?" She pushes slightly.

Carice hovers over her. "I have a sense here, Mia . . . if that's even your name, that interviewing top galleries in Europe is not your real story, is it?" She plants her hands on her slim hips. "I would like the name and number of your editor immediately, and then please leave."

Oh shit. Give her some version of the truth.

Jules stands. "Okay. You're right, Ms. van der Pol. This is not exactly the story." She pauses and swallows hard. *Think, think.* Dan hasn't even given her the go-ahead to start the stolen art piece. What if mentioning it somehow hurts the Bram Bakker angle? Protect the real story. She scours her brain as though speed-rotating through a Rolodex. *Trendy. Go with trendy.* "I'm working on an investigative piece about sexual abuse. Art gallery employees being used as bait to lure clients to purchase expensive art." She grinds her toe into the floor. "A #MeToo story in the art world."

The woman's face goes blank, but those cobalt eyes pierce like laser beams. "Then why exactly did you come here?"

Jules takes a bold step forward. "Some of the top dealers are being accused of sexual exploitation."

Carice exhales deeply, painfully. "Margaux de Laurent."

She said it, I didn't. And just look at the woman. She is scared. There is something there. Maybe not the story Jules is looking for—but definitely a story. *Don't think about Dan right now. You'll deal with that problem later.* Jules squares her shoulders. "Margaux is one of a dozen top dealers on my list."

Carice gauges Jules closely. "Is this the truth, Mia? Or is there something else here?"

She is telling me that there is something else. Stay vague. "Perhaps there is . . ."

Carice nods to herself. "Am I to remain anonymous?"

Thank God. Here it comes.

"One hundred percent. This meeting never happened."

The woman's porcelain skin looks ashen, and her cool demeanor falls by the wayside. And then, in a flash, the moment of revelation is gone. "How can I be sure?" Carice shakes her head, reclaiming whatever information she was about to give. "You wanted to tape me. Let me see your recorder right now."

"I use my phone." Jules hands it to her. "Here, look, nothing. It's turned off."

"You really need to leave."

But Jules maintains her ground. There is more here than meets the eye. *The story behind the story.* Give her something to put her at ease. "Here is the full disclosure." *Partial disclosure.* "Several years ago, I broke up a ring of sex traffickers. I was used as the bait, and the bad guys were caught. My work saved lives. But the story is not over for me. That's why I'm here. I thought maybe you could help." Real tears well up in Jules's eyes, and she knows better than to wipe them away. Carice sees them too.

Perspiration breaks out across the woman's lineless forehead. "And you came to me because . . ."

"You know why I came," Jules whispers.

The light in Carice's eyes goes out. Her tone is hostile. "Margaux de Laurent should be placed number one on your hit list. She uses her employees, sleeps with them, controls them, abuses them, drugs them . . . It's a game for her, destroying people's lives. She blacklisted me in the art world. She has that kind of power and reach."

"Why?" Jules interjects. "What happened between you two? Was it that night on the yacht?"

"I don't know what you're talking about." But by the redness spreading across Carice's face, it's clear that she does. "I suggest for your own safety you find another topic, Miss Clark. If my name or gallery are used in any form in this investigation, you will put me and my family at a grave risk. This isn't just a story—or a headline—it's my life. I have a young daughter. Are we clear? Do not come here again." She points to the exit. "Leave. This is over."

The woman's eyes are wide with fear. *Not over,* Jules thinks as she turns to go. *Just beginning.* Her analysis of Margaux de Laurent is writing itself. One thing is certain—there's a lot more at stake than just *Woman on Fire.*

EIGHTEEN

TWO HOURS LATER, Jules meets Dan at the Cobra Café on Hobbemastraat, a two-minute walk from the Rijksmuseum. They are alone. Ellis left Bram Bakker's apartment and headed straight to the Anika Baum showcase for Fashion Week. They'll meet up with him later this evening. The intermittent rain has passed, so they decide to sit outside on the terrace with a perfect view of the Museum Square.

But Jules's head is elsewhere. Panicking about the Carice van der Pol situation, she immediately orders *patatje oorlog*, Dutch fries, because she's starving, and a pale lager, a popular Dutch beer, because she needs it. She is fully aware of Dan's probing eye and tries to avoid it.

"Day drinking?" His good eye seems to darken.

"Hah." She smiles at him, then busies herself reorganizing the condiments to buy some time. It's like he knows. Of course, he knows. Dan and his wicked sixth sense probably knew even before she visited that woman at the gallery.

"How was the Anne Frank House?" he asks, slowly sipping a Coca-Cola while focusing on her beer. Her first mistake. She shouldn't have ordered it. She should have been more sensitive to him. But the way he is eyeballing her makes her nervous. *Yes, Dan. Guilty as charged.*

"How was Bram Bakker?" she asks instead.

"Answering a question with a question," he replies.

"Okay, fine." She throws up her hands. "You win. I didn't go."

He shakes his head at the obvious. "I figured as much. Then where were you?"

No way out.

"Why didn't you let me join the meeting with Bram Bakker?" she presses him. "I thought we were a team. I thought you valued my work."

"We are and I do."

The waitress serves the fries inside a newspaper cone, accompanied by mayonnaise and a spicy sauce. They both dig in. "It was what Ellis wanted. Today was very emotional for him. But to be honest, I preferred it that way too. It's best that Bakker doesn't know everything we are working on—meaning the Margaux de Laurent end of it." He pauses. "Like I said at the cabin, everyone's got a role to play here. I have mine, you have yours. Bakker has the art underworld contacts that will help our search. What matters is that one person—*me*—monitors all sides and keeps the machine going. There are rules . . ."

Oh my God, the rules.

"Rules, Jules," he emphasizes, and she hears the ridiculousness of the rhyme as he says it, but also sees the accusatory glint in his eye.

Her phone rings right on cue. Jules glances at it. *Her mother.* Of course, it is. It's like she knows precisely when Jules is in trouble. She hits decline and releases a deep, hard breath. "You're not going to like this, I mean, one bit."

"Jesus, don't make this a reality show. Where the hell were you?"

Carice van der Pol. The gallery. The warning to stay away from Margaux. The fear in the woman's eyes . . . She divulges it all while desperately trying to control the tears filling her eyes, because more than anything in the world, she doesn't want Dan to kick her off the story.

Folding and unfolding his arms while grunting his feelings, his gaze veers from Jules to the half-finished beer in front of her plate. She carefully moves it behind the sauce as a blocker and braces herself for the worst. "First, you don't run off and do your own rogue investigation. Period." He thrusts the saltshaker at her. "You think you know better, but you don't. When I was young and fearless and, yes, goddamn stupid—I would walk through minefields just to be the bearer of the truth." His voice dims and Jules knows he's about to blow. "I didn't want you in the meeting not because you're not part of it, but because I must protect the scope of what *we* are doing." His nostrils flare as he bangs down the shaker. "Second, visiting that woman without clearing it with me might have put the entire investigation in jeopardy. How do you know that this Carice person hasn't already contacted Margaux de Laurent? You don't know anything about their relationship. Poor judgment across the board." Dan's voice rises embarrassingly, and people turn to look. "If I didn't need you, I would fire you immediately. Do you understand the magnitude of what you did here?"

Dan's stare is intense, and Jules feels pinned down by his anger. But the thing is . . . she knows she would do it all over again. It's that force inside her that is unstoppable. An inexplicable magnetic pull that compelled her to walk past the Anne Frank House and get into a cab to stake out the gallery. That pushed her to go to Englewood, the most dangerous neighborhood in Chicago, alone and find the shooter's mother. That lured her to be used as bait as Anonymous Girl. And, if she's totally honest with herself, that coerces her to push the envelope on every single story she is assigned. Every single time.

"I saw her face," Jules blurts out defensively. "Fear, Dan. That woman is afraid of Margaux de Laurent. Terrified. She warned *me* to stay away from her. I think the warning is evidence of—"

"Didn't you hear a damn word I said?" he explodes. "Let me tell you what happens when you don't follow the rules . . ."

A chill courses through her. *El Paso happens.*

"People die. People get blown up because they think they know better. Cowboy antics. I need to be able to trust you implicitly." He leans forward, and his voice lowers menacingly. The couple sitting at the nearby table are obviously listening in and pretending otherwise. "Or else, you're off this story. Got that?"

"Got it."

"Let's hope you do." Dan wipes his forehead, and the fumes appear to die down. Sighing with relief, Jules knows she won't get a second chance.

Dan pulls out his notepad from his briefcase and grabs a pen from his breast pocket lineup. "Now that we're clear, I want every detail about that gallery, about this Van der Pol woman. Slowly, so I can think it through. Most importantly, what made you go over there in the first place?" His lone eye turns telescopic, and Jules wants to cover herself as though she were sitting across from him naked. "There's clearly more to this story. What are you leaving out here?"

The thing that I found out in Missoula; the thing that I can't divulge but wish I could.

DAN WENT TO the Internet café in the town of Missoula to do research while Adam and Jules stayed back at the cabin for her art tutorial. Jules decided that morning to wear her hair down, allowing her riotous curls to topple freely down her back in untamed auburn coils. Adam did a blatant double take when he answered the door. Self-conscious, knowing her hair is her best feature, Jules immediately put it back up into a topknot.

"Did you sleep okay?" he asked, gesturing her inside. He wore jeans and a white T-shirt and stood barefoot. "Coffee?"

"Yes, and yes, please." She lied about the sleep, but not the coffee. "Let me help you."

"No, go have a seat outside." He pointed out the window to the Table for One. "I will bring us something to eat, and then we can get started." He glanced down lovingly at the dogs clamoring around him. "Would you mind taking the monsters out there with you?"

She clapped her hands and the dogs followed her out the back door as though she were the Pied Piper. She wondered if Adam was watching her through the kitchen window as she sat down at the table with the dogs curling up at her feet. Several minutes later, he emerged balancing a breakfast tray in one hand and a fold-up chair in the other. Smiling, he sat down. Jules eagerly grabbed a mug of coffee. She had hardly slept the night before, instead staring at the wall filled with his paintings.

"You're the journalist." He reached for a piece of toast. "Humor me. What's your opening question?"

She laughed. "Oh, we're going to play a game?"

"I'm serious and admittedly curious." He sipped his coffee

while studying her, and she felt self-conscious again. "Because then I get to ask you some questions. If we're going to play 'How to Dupe Margaux de Laurent,' you will need to know exactly how this works, how she works. It's all games." He wiped away the coffee droplets that had gathered on his upper lip. "First thing to note is that she's a psychopath. She's got everybody fooled with her beauty, brains, and charm. But she's a master of mind games. That's what gets her off. She lures you in and makes you believe whatever you do is your idea, when it's hers all along."

He paused to eat his scrambled eggs, downing them in three bites. "For example, she always keeps a painting she's intent on selling hanging behind her desk when a client arrives for the initial sit-down meeting. Nine out of ten times the painting is sold right then and there. I've seen it with my own eyes. She also pairs clients with gallery employees as though wine with food. She pimps out her female workers to wealthy men to make sales. The older the man, the younger the woman assigned to sell him the painting. And it doesn't stop there. 'Margaux's Girls,' as she calls them, know they need to go the distance or their jobs are on the line . . . What that distance is, you can only imagine." Adam shook his head with disgust. "If the collector is a gay man, then Margaux assigns one of her boys on staff—young and handsome. She uses sex and manipulation to sell her art. She knows every vital detail about the client's lifestyle, sexual preferences, fetishes, etc." He waved his buttered toast in the air. "Like I said during our meeting, she has a former FBI agent doing background checks, taking pictures. For her, a client is not a human but a composite of needs, wants, and desires." He finished off the toast, then leaned forward. "So, Jules—what's your first question?"

She lifted her knees up, squeezed them tightly against her

chest, and eyed him with slight trepidation. "Why heroin?" The zinger. No warm-up.

He looked as though he'd been struck. "Well played. I knew there was a sharp knife in there somewhere." His green eyes lit up like one of those Marvel characters who appear normal, but then a second later their enlarged pupils glow neon. "Fair question. I'll get to that, but let me ask you this first: What does it feel like to find that perfect story? Describe it."

She smiled. "I'll show you mine, if you show me yours?"

"There's a point to this."

She felt the intensity of Adam's stare. What she really wanted to tell him was that she likes being a journalist because *she* gets to ask the questions and doesn't have to answer or reveal anything about herself. There's no quid pro quo—that's the beauty. *I ask, you tell.* But the way he was looking at her . . .

"Okay," she began, feeling both flushed and fired up. "The feeling is kind of indescribable—like you will die if you don't write it. There was one story that came my way, as though it was looking for me. It was my first, and—"

"A girl never forgets her first."

She laughed and then stopped abruptly when Rick Janus's face appeared in her head. *Don't go there.* She sipped her coffee to buy herself time to regain her composure. "So . . . I was the editor of my high school newspaper and at a party. Everyone was drinking and hanging out, but there was this girl, alone, crying in the basement bathroom. I walked in on her accidentally. We weren't in the same friend group—but we'd say hello if we passed each other in the hall. When I asked her why she was crying, she looked at me in this desperate way and began sobbing uncontrollably. I got down on the floor next to her and waited it out.

She was a bit drunk but finally admitted to having been lured by some older guy online claiming to be a scout for models and wanting to take pictures of her. It went from that to naked pictures to sex to trafficking her out to other men to blackmailing her, threatening to post those pics online and tell her parents. He would circle her house late at night just to terrify her. I saw cut marks up and down the girl's arms. There were other girls involved too, she admitted. She said she was thinking of killing herself because it was her only way out. Anyway, I made a deal with her. If she promised not to hurt herself, I promised I would do whatever I could to expose the man ruining her life. We met every night that week and she gave me all the information I needed." Jules paused for a breath and could tell Adam was captivated by the story. He wasn't blinking, and he'd put down his coffee. "I knew the only way to get this guy was to entrap him myself. But I wasn't stupid. I knew I couldn't do it alone and needed backup, so I contacted the investigative team at one of the major Chicago newspapers and brought them the story." Jules relived the thrill of that moment as though it were happening in real time. "Describe that feeling? I knew the second I met the girl in the bathroom that this was *my* story. I remember feeling a rush overtaking my whole body, like I was on the verge of explosion— like I could make a difference."

"You were not just reporting the story, you *were* the story," Adam said.

"Exactly." Her eyes widen. "That's what I love most about investigative reporting—the digging as far as you can possibly go, only to find that you can still go deeper. That story was exhilarating, knowing I was in the danger zone but still the one in control." Jules had never said this aloud until now.

Adam was silent and unreadable. Jules waited, taking in everything around her at once: the morning sun, the mountain air, the dogs at her feet, the burnt coffee aroma, the remnants of buttery eggs, and even Adam's soapy scent from across the table. Feeling slightly light-headed, she said, "Your turn. Tell me about the heroin."

Adam looked past her, at the mountains and the river running through his land. Jules studied his perfect profile as he spoke. "It was the same. Heroin was an indescribable rush, like a dam breaking inside me, water filling every crevice of my body. I felt euphoric and calm simultaneously. Heroin took away the anxiety, the depression, the stress, all the constant demand. It was a powerful climb and then a slow free fall. When I used, I felt like I could do anything. I was in it. But the real magic happens on the way down." He paused and turned to her. "Margaux was there. I was not in control—she was. She'd stick a canvas in my face and a brush in my hand right at that perfect-storm moment. She knew precisely when."

"Margaux . . ." Jules trod carefully. "She gave you heroin that first time?"

"Yes . . . and the last time, and nearly every time in between." His fists clenched, then unclenched. "She was my dealer and my handler. She nearly killed me—but I allowed it."

"Yet you painted before the drugs," Jules pressed him. "Your talent was there before."

"That's true, but with the drugs, I was on fire. I made some very bad decisions." He wasn't letting himself off the hook. "But let's get back to you. You took on a nationwide sex-trafficking ring and you were only in high school. You're Dan Mansfield's right hand. And that guy is tough. I'd say you are pretty damn badass, Jules. A good match for Margaux." He played with his coffee mug, spinning it around. She stared at the lined-with-paint fingernails, the long, slim fingers, the protrusion of veins. Her heart thumped wildly, and she couldn't stop it.

"Margaux's one weakness is *Margaux*," he continued. "What drives her is the fear of losing, falling from her pedestal where no one can touch her. It makes her do very bad things. When and if you meet her, don't kowtow to her. Don't act impressed. Don't look at your feet. Meet her eye to eye. She loves challenges, the idea that she can break you, reduce you, make you feel less than, and win. In a nutshell: You approach Margaux by showing up as *Margaux*, and *you* will win."

Jules filed that in her head. "Do you really believe she has the painting?"

He nodded. "I have no doubt. I don't remember much about our deeper conversations, except that her grandfather was the only person Margaux ever loved, or at least cared about. Getting that painting back would avenge him and give her the victory she craves. But stealing that Geisler treasure trove—now, *that* has her fingerprints all over it. That's her sweet spot." His gaze was penetrating. "She is involved in this. At what level, in what capacity, I couldn't tell you."

"Did you . . . love her?" Jules whispered what was in her head before she could stop it from coming out, picturing that naked image of Margaux inside his studio.

"Love?" He let out a belly laugh. "'Love' is certainly not how I'd describe it. I was her possession, the masterpiece she created— a strung out art world sensation. She was my Dr. Frankenstein. I depended on her for my existence, and she depended on me to keep her on top . . . relevant."

Jules noticed that Adam's hand, the one wrapped around the coffee mug, was shaking slightly. "I know you said yesterday that you need to do this. But how are you going to go back to her and stay sober? It seems . . ."

"Impossible." He finished her sentence, then rubbed his hands together as though they were cold and pressed them to his lips. "See, I'm not that same person anymore. I'm stronger. At peace. Or at least close to it. I've done the work. I've spent four years alone here in the mountains doing the work. If I go back—I know—no, I can *guarantee* Margaux will try to break me down, to control me once again. She can't help herself. That's who she is. All I have to do is present the challenge to her, to let her think that she has me . . ." He looks at Jules point-blank. "Then I'm going to get back my grandfather's painting. And I'm going to be the one to win this time."

Win what, exactly?

"Adam," Jules said carefully, following her gut, "is there something else about Margaux that I need to know, that you didn't mention in the cabin meeting?"

He swigged the rest of his orange juice and gently placed it down. "Off the record?"

Off the record. If she agreed to that, then she would have to keep his secret from Dan. Her eyes locked into his, and neither looked away.

"Can I trust you, Jules?" he pressed.

She exhaled deeply and cut the deal. "Yes."

DAN HAS JUST finished his second glass of Coke when his phone rings. It's Bram Bakker. "No," he tells the detective. "Can't tonight. Ellis is tied up through the evening. But yes, tomorrow morning we can meet. Nine a.m. Perfect. See you then." He turns his attention back to Jules, and his tone is stern. "Now what is it you *want* to tell me?"

Her upper lip breaks into a sweat. "Carice van der Pol was on the yacht the night Margaux's father died . . ." She pauses. "I found it in a French police report. She was with Margaux. That's why I went there."

It's the way Jules pauses that catches Dan's eye. It's like that one eye carries the power of ten pupils. She feels a pit forming in her stomach as she struggles to keep her expression blank and honor her promise to Adam.

Can I trust you, Jules?

"And who else was on that yacht?" Dan demands, leaning across the table.

The one person she wishes with all her heart had not been there: Adam Chase.

NINETEEN

ELLIS CAN NO longer maintain his cool composure. The possessive way Bram Bakker clings to the new information, his eyes playing ping-pong from his laptop to the stack of papers at his side, is infuriating. "Please," he urges the detective. "Just tell us. I couldn't sleep all night after Dan told me you found out something important related to the painting."

Bakker looks up from his paperwork, removes his reading glasses, and sets them aside on the dining room table. "Yes, just checking a few facts. I mentioned yesterday about a friend in Switzerland, a prominent auctioneer from Zurich. His father was an auctioneer, as was his grandfather. Anyway, the grandfather's close colleague back in the thirties was none other than Theodor Fischer—the very same auctioneer for the infamous Lucerne auction." Bakker sips his coffee and nibbles at a cookie, and the blatant suspension is literally killing Ellis.

Spit it out, man.

"After our meeting yesterday, my friend made several discreet calls as a favor to me," he continues. "He contacted me, late afternoon, and gave me the name of the anonymous buyer of the painting at the Lucerne auction." Bakker's gaze waxes bright. "We have the name."

"Who, damn it?" Ellis blurts out.

"Ellis, please." Dan shoots him a look.

"Dan, it's okay, really. I understand." Bakker pushes the papers out of his way and shuts his laptop. "The buyer's name is Otto Dassel—*was*. He's dead. He was one of the top executives at Hugo Boss, Berlin branch. So now we have another leg on the painting's journey: It traveled from Berlin to Paris to Switzerland and then back to Berlin. I did a little research, and Otto's grandson Stefan Dassel is very much alive. He's a filmmaker based in Berlin. It's a lead and, as we know, only part of the painting's story. A pit stop, perhaps. Ultimately, the canvas, we believe, ended up in Helmuth Geisler's hands." He pauses and writes something down. "I will check on that as well. Apparently, there was a private court hearing after the war disputing precarious art collections of prominent Nazis—Helmuth Geisler's, of course, being one of them. Geisler, as I'm sure you already know, was one of four art dealers appointed by the Commission for the Exploitation of Degenerate Art to market confiscated works of art abroad on Hitler's behalf. And from my understanding, the Allies at first seized Geisler's entire collection, and then later returned it. Why? I don't know. But I'm certainly going to find out. For now, we have a name." He eyes both men squarely. "This is excellent news."

Otto Dassel. Hugo Boss. The sole reason Ellis doesn't wear that brand, doesn't own a single article of Hugo Boss is based on principle: Boss designed the Nazis' uniforms. Hugo Boss will never have a place in his closet. Ellis feels sick to his stomach. *And now this.*

"Perhaps I can arrange a meeting with Stefan Dassel while you're still in Europe?" Bakker asks.

"Yes," Ellis responds immediately.

"That would be a yes for me," Dan says. "But Ellis needs to return home for health reasons." He conveys with a shake of his head that it's not a good idea for Ellis to travel to Germany. "I will bring my associate."

"I'm coming," Ellis announces with a sharp chin thrust, using the same authoritative tone he employs when telling his shoe designer that he dislikes a particular design and they must return to the drawing board ASAP.

"Well, you two can figure that out," Bakker says, trying to minimize the tension. "But who is your associate, and why didn't you bring the person here?"

Dan and Ellis exchange quick glances. Bakker catches the look, then eyes both men like a high school principal about to scold two troublemakers. "Is there something else I need to know before I delve into all this?" A vein in the middle of his forehead bulges. "I don't like surprises. It's a waste of my time and yours."

Dan turns to Ellis, who nods his consent. Dan clears his throat. "We suspect Margaux de Laurent—I'm sure you know who she is—may be connected to the whereabouts of *Woman on Fire* and perhaps Geisler's stolen collection as well. Her grandfather, as we discussed earlier, once possessed the painting. She may have a stake in this—perhaps even a legal claim."

"Margaux de Laurent?" Bakker is unable to mask his shock. "I know her fairly well."

"Not surprised," Dan says. "That's why I was hesitant to say anything. The art world, I'm finding, is extremely small."

"And you weren't sure I am trustworthy." Bakker leans back in his chair. "Margaux is one of the most well-respected art dealers—especially after her father's death, when she took over all the galleries at such a young age. I even contacted her a few years ago in connection with a painting I was hunting down in Buenos Aires. She immediately put me in touch with the right people." Deep in thought, Bakker points to the sitting room, where there are comfortable-looking couches and a fireplace. "Let's go sit over there. I gather you have a different perspective of her. I need to know why."

Dan's lips are pressed together in a slight grimace. "All I can say is that she is not who she pretends to be."

"Vague. What I'm understanding is that you've handed me a partial investigation." Bakker says. "You gave me one road to travel, while you intend to explore another."

Dan nods uneasily. "Please understand that full disclosure would put certain people at risk."

"You don't know me." Bakker crosses his arms. "I don't work half-assed."

"I don't know you," Dan agrees. "I know *of* you. Your success, your determination. Your—"

"I don't need compliments," Bakker interrupts. "I know my worth. But if Margaux de Laurent is indeed involved, all this becomes much bigger than just one painting. For me to successfully assemble the puzzle, I can't start off with missing pieces. It's like—"

"Working with one eye," Dan interjects. There's a suspended silence in the room.

"Exactly," Bakker says frostily. "A real shame when we have an opportunity to have *all* eyes on the prize. You have a choice here. Do you want this investigation to slow down or speed up?" He peers sharply at Ellis. "The more I know, the faster we move. *Het komt allemaal in één maag.*"

"What does that mean?" Dan asks.

"It's a Dutch expression: 'It all goes into one stomach,'" Bakker explains. "I highly recommend you let me fully inside. Let's maximize our time, resources, and brainpower. Trust me with the whole story, gentlemen, and we shall see if your hunch has teeth—if any of these forked roads leads to Margaux de Laurent."

TWENTY

MANHATTAN

GRIFFIN FREUND AGREED to meet at their usual spot for brunch in SoHo. He never says no to Balthazar or to Margaux. And by the flirtatious look he gives the handsome young host, Margaux is certain that Griffin either has slept with him or intends to. Who hasn't slept with Griffin? Even she slept with him years ago, after a hugely successful art exhibit on emerging graffiti artists that they put together when he was a rising star at MoMA. "And why shouldn't two triumphant bisexuals celebrate their first major victory?" Griffin told her later that night in bed. It was just once. They were drunk, it meant nothing—they laughed their way through it. Unlike their other collaborations over the years, which have meant *everything* to them.

Sitting at a corner table, Margaux faces out to the restaurant. She likes to see who walks in, and she likes to be seen with Griffin. He's a fixture in the art world and has never shed his enfant terrible reputation, which works to their mutual advantage. Griffin is all about the money, always has been. She respects that.

"So, tell me." He leans forward. "Is it true?"

She smiles knowingly. "Yes . . . he's back. Cleaned up, boring as hell, but not even sobriety can ruin that kind of talent."

Griffin clucks his tongue. "I've always envied you. What I would have given to spend one night in bed with Adam Chase." He laughs. But he's serious.

"Adam has a new series-in-progress on women—abstract, different from his past technique, but extremely relevant. I can't wait for you to see it." Margaux takes a dramatic breath, thinking, *I can't wait to see it.* "It's genius."

"More importantly, are you sleeping with him again?"

"Soon." She cocks her head with a sly grin. "Very soon."

"No doubt . . . And you're here why? Cut to the chase, Margaux. I have a nooner."

"But the chase has always been your favorite part," she teases.

"No, the money is my favorite part," he retorts with a wink. That's why she and Griffin are so compatible. It's not about the art, the sex, the banter—it's what lurks behind the curtain. *The reward.* The money, the power, the control over others. It's truth *and* dare simultaneously; a propulsive, high-stakes game that they both need to win. Every single time. Even now. She feels their umbilical connection across the small table, the internal green light flashing, egging her on.

"You're going to love this . . . I mean, *love.*" She pushes away her untouched omelet. "Now that Adam is having his come-to-Jesus moment, I want *you* to deliver his official resurrection for me. He must headline at Basel. Picture it: Drugged-out bad boy rises from the ashes. It's an Art Basel wet dream. And you will use that well-connected big mouth of yours to make it epic."

"No can do," Griffin counters. "Basel is less than two months away. Everything has already been set. The best venues are taken, deejays, drug deals—all done. I don't need to tell you that you're at least six months late in the game, my friend. Invitations went out to all the events that matter—including two of your very own artists."

She rolls her eyes. "What's it going to cost me?"

"Way more than you can afford. Let's see." He starts enumerating. "First, I will have to sleep with at least three key people to make it happen, and then—"

"Let me remind you," Margaux interrupts. "Five years ago, there was a line out the door just to glimpse Adam's paintings. It was like a bloody rock concert. His comeback tour is bigger than anything you've got going on. Do what you have to do."

"Five years is five *hundred* years in Basel time. It's going to cost you plenty." Griffin leans back, his arms folded over his chest in a hard pose. His distinctive good looks make him instantly recognizable. One green eye, one brown eye; sharp, strong cheekbones; smooth brown skin; and his signature long dreads trailing down his lanky back. But his striking appearance, photographed in countless arts and culture magazines, is deceiving. A human encyclopedia when it comes to art, Griffin Freund is perhaps the most brilliant, albeit ruthless, art adviser around, an unrepentant shark dressed in head-to-toe Gucci. And right now, Margaux can tell by his unblinking gaze that he has already calculated his next move. He glances around the restaurant, then whispers, "And when I said you can't afford me, I meant it."

Margaux freezes. "What are you talking about?"

"I say this as your friend. You and I both know that rumors are currency—especially in our world. Delicious only when they're vicious. Word on the street is that you're deeply in debt.

I've heard from three reliable sources that you're running around the world secretly selling off your family's prized properties just to stay afloat. That the Chelsea gallery construction has a stop order and DLG checks are bouncing all over town. Is it true?"

The bitterness shines through her eyes. She can't help it. Nor can she stop the heat from oozing through her entire body. "Where the hell did you hear that?"

"It's not like you to be so jumpy." He eyes her suspiciously. "A little telling. Ice queen melting. Not your best look."

If they weren't in a restaurant, if she didn't need him, she'd strangle Griffin with his own gray wool jacquard scarf. "Hmm, coming from the drag queen."

"Bitchy, bitchy." He waits it out. He wants an answer. Margaux sees it in his fierce, unrelenting expression.

"Look, it's no secret that my father lived way beyond his means. But my grandfather planned well. Lots of reserves. Don't worry, all is well in the House of De Laurent. And things are moving forward with the Chelsea gallery. There were a few glitches, I admit, but it wasn't a money issue, it was a design issue. Whatever you heard is total rubbish." She makes a mental note to herself that no matter what it's going to cost her, the first thing on her agenda is to get the Chelsea space up and running and quash those rumors immediately. "Recheck your facts. Besides, if there were problems, you'd be the first person I'd tell." *As if.* The last thing she would ever do is give Griffin Freund verbal ammo of her financial troubles.

But he's not done. She can see it by the sharpening glint in his eyes. He's just getting started. "Your father was not just living beyond his means, buying real estate left and right, sleeping with everyone, drinking away the storybook legacy—he was running your profitable galleries to the ground with his outrageous spending. Another yacht. Another party. All those prostitutes for his clients. The gambling. Everyone knows that. And—"

Margaux holds up her hand, keeping her voice steady, though inside she is verging on volcanic. "Enough. This is beneath even you. I don't have time for gossip and jealousies."

"Let me finish . . . I will get you Adam Chase at Basel. Consider it done. But you are going to need a hell of a lot more than that. You are in dire need of a grand gesture. Something internationally newsworthy—bigger than Chase. Something colossal to put you back on the map and crush the pricks who are trashing your name. I'm telling you this because . . ."

Because my business affects yours.

Their eyes lock across the table, and it's kinetic. They have looked out for each other over the years. It's their version of friends with benefits. She nods, filing his warning in her head, but that's all she gives him, and she quickly changes the subject. "Speaking of grand gestures, I have something else for you. Two paintings . . ."

Griffin's fork filled with mixed berries stops in midair. "Now we're talking. How major?"

"The kind of major that gives you a hard-on."

He smiles. "And the artist?"

"*Artists.* Once you place these paintings, you will make ten percent off an obscene amount. Let's start there."

"Twenty-five, you mean, given these are obviously hot."

"Twenty-five?" Margaux scoffs. "You're out of your mind."

"Perhaps," he purrs. "But you know what Andy used to say: 'Making money is art, and working is art—and good business is the *best* art.'"

"Yes. And Andy Warhol also has the unique distinction of

being the lone guy in New York who hasn't been in your bed. Fifteen percent," she counters.

"Andy's dead or he would have been. Eighteen, and I will buy breakfast."

"Done."

They clink cappuccinos. "If you're successful placing these . . ." Margaux pauses. "There's more where those came from. Consider this a test." Griffin is a thief, a very talented highway robber. But thieves, Margaux has found, if they give you their word, are the most trustworthy of all.

Griffin checks his phone, sends a text, and signals for the bill. "What do I need to know about the paintings?"

"Nothing, except one happens to be a Gauguin, the other a Cézanne. And neither has seen the light of day in eight decades."

His eyes pop wide. They both know what that means. "And their questionable provenances?"

"A 'revised' history comes with the paintings, don't worry," she assures him. "Your job is to place them with the right collector—someone who has no guilt and no regrets and will hang the artwork in a very private manner."

"Basically, that's everyone on my contact list." He laughs. "Fine. What else?"

"Leave me off the books completely. I'm a silent partner. My name doesn't exist."

"Hmm . . . the buck stops with me. If something goes wrong, it's my *good* name." He sniffs. "Reset. My rate just shot up to twenty percent."

"You're an asshole."

"I'm *your* asshole. I take that as a YES."

Margaux makes a panoramic scan of the packed restaurant—

fashionistas, grungy journalist types, an older man sitting alone with his newspaper and delicately tapping his hard-boiled egg in an old-fashioned eggcup as though it were a Fabergé, a matchy-matchy touristy couple, and random twentysomethings trying to look French and unaffected. "Fine, you've got your asking price, but there is one more thing that you're going to throw in for free." She picks at her breakfast. "I want you to connect me with Milo Wolff."

"Milo Wolff." Griffin lets out a long, low whistle. "Oh, I see we're playing *really* dirty."

"I thought that's our thing." She jokes but not really. Margaux has a thick file on Griffin Freund and all his underhanded dealings. Nobody does gutter better than he does. She also knows he has the goods on her—but only a small percentage of what he *thinks* he has—and he likes to remind her any chance he gets.

"Wolff just got out of jail after serving five years," he tells her. "I'm sure he has a waiting list a mile high for his services."

"I've heard. Get me to the front of the line. I want to meet with him next week."

"Sounds intriguing." Griffin lights up a cigarette, hands it to her, and lights another for himself. *Gitanes.* Of course. They share a penchant for the French variety. They smoke openly even though there's a small sign that says NO SMOKING. As if that matters. "Would you like to tell me more about it?"

An unkind smile spreads across her face. "Then I'd have to kill you."

"Be careful, okay?" Griffin appears to care. Margaux shrugs it off. She knows better. The guy would sell his mother for an extra ten grand.

"I've just upped your cut back to your original twenty-five

percent," she says. Enough with the banter. She needs to lock this down, and it better be worth it. "To be clear, this includes Adam's Basel comeback, selling the paintings, and setting up a meeting with Wolff next week."

"A package deal? I'm in."

They both stand, and he kisses her fully on the lips. His mouth is surprisingly soft for all the hardness that spews out of it. The kiss, like everything else between them, is purposeful, in perfect view of that hungry Page Six reporter who is pretending to check her phone when she's really snapping a picture of them. *So obvious.* They both saw her walk in and sit down two tables over ten minutes earlier.

No more words are exchanged, no handshake, no signatures necessary, no NDAs. *Just that.* A deal forged between a meeting of mouths, sealed by two highly skilled art thieves. Or, as Margaux likes to call them, the most honest humans in the world. No pretense, no deception. They are, for each other, exactly who they are.

TWENTY-ONE

BERLIN

ELLIS'S PRIVATE PLANE lands smoothly at Berlin Brandenburg Airport. But as everyone gathers their things, he sits glued to his seat, staring out the window. His regal profile is stony, reminding Jules of a granite face carved on Mount Rushmore. She touches Ellis's arm. "It's time," she whispers. "We're here."

He turns slowly toward her. His sharp eyes are dulled and disoriented. "I—I don't think I can do this."

"I will be there, Ellis. We all will." Jules motions to Dan and Bram Bakker, who are listening from across the aisle but letting her do the talking. "I can't even begin to imagine how hard this is for you. I won't leave you for a minute."

"I appreciate it. I thought I could, but . . ." His lips tremble. Ellis in his eighties suddenly transforms before her eyes. So young now, and scared, a man-boy at the end of his life feeling the beginning of it.

"Perhaps stay here on the plane with the pilot," she suggests gently. "And if you change your mind, we will come back for you. No pressure."

"Don't stay here alone," Dan interjects. "I was wrong before. You were right, Ellis. You *need* this. If this guy Dassel has information about the painting, I want you to hear it first. You deserve that. Please come . . . Like Jules said, we won't leave you for a second."

Dan extends his hand across the aisle, and Jules is struck once again by Dan's tenderness toward Ellis. He can be so crass and difficult, and yet with Ellis every good quality he possesses rises to the surface.

They all wait several minutes in silence, giving Ellis time to collect himself. As the early-afternoon sunshine lances through the airplane window, Jules sees the light slowly return to Ellis's eyes, the tightness in his jaw loosening, his stiff shoulders relaxing. He adjusts his tie. *Yes*, she thinks, *the man is wearing a suit and a tie to meet the Nazi offspring.* When he finally stands, she glances at Dan, who nods back at her. *Ready or not—here we come.*

STEFAN DASSEL IS nervous, Jules thinks, as he ushers them into his sprawling office, housed above a packed hipster café in the Kreuzberg district of Berlin. Midforties, wiry, with weathered skin, hooded dove gray eyes, and stringy salt-and-pepper hair, Dassel has that documentarian vibe down pat. Walking behind the group, Jules stops briefly to check out the flashy surroundings. The office walls are plastered with neon graffiti art like the inside of a subway. It's shocking to the system. She hears Dassel instruct his fluorescent pink–haired assistant (who perfectly matches the walls) to bring coffee and water to the adjoining conference room.

"Well, you've certainly traveled a long way to meet me," Dassel says as he sits at the head of the table. He switches from German to near-perfect English. "How can I help you?"

Bram Bakker takes the lead and formally introduces everyone. "Thank you for meeting with us. We know how busy you are. As I mentioned on the phone, we are searching for a painting by Ernst Engel. It has come to my attention from a colleague in Switzerland that your grandfather purchased this work back in 1939. We are eager to learn more about the painting's history, in hope of finding it." He glances at Ellis, who is staring at Dassel with wide, unblinking eyes. Jules, sitting next to Ellis, wishes she could wrap her arms around him and protect him somehow. This is clearly too much for him. Perhaps he should have stayed back on the plane.

"You mean, eager to *learn more* about my Nazi grandfather." Dassel fidgets with his pen, shifting it back and forth from one hand to the other. "Look, you're not the first who has inquired about his past, nor will you be the last. It's no secret that my grandfather earned his fortune as a top executive at Hugo Boss when they designed and supplied the Nazis with their uniforms. He worked closely with Hugo Boss himself, a rabid anti-Semite and Nazi loyalist. I know exactly where you're going with this, Mr. Bakker, using the painting as the segue to what you really want to find out. Been down that road more times than you can count." He drops the pen to the table and stands. He's jittery. Jules wonders if he's on something. "It's not a proud family legacy to have, believe me."

"This is not about your grandfather," Dan assures him. "We're not here to do a Nazi exposé. This is *only* about the painting, Mr. Dassel. *Woman on Fire*. That's what we care about."

Dassel returns to his chair. Dan's words seem to placate him somewhat. "Fine. Sorry, I'm just so tired of this . . . Like I told Mr. Bakker on the phone, I do know of that painting. Not many details. I've never seen it. From my understanding, my grandfather had it in his possession only for a very short time." He pauses awkwardly, as though trying to filter his thoughts. Jules watches his leg bounce anxiously. "My grandfather had a vast art collection. But this particular painting . . ." He looks away briefly. "Here's the thing—there is a story connected to it . . . That's why I agreed to meet with you."

Jules reaches out and takes Ellis's hand inside hers beneath the table.

"My grandfather, while supporting the Nazi cause, actually hid a Jewish family in the basement of his home during the war. Yes, it's true. He hid his best friend, a prominent Jewish banker, who came from a long line of Jewish bankers, and who, ironically, had helped finance the launch of Hugo Boss. His name was . . ."

"Arno Baum," Ellis whispers, his voice barely audible as he rises. "Arno Baum." He squeezes his eyes shut, clutches his chest, and falls backward onto the chair as though cut off at the knees.

As Dassel confirms the name, Dan pops up and hovers over Ellis. "Somebody bring him some water now!" he shouts. "Ellis— are you okay?"

Ellis raises his hand, coughs it out, ignores Dan as the pink-haired girl races in with water. "That banker was my father. Arno Baum was my father." His booming voice echoes throughout the room. "Please, Danny, stop fussing over me." He swats Dan's hand away, takes the water, his breath thickening with emotion. "I was separated from him when I was just a child."

Dassel is silent, staring at Ellis. "The name, of course . . .

Baum—a common surname here. Like Smith." His gaze sharpens with clarity. His words tell one thing, his eyes another. "Your father, I see . . . Like I said, there is a story behind this painting. My father, Franz, passed away a few years ago and told me and my siblings the story of the Baum family just before he died. We'd never heard it before then. He was in hospice and called us all together. He was delirious at the time, feverish, and we weren't sure what was real, what wasn't. I had to swear to him on his deathbed that I would never make a film out of what he was about to tell me and to keep his confession between the family members in that room." Dassel runs his hands roughly through his hair, pausing midway as though pulling it, clearly conflicted. "You have to understand that it's taken my family a long time to heal from our Nazi past. My siblings and I suffered a lot because of it."

"Mr. Dassel," Bakker interjects carefully, "we are not looking to exploit your family. We understand the situation. This is only about the painting, about a man"—he points to Ellis—"trying to piece together his past and reclaim his artwork. If you know something, anything will help."

"Ellis Baum is not *just* a man," Dassel counters. "The entire world knows who he is, and that's the problem I'm having right now. I didn't realize until this moment that this painting was connected to him. Look, I'm not trying to hide relevant information; I just don't want to put my family through more hell by opening Pandora's box, and I did make that promise to my father. And believe me, I've wrestled with this myself. I try to make provocative films that convey moral dilemmas. Films that make you think. I thought to myself, if only I could share the secret story of my grandfather, a Nazi *saving* a Jewish family, perhaps it would clear the family name. But you see, the more I learned, the more complicated it became." He waves his finger in the air. "Is saving one family good enough to wipe out the rest of your horrific Nazi past? The answer is no. And especially because I'm afraid, Mr. Baum, in the end . . ." He shakes his head, stops himself.

"Tell me what you know," Ellis pleads. "The war is long over. Everybody involved is dead. I'm dying. I've been tortured by too many unanswered questions. Please, I'm asking you . . ."

Dassel guzzles a full glass of water as though he's been thirsty his whole life. Ellis straightens his back, positioning himself for battle. Everyone in the room knows that this is a story not just about a painting but about the lives around it. Dassel looks as though he could burst open with one pinprick. It's the truth, Jules thinks, feeling chilled, the story of Ellis's life—a life for him that stopped at eight years old.

TWENTY-TWO

BERLIN, 1938

ARNO BAUM KNEW that Anika was not expecting him to come to the apartment that night. He was supposed to be spending the evening with his family, his wife and their two daughters. Not his mistress and their son. But he couldn't sleep. The pressure, the worries, the constant fear. The dire political situation was worsening by the day. Jews were being targeted everywhere, and the Berlin branch of his family's bank had been seized by the Nazis the week before. He'd gotten word that the Munich branch was next. He had tried everything in his power to protect his banks and his family. But bribes and payoffs were no longer enough to pacify those monsters. He had to get his family out of the country immediately. But what of Anika and the boy?

Tossing and turning, sweating between the sheets, Arno got out of bed, put on his clothes, and snuck out of the bedroom while his wife was sleeping. He needed to see Anika, to feel her beautiful body wrapped around him one last time. He yearned to forget his problems for a few stolen moments. And then, he would tell her tonight that he was leaving.

As he drove to the apartment in the Prenzlauer Berg neighborhood, his heart ached with a pain so profound that he could barely drive. His best friend, Otto Dassel, a top executive at Hugo Boss, was secretly working on securing safe passage for him, Evelyn, and their girls to Switzerland. *Otto . . .* he thinks, *how he got caught up in this Nazi mess I will never understand.* The goal was to pay the Nazis' mandated "flight tax"—25 percent of all his earnings—and leave Berlin by week's end if all went according to plan. Tonight, he would urge Anika to take the boy and leave Germany right away as well. It didn't matter that she wasn't Jewish. None of it mattered. She was his mistress; the boy was his. Anyone who lived in her apartment building knew about them—the Jewish banker, his celebrity mistress, and their bastard son. Anika was in danger. People throughout the country had lost their minds and their hearts. He had no doubt that someone would turn them in. They needed to move fast. Arno patted his coat pocket, which was thick with cash. She would have more than enough to get out safely.

When he arrived at the apartment, Anika didn't answer the repetitive knocks at her door. He didn't like to intrude on her, even though he had a key. He respected her space. She was that kind of woman. But it was late; perhaps she was already in bed. Changing his mind, he used his key and quietly opened the door, entered the foyer, and stopped cold when he heard laughter and Beethoven coming from the guest room at the far side of the large apartment. His stomach lurched the moment he perceived a man's voice above the music. Anika was not his wife. He had no claims on her. But they were in love, and he'd been planning on leaving Evelyn until Hitler got in the way. He hadn't meant to fall in love with Anika. Hadn't meant for the affair to go on for nearly seven years. He was not that kind of man. He was loyal. He had integrity. He always tried to do the right thing. Except for this . . . this was wrong. A sin. But he couldn't stop, didn't want to end it. And now he had no choice.

Countless times over the years Arno wished he'd never laid eyes on Anika Lang that night at Otto and Klara Dassel's ten-year anniversary party. But he had. Their eyes met across the room and locked as though they'd never been apart. He yearned to look away, to ignore the electrical charge overtaking him at the sight of her. She was a celebrity and twelve years his junior. Miss Germany of 1927. She was in magazines, a model. And who was he? A conservative banker from a prominent family, married with children to a woman he greatly cared about. Married, he reminded himself as Anika sluiced toward him in that lacy, formfitting white dress, *married*. Evelyn was at home that night because their eldest was sick. He had come to the party without her only because Otto had begged him to be there, to just stop by at the very least. But in that moment, Arno knew before even exchanging a single word with Anika that this woman was about to change his life forever.

Otto was the only one Arno trusted with details of the affair. And there wasn't a day that passed in which Arno's conscience didn't get the best of him. And yet, he kept going back for more. And then, eight months after their first night together, Anika became pregnant, an accident—and she birthed him a son. Arno gave the boy his last name, but only in secret. He went by Ellis

Lang, a beautiful, sensitive child who looked just like her. Anika loved Arno fiercely, and she accepted their unconventional lifestyle even when he could barely endure the situation himself.

As Arno strode heatedly past his sleeping son's bedroom door toward the sound of those voices, his heart ached. What rights did he really have? He knew he should turn around. *Leave now.*

But he couldn't. He had to know who was lurking on the other side of that door. He stood in front of it, gathering his breath, then opened it slightly and was shocked by what he saw. Anika, naked, posing in the center of the room like Aphrodite. Across from her was not a man entangled in her arms, as he'd pictured, but rather a concentrated man painting. Arno was mostly relieved, partially betrayed, and admittedly intrigued. From his vantage point, the large canvas faced him, and it was glorious. Perhaps even more stunning than Anika in real life if that were even possible. With broad, fluid strokes, the artist had captured her billowy golden river of hair, the cerulean sparks in her eyes, the moist lure of her full lips, the confidence exuding from her strong face, the voluptuous curves of her body—so much movement on that canvas—it was practically alive. And then suddenly, the artist turned in Arno's direction. *Ernst Engel.*

Arno knew him. Not personally. But everybody knew of him. Like Anika, Engel was once considered the pride of the nation, one of the founders of Germany's most progressive movement of art—Expressionism. In fact, Arno had purchased two major Expressionist works for his office at the bank—one by Paul Klee, the other by Emil Nolde. Both paintings were now gone, confiscated once the Nazis seized the bank. But Engel was the leader of the Expressionist pack, the first to be declared a "degenerate artist"—an enemy of the state. Arno's initial admiration quickly flipped to fear. *What is Anika doing with him? Why didn't she tell me about this?* She is putting herself and their son at grave risk by having this man in their home, painting her. Arno's chest constricts tightly. He must get Engel and that painting out of here immediately.

Eyes blazing and fists curled, Arno stormed into the room. "Anika!" he shouted over the music, moving toward her as she once walked toward him that very first time. Eyes locked, the key thrown away. "This ends here."

STEFAN DASSEL STOPS speaking, yet the resonance of his voice fills the air. Ellis, mouth open, is silent. Jules feels his hand trembling inside hers.

"What happened to Arno Baum and his family?" She blurts out what everyone else is thinking.

Dassel sighs heavily. "All I know is that the Baum family hid in the basement of my grandfather's hunting retreat in the Grunewald Forest for a short period of time. And that my grandfather purchased that painting by Ernst Engel. Perhaps for your father." He looks at Ellis. "But the painting was only there for a short period. Before—" He cuts himself off.

"Before what, damn it!" Ellis cries out. His elegant persona falls by the wayside. Jules can tell he is on the verge of losing it. "This is unbearable. It's clear to everyone here that you know more than you are sharing. You're tossing us dog bones. You know more!"

"Ellis, please," Dan says, trying to calm him down. "I know this is difficult."

Perspiration breaks out across Dassel's forehead. "I'm sorry, Mr. Baum. You're not wrong. There is more. But it's confusing.

I'm not sure if my father was even coherent when he told us the rest of the story. Minutes before he died, he brought us together again. He confessed that *he* betrayed the Baum family. He said he was a jealous, silly boy of fourteen who'd been rejected. You see, one of the daughters . . . the younger one, Lilian . . . he liked her, and she didn't like him back. He retaliated by telling the headmaster at his school that there were Jews hidden in his family's home." Dassel's eyes turn glassy. "The Baum family left my grandfather's house that very same night . . . but they didn't make it. I'm sorry, Ellis. They were stopped and taken."

No one speaks. There is nothing anyone can say. It is clear Dassel, as the son of the man who betrayed Ellis Baum's father and now must face him, is racked with guilt.

"And the painting?" Bakker jumps in after sitting in silence taking notes. "You said it was there just a short time. What happened to the painting?"

But no one in the room other than Bakker is even thinking about the painting. *Bakker is used to this*, Jules thinks. *He's dealt with similar situations many times before, the cruelest of combinations . . . lost paintings and the overwhelming pain that goes with them.*

Dassel swallows hard, and Jules feels the weight of his guilt. More dog bones are coming. All they need to do is wait it out and this guy will probably end up revealing that the painting is here, hiding in the office. "They came for it," he whispers. "Actually, *he* came for it. Shortly after the Baum family fled my grandfather's house, Helmuth Geisler—yes, I'm sure you know who he is—showed up. My father told us that Geisler came to the house alone, which is odd. Nazis never arrived anywhere without their pack, guards, posse of intimidation. But that night, it was just

Geisler himself. My father told us that he was eavesdropping at the closed door of his father's library when he heard words exchanged between the two men."

⟨⟩

"So is this surprise visit about the painting or my son?" Otto Dassel demanded of Geisler.

"Both," the man responded. "This is about me covering your ass after your son told the headmaster of his school that you're harboring Jews."

"Lies," Otto roared. "Lies."

"Maybe yes, maybe no. You are important to the Party, Otto," Geisler began. "And to me personally. You were the first one to support my plan to build the *Führermuseum* complex. Others had doubts, but not you. I don't forget those things."

"Is that why you're really here?" Otto asked. "Surely you're not planning to put an Ernst Engel painting in Hitler's prized museum."

"No, this is personal. I want the painting," Geisler said. "I wanted it before I was *forced* by Goebbels to put it up for auction in Lucerne."

"And if I don't hand it over?"

"Well then, I will have you arrested for sheltering Jews. One word from me saying that your son was lying just to impress his friends and to get into the Hitler Youth program will change all that. What'll it be?"

"Why this particular painting?"

There was an elongated lull in the conversation. "Ernst Engel was my . . . Just hand me the damn painting and control your family."

"Can I keep it for one more week?" Otto asked. "And then you can take it."

"Why?"

"The same reason you want it. I've never seen such beauty. In times like these . . ." His voice drifted, waned. "Just seven days, Helmuth. And then she's yours for the rest of your life. I will sign the painting over and prepare all the paperwork for you during that time as well."

"One week," Geisler conceded. "No one can know. That's the deal."

"No one will know."

"And that was it." Stefan Dassel stands up, signaling the meeting is over. "Geisler came and took the painting exactly one week later. He kept up his end of the agreement with my grandfather. I never learned why that painting was so important to him. But our family was left alone, my grandfather continued to support the Reich, and my father rose to become a leader in the Hitler Youth movement. How's that for a history lesson." He wipes the sweat off his brow with his sleeve, reaches into his pocket, and pops a pill. By the looks of him, Jules thinks, probably one of many. "I think we've all had enough for the day. I certainly have."

"That's everything?" Dan presses him, eyeing Ellis from the corner of his eye with worry.

Dassel shrugs. "Everything."

A lone tear runs down Ellis's cheek, and it's crushing. *He's breaking*, Jules tells Dan with her eyes. He nods back. *Yes, it's enough.* She stands, gently bringing Ellis up with her. Dan supports him at his other side, while Bakker busily gathers his papers. They are done here. They learned one more crucial piece of the painting's journey. They can now confirm that the painting indeed landed in Geisler's hands. The hunch, the rumor, is now fact. But by the relieved look in Dassel's eyes to see them leaving, it is obvious the man knows more, and Jules intends to find out exactly what it is he's holding back.

Once they get to the car waiting outside the building for them, Dan pulls Jules aside. "That was a lot to handle. Even for me. I'm not religious at all, but I found myself thinking of my Jewish grandfather. I feel sick inside. For Ellis . . . it was beyond traumatic. We could all see that. So . . . change in plans. Instead of coming with me to Munich, you're going to travel with him back to New York and make sure he gets home safely. I will go to Munich alone. First, I plan to debrief with Bakker here this evening, then I will take a train to Munich tomorrow and meet the *Spotlight* editor the day after as planned." He glances back at the waiting car. "I'm sorry, Jules, but Ellis needs you."

"But . . ." she begins, then stops herself.

Dan reaches inside his wallet and hands her a credit card. "You seem to be the only one who can calm him." He gestures over his shoulder with his head. "He looks terrible. I don't want anything to happen to him. Take him back. Adam is there in Manhattan. Fill him in on his grandfather, Bakker, and Dassel, and get an update on his end with Margaux de Laurent. Then I want you to fly back to Chicago. Research everything you can about the lovely Dassel clan, and the Baum family as well. There's obviously much more going on here. When I return at the end of the week, we'll regroup. Got that?" Dan's gaze intensifies. "No going rogue. The rules, Jules, don't forget. And save your receipts."

TWENTY-THREE

MANHATTAN

MARGAUX KNOCKS LIGHTLY on Adam's door. He is staying in a walk-up apartment in the Village. She wants to see him before she takes off for France again tomorrow morning. He isn't expecting her, but she knows he is there. She's had him followed the past few weeks, since he returned to New York. She knows he picked up his morning coffee, strolled around Washington Square Park for an hour, and then returned to his apartment. Adam's lifestyle is surprisingly low-key, from the reports: long walks, café stops, window-shopping around SoHo, museum visits—the Guggenheim, the Met, MoMA. But mostly, he holes up in that apartment, where he is probably painting. No nightlife. No drinking or partying. No meeting friends—if he still has any. She's not used to this introverted version; doesn't recognize him at all.

Adam answers finally, and the sight of him wearing joggers, an opened flannel shirt, and a black beanie sends a warm shiver to the base of her spine. *I still want you.*

"What are you doing here?" Adam's surprised expression is

grim. He clearly doesn't look happy to see her, nor is he inviting her in. "More importantly, how did you find me?"

You know me better than that. She forces a smile. "And hello to you. I was taking a walk in Washington Square earlier and saw you from afar—and, admittedly, I followed you here." Two lies packed into one. She switches subjects quickly. "I came to tell you some good news in person before I leave for France tomorrow. And, of course, I want to see the paintings."

"How 'bout calling first?" he huffs, folding his arms. "And really, *you* took a walk in Washington Square. In those boots?" He points to her four-inch heels.

"Yes, I walked." She gestures inside the apartment. "Seriously? You're not going to invite me in?"

He steps aside, and she strides past him.

"I could have called, but it's not my style." She tries to make light of it. But he's not light anymore. When Adam was high, he used to laugh. He was fun, until he came down from his high. But this Adam, off the roller coaster, is sober and humorless.

She walks around the sparsely furnished one-bedroom apartment and shakes her head. What a dump. This place is perfect for a struggling NYU student—not *the* top-shelf artist of Chelsea, who once lived in a decked-out duplex. Scanning the chaotic room, she sees clothes, strewn paint supplies, blank and half-started canvases, coffee cups everywhere. A mess—but it's also a familiar and admittedly comforting sight of Adam hard at work.

In the far corner of the room, Margaux pauses in front of a large board of pinned-up black-and-white photographs of women's faces—close-ups. He's captured images of women of all ages and ethnicities. The light from the window illuminates their natural expressions. Excitement shoots through her. Sober or wasted—that's still Adam's technique, his foreplay. Photographs first. Black and whites—subjects to inspire him, push him to think, and when he's ready, when he can't hold back anymore, he lets the color rip on canvas.

"I see you're taking pictures." She returns to the couch as he removes a clean pile of folded laundry from the cushion to make space for her to sit down, then sits on the chair across from her. So that's how he wants to play it. Crossing her legs languidly, she studies him. There's a resilience about him now, an armor that he never possessed before. And he's more muscular than she remembers. Back then, he hardly ate.

"Yes." He acknowledges the photos. "I've got several finished pieces as well that are being shipped from Montana. I've been spending my days hanging around parks, prepping. So, what's in France? The Paris gallery, or are you heading south?"

She tosses her purse next to a pile of newspapers. "Both, actually. Making my rounds. I plan on checking in on the gallery first. Some new paintings have just come in and they want my approval for an upcoming exhibit, and then I'm heading out to Correns to inspect the vineyard. Grapes and masterpieces—what else?" Her laugh is controlled, and he smiles back with a closed mouth, as though doing her a favor.

"What kinds of paintings?" he asks.

"Why do you care?" Now it's her turn to arch a brow. "You never cared before."

"I don't," he says nonchalantly. "Just making conversation. Whatever. Why are you *here*? Shooting the shit is not your thing."

Rehab really sucked the life out of him. "No, I suppose it isn't. Well . . . you know Griffin Freund."

"I wish to hell I didn't." Adam cracks his knuckles loudly,

then pushes up his sleeves. That habit she remembers. It annoyed her then; still does. She sucks in her breath when she notices the faint pinkish scars from the needles lining his arms—*her* artwork. And the one scar protruding from his top lip that she'll never forget. It's a remnant from the night of the overdose when he fell face-first to the floor. She swallows hard, looks away. "What about Freund?" he asks.

She reaches for her purse, grabs a pack of cigarettes, and sees Adam flinch. Is he living *that* clean? She sparks up anyway. She needs it. "Griffin got you a major showcase at Basel. And not just any exhibition. It's at the Versace Mansion, and it's going to be big. Everyone is coming. And I'm planning on adding a few extra touches of my own to make it *really* big."

She doesn't appreciate the way he is looking at her. Like she's guilty of everything. He seems much angrier than when she saw him for dinner. He's always been moody. She stands, cigarette in hand, walks around the room, observes the photo board up close, then pivots around slowly. "I also came to tell you that you have six weeks from today to get me the series that you pitched so vehemently the other night. The deadline is tight, I know. But I've seen you pull off shows with much less time. We want and *need* Basel. It is *the* prime venue to relaunch your work. No matter what you feel about Griffin, I pulled a lot of strings to make this happen. The publicity team is spreading the word next week." She opens her arms wide, as though expecting applause. "Don't disappoint me."

"What's in it for you?" He leans back in the chair, looking at her like she owes him, like she'd better not disappoint *him*.

"That's your response?" She wants to slap him. "The obvious, asshole. Publicity and sales—what else?"

"What I mean is, what did you promise Freund in return

for all the bells and whistles?" Adam has never liked Griffin—but there's something else going on. She detects it in his face—restrained, angry, but trying too hard to keep his emotion on a tight leash.

"I thought you'd be thrilled." She sighs.

"I am, but I don't like being controlled. Not anymore." He leans forward. "You know exactly how I feel about Freund and his merry band of drug dealers. I don't want that garbage anywhere near me."

"Griffin is good for business," she counters. "That's all I care about."

"Yeah, what's he done for you that's so great? His clients are lowlifes—cartel, mafia, hedge fund cokeheads, the dregs. That can't be good for your reputation."

The same people that Adam used to celebrate, beg her to see. "Yes, but lowlifes with a lot of expendable cash are a boost for my bank account. They're all buying up expensive art to show off to their depraved friends to raise their status. Who cares? It's a win for me."

"What paintings are you selling Freund's drug clientele?"

I'm selling him more than one hundred million dollars' worth of stolen art. Where is Adam going with all this? "You know that's confidential." She grinds out her cigarette in a random paint lid. "Tell me, if you're so critical of my methods and to whom I sell my paintings, then why did you come back to me?" She knows she sounds defensive, but she must know.

Adam pauses; his eyes and mouth don't match up. It's like one is lying and the other is telling the truth—which one should she believe? "Because I'm ready, and it's better to be with the enemy you know."

She points her manicured nail in his face. "Now I'm the enemy? You know damn well that I'm the only one who could handle you, who knows your work better than I know my own body. The right answer—the one you told me over dinner—is that you came back because we are on the same team. No matter the history between us. We've always been unstoppable. Admit it."

Adam grits his teeth. "Unstoppable indeed. Quite the team in the South of France. I wonder what your father would say to that."

Margaux's face drains of color. "He drowned, Adam. Drowned."

"Drowned with a twist and push." Adam is not letting up. "I may have been strung out, but once I sobered up, the memories came back to me."

"Where are you going with this?" Her eyes feel fiery. "What's past is past."

Adam doesn't say anything for a long while. They both sit in heavy silence, glaring at each other. What's past is still present—all of it. "I came back to you, Margaux . . . because you're right, nobody knows art like you. And nobody knows *my* art like you."

She smiles tightly, somewhat relieved, but not really. "That's better."

"Look, you came here to share good news, and I appreciate it. What I don't need is having to deal once again with pricks like Freund," he tells her. "And another thing . . . Get whoever is following me off my tail, or this ends right here. You think I didn't see that guy loitering behind me in the park? I may have once been your devoted heroin addict, but I know you. I witnessed all your tricks firsthand." Adam stands, arms pressed against his chest. "I'm all in, Margaux. But I'm not going back to what was, no matter what."

She stands too, points at him. "You want out of Basel? Say the word."

"No, I want *in* Basel, but without the noose around my neck." He gestures to the photo board behind him. "Like I said, we can do this together, and it's going to be great. But no more showing up here like you own me." His tough tone eases up. "So, clear?"

"Perfectly." They face off in another round of silence. His eyes dart from her throat to her torso. She knows what he sees now that he's finally looking at her. She dressed carefully for this. A simple light gray pinstriped long suit jacket that doubles as a minidress, with thigh-high black boots. She knows Adam's taste. He likes when she mixes feminine and masculine. Even this new, self-righteous Adam isn't immune.

"My turn to ask you something." He measures his words. "You have a thousand cutting-edge artists who would kill for you to represent their work. Why make me your showcase at Basel? You don't need me."

I do need you. That's the problem.

"Please don't tell me you've become one of those needy artists requiring an ego stroke?" She rolls her eyes. "I've got more of those than I can handle." She takes a bold step toward him. "I'm only going to say this once, so don't ask again. Not a single artist I have seen in the last decade possesses anywhere near your level of talent. That's the truth, and why I'm still standing here."

She wants to touch him, to feel his skin against her hands. Reaching out, Margaux slowly runs her fingertip along his scruffy jaw. "I won't lie. I came for this too. Tell me you don't miss it; miss us."

Closing his eyes briefly, Adam intakes a sharp, concentrated breath. He then looks up at her and places his hand over hers.

"You're beautiful. Sexy. But I'm not going back to what was." He removes his hand and hers.

"I'm not asking you to go backward. How about joining me right now?" She glances down at his joggers, at the obvious strain against the cotton fabric. Her face splits into a wry smile. "You can't hide that."

He turns red and can't hide that either. "That's just a Pavlovian response to you. But the real me"—he taps his heart and then his head—"knows exactly where we've been, and that place was pure hell. So do you want me to paint, or do you want me to fuck—which is it, Margaux?"

"Both." He still wants her. It's so obvious.

"Then you need to leave." The chill in his voice surprises her. "Or I will."

Margaux feels an unfamiliar pang in her chest. A loss of control. She pulls back her shoulders. *Fine, play it that way for now.* Because she's not giving up his Basel comeback. She needs to make a huge splash this year and quash all the rumors, proving that she is not only still in the game—she *is* the game. This is rehab talking, not the real Adam. Give him time. He will be back in her bed soon enough.

She turns away, walks over to the couch, grabs her purse. "I'm returning a week from today to check your progress. Same time, so expect me. But I do need to know this . . . and I'm not messing around here. Can you still paint without the drugs?"

Adam clenches his jaw. "Yes, actually, I can."

She heads toward the door, puts her hand on the knob, then changes her mind. If she can't sleep with him, well then, let him see what he's missing. Turning to face him, she undoes the lone button holding her jacket together. She's wearing nothing underneath and lets the garment drop to the floor, then kicks it aside. "Changed my mind. I want to see what you can do with my own eyes. Consider this a test. Paint me now . . . just like this. You said you were focusing on women not as objects but as moods." She struts toward him and stands in the middle of the room, hands to hips. "Here's mine. Angry, rejected. Let's call it *Woman Un-Fucked*. How 'bout that?"

"Jesus Christ."

But his eyes move greedily over her. He can't help himself. She smiles knowingly. She can see his mind twisting, working its magic, beginning to paint her in his head. The sensual curves of her body, the defined contours of her face. She observes Adam flexing his fingers, biting down on his tongue, conflicted. *This*, he can't resist.

TWENTY-FOUR

E LLIS TELLS HIS driver to stop the car on West 52nd Street. He gets out of the vehicle and stands in front of the boutique. All thirty of his locations are special to him, but this one is his firstborn, fifty-three years old, the original freestanding Anika Baum store. He grew up with it. He got married and launched his first store in the same year. He smiles tenderly at his reflection in the glass window showcasing the new Fall collection. So many precious memories.

He sees Paul parking across the street, waiting for him as he enters the store. He looks around. The shoe display is perfect; each shoe is positioned at an exact 45-degree angle, as mandated. Ellis knows each sparkling stiletto personally. They are part of him. The heel, the elegant dip of the body, the embedded jewels, the golden sole, the buttery leather. But the store, he thinks, looking around, is sadly empty. Just one customer and what appears to be her daughter, with two salesclerks pushing the sale. His accountant has been telling him for the past five years to shut down this location. It's losing money. But Ellis simply can't pull the trigger. Everyone stops talking at once when they see him.

"Good morning," he says cheerily, used to this reaction among his employees. "Lovely day, ladies. I was driving by and . . ."

There's no need for an explanation. He is Ellis Baum. They are all standing with openmouthed, shocked expressions. The senior saleswoman gives the younger one a hard look and the girl scurries off to make him a cup of green tea with honey. It must be in the employee manual. Everyone seems to have his favorite tea ready for him whether or not he wants it. He doesn't want it right now but takes it anyway from the girl's trembling hand.

"Thank you, it's perfect. I'm going to go down to the studio for a bit," he tells them as he makes a beeline for the basement.

The basement studio was once his premier laboratory, where he'd draw his exclusive one-of-a-kind shoe designs. Now they use the company's corporate headquarters in Midtown for all their projects. But designing in his first store's basement had been Ellis's ritual for decades. Twice a year for the Spring/Summer and Fall/Winter collections, he'd lock himself down here, in the sprawling, state-of-the-art windowless studio for days at a time. It has a comfortable daybed, a fully stocked refrigerator, a surround-sound stereo system, and all of his favorite amenities. Vivienne knew that when Ellis was in design mode not to bother him unless there was an emergency with the kids. When he was immersed in his Shoe Cave, as she called it, the outside world ceased to exist. Using sable brushes and watercolors, he'd sit and freehand sketch for hours without stopping. Once he completed the collection, he'd hop on his plane to his factory in the Le Marche region of Italy—better known as the Shoe Valley, where Luigi, his crusty old cobbler, an artisan with mystical hands, would spin his sleek renderings into gold.

Unlocking the studio door, tranquility washes over Ellis as he enters. He was always most at home in this simple sacred space.

And after the Berlin experience, he needed this to ground himself. Has it been more than a year since he's been back? After his lung cancer diagnosis, he reluctantly handed over the design reins to his creative director. He moves around the no-frills studio, taking inventory like a kid in a candy store who just got paid his weekly allowance. White-walled, spotless, with an elegant yet understated Art Deco crystal chandelier at its center. Colorful baubles and shoe accessories fill his customized color-coded bins like an arts and crafts center. But it is dusty, he notes critically. He will take care of that later. There are no pictures of his family or friends or any of his myriad fashion awards, just hundreds of photographs of his shoes lining the walls. And one lone framed painting. He walks up to it, touches it. *Adam's painting.* The one he created when he was just ten years old. A tornado—a violent, rotating column of charcoal and black with a woman's face embedded inside of it and a swirling debris of color at its base. It's so much like *Woman on Fire. How could the boy have possibly known?* But somehow, he did.

Pulling himself away from the hypnotic canvas, Ellis sits down at his long industrial table. He spots his special last perched on the closest shelf, where he left it. He named the wooden shoe mannequin *Helga*—an ugly, albeit befitting, name—because she is as old as the store, sturdy, scratched from overuse, at times brutally demanding, and always unapologetic. But Helga is his good luck charm. He has used her as a model for all his most famous stilettos. Each Anika Baum shoe is given a special name—*The Vivienne*, of course; *The Hannah*, named after his eldest daughter; and on and on. Each name is deeply meaningful to him. And today, his newest design will be called *The Jules*.

Yes, he thinks, smiling to himself, *I have a crush.* He recalls Jules's kind face back in Berlin just a few days ago, protecting him, reluctantly leaving Dan just to make sure he returned safely to New York. She held his hand the entire way home, talking him through what happened at the Dassel meeting, and Ellis thought to himself as he looked at her: *You are going to be unforgettable one day, young lady.* Jules is smart, quick-witted, strong-willed, modest, confident, and nobody's assistant. Not to mention the way his grandson stared at her in Montana. He smiles again. That girl is so full of energy and ideas, she will surely soar past Dan one day.

Ellis is inspired to create a different kind of shoe, something totally original, something his mother would have appreciated—a strong, working woman's sophisticated yet *practical* shoe—a first for him.

Time passes. How much, Ellis doesn't know. An hour, perhaps? Two? Three? His phone is full of messages and missed calls, but he ignores them all. When he's finally done, he takes the sketch and holds it to the light. *Yes . . .* he thinks. A caterpillar turned butterfly. *Perfect.*

And just as he reaches for Helga to translate his sketch to the shoe, the chest pain begins shooting at him like a shrew with a machete—shrill, precise, and relentless. He drops the sketch to the table, and his elbow knocks the green tea to the floor. Ellis tries to will away the excruciating pain, but it only digs deeper, harder, meaner. Clutching his chest, gasping for air, he is rendered speechless as he falls to the floor, unable to call out for help. He is bleeding profusely from his forehead. His vision becomes blurry, until he no longer sees what's in this room. Until it spins into another . . . the familiar yet faraway images swirl around him violently, like the tornado in his grandson's painting.

It was night, way past his bedtime, and the very last time he saw his father . . . Ellis heard the cries, his mother's screams, saw her long blond hair flowing behind her as the bell sleeves of her burnt orange floral silk robe flapped with each accelerated stride. He hid behind his bedroom door, slightly ajar, and watched the skewed images flash by like a scene from a passing train. Ernst Engel carrying that enormous canvas out the door, his mother crying out for the man to stay, his father behind her yelling to let Engel go, that the artist's presence was too dangerous. And once the door slammed shut behind the famous artist, his parents fought it out until they exhausted themselves and fell into each other's arms, that silky robe falling gracefully to the floor like autumnal foliage. He recalls his father's face, part agony, part ecstasy, eyes squeezed shut, embracing his mother so tightly that their bodies became one person.

The image leaves Ellis as the growing pain inside his chest overpowers the memory, which shrivels up until it is barely discernible. Did that even happen? If he were an angel watching from above, he would have seen the balletic way he tumbled from the chair to the floor, clutching his chest like a Balanchine-choreographed death, albeit the landing was flawed and harsh, his face now pressed to the cold tile. *Am I still alive?* he wonders, hopes, as he desperately clings to life. He's not done here . . . *His mother . . . the painting . . . he must see her.*

Somewhere in the distance, Ellis hears the shrill sound of a siren wee-wooing, and then his mind blanks out, the whiteness of his firstborn store blinds him, and what's left is murk, a total eclipse, and then nothing at all.

TWENTY-FIVE

CORRENS, FRANCE

MARGAUX PACES THE entire first floor of the château. Milo Wolff, the art forger, was supposed to have arrived over an hour ago. She despises those who aren't punctual, especially when it comes to wasting her time. But she needs him. She walks into the Drawing Room, glances at *Woman on Fire* leaning against the wall, then heads into the Great Room only to find Wyatt Ross sitting in her grandfather's favorite chair, smoking, as if he belongs there.

"Get off that chair," she barks at him.

"Jesus, Margaux, relax." He stands and moves to the uncomfortable-looking needlepointed armchair across from it. "I promise, Wolff is coming soon. The driver texted that he picked him up at the airport in Aix thirty minutes ago."

Margaux glowers at him. "I've changed my mind. I want to meet the forger alone. Without you. Let's meet up after he leaves, okay?"

Wyatt nods, stands, and gestures toward the kitchen. "Fine.

You know where I'll be. Remember—let the forger talk. Let him brag. Feed his ego. This is a guy who fooled the world for fifty years until he finally got caught. He calls his paintings 'method acting on canvas.' The guy is brilliant. He was actually put in jail for selling a fake Renoir to the chancellor of Germany." He laughs. "Doesn't get ballsier than that. Just don't act"—Wyatt presses his lips together—"superior, or you will lose him." With that, he leaves the room, and she hears the not-so-subtle slam of the kitchen door.

Superior. Margaux clenches her teeth and continues her pacing, until the doorbell finally rings twenty minutes later. She answers to a tall, beefy man, sloppily dressed, who looks like an aged Viking with his long, streaked blond-gray hair, prunelike wrinkles, and crazy eyes.

"Come in." She ushers Wolff into the Great Room. "I'm sure you are tired from traveling."

She glances down at his mud-caked boots traipsing across the hardwood floor. All his millions, and the guy could easily double as a grape picker from the vineyard. He looks around and lets out a whistle. "Reminds me of Versailles. You've done well for yourself, Mlle de Laurent."

"From my understanding, so have you." She tries to ignore the dirty shoes and offers him a scotch. The forger is clearly not the wine type. And she's pegged it right. He downs the vintage Macallan in one dramatic swig, like a Russian throwing back vodka. She thinks of Wyatt. "I'm a big fan of your work, Mr. Wolff."

"I find that hard to believe, since you're an art dealer. I'm basically your nightmare." His face breaks into a wide, gap-toothed grin. "For the record, I am the best."

"So they say. Just curious, what makes you so good?" she asks, stroking what appears to be his enormous ego. Wyatt was right.

"There are rules I follow that separate me from all other forgers," he explains. "Rules are the reason I wasn't caught for more than fifty years. And the only reason the Renoir was discovered to be a fake is that one of my employees, who I fired because he was stealing, wanted revenge. But there are rules . . ." He points a hostile finger at her.

"Sounds like this is going to be interesting. Do tell." Margaux forces a smile. Instantly, the forger's body language shifts, morphing from stiff to relaxed. He clearly likes an audience. "I apologize about the floor." He points to his boots. "I was working up until the time of the flight, running late as usual. I realized once I got on the plane that I was still in my work boots."

"Didn't even notice." *Keep buttering him up.* Wyatt told her that Milo Wolff doesn't take on a painting unless he feels a connection. Apparently, he can't be bought. Except that everyone can be bought. "Your top five rules, Mr. Wolff," she gushes.

He leans forward, and Margaux can see the bushy blond chest hair poking out over the top of his wrinkled blue work shirt. An oaf, most likely demanding and selfish in bed. "First, you need a convincing backstory. Staging is everything," he exclaims. "When I painted the Monet—you know, the one from the *Haystacks* series that sold for eighty million? My wife dressed up in elegant clothing as though she was from the late eighteen eighties, the exact period when the real painting was created. Then a photo was taken of her in a fancy château very similar to this one with the forged painting hanging behind her. Our photographer used an old box camera and developed the image on prewar photographic paper." He slams his fist down on his thigh. "Authenticity is everything. The right materials must be used—the canvas especially. And the frame must come from the exact time of the original artist. We actually stain our canvases with teabags to give them an aged look," he explains. "Most forgeries are caught due to the type of paint utilized. Pigment *must* be chosen from when the artist was still alive. Chemical checks can verify this. The aging process is key." He pauses to pop a lime green macaron into his mouth from a sizable platter of desserts Margaux had set out on the coffee table. His large hands—seeming to belong to a welder, not a painter—flail through the air animatedly. "My wife actually blow-dries the painting, and then we bake it in a special oven we designed ourselves to give it a certain aging effect. We aren't forgers—we view ourselves as historians." His gaze intensifies. "Tell me, why am I here, Mlle de Laurent?"

Margaux puts down her drink. "Come. I want you to meet her."

He follows Margaux into the Drawing Room and stands near the entrance in awe. "Ernst Engel," he whispers, his voice barely audible.

She nods. "Yes, his very last known work."

"There were rumors of this one . . . but no one has seen it since it sold at the Lucerne auction." He approaches the canvas slowly with naked anticipation, a groom to a blushing bride, stands back, and takes her in. "Leave the room. Now. I need to be alone. I must see her, feel her, understand her."

Margaux pauses with uncertainty. *Does he need to steal her too?* There's a gun in the other room that she keeps in the desk in her grandfather's study. "I will be back in a few minutes."

"Thirty," he commands, not looking at her.

"Fine." She watches him for a few moments, stripping *Woman on Fire* with his eyes. "Thirty minutes."

TWENTY-NINE MINUTES LATER, Margaux reenters the room. Enough with the games. "Well," she says, "can you paint this?"

Wolff is sitting in a chair that he moved from across the room to face the painting. He is immobile; his voice is flat. "You insult me. I don't paint from copies. Only originals." He turns to her with clenched fists. "I stopped my important work for this garbage?"

For a long moment there is only dead air. Margaux presses her hand against the gun hidden at her side. "What are you talking about?"

Wolff stands and swipes his hands against his dusty pants. "This *is* the forged painting. It's not the original."

"What the hell are you saying?" Margaux will murder this Neanderthal with her bare hands.

He walks up to the painting and touches it. "Look here. It's all in the brushstroke, my dear. It tells the whole story. The one rule I didn't mention: *Know thy fucking brushstroke.*" He signals Margaux over to the painting. "This was painted by a right-handed forger. Ernst Engel was a lefty. There's a difference. I can tell by the pigment, the texture, and even the slightly vinegary smell—remnants of old varnish—that this was indeed painted during the nineteen thirties. That part is real. But the stroke?" He laughs sardonically. "Forged!" he shouts. "Look at the signature, the way the L loops and the angle of the T—clearly right-handed. You, Mlle de Laurent, are in possession of a high-quality copy. Not the real painting." He stands and walks toward the door. "I will show myself out."

Margaux doesn't move, doesn't breathe, and what happens next after the man leaves, she will barely remember. Just the feeling, the fury, creeping through her body, rising and shapeshifting until it overtakes her, until she becomes a human inferno. Like the forged painting herself.

NOT HEARING FROM Margaux, Wyatt Ross returns to the château a few hours later and witnesses the aftermath of the disaster, as though an explosion took place. *What did she do?* The Great Room is trashed, like a heavy metal rocker had his way with it after a drug-induced performance. The wall-sized antique gilded mirror is shattered; shards of glass are scattered everywhere. Vases were thrown, fresh flowers lay belly-up amid puddles of water, drawers have been emptied onto the floor, her grandfather's favorite chair is tilted on its side, the coffee table was flipped over, and the walls are covered with a buffet of pastries and cakes. Wyatt doesn't know where to look first. He finds Margaux in the Drawing Room—also in disarray, littered with debris—staring at the painting. She is barefoot, and her feet are bloody, as though she walked across the broken glass. She doesn't even turn when he calls out her name.

"Margaux," he repeats, feeling a sharp twitch at the hinge of his jaw. He walks toward her and pulls her around to face him. Her mascara is smeared across her face, as is her lipstick, and her hands are bloody. "Christ, what did you do to yourself?"

"How did *you* miss this?" she sneers at him.

"What did I possibly miss?" he counters defensively, hiding the papers that he brought to show her behind his back.

"You should have known, damn it. She's a fake!" Margaux's

face contorts as she points to *Woman on Fire*. "Everything I have been planning . . . destroyed."

How would I have known it's a fake? "We can fix this," he says, treading carefully, knowing better than to avert his eyes. Meeting her wrath head-on, Wyatt is uneasy about what she is planning to do next, especially after spotting the grip of a gun protruding from her waistband.

Sparks fly from her eyes. "Just fix this!" She pushes him roughly out of her way.

"It's a setback, that's all. We just need to regroup." He steadies himself. "We will find the real painting."

"There is no regroup. This is not a corporate takeover," she yells. "Don't you see—it's ruined."

"It's not ruined. We have hundreds of other masterpieces in our possession."

"This painting is the only one that matters." She kicks her way across the room, through the debris, not even flinching as she steps onto shards of glass. Wyatt doesn't know what to do.

Margaux's hair, usually glossy and coiffed, is sticking out in strange places, like she pulled it herself. Her face seems to distort as the anger consumes her. He wishes he could look away, but he can't. Admittedly, he is fascinated by the transformation. Her beauty is suddenly monstrous. Her brows, dramatically arched, look grotesque; her nose, long and straight, appears witchy. The sheer disbelief that she has been one-upped by some unknown forger from the past has derailed her. None of this is Wyatt's fault—but it doesn't matter.

"Just get out of here!" she hisses. "I need to figure this out on my own."

This time Wyatt does not leave. He stands right where he is. "Let's plan our next move."

"*You* have no moves!" she screeches while eyeing the papers he's holding. "What's in your hand?"

He glances down at the documents sheepishly. "This can wait."

"Tell me, or I will fire you immediately."

Wyatt breaks out into a sweat. "Carice van der Pol. As you know, I've had her gallery in Amsterdam tapped since . . . the accident. For nearly five years there hasn't been a peep out of her. But I just got some audio that you're not going to be happy about. There's a young reporter who came to her gallery. She's doing a story and asking about you."

Margaux's face is inflamed. "A reporter? Who? What did Carice say to her?" She shoves Wyatt hard again, and this time he loses his balance and falls to the floor. She hovers over him. "You should have gotten rid of that woman long ago when we had the chance."

Wyatt stands, shocked by the push. "Enough. We're on the same team here. Carice did not say a word about that night, because she doesn't want to implicate herself. She tried to get the woman out of her gallery." Wyatt refrains from telling Margaux that he obtained only a partial recording of the interaction and then it cut off.

"Who is the damn reporter?"

"She's from Chicago. The name and newspaper she gave Carice were fake. But there were cameras in the area that captured the young woman waiting in front of the gallery. With facial recognition, I was able to identify her. Her name is Jules Roth. She works for the *Chicago Chronicle*." But Margaux is no longer paying attention. Her gaze is focused only on the painting. "Did you hear me?" Wyatt asks.

"Hear you?" Margaux snaps at him, then reaches for the Chinese vase perched on the mantel next to the painting—a Qing dynasty piece—and whips it with all her might at the far wall. They both watch as the priceless vase shatters into a thousand little pieces. She glares at Wyatt. "Did you hear that? Now get the hell out of here. I need to think."

"Do you want me to take the painting back to the vault?" he whispers, pointing at the canvas.

Margaux pauses, her ebony eyes recalibrating, her voice deceptively calm. "Keep the forgery but get rid of the forger."

TWENTY-SIX

LATER, AFTER SHE calms down, Margaux meets Wyatt in his office. He avoids mentioning the disaster that took place earlier in the day as he hands her a stack of papers, but it's there like an unwanted house guest between them. "An update . . ." he begins carefully. "The journalist who met Carice in Amsterdam works for Dan Mansfield at the *Chicago Chronicle*."

Her mouth drops open. "The investigative reporter?"

"Yep, him," Wyatt affirms. "Except that his investigative team was disbanded a few years ago, apparently after a mishap. Now Mansfield has a desk job. From what I gather, he's gone rogue, and undercover investigations are his side hustle. I've gone through hundreds of emails, but Mansfield's very cautious about what he puts in writing . . ." By the melodramatic pause Wyatt takes, Margaux knows this is going from bad to worse.

"Just say it."

"Sit down," he says forcefully, and, surprising them both, she does.

"It seems Mansfield has assembled a team—Jules Roth, a woman named Louise Archer, who works with him at the newspaper . . . But there are others . . ." Wyatt clutches the edge of his desk, as though bracing himself. "And . . . Adam."

Margaux's eyes pop, the name spinning in her gut. "My Adam?"

"Yes . . . And his grandfather, Ellis Baum, seems to be involved as well. It appears they've joined forces to find *Woman on Fire*. Why, I couldn't tell you. But it's happening. And from what I uncovered in a recent email exchange, Mansfield is in Munich right now. My sense is that—"

"Wait—*Adam?*" Margaux's mind races in a hundred directions. She thinks back to his apartment several days ago when he painted her naked. When he didn't touch her—as though she had leprosy. She covers her mouth with her palm, and her eyes bulge. Adam didn't return to her to make his art world comeback. *It's the painting he's after.*

"I think that—"

"Just shut up. I'm the one who needs to think right now." She stands and begins to pace. From the corner of her eye, she sees Wyatt guarding his state-of-the-art computer system, quickly turning off various systems, as though anticipating her going postal on him again. "Don't worry," she says icily. "I only break things once a day."

Wyatt knows better than to respond. Instead, he walks over to the bar and, bypassing the family reserve, reaches for the scotch and pours them each a glass. She accepts it.

"Back up," she says, swigging hard. "What is Mansfield doing in Munich?"

"I believe he's meeting with the editor of *Spotlight*."

"*Spotlight?*" Margaux slams down her glass on Wyatt's desk, not caring that the scotch spills over his papers. "That's how we originally got the tip about the Geisler treasure trove . . ."

"Yes, exactly. From Munich, he's scheduled to fly back to Chicago in two days and—"

Adam, fucking Adam.

Wyatt stops speaking, cleans up her mess, then clears his throat. "None of this is good news, but we can handle it, make the tough decisions."

Margaux lights up a cigarette; doesn't offer him one. She leans against his desk in silence, staring at the far wall.

"I'm not going to lie to you," he continues. "There's more . . . Mansfield, Roth, and Ellis Baum recently flew together to Amsterdam to what appears to be a meeting with Bram Bakker—the art detective. He may be part of this as well."

"Bram Bakker!" She whips around with a shriek. "What the hell! You know Bakker—whatever he touches makes headlines. What's your plan now? Still regrouping?"

Wyatt, silent, shuffles his boots against the floor.

"Say something, damn it!"

"I'm working on it," he yells back in frustration. "The trail went dead from there. I also placed a call to your FBI guy, who's been keeping tabs on Adam, to send us anything he's discovered in the past few days, and—"

"Wait, stop talking," she interrupts, snapping her fingers. "There is another piece. Griffin Freund mentioned to me the other day that he's just started seeing someone. An old lover. He laughed, saying he snagged the guy right out from under Ellis Baum's nose. Christ, we are being ambushed."

Wyatt's eye tic is now off and running. "Okay . . . none of this is good. But think about it. We have an opportunity here to manipulate all of this to our advantage. We can use *them* to do the work for us, to find the *real* painting and foil whatever they *think* they know about the Geisler collection—especially if they don't know that we are onto them." He walks around his desk, stands close to Margaux, takes her hand. "I've got this."

She yanks away her hand. "You've clearly got nothing. I'm sure as hell not going to wait around like I'm target practice. We are going to be proactive and eliminate the problems one by one, my way. *We* do the work—not them. Got that?"

He nods.

"First . . . the forger?"

"Already handled." Wyatt rubs his hands. "Milo Wolff never made it home from the airport . . . I got his wife's Tesla up to one twenty, then disabled the brakes."

"Be sure to send flowers." Margaux nods approvingly. "Two . . . Bram Bakker?"

Wyatt shakes his head. "Untouchable. He's too well-connected—with police, international authorities, and criminals. And his accounts are firewalled in titanium—I've already checked. I can't break through easily, but I will get there. In the meantime, I plan to keep Bakker very busy with my diversion plan. He will soon learn that several stolen works from Geisler's collection are now in the hands of the mafia and neo-Nazis. He will follow that trail, and I will manipulate it."

"And I've got number three." Margaux grabs her coat off the chair. "Find out the location of Mansfield's hotel in Munich and fire up my plane and the crew. He's not going back to Chicago."

TWENTY-SEVEN

MUNICH, GERMANY

D AN POPPED ANOTHER painkiller a half hour ago, because more than anything, he wants a drink. The chalky pill exploded through his system, and he hopes it will numb out his darker impulses once again. He adjusts the lamplight on the hotel room desk. Normally, he'd keep it on dim to prevent the migraines, but not now. He switches the light to its brightest level. He wants to fully see, smell, feel the gem that has landed in his hands. Two seconds after the *Spotlight* editor gave him the photo during their meeting this morning, he knew.

I've got her.

Dan scrutinizes the enlarged image from top to bottom, thinking, *This is the magic. This is why I don't sleep or see my kid.* A story unexpectedly comes to life, gift wrapped in a bow. *Like Christmas.* The unexpected is why he's still in the game. It's why they can't keep him down or relegate him to a corner office. Margaux de Laurent, disguised in a blond wig and sunglasses, is standing directly across the street from Geisler's apartment building, clearly casing the place, two days before the old man was found dead. The picture was taken from a car circling the building. It wasn't just any car, the *Spotlight* editor told Dan—it was hired out by their investigative team when they knew they had a story, a huge story that was initially quashed, killed before it saw the light of day.

The editor explained off the record that key members of the German government knew about Carl Geisler's existence and the vast amount of art the man was hiding, and that his dead Nazi father—Helmuth Geisler—bequeathed the stolen masterworks to him in the seventies when he died. They knew all this and did nothing about it. Most likely because they didn't want the public relations nightmare. The news magazine only got wind of the story because one of their junior reporters happened to be on the same train as Carl Geisler, who was traveling back to Munich from Salzburg—apparently visiting his mother's grave on her birthday. The old man was anxious and jittery, so the authorities questioned him as he was getting off the train. They caught him with nine thousand euros stuffed in an old briefcase. He told them he'd sold a drawing there, but was so disoriented that they decided to investigate him further and found that he hadn't paid taxes in twenty years. They also confirmed that he was indeed Helmuth Geisler's son. They knew right then exactly what Geisler was harboring in his apartment, and yet they sat on it. The editor told Dan that just before *Spotlight* was going to print with its exposé, a posse of government officials came to the paper, and one hour later, the publisher pulled the plug on their biggest story ever. But then, just a few days later, Carl Geisler was murdered, and his editorial team defied government demands and went with its story anyway—full out but with no bylines—to protect its reporters from backlash. The editor alluded to the fact that the junior reporter who saw Geisler on the train abruptly quit the paper and disappeared. He was convinced but could not confirm that someone had threatened the young journalist.

Dan stares at the prized photograph, and the achingly familiar adrenaline rush overtakes him, the indescribable elation of blood moving through his body whenever he discovers a major lead, a continental shift from getting nowhere to arriving on target. This is what his ex-wife, Pam, was never able to comprehend, his insatiable need to nail down the truth, no matter the cost. Once Dan closes in, there's nothing like it.

He gently places the photo on the desk and checks his phone—there are five missed calls from Jules and a half dozen desperate texts to get ahold of him. He'll see her in a couple of days and fill her in on everything. Right now, he needs a breather, just to think this through and strategize. He removes his laptop from his briefcase and fires off a quick, carefully constructed email to Jules just to let her know that he's alive and kicking.

J—Sorry for the delay. Will be back at office in two days. Something important to show you—D

It was a helluva good day, Dan thinks triumphantly, eyeing the minibar and trying hard to look away. He's starving. Maybe there are snacks in there? He opens the fridge, his heart pounding, knowing he's lying to himself as he confronts the enemy. A blitzkrieg of tiny bottles dares him to cross the line. He reaches past the Jägermeister for the vodka behind it and presses the cold, familiar glass to his lips. One tiny drink to celebrate can't hurt. He then sees Ellis's face pop up in his head and drops the bottle onto his lap and stares at it. His eyes blur. *Who am I kidding? One tiny drink will kill me. The rules. Don't break the damn rules.*

He tosses the vodka back inside the fridge, hears the clackety-clank of bottles knocking one another down like bowling pins, and slams the door shut. He then takes the armchair from the corner of the room and shoves it up against the fridge in a feeble attempt to lock himself out. He laughs—*as if that would stop me.* Changing his mind, Dan starts to remove the chair, but then he hears a crashing sound coming from the bathroom.

He heads to the bathroom to check out the noise. Nothing—his Dopp kit had just fallen off the sink counter to the floor. He picks it up, then skips brushing his teeth and opts for mouthwash. He strips down naked, leaving the pile of clothes right there on the bathroom tile, and searches around. Where are his painkillers? He is certain that he left them on the counter. He is hoping to take one more just to knock out quickly and prevent himself from reopening that fridge. Is it on the nightstand? He walks toward the bed and doesn't notice the slim shadow emerging from the closet next to the bathroom. Exhausted, he skips the pill search, climbs into bed, closes his eyes, and thinks he's dreaming when hears a velvety voice echo against the darkness.

"Rough night?" The accent is British, but not exactly. Dan freezes, and the lithe silhouette appears before him as though jumping straight out of the photograph. Wearing black with a pale blue scarf wrapped around her neck, her dark hair pulled back in a severe bun, Margaux de Laurent holds a gun and his bottle of Percocet—hence the crash. He reaches for the light.

"Don't."

Dan's arm drops limply to the bed, slowly comprehending.

"So, this is how we meet?" His composed voice belies his fear. "No blond wig this time?"

She smiles. He can't see it, exactly, but he feels it. Dan contemplates his next move. He used to carry a gun back in the day. But that gun is tucked away in the basement safe in his old house that no longer belongs to him.

"I thought we'd have a little chat first." Margaux sits on the edge of the bed, gun pointed at Dan.

"First?" Dan retorts, utilizing the mantra from his days spent out in the field: *No matter what happens, never show weakness.* "I prefer to know what's last."

She laughs, and the delicate, girlish sound does not match her. "Oh, I think that's obvious," she says simply.

The truth is death doesn't scare Dan as much as his life ending without answers. "Why are you in Munich?" he asks quickly, trying to buy time. "And how did you know I was here?"

"It's a new world, Dan. Hackers rule, haven't you heard? But I will give you the truth, because that's the kind of guy you are, the kind of girl I am. I got wind of what you're up to through the antics of a nosy young journalist asking about me in Amsterdam. She's working on a story, and apparently, I'm her focus. And you're behind it, right?" She laughs again. Only this time the sound is stronger, condescending. Dan's heart sinks. *Jules. That one mistake is going to cost me my life.* "I'm here in town protecting my interests," she adds.

"Your interests?" Dan baits her. "Tell me, why do *you* need to steal art? You're one of the top art dealers in the world, from an art dynasty. Either you're a psychopath or in dire financial straits and don't want the world to know the truth."

"Or both," Margaux suggests. "Could be both. If I were you, I would be hoping for the dire straits option? I mean who would want a psychopath in his hotel room with a gun to his head? I know I wouldn't."

"Why now?" he asks.

"I'm very busy. Your little investigation is not only annoying, but also, I don't have time for it or your sloppy young reporter dragging my name through the mud. I've got full access to your phones, your computers—meaning all of your accounts and *everyone* you've been in contact with." She allows Dan a few moments to absorb her words, the fact that Jules, Ellis, and Adam have all been compromised. Edging in, Margaux's body is now pressed against Dan's covered feet, the gun still aimed at his face, only closer.

"What did you expect?" Dan maintains eye contact, though he can barely see in the darkness; he just feels the warm stream of her breath. "That you could murder the son of a Nazi who had a massive amount of stolen art and rob him blind, and no one would notice or figure it out?"

"Your contacts at *Spotlight* noticed," Margaux sniggers. "And members of the German government noticed long ago that Geisler was hoarding confiscated masterpieces, and they did nothing. Someone had to make a bold move. And good for you. You figured it out, and here we are." She points the pistol between his eyes, and Dan can smell the gun oil. She must have just cleaned it. "What exactly is your connection to the Geisler heist?" she demands. "Why are Ellis Baum, Adam Chase, and Bram Bakker in on this? I want details. Tell me, and just maybe, if I'm satisfied, I'll let you go."

Just maybe. Dan remains silent. This psychopath will never be satisfied, and she certainly has no intention of setting him free, no matter what. Look what she did to Geisler.

Margaux tilts her head and assesses him. "I do admire your allegiance, but it's not going to help you or your friends. Look at you, naked and powerless." She glances at the opened bottle of pills in her hand. "Knocking down painkillers, right? Another addiction to add to your repertoire. Yeah, my hacker told me about that too. I've got paperwork from your rehab to prove it. You're a drunk. I guess I'm not the only one with secrets." She points to the chair shoved up against the minibar. "Were you planning on celebrating? What do you really want? Just say it. It's the painting, right? *My* painting. I want to know why."

But Dan remains monk silent.

"That's how you want to play it? The way I see it, you have no options left here."

"You are a disgrace to the art world." Dan tries a different tactic. "You, a Jewish woman laundering Nazi stolen artwork. Your grandfather was known to have saved many works of art during the war. He was a hero. No shame?" he prods.

Margaux sneers. "Half Jewish and raised without religion. Or morals, for that matter. And you're right—no shame. I'm fiercely loyal to only two things: myself and my galleries. I will do whatever it takes to make sure both are well-positioned. That's what matters to me."

If Dan could see Margaux's face clearly in the light, the slight blanching of her olive skin, he would know that he just activated her. He would know that by mentioning her grandfather, he has ended his life a good ten minutes earlier than she intended.

"But there is another possibility," Dan interjects carefully. "Let me live, and *I* will gather all the information you need and skew a news story to give you what you really want—recognition, a mythological stature to reinstate your family's name—a name that your father nearly destroyed. I know you're having financial problems. I've seen the documents. I also know you've had bad press the past few years, a series of artists who've fallen flat. But you can change all this easily. You can emerge a hero. Picture it—the woman behind *finding* the treasure trove of stolen art—instead of the one profiting from it. Think of the worldwide headlines, the positive publicity," he presses her. "I can give you that—nobody can write it like I can."

"You?" she howls. "Really? The great Dan Mansfield volunteers to become my lapdog, my publicist. Is this how they teach you to plead for your life in journalism school? And it actually works?" She places her hand holding the pills against her chest with feigned surprise. "Honestly, I'm disappointed. I gave you much more credit than that." She shakes her head. "Here's the beauty of all this. I don't need you anymore. I will soon have your loyal assistant at my disposal to do whatever I please, to skew any story in my favor, as you say. Seems like you put a lot of faith in that girl, according to the emails and texts I read. She's not you, but I've decided she will be much easier to manipulate over the long term."

Dan pictures Jules being harmed by this monster. He may not have a chance here . . . but Jules. "For what it's worth . . ." He struggles to keep his voice even. "She's young, unseasoned. Has only been working with me a couple of months. Makes stupid mistakes. There are many things she doesn't know and obviously I don't let her in on. This is *my* story, not hers." He points to the gun. "This is between you and me."

"Oh really?" She raises a brow. "Well, your precious Jules seemed to think she knew what she was doing in Amsterdam.

Not to mention that she just received this email from you"—
Margaux checks her Apple Watch, as though Dan's emails are
streaming in as she reads it aloud—"About nineteen minutes ago
exactly. 'J—Sorry for the delay. Will be back at office in two days.
Something important to show you—D.' Sounds like you two are
partners here. Your problem, Dan, is that you underestimated
me. We're done here."

She hovers over him and jams the gun to his throat, clearly
enjoying hearing him gasp. The flowing ends of her silky scarf
tickle his bare chest, and Dan seizes the moment. He grabs the
scarf and yanks hard, choking her, quickly turning the tables.
The gun drops from Margaux's hand, and Dan's pills fall and scat-
ter across the bed. He pins her down with his knees digging into
her chest. She is now under him, his nakedness exposed—one
tight pull and it's over. He stares deeply into her coal-fired eyes.
She is dangerously beautiful, even as she struggles beneath him,
kicking, begging him to stop.

And then he hesitates. If he kills her now, he will never know
what she is planning to do, or if it's already in motion. Dan loosens his grip for a mere indecisive second, forgetting the single
most important rule that he learned on the battlefield of war reporting: *Never pause.* It can mean the difference between life and
death.

Still choking but unwilling to succumb, Margaux seizes her
moment and knees Dan hard in the groin. He falls backward
onto the bed, clutching himself in pain. She quickly grabs the
gun that fell onto the twisted sheets and expertly wraps the scarf
around his throat. She yanks the scarf hard, until Dan is struggling for air. She leans in with a conspiratorial whisper. "Oh, and
just to mention before you go, I have excellent backup on the

way. This is going to be a hanging and pills combo. Think of the headlines . . ." Her smile bares her white, glistening teeth. "'World-renowned investigative reporter dies by suicide.' And in case you needed confirmation, I do have Geisler's paintings. *All* of them. Just not the one I want. But your girl Friday is going to help me find it." Margaux's mouth burns against his skin. She stops choking him, and as he takes his final breath, she reaches for the handful of Percocet tablets scattered on the sheets and shoves them deep into Dan's mouth and down his throat.

TWENTY-EIGHT

MANHATTAN

ADAM STARES OUT his apartment window, posing like Julius Caesar contemplating the fate of Rome. The sunlight spilling in catches his profile, and Jules sees the tension clicking in his jaw. *He's stuck*, she thinks. *We both are.* Ellis is in a medically induced coma, Dan is AWOL in Munich, and she is sitting in Adam's apartment not sure what to do next. She traveled with Ellis on his plane back to New York three days earlier at Dan's behest and then took a flight home to Chicago later that same night. Ellis told her to return home, that he would update Adam on Amsterdam and Berlin himself. Then Ellis had that freak accident. Now she's back here. The worst part is that Dan doesn't even know. Not for lack of trying. All she's gotten from him is one cryptic email, and nothing else.

"Still no answer," Jules announces from Adam's couch, pointing to her phone. "I've tried him at least ten times. This is not like Dan. I'm really starting to get worried. I know when he gets involved in something, he's all in. But I don't want to leave him a voice mail or a text about Ellis's condition." Adam is not listening. "Hey—are you with me?"

Adam nods, walks toward Jules, and sits in the chair across from her. "I really don't know what's up with Dan, but I asked you to come back to New York because, given the circumstances with my grandfather, we don't have a lot of time . . . I think we need to speed things up." The stoic veneer falls and tears fill his eyes, and it kills Jules to see him like this. "He's going to come out of this. He has to," Adam whispers, as though reassuring himself.

"I know he will," she says softly. "Your grandfather is so strong and determined. I agree, he would want us to stay on course." *No matter what.* Her heart sinks. Chances are slim that Ellis is going to come out of this okay. The spreading of his lung cancer, his body organs shutting down, his kidney failing, plus the concussion from that fall . . . a nightmare. And she can't even visit him at the hospital, because as far as his family is concerned, she doesn't exist. *The rules.* She wishes Dan would just answer the phone.

Adam slaps his palm against his forehead. "I just realized that with everything going on, I forgot to mention that Margaux showed up here last week unannounced. I never gave her my address. But I think she's having me followed. She does that sort of thing, spying on her clients and her artists. I'm an idiot for telling you to meet me here. I should have been more careful. You may have been photographed. I'm so sorry. I wasn't thinking." He leans forward, cupping his chin. "My fault if this messes things up."

Jules's mouth drops. She should have thought this through as well. This could blow her cover. Dan will really be mad that she just hopped on a plane back to New York without consulting him first. And now this. But Adam looks so distraught that she tries to keep her voice steady, confident. "We just need to figure out plan B, and fast."

There's an awkward silence between them. So much to consider. Over Adam's shoulder, in the far corner of the room, Jules sees a large board filled with black-and-white photos depicting dozens of women's faces, close-ups. It's kind of freaky. "Who are those women, by the way—old girlfriends?" She forces a smile to break the tension. "On your hit list?"

He turns to look and laughs despite himself. "I know, weird, right? It's kind of a thing I do. I love photography almost as much as painting, so I combine both when I'm working. For this series, I took pictures of women walking through the park from the same spot, same time of day, over a week-long period. It's an amazing study of human nature. I find patterns, a thread, and it becomes the inspiration for my work. It's complicated."

"It's your process," Jules says, noticing the windows: wide open, with everything visible. "Do you mind if we close the curtains?" She points. "Just in case someone *is* snapping photos."

"I got it." Adam gets up, walks across the room, and draws all three window curtains. He spins around. "I just had a crazy idea. What if instead of the stolen art cover story that Dan wants you to do, you model for this series? That way if Margaux pops by unexpectedly again or should your photograph somehow land on her desk—we have a legitimate reason as to why you were here." He waits. "It's not perfect . . ."

It's not bad, Jules thinks. But Dan wants the stolen art story because it would give her freedom to explore the subject out in the open and it's a natural cover. And she's not a model by any means. *No cowboy antics*, she warns herself. Not to mention the small fact that she is attracted to Adam. His painting her would just be too intimate, and she's got to be careful. Her heartbeat quickens. "I'm not sure . . . but if Margaux does somehow get a photo of me in your apartment—there's no question, my cover is compromised."

"I think we need to accept that we *are* compromised." He returns to the couch, sitting closer to her than where he was before.

He's right. "Until I talk to Dan—if he ever calls me back—I'm not going to drop the stolen art piece," she says adamantly. "But let's do the painting thing since I'm already here, just in case he does agree with your idea." She pauses, somewhat embarrassed. "I've never modeled anything . . . what do I have to do? Can I wear what I'm wearing?"

"Yes, you're fine." He grins. "And you don't have to do anything at all, except be still. My sense is that that might be the hardest thing for you to do. And by the way, artists' models aren't meant to be runway models. Quite the opposite—real women are much more interesting." He gestures to the inspiration board. "This series is about mood. Look at their faces. Real." He blushes slightly. "You're real, Jules. I can see why my grandfather has a crush on you."

Bam. And she's off. She feels her cheeks flaring up. How does he manage to do that to her? "Well, the feeling is mutual," she says, adding quickly, "toward your grandfather."

Adam beams, and Jules feels the warmth spreading through her entire body. "When he arrived home from Berlin, he told me everything you did to bring him back safely. Dan is brilliant, everybody knows that, but from what I've seen, so are you." Adam pauses. "I want to capture that intensity on canvas. That emotion. Will you let me?"

The way he's looking at her . . . Jules hopes he doesn't see *that* emotion.

Adam's leg grazes hers in the same way it did back in the cabin. She feels the heat between them as he gently reaches up and lightly pulls the black scrunchie out of her hair, freeing the loose topknot and releasing a waterfall of unruly curls. She doesn't stop him. Her eyes close briefly.

"Let me paint you as I see you," he whispers with a glimmer in his eyes. "I *have* to paint you."

ADAM BEGINS WITH brown pigment, and then comes red. He sniffs the paint bottle as though it were wine or perfume. Auburn, Jules thinks. He's enriching the brown. *My hair.* An hour later, he mixes equal parts red, yellow, blue, then adds in white with flecks of yellow. *My skin.* Smiling slightly at him, she feels the cool breeze ease over her through the partially opened window. The curtain billows beside her, brushing against her arms. She can't remember the last time she's sat still this long not having a computer in front of her or a phone in hand. Not doing or accomplishing anything—*just being.* And yet in this sedentary, unproductive state of immobility, she feels strangely alive. And she gets to freely observe Adam as, with concentrated intensity, he puts down his brush, picks it up, chews the end of the brush, lightly dabs his canvas, and then presses hard with knifelike stabs. He closes one eye as he assesses her. This pattern goes on for what feels like hours, and then, in the early evening, it stops.

Adam lays down his brush, stretches his arms overhead, and stands. His eyes lock with hers as he walks toward her. Jules doesn't move, barely breathes as he approaches her.

"You were perfect." His voice lowers huskily. "I got what I

need for today. Let's take a break." He reaches for her hand. "I'm lying. I stopped because I could no longer paint you without touching you. I know this is wrong on every front and Dan would have my head, but . . ."

Jules feels the persistent pounding of her chest as he struggles to get the words out.

"There hasn't been anyone else," he stammers. "I couldn't . . . after the overdose. I wasn't ready. I had a lot of damage to repair. But now . . ."

"Adam." His hand feels so safe and toasty. She begins to fight with herself as the muscle memory kicks in, flashing a neon warning—that night with Rick Janus. *The Rules.* Do not get involved with anyone on your story. Jules listens to the voice and reluctantly pulls her hand away. "I can't. We are working together. This could really ruin things."

"I know. Believe me, I get it. But what if it doesn't . . . ? What if we are the exception?" He presses his leg against hers, and this time she doesn't move. "I felt a connection between us in my kitchen that very first day, when we were washing dishes together. Not my most romantic moment, but somehow it was, right?" His wistful expression begins to melt her resolve. "Did you sense something too? I'm not crazy here, am I?"

Jules is acutely aware of her body and mind partnering now. "Not crazy . . . but it's not just about Dan and his rules," she tells him. "I once had a really bad experience and promised myself I would always put the story first, no matter what." His heart is beating so fast, she can hear it—*or is it hers?*

"I just want to be close to you." Adam takes her hand once again, and this time she lets him. He searches her face. "Is that a yes?"

"It's not a no." She laughs nervously as he embraces her. Closing her eyes, she allows herself to sink into him, knowing she should pull the plug immediately. But the desire to be close to him too is stronger. Her breath shortens. There have only been a couple of other guys since that horrible night with Rick Janus. No one she's cared about, no one who mattered. *But this . . . If it doesn't work out, there's a huge risk. Ellis. Dan. The story. It matters.*

And then Adam's lips graze her neck and quickly dispel her doubts. Inhaling deeply, she smells the piney Montana scent embedded in his skin, and it's intoxicating. He leans back, his eyes never leaving hers as he slowly removes his shirt. Jules reaches out, she can't help it, and touches the smattering of see-through golden-brown hairs dancing across his muscular chest. She fans his biceps with her fingertips then slowly traces his arms but pauses when she sees remnants of track marks. She meets his eyes again, and this time, she sees pain. Leaning over, she presses the damaged skin to her lips and kisses the pale pink scars. He tenses, then loosens up, reaching for her, and then gently removes her turtleneck sweater.

She notices that Adam's hands still have drying paint on them as they both begin to explore each other's bodies. Naked, he is like a Rodin sculpture with his sculpted cheekbones, carved torso, and raw defined masculinity. She feels the swell of his desire against her as she runs her fingers through his hair. *Yes, it's good*, he whispers. *Just like that.*

Lifting Jules in his arms, Adam carries her into the bedroom, and slowly, carefully, it all begins again. First the kisses, the neck graze, her breasts, his chest, and then his tongue makes its way down her torso. He looks up when he comes to the edge. Meeting his sensual gaze, she gives him the go-ahead. He begins with light kisses between her thighs, then buries his face deeply, hungrily inside her. Every inch of Jules is ignited, everything else—the story, Dan, Ellis, the rules—fades away until it is all nothing but a vanishing point.

As Jules spreads her legs wider, Adam slowly enters her. "Look at me," he commands, and his bright eyes sear through her. "God, you're beautiful. I want to remember this."

He is painting me, she thinks, drawing him deeper inside, their bodies moving in sync. Suddenly, he stops midthrust, waits for her to catch up, and only when she is ready—only when she says, *I'm with you*—does Adam let himself go completely and take Jules with him.

He's right. What if we are the exception? she thinks afterward, eyeing Adam's satiated face, just inches from hers. His lips are parted in deep sleep, and his arm is slung lazily over her breasts as she stares out the bedroom window and identifies the outside sounds. Cars passing, blurred voices, radios blaring, honking, an ambulance. As the evening morphs into night, she listens to Adam's comfy snore and watches the symphonic rise and fall of his chest.

Thirsty and starving, Jules detangles herself from his body and tiptoes naked into the main room toward the kitchen but makes a bathroom stop. Between the bathroom and the adjacent linen closet, she notices the back of a medium-sized canvas wedged against the wall, the colors peeking out from its sides. Curious, she stops and flips it around. It's still slightly sticky, newly dried. She lifts it to the light in the bathroom and absorbs the abstract composition. A woman, of course, with wild black strokes of hair, penetrating ebony eyes, flawless olive skin, creamy round breasts tipped with rose, an omnipotent smile, and long, bare legs adorned with high black boots. Naked and seductive; a femme fatale. Jules recalls a similar canvas that she saw in the cabin. *Her.* He painted Margaux de Laurent naked. *Here.*

It's as if somebody has shot a bullet straight through her chest. Margaux didn't just show up at Adam's apartment unexpectedly last week. He had sex with her in that very same bed. Sexual images of the two of them bulldoze through Jules's brain. She leans against the nearest wall to brace herself. The whole I-fell-for-you-in-the-kitchen story. *What a blatant lie*, she yearns to scream. *I'm an idiot, a rule breaker.*

Abandoning the painting on the bathroom floor, Jules doesn't feel, doesn't think. She quickly gathers her clothes from the bedroom and her small carry-on bag and purse that are near the front door and sneaks out of the apartment. Still naked, she puts on her clothes in the hallway, not caring if anyone passes by or sees her. She feels nothing and everything at once as she races down the two flights of stairs, her Converse still untied as she hails a taxi to take her straight to the airport.

TWENTY-NINE

CHICAGO

IT'S BEEN TWO days since she left Manhattan and Jules can barely bring herself to get out of her bed. Everything has fallen apart. *"Dan's dead. Dan's dead,"* she cries out repeatedly inside her bedroom, but no one is listening. Her mother is already up and out. Jules felt her light kisses against her forehead earlier while she was still half asleep, followed by a murmur that she was heading off to work but would stop back home at lunchtime to check in on her.

Wiping the crusty tears from her eyes, Jules leans up against her headboard, stares at her wall, feeling lost and abandoned. Dan would never have left the world like that—by his own hand—with no closure, in the middle of an investigation. He was too passionate, too unstoppable. He cared too deeply. She didn't know him very long, but for the past few months of working closely together, they have been intensive, emotional, and totally dependent on each other.

She knew about the alcohol and even the painkillers. She'd

see him popping those pills when he thought she wasn't looking. He'd substituted one addiction for another, and there was nothing Jules could do to stop it. She also knew that his relationship with his daughter and ex-wife was strained—she overheard some rough calls between them—and that it was hard for him. But suicide? No way. He was too jacked on this story, too determined to get the painting back for Ellis, clearly a substitute father. Dan was smack in the middle of doing what he loved best—and there is no way in hell that he'd kill himself.

Someone did it for him—evidenced by the one email he sent her that said he was planning on returning. Jules keeps replaying the message over in her head, trying desperately to find a clue between the lines.

> J—Sorry for the delay. Will be back at office in two days.
> Something important to show you—D

He discovered something important that someone clearly didn't want him to know. No matter what the authorities or the papers say, Dan would never have abandoned the story. *Never.*

A detective with the Chicago Police Department who is working closely with the Munich police questioned her at length yesterday afternoon at home. She purposely kept her responses brief but with just enough detail to satisfy the investigator. Yes, Dan took painkillers for his injuries. And yes, he was working on a story outside of his managing editing responsibilities. But no, it was not a story for the *Chronicle*. It was a personal investigation on stolen art that he was working on independently, but that's all she knew. She purposely didn't mention any details about their off-the-books team. Didn't mention Ellis or Bram Bakker or

Adam. Not just to protect them but also because she intended on finishing what Dan had started.

Dan would want that more than anything. She could hear his voice banging inside her head: *Do whatever it takes. Find the painting and expose the goddamn truth.*

Tears roll down Jules's face as she gets dressed and heads over to the newspaper before the police arrive there later this afternoon, as the detective mentioned to her that they will. Whatever Dan had wanted to show her, she is determined to find it—if the evidence exists—before they do.

WHEN SHE ARRIVES at the *Chronicle*, Louise is already there, of course. She lives at the office. Just like Dan once did.

"Louise," Jules whispers her name as she enters the office, swallowing hard when she sees Dan's door open and his outdated Members Only jacket still hanging over the back of his chair.

Louise looks up from her desk. Her eyes are red-rimmed and swollen. "It doesn't make sense, does it, Dan dying like that."

Jules blinks back tears. Everyone knows that Dan was the soul of the *Chronicle*, a tour de force. Louise keeps things running smoothly, but when Dan walked into the newsroom, he owned it.

"I would see him taking those pain pills, you know." Louise's voice is strained. "But he would never have killed himself. I worked by his side for more than twenty years and I've never known anyone more alive, with more fight and passion." Tears pool in the corner of her eyes. "You don't think he did it either, do you?"

"I know he didn't." Seeing Louise so broken is unbearable. "I tried calling you and didn't want to leave a voice message, but a detective came by my apartment yesterday to question me, and the police are coming here later today."

"I know, I got a call about it this morning."

Jules scrapes her hand through her hair. "The detective told me that Dan was found hanging in the hotel bathroom pumped with pills and that there were emptied bottles of alcohol everywhere, but I don't believe a word of it."

Louise shakes her head. "This all has to do with that damn art story, right? That woman."

"Yes." Jules wonders how updated she is.

Louise rubs her temples, then blows her nose loudly. "I spoke to Dan the day he died. He called from the hotel after his meeting with the *Spotlight* editor. It's no secret that he doesn't know a thing about computers, or anything technical, for that matter . . . so he contacted me."

"What did he want?" Jules edges in closer.

"He said, 'Louise, it was a day for the books.' Not the words of a man about to kill himself, right? In fact, he sounded a bit tipsy, to be honest. Not drunk, but euphoric. He gets like that when a story is going his way. When I asked him if he'd backed up whatever he was working on, he laughed and said, 'Don't worry, I took a picture of it. I'm sending it to you now. Put it in the folder.'" Louise pauses and points to her computer. "It's in there. I made a secret folder for him long ago. Our most important documents. It's called 'Emily'—his daughter's name."

Her palms sweating in anticipation, Jules stands behind Louise as she opens the folder and zooms in on the image. "Does this photograph mean anything to you?" she asks.

A blond with dark sunglasses stands in front of a white apartment building, and in the far left-hand corner of the photo there's a storefront with what looks like German lettering. Jules gets goose bumps. *It's her. Fake hair, but same nose, mouth, body type.*

But where is she? What building is that? This must be what Dan wanted her to see—only he had been planning to accompany that photo with an explanation. "It means everything." She leans over to whisper directly in Louise's ear. "Meet me outside the building now. Leave anything with wires here and turn off your phone," she instructs.

Five minutes later, the two women walk through the building lobby, head outside, and walk down Michigan Avenue. "I take it you've seen all of Dan's notes, his research, his emails, and his backup—not just that photograph—am I right?" Jules grills her.

"Of course," Louise responds. "I do all his paperwork. I've copied all his files on backup discs. I even make sure he uses an old Polaroid camera to back up the most important photos and documents, and I hide them in a safe-deposit box. When you do investigations that are not part of your job description, you go old-school," she emphasizes. "So, yeah, everything."

Jules checks her watch. The police should be at the paper sometime soon. "I need you to do something for me as quickly as you can. Can you get everything relevant to this story off his office computer and yours? Until I can figure out my next move. Make copies on backup discs, hide them, and then later, when you can, put them in your safe-deposit box for safekeeping." She eyes Louise closely. "Can I trust you to keep all of this under wraps, no matter what?"

Louise pushes her floppy bangs away from her freckled forehead. "I'm a vault, but I want to know why."

"I'm sure the police will ask more questions relating to Dan's work habits, his most recent stories—particularly the art story. Our stories must match. Just say you know that he was working on a piece related to stolen art, but he kept you out of the loop." Jules looks up and down the street. "I need time to investigate what's really going on here. We both know this is what Dan would want. The woman in that picture is Margaux de Laurent, as you probably know. I need to determine what she was doing in Germany and when and where exactly that photo was taken. And most importantly, whether she is directly involved with the stolen paintings or Dan's murder—or both or neither. If she is, which is my guess, right now she thinks she got away with all of it. That everyone believes Dan is a drug addict alcoholic who killed himself. And we *need* to let her think that so I can buy time and keep working."

Louise's face scrunches up, and Jules gets it. "I know what I'm asking you is wrong, Louise—especially the lying to the police part," she says, pleading her case. "But . . ."

Louise glances up at the sky with an ugly twist of her mouth as though scolding Dan. "Always the damn story." She turns and heads back to the building. Jules takes that as a yes.

Walking aimlessly for a few more blocks, she tries to organize her thoughts, the puzzle pieces, her plan of action. She stops at a relatively empty side street off Michigan Avenue, turns her phone back on, and knows she must call Adam, whose calls she's ignored for the past few days. He answers on the first ring.

"I heard." His voice is filled with concern. "I'm so upset. I've been trying to get ahold of you. I've been calling you around the clock since you left . . . Are you okay? Are you—"

"Not okay." She cuts him off. "Just listen to me. There isn't time. Do not tell Ellis about Dan. If—*when*—he wakes up from the coma. Don't tell him. Even if you must lie. And if somehow you are questioned about Dan—the art story, whatever—you have *no* knowledge of any story relating to stolen art or to Margaux de Laurent. Got it? You *have* to lie—which clearly shouldn't be a problem for you," she adds because she can't help herself.

"Jules . . . c'mon. That's what I wanted to talk to you about. It wasn't like that."

"Whatever. Doesn't matter. This is my priority now. Just do this for Dan, all right?"

"Yes, but—"

"I'll be in touch." Jules hangs up before he feeds her more lies. She steels herself as she sees two police cars in the distance sidling up in front of the *Chronicle*. She walks quickly toward the building, squaring her posture, soldiering up. Her mentor died chasing the truth. This story is no longer about the painting. This one's for Dan.

THIRTY

MANHATTAN

THE CHELSEA SPACE is back in action. The first thing Margaux did after Griffin Freund sold four of Geisler's paintings was get the construction ball rolling again. She paid the contractors double to work overtime to finish the job as quickly as possible. The mammoth fifty-thousand-square-foot space on West 25th Street, known as DLG Tower, is now up and running with only minor details still in progress, and it is easily Margaux's favorite of all twenty-two DLG galleries.

The ornate seven-floor building is topped with an expansive open-air terrace for entertaining: exhibitions and parties. Wealthy clients, her grandfather used to say, like to be reassured by signs of prosperity and extravagance in their art dealers. The most important dealers don't just sell their art, they sell their personal style and taste. In its heyday back in the seventies and eighties, DLG's flagship location in SoHo had all the luminaries under its wing: De Kooning, Rothko, Warhol, Schnabel, Ruscha, Pollack, Mitchell, Krasner, Johns, Smith, Hockney—everyone who mattered in the contemporary art world. But her father squandered it all, both the gallery's profits and its reputation. It was a slow, torturous demise, and artists began to drop DLG one by one. And the worst part: the competition came hunting like vultures scavenging the carcass, snatching the gallery's top-tier clients left and right. DLG had become a shadow of its former glory. Until Adam Chase came along—then Margaux's juju changed, and her relaunch campaign began.

Adam's work was so original, awe-inspiring, and socially relevant that it quickly propelled her back on top. Everybody wanted a piece of them. But it was all smoke and mirrors. Margaux knew that beneath the surface, like diseased soil, DLG's financial issues persisted, despite one artist's tremendous success. It became apparent that her father had leveraged the galleries to pay off his massive gambling debts. The truth, she learned from her accountants, was much worse than the rumors.

But the tables are now turning. Overnight the money poured in, thanks to Geisler's tainted pot of gold. Bills and creditors are being paid off, and Margaux's surprised accountants have told her that it is simply a miracle that DLG would soon be in the black. *A miracle—hah!* And Adam's Basel showcase is now the talk of the town. Her phone has been ringing nonstop with the top art reporters working on what appears to be this year's hot story— there's always one—and it's hers. *I'm so back.*

Margaux checks her appearance in her office mirror for the third time that morning. Adam should be here any minute with new paintings to show her, and she can hardly wait. It's been over a week since she returned from Munich. She hasn't bothered him but has monitored all his activities closely. Her private detective confirmed that Adam has barely left the apartment, which means he's been compulsively painting. That's all she needs to know. And then, of course, there's the other thing. The thing she almost wishes she didn't know. *Lies and games.* She applies more red lipstick. *Bring it on.*

She hears Adam's voice from her intercom as he enters the gallery. Her newly hired gallerina, yet another interchangeable waiflike girl with opaque tights and an art history degree from an Ivy League school, is welcoming him. Margaux had a hidden camera installed in the reception area on the first floor that connected directly to her new office to monitor the gallery's comings and goings. She hears the young woman's flirty voice, and it irritates her. No one is immune to Adam's charm.

"Margaux, Adam Chase is here," the girl announces on the intercom.

"Send him up."

Minutes later, Adam struts into her office wearing faded jeans, a crisp white V-neck T-shirt, and that same leather bomber jacket and carrying a large portfolio. His uniform. "Hey."

"Hey yourself." She smiles back, eyeing the portfolio hungrily, then looks up at him. "You shaved. A good sign."

They lock eyes. She knows his patterns, his eccentricities. They were once married, mind, body, soul, drugs, art. Not anymore. Now Adam is part of something else—a secret investigation—to take her down. Let him think he's playing her. Let him think she's stupid. She will collect her due at Basel and then crush him. *But damn, look at him.* Her heart races. No matter how hard she tries, Margaux can't pretend that she feels nothing. It's the something she *still* feels that she needs to destroy.

"You look good," he notes. "How was your trip?"

"Productive," she tells him.

"Anything interesting?" he presses, eyebrows cinching.

Yes, I took a side trip and got rid of your fearless leader in Munich. "It's all interesting, but not important right now. Show me the paintings." Margaux walks around her desk to face him up close. She's wearing her new Stella McCartney minidress with gold chain detailing and a see-through tulle neckline. It fits her like a glove. She observes him staring, hears the unmistakable intake of his breath. She smiles to herself. *Let's see how long you can keep this up. You will break. In more ways than one.*

"I went a different route," Adam explains as he unpacks five paintings and lines them up along her windowsill, where the light is just exquisite at this time of day, the golden hour. Margaux is silent as she walks toward the canvases, always trusting her first emotion. That's the one that matters, the one that sticks, the one that sells. She is never wrong. Never mind that she was wrong about the last few artists she signed. That was then.

She takes her time observing each one. Adam's brushstrokes, as always, are flawless and boldly dramatic. The texture of the paint, color upon color, the exact right amount of layering, stimulates the senses. She can smell it, practically taste the mix of oils on her tongue. The model, though abstract, is young, fresh. The paint is smooth and creamy around the oval of her face. The eyes are neither innocent nor jaded—rather deeply intelligent and highly inquisitive. Her sensual mouth appears hungry, starving for more. *More of what?* she wonders. And that cascade of chestnut curls fills the canvas, tumbles and twists down her body, all curves and carnal lines.

Margaux can barely breathe as she imbibes each canvas depicting the same young woman in various abstract poses. And the detailing is so intimate—as if you walked in on her unexpectedly—showering or changing or masturbating. The work has an anticipatory pull, seductive and beguiling, as though Rodin were sculpting Camille Claudel for that very first time just *before* they become lovers. These paintings are bursting with so much passion for his subject that Margaux realizes that her new minidress, heels, and La Perla bra and panties are irrelevant.

And those black-and-white photographs of women from the park filling his inspiration board back at his apartment—he's ignored them all. His whole *Tunnel Vision* mood pitch—*not this*. No, these canvases tell a totally different story. Margaux can smell it, sniff out and separate the pungent notes, like rotted grapes from the vineyard. That's not just any face—but that of the young journalist snooping around Amsterdam. The face of the woman who was in Adam's apartment while she was in Europe—she saw the photographs her detective handed her. Margaux can barely breathe seeing it all displayed so blatantly. *As if I don't know.*

The artwork reveals more truth than words could ever accomplish. They expose Dan Mansfield's so-called unseasoned protégée for not only working against her but also stealing Adam's heart right out from under her. Margaux is unable to peel her eyes away from both the woman's beauty and Adam's brilliance.

"I know it's not what we discussed before," Adam says sheepishly, gauging her reaction. "But these images are so much stronger. Just the first five in the series, and—"

"They're perfect," Margaux murmurs, cutting him off. Quickly turning away, she obscures her real reaction from Adam's view. If he peered into her eyes right now, he would see the irreversible decay taking root inside her. "These paintings are absolutely perfect."

THIRTY-ONE

CHICAGO

JULES WORKS EVERY portal at once, like a one-woman rock band. Her home computer, her laptop, her phone, and her iPad. The devices are placed in various positions in her bedroom. She decided to start from the beginning. That's what Dan would do. You get stuck, go back. Retrace your steps and see what you missed.

Day One . . . Jules eyes the four-hundred-plus pages Dan gave her that very first day, and it makes her sad. She forces herself to walk around her bed and focus. She's divided her research into categories and subcategories: WWII/Stolen Art, "Degenerate" Painters, Ernst Engel, the De Laurent Galleries, Charles de Laurent, the Lucerne Auction, Young Ellis/Anika Baum/Arno Baum and Old Ellis/Anika Baum Inc., the Dassel Family, Helmuth Geisler Before and After the Nazi Rise to Power, Carl Geisler, Margaux de Laurent Art/Social/Cultural/Financials/Personal, Adam Chase Before/After Overdose, Bram Bakker, and the minor categories, including Carice van der Pol, Sébastien de

Laurent, and the *Spotlight* investigation. She jots down a note to herself.

Contact Bakker and *Spotlight* editor.

"There," she says aloud, swiping her hands with satisfaction, surveying the hundreds of colorfully organized sticky notes, the large whiteboard pushed up against her window, the multihued markers and pens lining her desk kinetically like an Agam print.

She doesn't hear her mother come in. "Jules, we need to talk—what the hell?"

Jules, deeply concentrating, whips around. Her mother stands near the door, hands to hips, mouth dropped open as she surveys her daughter's situation room. "Are you working for the CIA? What is going on here?"

"You shouldn't be in here, Mom. And what about knocking?"

"'Shouldn't be in here'?" her mother repeats with an incredulous expression. "What is going on under my roof, and what *exactly* are you involved in?" She walks slowly around the room, observing each portal closely as though it were a food station at a wedding. "Let's see, we've got World War II, Nazis, art, and Ellis Baum? I want to understand this. And let me be clear: I'm not leaving this room without an explanation." Her gray-blue eyes turn cloudy. "Go."

Jules remains obstinately silent.

"Really? Here's what I do know . . ." Her mother is now working the courtroom. "Let's see, your boss with whom you traveled was found dead in Munich just a few days after you returned home. And not just any boss, but one of the world's most celebrated journalists." She points a loaded finger. "You have never lied to me before, but since you started working for Dan Mansfield, you've done nothing but lie and evade. News flash: I'm a lawyer." Jules rolls her eyes. "Yes, honey, I read faces for a living. But most of all, I'm your mother, and your face is the one I can read with my eyes closed. I'm not leaving this circus of sticky notes without the truth."

Her mother plants herself at the foot of the bed. Jules observes that she is sitting on the Dassel family category. When her mother gets like this, there is no point in arguing. "You're right," she admits, grinding her toes into the shag carpeting. "I have been lying—well, not exactly lying, but filtering."

Her mother throws back her head. "Give me a break. Same damn thing."

Jules lowers her voice. "Okay, fine. Dan's death was not a suicide, and—"

Her mother's eyes amplify. "You think he was murdered. Do you have evidence?"

"Yes . . . and no. I have working theories pointing in that direction."

Her mother springs from the bed. "Then I want you off this story. I know you think you know everything. But if someone of Dan's caliber was *murdered* over an investigation that you are *still* working on—you are clearly in danger."

Jules can't fight this. Her mother isn't wrong. "I get that you're scared, but I'm not. See, that's the thing . . ." It's now Jules's turn to present her case. "Let me ask you this, Mom. Are you ever afraid when you are prosecuting a murderer, a rapist, or any kind of criminal?" She pauses dramatically, waits for it. "No, right? Because that's *exactly* when you rise to the occasion. That is *the* single moment you fight your hardest. I'm just like you. Can't you see that?" She reaches for her mother's trembling hand. "I am not walking away from this, and you more than anyone understand why. Getting the truth—doing what's right—is a nonnegotiable for me. Just like it's always been for you." She points to her bed covered in categories. "I am trying to sort everything out—can't you see that?"

"Oh, I can see all right," her mother responds frostily. "But when I'm fighting a hard case, I don't go after or represent anyone alone. There's a team in place. There are checks and balances and accountability. Dan is dead. You're just twenty-four years old with your whole life ahead of you. This is your first real job. Who's your team, Jules? It looks to me like you're flying solo here."

Me, Jules shouts inside her head. *I am my team.* But her mother needs to hear about a group effort, or she will never win this. "I do have a team. Louise Archer—Dan's right hand of twenty years—and an expert investigator in Amsterdam, plus two people working on this in New York," she argues, thinking, *Never mind that one of them is in a coma and the other is sleeping with the person of interest.* "I am not working alone. And I'm not stopping either." She bites down on her bottom lip and crosses her arms defiantly.

Her mother's eyes blink rapidly, and Jules knows that she is ramping up her case. They are mirror images. *Same stubborn woman.*

She rises, meeting Jules practically nose to nose. "Well then, you are certainly not working this investigation from your bedroom. How do you know that you're not being followed? How do you know we're not bugged? How do you know your phone hasn't been cloned? How do you know there isn't a hit out on you already? I heard you talking to that detective That's right. You think I didn't listen in? All I have been doing the past few months is searching for clues." Her eyebrows hitch. "Out with it."

Deep breath. "I'm trying to locate a stolen painting from the Nazi era."

"A painting? This is all about a painting?"

Jules nods. "More like a masterpiece. I'm sorry, Mom, that's all I can tell you. I know this is hard, but I'm going forward with the story."

Her mother, who never cries, begins to tear up. "Please don't do this to me, to us."

Jules's heart sinks. "I'm not doing this to you . . ." But her mother is right about one thing: she needs to put more precautions in place. It's not enough that Louise has copies of Dan's files hidden away. Most likely, someone else has his files as well, and possibly hers too. When she asked about them, the detective told her that there was no laptop or briefcase found in Dan's hotel room. Dan never went anywhere without that beaten-up briefcase, which he called his "traveling closet." Whoever murdered him must have it, and the laptop as well. Dan is dead, and she is most likely in danger. Holding out her hands, Jules surrenders. "I'm open to taking more safety measures. What do you suggest?"

Though her mother still looks troubled, she also seems somewhat relieved. Her game face suddenly appears, which is a good sign. "I suggest you gather all of your things and work from my office—not my office per se, but in a special division that we use for highly classified information. It has firewalls, security, research resources, and nine yards of protection. I will clear it with Steve first. He knew Dan personally and he won't say no. If I can't stop you, Jules, then I'm sure as hell going to protect you, and you're going to let me." Her mother has her "make your bed or die" look.

"Fine."

Her mother points to photocopies of Anika Baum's stilettos

in the Ellis Baum pile. "And why do you have photos of Ellis Baum everywhere? What in God's name do his shoes have to do with Dan Mansfield's murder or a stolen painting?"

Everything, Jules thinks. *Everything.*

BRAM BAKKER BEATS Jules to the punch. Her phone rings two hours later while she is paying for her cappuccino. She eyes the Unknown Caller and throws down money on the counter and bolts out of the Starbucks.

"Jules, it's Bram." He sounds a million miles away. "I heard about Dan. I'm very sorry. You must be devastated."

She squeezes the coffee cup and watches the foam protrude through the to-go top opening. "I am."

Bakker speaks quickly. "I'm on a secure line, but you are not. I want you to download a particular app right now and then do exactly as I say. We need to talk. It's important. Write this down, and not in your phone—separately."

Jules writes the information on a Starbucks napkin and decides to call Bakker while walking back home along the lakeshore instead of taking her usual route through the city. She zippers up her coat and pulls the hood over her head. It's colder by the lake, and it's windy but still quieter. And from what she can see up ahead, the beach area is practically deserted, except for a few old men playing chess.

"Bram, I'm here," she says after she dials in five minutes later.

"Good, yes." He pauses as though checking something. "It wasn't suicide." His Dutch-accented English is heavy and slightly hard for her to hear.

"Not suicide," she concurs. "Speak louder and slowly."

"Dan interviewed the *Spotlight* editor just hours before he died," he says. "You should follow up and call the editor, tell him who you are, and try to get information on what happened at that meeting. If you're uncomfortable with that—I will do it."

"I'm comfortable, and that was already my plan." She checks her watch. "But it's Saturday and nearly midnight, Munich time. I don't have his information. I will have to wait and call *Spotlight* Monday morning."

"That's not a problem. I will get you the editor's personal cell within ten minutes. Don't wait until Monday. Call him tomorrow morning first thing, using this app. Anything important, I suggest, stays off the grid."

"Got it."

"And Jules . . . I know this is a hard question, but are you planning to continue working on the investigation anyway, or—"

"Of course, I am."

"Good, because I've learned from a source that four paintings allegedly from the Geisler collection are now on the black market. Whatever I find out, I will let you know."

"Thanks." She pauses. "There's something you should know . . . Ellis is in the hospital, in a medically induced coma. Somehow the family has managed to keep it out of the press. He had a bad fall, and his cancer has taken a turn for the worse." She gathers her breath. "I don't know if he's going to come out of it. But if he does, I plan to do everything possible to get him the painting. He deserves that. Dan would want that."

Bakker pauses. "So it's just you."

She thinks of Adam and shakes it off. "Just me."

"Be careful. I'm here to help. Whatever you need." He clears his throat. "There is something else, perhaps the bigger item . . . After I left Dan, I did my own little investigation into the Dassel clan. There's quite a lot more to digest. Stefan Dassel's story only *half* checks out . . ." Bakker's voice fades.

"And the other half? Louder, please," Jules presses.

"The other half is what may be the important piece. Stefan neglected to mention in his confessional that not only did his father, Franz, become a leader in the Hitler Youth, but he also later *joined* the *Reichskulturkammer*—the Reich's Chamber of Culture—a plum post reserved for the Nazi elite. Helmuth Geisler was an integral part of that department as well."

Jules thinks about her Stolen Art category with the purple sticky notes still laid out on her bed. "I know exactly what that is."

"What you don't know is that Franz Dassel was actually Joseph Goebbels's assistant."

"Goebbels's assistant?"

"Yes," he confirms. "Franz saw it all . . . but there's more. Franz, if you remember from what Stefan revealed, was rejected by one of Arno Baum's daughters, and because of that, he exposed the Baum family. He must not have gotten over that rejection, because he later used his influence to pluck the very same girl—Lilian Baum—out of Auschwitz. He saved her. She was the only Baum family member to survive the camps."

Jules stops in her tracks. "Are you kidding me?"

Bakker continues. "I know, it's unbelievable. Lilian Baum was then around sixteen or seventeen, and it appears that she became the Dassel family maid and then . . . This is the part, Jules . . ." She hears Bakker blow air out into the receiver. She clings tighter to her phone. "Lilian wasn't just the maid. Or maybe she was, but she married Franz Dassel and divorced him a few years after the war. No kids. Stefan's mother is actually the second wife."

Jules stares at the two old men near her, intensely playing

chess despite the freezing weather. "How could that possibly happen?"

"I don't know, but it did," he says. "To be honest, after years of searching for stolen art, nothing fazes me anymore. And Lilian is still alive. In her nineties. I have her contact information. An address and a phone number. I don't know where this will lead, but you never know. Here, take it down." He pauses, and she hears a loud exhale. He's smoking. "I really liked Dan."

"He liked you too," Jules returns. "And he doesn't like a lot of people."

"Thank you . . . I really appreciate that," Bakker says before he hangs up.

Jules stares at the name and address that she's written down on the backside of the same Starbucks napkin. She heads farther down toward the lake and plops onto the cold damp sand at the water's edge, the toes of her boots getting slightly wet. Staring out into the foggy abyss, she hopes for some clarity. But everything around her is gray, dreary, and blurred. Even the skyscrapers in the distance have been eclipsed by fog, as though beheaded. Too many moving parts. *What am I even investigating here?* A stolen painting? Dan's murder? A criminal art dealer? Over a billion dollars' worth of stolen art? Ellis Baum's lost, messed-up family?

At least ten times a day, she asks herself, *What would Dan do?* But Dan is dead. It's all on her. Picking up a smooth rock, she throws it as far as she can into the filmy lake but doesn't see it land. *Choose one lead*, she tells herself as she gets up to leave. *And if you're lucky, that one will help solve the others. And if you're not . . .* But she pushes the contrarian right back down where it belongs, as far away from her as possible.

THIRTY-TWO

JULES WAKES UP from a deep sleep, disoriented. She wipes her eyes, thinking that her mother was in her dream. But she's wrong. Her mother is live, standing in her bedroom, hovering over her, and the familiar scent of coffee mixed with toothpaste mixed with Giorgio Armani fills her nostrils. She is saying something about a young man named Adam Chase being in the lobby.

"Mom, wait, what?" Jules sits up so fast that she knocks over the glass of water on her nightstand.

Her mother picks up the glass. "Yes, Owen just called up. He says there's an Adam Chase here to see you. This early?" Her lips tighten. "Who is he? Another sticky note category?"

"Here? Like in the apartment building?" Jules's first thought is the dried zit cream all over her face. "He's . . . an artist. Ellis Baum's grandson. Just tell him I will be right down."

Adam is here. How does he even know where she lives? She glances quickly at her phone on the pillow next to her. Three missed calls from him—one late last night, two early this morning. She has been avoiding his recent calls; the onslaught of texts too. And now he's here in the flesh, refusing to be ignored.

Jules kicks off her covers and quickly hops out of bed, catches a glimpse of herself in the passing closet door mirror, and groans. *Christ, what a train wreck.* Her eyes are puffy, raccoonlike, from spending practically all night at her mother's office yesterday investigating Lilian Baum and the Dassel family with their Nazi history as thick as a phone book, as well as that photo of Margaux de Laurent in disguise. A long, tedious night staring at the computer, stuck in research quicksand, but highly productive.

Jules also took Bram Bakker's advice and had a brief conversation yesterday morning with the *Spotlight* editor, who initially gave her no new information about his meeting with Dan except to say how sorry he was and that, yes, he had given Dan a confidential photo but would not be able to provide her with more details or comment on it. She pressed him hard about the photo, saying she worked closely with Dan and already has the image in her possession, but needs a basic explanation. He finally relented, admitting that, yes, the photo was taken on German soil. And after further prodding, Jules got an *in Munich* out of him and a date that the picture was taken. With the Munich detail, she was able to pinpoint the exact location of the photo. By 1:30 a.m., Jules found the small produce market pictured to the far-left side of the photograph, next to the apartment building where Margaux was standing in disguise. It is called Müller's Markt, in the Schwabing neighborhood, and is located on the very same street where Carl Geisler once lived, proving that Margaux was clearly staking out the place, standing on his street two days before the murder-robbery. That must be what Dan had wanted to tell her.

Of course, the information leads to more questions: Did Margaux steal Geisler's treasure trove with *Woman on Fire*, or without it? Did she murder the man? Or hire someone else to do the dirty work? Did Margaux discover Dan was onto her and kill him or have him killed?

And then there is the twisted tale of Franz Dassel and Lilian Baum. After an intensive search through the Library of Congress files, browsing through hundreds of documents and clippings from old German newspapers, tattered microfilm and public records, Jules finally found a marriage certificate dated November 1945 and a divorce certificate dated three years later. It was all right there in faded sepia. Franz Dassel remarried in 1951—Stefan's mother. Did Lilian ever remarry? Have kids? Work? She found no other information. And Arno Baum . . . Stefan Dassel said that he came from an important banking family. After examining more than one hundred banking-related photos taken during the 1930s in Berlin, Jules unearthed a single image published in the *Berliner Morgenpost* at a BKommerz bank branch twentieth-anniversary celebration in 1932, taken at one of Arno Baum's banks. Arno was photographed there with his young family standing behind him. Two small daughters flanked his wife in black and white. Zooming in, Jules saw that Lilian, even as a young girl, looked just like her father and had the same penetrating eyes as Ellis. Jules searched everywhere but found no photos of Anika Baum. What was her maiden name? Who was she? If only she could ask Ellis.

Jules also followed up on Bram Bakker's information and discovered that one Lilian Dassel—she kept his last name—lives in Baden-Baden. And not in a single-family home; rather, a convalescent home. She is ninety-three years old. No living relatives. If only she could talk to Lilian. If the woman still has her memory. *So many ifs.*

After nine straight hours of research, Jules turned off the computer, having chosen her lead, the one road to follow. It breathed.

She felt it in her bones. And now Adam is here on her doorstep, about to complicate everything. Her brain hurts from all the thinking. She tosses back two Tylenol and scrounges around her drawers for her favorite black yoga pants and a clean sweatshirt. She splashes water on her face, gargles mouthwash, topknots her hair, slips on Uggs, grabs a jacket just in case, and heads out the door. As angry as she is, a tiny, hardened part of her begins to thaw. *He showed up.*

ADAM SITS, ELBOWS to knees, staring at the floor on the bench across from Owen, their doorman of fifteen years—who is more than just a doorman, her mother always says. Owen is their guardian angel, their protector, always watching out for them. Adam looks up with a hopeful gaze as Jules slowly exits the elevator and walks toward him. She realizes that it's no longer anger she is feeling. It's deep hurt.

"Hey," she says, because nothing else comes out.

Adam takes a hesitant step toward her. His words are slow in coming. "Hi . . . I know this is weird that I'm here. I came because you wouldn't answer any of my calls."

A beat of silence. A hundred thoughts merge into one. "Is it Ellis?" she asks. *Please say no.*

Adam swallows hard. She sees the rocklike protrusion of his Adam's apple. "He's still in a coma, but hopefully they are taking him out of it as early as next week . . . we'll see. No one knows anything for sure. It's all up in the air. My family hasn't left his side." He shuffles his feet, clearly trying to keep it together.

"I'm sorry," Jules says sincerely. *And yet you're here.*

His gaze bores into hers, and it feels like he's trying to talk to her through his eyes. He is so handsome, but painfully shy, like an awkward boy who grew into his good looks too late. She saw that the very first time she met him in Montana. She remembers thinking that his introverted, self-conscious demeanor didn't match the wild stories written about him.

"How did you find me?" she asks, wishing her heart would just stop pounding so damn fast.

"It wasn't hard. Google." He holds up six fingers. "Did you know that there are a half dozen Jules Roths in the Chicago area, and two happen to be in elementary school?" He glances at Owen, who is eyeballing Adam like a provoked pit bull.

"Impressive." Jules laughs, despite herself. "For an artist."

He smiles back, and then the corners of his mouth turn downward. "I know what you think you saw at the apartment. But *that* didn't happen."

The seductive brushstrokes, your basic all-around sex on canvas. "I know *exactly* what I saw. I didn't think it," she counters.

Owen is still glaring at Adam. Jules sees it, smiles appreciatively, and waves that all is okay.

"Is there anywhere else we can go to talk?" Adam asks.

"Say what you have to say right here." She knows her icy tone belies all the mixed feelings swirling inside of her.

"Okay, fine." He sighs hard. "I didn't sleep with Margaux. I painted her. She tried to seduce me. She took off her clothes and tried, but nothing happened."

"And yet you painted her naked." Jules states the facts. She thinks about the other painting at the cabin. Margaux standing nude on the globe in stilettos. "And that's not the first time . . ."

"No, it's not." His voice is a hoarse whisper. "But it's definitely the last." Jules doesn't say anything. He tugs nervously at the scruff on his chin. "Look, I was really upset when I found the painting on the bathroom floor and you took off without saying goodbye." He gives her a pained stare. "How can I make you believe me that it was nothing?"

"It wasn't nothing to me. You once told me, 'Every painting has a story.'"

He rubs his eyes, which are red streaked, as though he, too, hasn't slept. "Okay . . . Just before Margaux left the apartment after telling me about my Basel exhibit, she took off her clothes, and like I said, she tried to seduce me—that's her way. She uses her body to get what she wants. It's not about sex—it's about control. I won't lie to you. It has always worked in the past. *Always*. Before, it was all about the drugs for me. It was our sick, codependent relationship. Yeah, that's what I got in therapy." His forehead perspires slightly, and Jules feels a little guilty. She knows she is making him work hard for this right now. "But everything has changed. Margaux has nothing over me anymore. I find her repulsive."

Jules crosses her arms, still not done with it. "So repulsive that you *had* to paint her?"

His upper lip is sweating. "I don't know how to explain this. But in that moment, I also saw her as an artist would . . . not as a man. Beautiful on the outside, but monstrously ugly, like Medusa. I wanted to capture that dichotomy. Not her in bed—*that*. There's a difference."

Jules remains quiet, letting his words sink in.

"It's the truth. Please believe me," Adam pleads. "I'm here. I care. You matter. That night mattered. What more can I say to convince you that I feel nothing but contempt for Margaux?" He reaches out and lifts Jules's reluctant chin upward. "Look at me. The night we spent together meant something." His gaze softens as his grasp on her chin tightens. "It was the first time in years that I made love sober."

Jules doesn't want to feel or let him off the hook, and yet . . .

"Sorry that I hurt you," he whispers sincerely, the hand on her face falling limply to his side.

"Okay," she says under her breath, so quietly that she only hears it inside her heart. He's telling the truth. It's not perfect, but it's real. She glances over at Owen. Still glaring. "Let's go to the lake. It's nearby."

Fifteen minutes later, they walk along the beach and sit on a large rock formation beside the water. It's much colder out than she anticipated. Jules zips up her jacket and digs her hands deep into her coat pockets. She's aware of their bodies touching, and of the way he is glancing sideways at her. "I need to tell you a few things," she says quietly. "I need to trust someone . . ."

He waits patiently as she draws in the cold air, glances up briefly at the cashmere-gray sky, then spills it all—Dan's death, the photo of Margaux in Munich, Lilian Baum/Dassel, her recent conversations with Bram Bakker and the *Spotlight* editor, her mother's concerns for her safety—*all of it*.

Adam's eyes pop at various points, but he says nothing. When she's finally done, he takes her hand inside his. "I'm going with you."

"What are you talking about? Going where?"

"Baden-Baden. The nursing home," he says. "That's your plan, isn't it?"

"Yes." She stops blinking. "It's my plan, but—"

"I'm paying for it too," he says adamantly. "And don't argue. The flights, the hotel, expenses, everything. I have money, Jules.

After all the drugs I consumed, all the waste, all the cash I blew . . . I never touched my trust fund, and it's substantial." He stares out at the lake as he speaks. "Full disclosure, I tried hard to get to that trust fund money to feed my drug habit, but my parents protected it and locked me out. I hated them for that. Not anymore. I'm grateful. It's all there, all mine, and available." He turns to her. "And it's more than enough for us—you—to do whatever we can to find the painting before . . ."

Before Ellis dies.

He nods silently as though hearing her thoughts. "You're not doing any more of this alone," he emphasizes again. "That part is over. And you can tell your mother that too. In fact, if I get a chance to meet her, I will do it myself." Just as Jules opens her mouth to protest, he lightly presses his fingertip against her lips. "It's my grandfather, remember. *My grandfather.* I have a large stake in this. Dan is dead, and I'm not going to let anything happen to you. Especially now, after everything." He throws a small rock far into the distance and they watch it plunk into the water. "Agree, or I'm not leaving Chicago."

Jules feels a warm flush rise in her cheeks. *I have my team.* "Fine, but I call all the shots." She straightens her shoulders. "Your money, my plan."

"Sounds fair." They both laugh.

She watches the muddy waves thrash against the rocks. "Here's the thing . . . you can't come to Baden-Baden. You just can't. You took a risk coming here and may have been followed. You have an exhibition coming up, paintings you still must finish. Most importantly, you need to continue the charade with Margaux, stay in New York—"

"You're not traveling back to Germany alone, no matter what," he argues. "Unless . . ."

"Oh god, don't say it." She shakes her head. *No way in hell.*

"Yup." He grins. "Take your mother with you. From everything you've described, she seems extremely capable, and most importantly, she will make sure you stay safe and not take any stupid risks."

Before Jules can respond, Adam leans in and wraps his arm around her tightly, and she sinks into the puff of his jacket, inhaling his scent, slightly pungent from travel and stress. And yet it is achingly familiar, as though she has always known it. They both stare out at the lake, where the waves that were surging just minutes ago have mysteriously flatlined. *Her mother?* No way. Though Adam may have a point. In terms of a cover, it's kind of genius.

As Adam's chapped lips touch the tiny part of her neck that is exposed, Jules cannot help but think how deceptively calm the water is right now—and how at any second it could all change.

THIRTY-THREE

CORRENS, FRANCE

MARGAUX FLEW BACK once again to Correns. One last hurrah before Basel to make sure everything runs smoothly, no loose ends. This trip, unlike all the others, is purely insurance. She refuses to leave anything to chance. After seeing Adam's paintings, she knows that they are onto her, and she needs the legal documentation to prove she is the rightful owner of *Woman on Fire*.

It's got to be here.

Rummaging through document after document in the Maison's archives, Margaux is determined to find the painting's original proof of purchase, the bill of sale—proving Charles de Laurent was indeed the legitimate owner of *Woman on Fire*. That he was *forced* to sell the painting during the war . . . which, in the world of restitution surrounding Nazi-looted art, means that no matter who finds the real painting, she has solid legal claim to the masterwork.

Her grandfather's extensive archives are painstakingly

meticulous—the definitive *catalogues raisonnés* of major modern artists, dealers, collectors, and curators compiled during World War II, after Charles de Laurent was forced out of Paris. He sought refuge in the countryside and worked closely with Louvre operatives to protect many of France's most important paintings. He used the Maison as a safe house to smuggle hundreds of paintings out of the country for protection, and every single covert movement was documented here.

Even after the war was long over, her grandfather never let up. He continued to compile pertinent intel on modern art and artists until his death. As Margaux digs through the infinite piles of certificates, records, and deeds, the fastidiously organized papers fly behind her in a mad disarray. In the distance, she hears the approaching stomp of Wyatt Ross's boots. *Not now.*

"Leave me alone!" she shouts out.

The Doc Martens stop in their tracks. "I need to talk to you," he fires back, his voice reverberating through the stacks.

"Later," she yells. "Just get the hell out of here."

His grating voice vanishes. *Good*, she thinks, *go back to your hacking cave.* She just wants to be alone. She gave Wyatt a chance to find the document on his own and he came up empty-handed. But she knows it's here. However long it takes her, she will find it. Eyeing the vast amount of information before her, Margaux is reminded of her days spent perusing the Bodleian Library at the University of Oxford, her alma mater. She used to relish checking out the impressive art history section, closing her eyes and randomly pulling out a book. She would force herself to read whatever it was she'd chosen—whatever artist or philosopher had landed in her hands. She savored the feeling of confronting something bigger, more powerful, more knowledgeable than she—and then conquering it.

Wiping the sweat dripping off her forehead with her sleeve, Margaux glances at the endless rows of cabinets and storage in front of her. There's got to be hundreds of thousands of documents stashed in this place. If only her grandfather were still alive to help her, how different things might have been. He would have kicked her philandering father out of the business permanently before he could destroy it, and the two of them would have conquered the art world together—her grandfather's brains, business acumen, and impeccable eye for detail teamed with her ability to find the next big thing and make it even bigger. Instead, she is left picking up the pieces of a drunken, gambling womanizer; a despicable *son of* who squandered all the family jewels that fell like manna into his slippery lap. *I hate him. My father's dead—and I still hate him.*

Hours pass, and the floor looks as though a tornado has struck, but Margaux is undeterred, poring through every classification she can think of. Ernst Engel's files—nothing. Helmuth Geisler—nada. German Artists—zero. Category after category—not a damn thing. Exhausted, she sits back against the nearest wall, spent and dehydrated, refusing to accept defeat. "Speak to me," she whispers, looking up at the arched, wood-beamed ceiling. "Enough games, Grand-papa, just tell me."

And then, like a faulty light bulb that suddenly flashes on—*she knows*. It is not the subject that she should be investigating—it is the man himself. This painting was not about business for her grandfather; it was personal.

Margaux's mind immediately shifts gears. She stands and

stretches her arms high overhead, feeling a surge of energy pump though her body, pulling her, guiding her. She kicks the piles of rejects out of her path as she makes her way to the farthest side of the archives. Her grandfather once told her that he believed this powerful canvas had kept his wife, the only woman he ever truly loved, alive. The painting filled her dying, deteriorating days with joy, and seemed to ease her constant pain. No, *Woman on Fire* would not be among the business transactions. It would be filed in a category of its very own.

She walks toward a file cabinet near the last row, simply titled: SYLVIE DE LAURENT. Her grandmother. Margaux knows even before she opens the files that the document will be there, waiting for her. *Woman on Fire* and her grandfather's beloved Sylvie would naturally be together.

Her whole body ignites as she retrieves the delicate, discolored, sepia-toned contract signed in her grandfather's elegant hand and, of course, with Helmuth Geisler's practically unreadable signature—just the H and G are distinctive. And the document bears yet another gift. Behind it, she pulls out a faded black leather diary. Evidence, in his own words. The heart attack that took her grandfather away from her too soon left her with only half a story. As Margaux opens the dog-eared journal, she knows she is about to discover the other half—the part that matters.

THIRTY-FOUR

PARIS, 1939

THE BANGING ON the gallery door was the kind that should have served as a warning. Loud, demanding, urgent. Charles de Laurent shook his head. *Impossible. All precautions had been taken.* He wasn't one of those people whose doors get banged on. There was a protocol, an etiquette, a respect for his position. He had protection, friends in the highest of places, and every important cultural institution in Paris revered his opinion. If Charles de Laurent declared an artist gifted, well then . . . Standing at his desk, clutching the edge of it, he listened to the continuous pounding. No one needed to tell him that this was not a courtesy call. His breath quickened and his eyes began to burn.

"De Laurent!" he heard someone bark. "De Laurent!"

Charles turned to his two young female employees, whose mouths were agape, standing frozen in their tracks. "Leave now," he ordered them. "Take your things and go out the basement door. Go! Be safe."

The banging continued like a petulant child refusing to give up. "De Laurent—open the goddamn door!"

French with a German accent. Charles's heart sank. *The paintings. They've come for them.* He broke into a sweat and felt his chest tightening. At least many of the important canvases were safe. Some were hidden at the château; others had already been sent to the United States; a third shipment was transported eight days ago to a colleague in Malaga, Spain. *Stay calm,* he warned himself as he walked toward the door and opened it. *Don't show them fear.*

Five men of varying ages and sizes faced him, a shadowy squadron in dark leather jackets. Keeping his voice even, Charles stood in the wide doorway. "Yes, gentlemen, how can I help you?"

The one in the middle, the smallest, pushed past him, entering the gallery as though he owned it. Charles knew exactly who he was and chided himself. He should have been more prepared. He should have seen this coming sooner—*him* coming. The man paused in the foyer, waiting for the others to traipse in after him. They entered robotically, filing one by one into a semicircle behind their leader, awaiting orders. The man ignored them, hypnotized by the magnificent gallery, known throughout Paris for its opulence. "Even grander than I imagined . . ." He pivoted slowly to face Charles, signaling his men to stay put, and gestured to the next room filled with paintings. "A word."

Charles followed him into the main gallery, his pride and joy, a sprawling sanctuary with a twenty-foot-high ceiling and, at its center, a dripping crystal chandelier, which cast a warm hue over his canvases, accentuating their color and beauty. Any new painting that landed at the gallery always began its journey in this room. If the canvas didn't sell after a month's time, it was moved upstairs to the second floor. But now, as the man circled the room silently with his hands clasped behind his back, Charles yearned to cover his beloved canvases, to protect them from this poisonous snake's view.

"Modigliani. Léger. Picasso. Cézanne." The man ticked off the names as though he knew the painters personally. "Priceless art. You're an enviable man, M. de Laurent." He glanced around. "But a man without guards—not smart."

No, Charles thought. *Not smart at all.* He did have two security guards, but they were taking their daily lunch break. Most likely, he'd been surveilled. *They knew precisely when I would be alone.*

"And you are?" Charles raised a curious brow for show. He knew exactly who the man was. Anyone who read a newspaper knew who he was.

"Yes, let's play that game." Geisler exaggerated a bow. "Helmuth Geisler at your service. You've heard of me, I assure you . . . Just as I've heard of you, Charles *de* Laurent," he sneered. "The 'de' part always makes me laugh, wondering how you, a Jew, managed to possess the coveted participle belonging exclusively to French nobility. Who did you pay off?"

Charles didn't flinch. "I thought you looked familiar," he quipped instead, knowing better than to show any weakness. "Only the Helmuth Geisler I once knew was the director of the König Albert Museum in Zwickau. Modern art was his specialty— his passion. The Helmuth Geisler I knew was a student of Expressionism, his teacher none other than Ernst Engel himself." Charles pointed a shaky finger in the air. "The Helmuth Geisler I knew *championed* Expressionists . . . and a few of my artists were exhibited in his very last showcase before he left the museum and betrayed the movement he once celebrated. The exhibit was called"—Charles snapped his fingers dramatically—*"Die Brücke and Blau Reiter: Expressionists, The New Generation of Modern Art. You*, Herr Geisler, were once the enviable man." Charles's whole body fumed with rage. "What happened to you?"

"I'd advise you to watch your step." But Geisler's face crumpled—he couldn't hide it. He was the worst kind of Nazi, Charles thought. A traitor to the movement. Not like Max Kruger, who *pretended* to work for the Nazis to save art. Geisler was leading Hitler's pack of thieves, vilifying and destroying the art and artists he once fully embraced.

"Where is she?" Geisler demanded, his eyes traveling over the gallery walls and pausing at the winding staircase in the center of the room, leading to the second floor. He pointed to the ceiling. "Is she up there?"

"Where is who?" Charles played dumb. But his calm demeanor belied the panic gripping his throat.

"Stop with the charade. I know all about Ernst Engel's last painting and the story behind it," Geisler told him.

The story behind it. Charles held his breath. Too many nights he imagined what it could be . . . Who was the woman, the muse, in the painting? This duplicitous pig knows it all. Of course he does. A turncoat who couldn't compete with Ernst Engel's brilliance and fame, so he became the leading curator of Expressionist art instead to make a name for himself. Charles knew about Geisler's rejections early on as a young artist. He'd even seen some of the man's inferior works. Geisler must have been so secretly jealous of Engel and his friends that when he rose to power, he made it his personal mission to destroy the man who once nurtured him and the movement of art that left him behind. There is no greater pain than being a rejected artist and no greater danger than payback. "And what story is that?" Charles had to know.

Geisler smiled omnipotently, purposely ignoring the question. "She's here with you, isn't she? I feel it. Let's make this easy. Your good friend Max Kruger is still alive, but barely. He broke under intensive questioning. His home was burned down. His paintings are now in our hands. His family has been arrested. Shall I go on? We caught him sending traitorous messages. Messages that went directly to you." Geisler's beady eyes gleamed like a demonic character out of Goya's *Black Paintings*, and Charles felt a sudden, soul-shattering chill.

"I want the painting," Geisler demanded. "And I'm not leaving without it."

Charles folded his arms and ground his wing-tipped shoes into the marble floor. "I will call the police if you don't leave immediately."

Geisler laughed so hard that his tiny eyes all but disappeared. It was a small man's sardonic sound, larger than his size and cruelly executed. "Save your energy. Your so-called brave French police are cooperating with us now. No one likes a smuggler. Especially a Jewish one. Certainly not the French, who place more importance on culture and couture than they do their own pathetic military." His nostrils flared. "Now, where is she, damn it?"

His heart pounding, Charles struggled to keep his face blank. "I don't have her anymore. She is in the United States for safekeeping."

Geisler wagged his finger between Charles's eyes. "You're lying. I do this day and night. An eye twitch, a mouth curl, a nervous shuffle of the foot. All three, de Laurent. All three. Here's how this is going to go . . . Either give me the painting, or the consequences will be severe."

He gestured with his thumb to the men waiting in the next room. "Those men—they wouldn't know a Rembrandt from a comic book. They are uncouth, animals. They like to set beautiful things afire and watch them burn. It's sport for them. All I need to do is give them the go-ahead and this splendid gallery of yours will be ash, and those paintings will find a new home with me." He pointed to the Picasso in front of him, an old man playing guitar doused in various shades of blue. "The Reich is coming to France. It's inevitable. And when we do, I will make it my personal mission to procure all your assets. All your paintings. And not just yours. I will confiscate your precious client list and their artwork as well."

He moved in closer. Charles could smell the man's last meal on his breath—the onions, the garlic, the cheese. "Is one painting worth all this?" he hissed. "Give me the painting, and the only deal I'm offering—and I don't negotiate with Jews—is that you will be left alone. Your clients will be left alone. Your prized gallery left alone. Your personal collection—minus, of course, a few choice items—will be left alone." He rubbed his hands together as though warming them. "What will it be?"

"Why this one?" Charles had to know. "Why come all the way to Paris just for this painting? Besides, aren't you people supposed to be getting rid of so-called degenerate art?"

Geisler paused, considering his response. "It's because of her . . . the model."

"The model?" Charles demanded. "Who is she to you?"

Geisler shook his head, not giving Charles another inch. "The real question is, who is she to Germany? See, that's the beauty of this. I don't have to tell you anything. I am authorized to take what I want, when I want it, for reasons of my own. That's power. *That* is art." He made an exaggerated sweep of his arms, and Charles knew that any deal engaged in with this godless man would be broken.

Geisler spun around on his shoe like a Degas ballerina, signaling his thugs to follow. "You've got one hour to decide, de Laurent. It's the painting, or everything else." He drops a pre-written contract on Charles's desk on the way out. "You will sign it and be paid accordingly. I never make a deal that's not legitimate."

The door slams. *Legitimate*—that thief. Charles looks down at the one-page contract. Two thousand francs for a painting worth a thousand times that. But his family, his clients, his artists . . . all his responsibility. With tears in his eyes, he reached for his prized Montblanc fountain pen, which was preening and judging him from the corner of his desk. *I've never signed a contract that I will regret for the rest of my life*, Charles thought. *Until now.*

THIRTY-FIVE

CHICAGO

IT IS NEARLY 7:00 p.m. Adam stands in the doorway of Jules's apartment, hesitating to leave for the airport. Owen called up just a few minutes earlier. The Uber is waiting.

"I'm really glad you came," she says, not wanting him to go.

Adam leans in. "Me too." His brow furrows and his voice turns fatherly. "Promise me. I want to hear it again. You are going to take your mother with you. You're not going to change your mind."

She points behind her at her mother, who is cleaning on the other side of the apartment, pretending not to be listening in. "You've met her. No one messes with Elizabeth Roth." She laughs. "For the tenth time—YES."

"Basel is in just a few weeks," he reminds her. "Like I said, I'll get through the show, and then after that . . ." His mouth is just inches from hers. She inhales the lavender vanilla bean scent of him. He used her body wash during the shower that he took after the lake, before her mom whipped them up an early dinner and then grilled Adam as though he were sitting for a deposition. They hold each other's gaze.

"Contact me when you get there," he says with finality.

"We discussed that, remember? If you're being followed—"

"We both agreed that I've probably blown that big-time with this trip, haven't I?"

"Yes," she says. It's the truth. If Margaux was suspicious before, now it's confirmed. "I'm not exactly sure what to do at this point except to just keep going forward." Jules turns away slightly to collect her thoughts. "Maybe I'll go back to the stolen art story as a cover. After this trip, I will figure it all out."

Adam pulls her in close once again. "I'm going to miss you and these crazy curls." He takes an untamed tendril, winds it around his finger, pulls it toward him, and lets it boing backward. Then he kisses Jules hard on the mouth, reluctantly releases her, and turns toward the elevator.

"Keep me updated on Ellis," she shouts down the hallway, watching him as the elevator arrives.

He holds the doors open with his body, straddling the threshold. As their eyes meet one last time, Jules feels a jolt inside her chest. Ellis is in a coma; Dan is dead. She shudders when the elevator doors close behind Adam. Bad things come in threes.

THE MOTHER-DAUGHTER TRIP turns out to be the best way to go. After Adam leaves, Jules immediately contacts the director of the assisted living facility in Baden-Baden and asks the woman if visitors are allowed, pretending to be closely acquainted with the Dassel family. She maintains that both she and her mother will be traveling around Germany for the first time, stopping in Baden-Baden, and wonders if Lilian Dassel might be available for tea?

At first, the director declines the request, saying how truly sorry she is but that only registered members of the family are allowed to visit. Jules quickly counters with the one thing she hopes will be foolproof: "My grandfather," she lies, "was a very close friend of Lilian's father *before* he perished in the camps during the war." She feels a little uncomfortable playing the "Holocaust card" but knows that guilt—especially in Germany—will surely gain her access to Lilian.

There is an awkward, thick pause. "Yes, well then, I think we can make an exception just this once," the director says with a scratchy cough. "A one-hour visitation. Ms. Dassel, I'm afraid, is not well, and that is all I can offer. We will see you in few days."

"One hour is perfect. *Danke schön*," Jules responds, pulling out one of the ten German phrases she knows. One hour is practically nothing. She will have to work fast and smart.

After the call, Jules preps for the trip by downloading a German language app and compiling numbers for the U.S. embassy, police, and medical emergency—all the essentials—and then walks toward her mother's bedroom. She stands in the doorway for a moment. Her mother's back faces her. Jules still can't believe she is accompanying her on the trip—not Dan. It feels like she is nine years old all over again, when her closest fourth-grade girlfriends formed a Princesses group—a special father/daughter meetup once a month—and Jules didn't have a father to bring. She remembers coming home from school crying that she felt left out because she didn't have a dad like the other kids. Liz Roth, game face intact, said simply, *I'm going. I can be both.*

It was embarrassing, walking into her friend Kaleigh's house with her mother. All the dads and daughters were sitting together in a circle when they entered the room. No one said anything, but by the looks in their eyes Jules knew exactly what they were all thinking. She felt her skin prickle with shame from head to toe. But her mother wouldn't allow the pity party to last beyond that very first meeting. *Buckle up, Jules. Some kids have no parents. You got me. I got you. And we got this.* Her mother steamrolled into the next Princesses gathering head held high. And everyone said that Liz Roth's Oreo cupcakes were the best snack ever.

Jules enters her mother's bedroom, sits on the bed, legs pretzeled, and watches her mother pack.

Her mother stands in front of her closet, contemplating which clothes to bring. "Let me get this straight . . ." She turns to Jules. "We are traveling four thousand miles for a *one*-hour meeting. Is this really worth it?"

Worth it? "Let me ask you this, Mom. How many miles would *you* travel for a key witness who could potentially make or break your case?"

Her mother's shoulders pull back and she exhales through her nose, the same way Jules has seen her do numerous times just prior to conceding a point to opposing counsel. "I would travel four thousand miles. Touché," she admits, then sits down on the bed next to her daughter. Her eyes are shiny. "I really like Adam, by the way, in case you were wondering."

"I like him too," Jules says quickly, secretly pleased but not wanting to discuss Adam further. She needs to be in her journalist's head right now—tough and focused—not replaying every second of Adam's visit.

Her mother wraps her arms around Jules's shoulders and pulls her in close. "Are you okay? I saw the way you looked at each other just before he left—like neither of you wanted him to go."

"I'm fine, but I really need to concentrate on this trip." Jules shuts her down, fully aware that her mother is evaluating her reaction and will push for more information later. Changing the subject, she points to the black dress on top of the heap in the small carry-on. "Where exactly do you think we're going—the opera?"

Her mother laughs. "Baden-Baden is a world-famous spa town. There's a casino and the Fabergé Museum—and have you heard of the *Festspielhaus*? It's the second-largest performing arts center in all of Europe. Let's have some fun while we are there—why not?" She crosses her arms defiantly. "So yes, black dress."

Jules shakes her head. *Fun?* "This is work. We are going for three days, two are for travel, and one of those is going to be spent in a nursing home. But if you want to bring your black dress—"

"I'm bringing the dress."

Liz Roth is bringing the dress. Jules eyes her mother's stuffed bag, thinking, *I can't believe I let him talk me into this.*

For a final touch, her mother carefully spreads her favorite red cardigan sweater over all the clothes in her suitcase as though she's frosting a cake. Zippering up the bag, she looks at Jules. "I'm also very capable. Put me to work. Give me files to go through. This is your show, but perhaps I can do more than just chaperone. As you know, my grandparents spoke Yiddish in the house when I was growing up. I learned to understand it, and it's close enough to German to get by."

Jules assesses her mother and thinks about the Dassel documents, the mounds of paperwork. Maybe she can be of assistance in the stolen art legal arena, particularly in the laws of restitution. And perhaps, using the law firm's vast resources, she could investigate DLG's finances as well. And Jules could certainly use another set of eyes and ears. Her mother is not only highly intelligent and competent, but also the best there is in finding the loopholes and the potholes. *Stop fighting it*, she tells herself. *Lawful Liz*—as her mother's office nicknamed her—just might be useful, in or out of that fancy black dress.

THIRTY-SIX

BADEN-BADEN, GERMANY

THE KLM FLIGHT lands at Frankfurt Airport in the morning. Jules and her mother slept hard, knocked out from Benadryl on the long flight over with one stop in Amsterdam. As the taxi driver takes them from the airport to Baden-Baden, Jules glances at her GPS and sees that they are going to be more than an hour early for their scheduled meeting.

Jules and her "team" (aka her mother) are not prepared for just how beautiful the drive is to *Haus am Meer*—House by the Sea. The driver gave them a choice of two routes to take—the A8 highway, hampered by construction and traffic jams, or the scenic route— longer but lovelier, a serpentine drive between the Rhine plains and the northern Black Forest, with its canopy of snow-covered ever- greens and trails and small outlying vineyards. Her mother grabs her dictionary and shouts, *"Szenisch!"* *Scenic.* Smiling, Jules doesn't argue, because they are ahead of schedule.

Opening the window slightly, she inhales the cold air against her face as they drive. None of the passing scenery looks real—

it's straight out of a "Winter Wonderland" storybook. The sky is overcast, but the forest around them is so dense and bright with white-dusted trees. *If only Adam was here to see this, paint this.*

Her mother predictably reads factoids aloud from her travel guidebook, and it's annoying. "Did you know what Mark Twain said about Baden-Baden? 'After ten minutes you forget time, after twenty, you forget the world.'"

"Did not know that." Jules points to what looks like a vineyard up ahead as they approach the outskirts of Baden-Baden. In the distance she sees Mount Merkur, the famous two-thousand-foot-high mountain peak that dates to Roman times as a monument to the god Mercury—her mother already provided the history lesson ten minutes earlier. "There—see that sign up ahead? *Haus am Meer.* That's it." She glances at her mother. "Let me do all the talking, okay? I have just one hour to find out everything I can. Remember, this is about the painting. Please, don't jump in."

Her mother laughs. "Yes, boss. I know this is the last thing you want to hear, but you remind me of me. I'm not used to being given orders. But don't worry, I will take it like an intern and shut my mouth, smile, and drink my tea. Unless—"

Jules shoots her mother a reprimanding look as the driver pulls up to the bottom of the long driveway. "There is no *unless*, and I love you."

Pulling up to the nursing home, the driver agrees to pick them up after the meeting and bring them back to the town of Baden-Baden, to their hotel—courtesy of the Adam Chase Trust Fund. They both stand at the entrance of the sprawling, snow-covered medieval structure with its Gothic façade, lacy spires, and gargoyles.

"This place looks like a royal retreat—definitely not a nursing home," Jules remarks as they walk inside. She wonders if there's a moat out back.

As they approach the front desk in the ornate lobby, her mother whispers, "Wow—it's like a museum. You have full permission to put me in here when I'm on my last legs." She gestures to the mosaic floor, imposing marble pillars, murals, and sculptures filling the reception area.

They provide their names to the receptionist, and the director appears a few minutes later, introducing herself as Johanna Lutz. She offers to give them a brief tour, which Jules readily accepts. Johanna is younger than she sounded on the phone and looks more like a flight attendant than the head of a convalescent home. Her bright blond hair is pulled back into a short ponytail. She wears black slacks and a crisp white blouse with a small bow at the top. She speaks to Jules and her mother in heavily accented English as she briskly guides them through the large dining hall, the exercise room, the small movie theater, the ballroom— *yes, ballroom*; Jules and her mother both raise their brows in sync—and, finally, the courtyard. This is a resting home for the rich and famous. Jules wonders how Lilian is paying for all this. Dassel family money from the divorce? Blood money to keep quiet about the family's Nazi past.

"Where are you from?" the director asks them. "To be perfectly honest, Frau Dassel has been with us for nearly five years and mostly keeps to herself. She barely associates with the other patients, and she listed no one—not a single person—in her visitors' profile. To say that I'm thrilled she has some contacts is an understatement."

"We're from Chicago," Jules says, and then adds quickly, "Surely someone must be in touch with you to pay for all this?"

The director proffers a tight-lipped, polite smile. "Frau Dassel paid in full when she arrived. Meaning, from arrival to departure."

There is an awkward silence, and Jules glances at her mother with a *Help me here* gaze. Reading her daughter's thoughts, Liz quickly interjects, "Tell me, how does Lilian spend her days—what does she enjoy the most?" she asks as though she's known Lilian Dassel for years.

The director's cool demeanor changes and she seems happy to answer that question. She presses her clipboard against her chest. "Frau Dassel thoroughly enjoys our art program. When she first came, she painted and would knit sweaters. She loves to be outside—no matter the weather. She has a favorite spot by a specific tree, and . . . What do *you* know about her?" she asks. "I'm always curious to learn what's not on paper."

Jules opens her mouth to speak, but nothing comes out. She isn't prepared for this part of the visit—a one-on-one with the director. Her mother eyes Jules, who nods, giving her the go-ahead once again. They both know that small talk to get pertinent information is Liz Roth's superpower.

"Lilian's family used to be in the banking industry," her mother begins, sticking close to the truth—always the best move. "My husband, may he rest in peace, was a banker as well. His family left Germany for the States just before the war broke out. He, of course, was born in America, but he heard the stories of Lilian's family . . ." She glances at the director, who tightens the bow of her blouse with a *We've all heard those stories* look.

"Yes, well, I'm sure you will enjoy your time with Frau Dassel," she says curtly. "Given it's such a surprisingly pleasant day for this time of year, I will have someone bring her out to greet you in the courtyard by *her* tree. We have outdoor heaters," she adds, as though that would make up for the war. "You will have your privacy. And please, just keep it to one hour. The rules . . . Thank you for understanding."

When the director finally leaves and they are sitting in the courtyard waiting for Lilian, Jules turns to her mother. "Thanks for the quick thinking back there. And sorry I was bitchy earlier."

"Happy to help." Her mother beams. "This next part is all yours."

Ten minutes later, a bundled-up Lilian Dassel emerges from the patio doors and is rolled outside toward them in a wheelchair. Jules and her mother stand as Lilian approaches with an aide at her side. She whispers something to the caretaker in German. The woman parks the chair, then abruptly leaves.

Lilian up close is so pale that she's practically translucent. Her thick hair is snowy white and long for a woman her age, like two puffy cumulus clouds framing her face. Her cheekbones are so pronounced that Jules can practically see the bones jutting through. She is ghostly, yet in a lovely, otherworldly way. Before Jules can say anything, Lilian gets there first.

"I don't forget anything. I have no relatives in America." Her voice warbles, but her English is concise. She points a finger. "Who are you?"

Jules and her mother are taken aback. Jules was prepared for vacancy, senility, a thousand-mile-away stare—but not this. This old woman is clearly lucid—a good thing; anything can come out of this. She feels the excitement welling up inside her. One hour, she reminds herself. One hour. *You got this.*

"You're right, Frau Dassel. You don't know us," Jules launches in. "I'm Jules Roth, a journalist from Chicago. This is my mother, Elizabeth Roth, an attorney. This may come as a shock—"

"I'm unshockable," the woman responds coldly. And Jules knows with every fiber of her being that Lilian is telling the truth.

She decides quickly that direct is best. "We are looking for a painting. Your . . ." *What does she call Ellis? Your father's mistress's son?* "Do you know who Ellis Baum is?"

"Should I?" Lilian asks with a razor-thin smile accompanied by a pointed look that tells Jules that Lilian knows exactly who Ellis is.

This is not going to be easy. "He is a friend of ours and he is looking for a painting."

Lilian's blue eyes pop open wide, and then the unthinkable happens. Her face distorts and she starts cackling like one of those witches in *Macbeth*. And then, just as quickly, the laughter dies, her eyes shrink to slits, and Lilian begins to cry.

"Jules." Her mother shoots her a look. *Do something.*

Jules collects herself. This is the moment. She knows it, feels it, smells it. *Don't pity her. That's not what this woman wants. She wants to talk. Wait it out.* Laughter turns to tears turns to confession— that's the train they are on. Jules has been on this track before, so she follows her instinct. She reaches for the woman's frail hand, delicate and covered with so many age spots that the bleached skin is nearly imperceptible. "Frau Dassel, what is it?" Jules presses gently as she carefully tightens her grip. "You can tell me."

The woman's tears stick to her face. "I know the painting . . . that cursed painting destroyed us. Destroyed my family—do you understand me, young lady?"

Jules notices the aide standing in the window watching them, looking concerned. Jules smiles at her reassuringly, then turns back to Lilian and kneels next to her. "More than anything, I want to understand."

Lilian's tone is bitter. "Little Ellis was the son my father always wanted." She studies Jules's face. "Lovely, aren't you. We were just his daughters, girls—unimportant—his *other* family. But we were there first. *First!* Not that impish child. I saw him once, you know. I went to the park where he was playing. I shouted some ugly things at him and that mother of his. Like a film star. But I heard her ending wasn't pretty. Franz told me what happened to her, paraded like a prostitute in the street . . ." Lilian's eagle-eyed gaze drifts elsewhere, as though her mind moves in fragments, clinging to drive-by images. "In the end, my father chose us. But there wasn't a day in that basement hiding like animals that we didn't all know how badly he wished he had chosen *them*. Anika and her son."

Lilian leans over the side of the wheelchair and spits to the ground, as though the name Anika were a curse. "That painting was *her*. Beautiful Anika Lang—Miss Germany—who secretly took my father's name. Can you imagine? He was still married to my mother! And that painting was larger than life. Otto Dassel gave it to my father as a gift. Guilt. Guilt. Guilt!" she shouts. "He brought that woman's image to the basement where we were in hiding so that my father could look at it every day. And my mother would cry. My sister and I had to live with those tears and the mistress in that painting every single day we were in captivity."

Anika Lang—that's her maiden name. Jules wants to interrupt, ask a hundred questions, but knows better. Her mother's gaze locks into hers. *Let her talk.*

Lilian leans so far forward that Jules is worried the woman is going to topple over. "And just before they came after us—and make no mistake, they did—Franz Dassel, then all of fourteen, apologized for betraying us. But I wouldn't look at him, wouldn't give him the satisfaction. And later, he saved me from an Auschwitz oven, but I never forgave him for the betrayal. Ever." She points a loaded crooked finger at Jules. "You think I married that man for love? A Nazi?" She laughs but it sounds like a growl. "He saved me from the camps to mend his own guilt. But it meant nothing. My family was dead. No—I married him for revenge. That stupid boy fell in love with me—a Jewish girl hiding in his family's basement who rejected his advances—and he never got over it. But I made him pay later for killing my beloved sister, for sending us to the camps, for being forced to watch my father shot dead before my eyes." She looks away from what is clearly unbearable. "Franz took my body and I felt nothing. And that indifference hurt him more than anything—more than hate or blame. And what did Franz give me in the end? What was his very last gesture before I left him for good? The damn painting!" she shrieks.

Jules shudders, then steadies herself. *Lilian has the painting.* She thinks back to what Stefan Dassel told them. He said that Helmuth Geisler came to the Dassel estate to claim the painting, secretly seizing the canvas for himself as collateral for not exposing Otto Dassel for harboring Jews. How is this possible? How did Franz Dassel have the painting if Geisler had already taken it for himself years earlier?

Jules must know. The woman is confused. Taking a deep breath, she goes for it. "I am truly sorry for all your loss, all your pain, Frau Dassel. But I need to ask you this. You said that Franz had the painting of the . . . mistress . . . and he gave it to you. How is that possible when Helmuth Geisler had already claimed the artwork for himself? Helmuth Geisler was the—"

"I know who that criminal was!" she shouts at Jules. "Don't be condescending, young lady." The woman's eyes are fierce. "Otto

Dassel gave Helmuth Geisler a *forged* painting. He must have recognized the importance of it and had it made. Don't forget we were hiding in the Grunewald Forest, where a strong community of artists lived and painted back then. But the real painting Otto gave to my father, his best friend. It lived with us, in that basement."

Jules works hard to keep her voice steady. "Frau Dassel—Lilian—who has the painting now?"

The woman's laughter like a deranged hyena erupts once again. The aide bursts out the door and makes a beeline for Lilian. Jules pleads with Lilian. "Please, just tell me."

The cackle continues, and her mother, using her authoritative voice, jumps in. "Lilian, this is your chance to get rid of that painting once and for all. You are innocent. You were just a girl who did what she had to do to survive. The painting is guilty—not you."

Almost instantly, the laughter stops, and tears begin to cascade uncontrollably, a deluge of pain and secrets, unspeakable things that Lilian has done to survive. As with all survivors, in the end, the perpetrators still win, and it is the survivors who are left depleted and destroyed.

"I have the painting." Lilian's voice is small, younger, broken. "It is all I have of the past, of my father." Her misty gaze looks beyond them. "You should have seen his face when he looked at it, the shine in his eyes. It is how he survived the degradation they put us through. He was once a proud, prominent man. Until they stole everything from us—our banks, our lifestyle, our humanity—and forced us to live in that cold, dark basement. I was just a young girl terrified of spiders. Scared all the time. But my father endure the was a man in love. That painting gave him the st unendurable—until the bullets finished him off. It took twelve to kill him—I counted." Lilian's voice tapers to a faint whisper as her aide comes to take her away. "I loved my father. And I know he loved me back . . . but he loved that painting more."

"Where is the painting now?" Jules presses, her heart racing. The hour is up.

"I buried it," Lilian says just as the woman wheels her away.

THIRTY-SEVEN

CORRENS, FRANCE

MARGAUX WALKS INTO Wyatt's office late at night in old sweats, beat-up sneakers, and the same white cardigan that she's been wearing for the past few days. "I'm heading back to New York tomorrow. A day early, since I found the paperwork I needed. Is the painting ready?"

"Packed and ready for Basel," Wyatt says, then his eye twitch begins spasming. *His tell.*

Margaux doesn't have time for this. "Out with it."

He leans forward over his desk. "You'll be happy to know that I discovered why Ellis Baum is searching for the painting. I just finished combing through Louise Archer's laptop—she was Mansfield's assistant for twenty years."

"And?"

"Ellis Baum's background materials claim he was born in Belgium to a prominent diamond-dealing family. It's a fabrication. Mansfield's personal notes that Archer kept in a secret file tell a different story. It looks like she tried to delete it, but when you don't empty the trash, it's still accessible. The woman in the painting—the model—was his mother. Baum is originally from Berlin . . . Her name is Anika. And . . ."

Margaux turns pale; she barely hears the rest of Wyatt's explanation. *Anika Baum. Anika Baum.* The namesake for the most famous shoes in the world is also *Woman on Fire*? "His mother . . ." She doesn't feel the words escape her mouth as she stares incredulously at Wyatt. "Whose claim is stronger—mine or his?"

Wyatt reaches for a cigarette, and Margaux clamps her hand over his and blocks him. "Don't lie to me."

"Ellis Baum is dying," he says carefully. "I've got more information on that too. The painting is yours."

She lifts her hand, points her finger between his eyes. "Don't fucking lie."

"Forced sales hold a lot of weight, but perhaps so does the actual woman in the painting." Wyatt looks away from her probing eyes. "It's his mother, Margaux. That's a pretty strong claim."

"There's more, isn't there?"

Wyatt snags a cigarette from the box and lights it quickly. "That photo we found in Mansfield's hotel of you in the blond wig in Munich . . . well, the *Spotlight* editor gave it to him. I'm not going to lie to you. This isn't good. There's a chance you may already be a suspect in the Geisler murder-robbery." He holds his breath, knowing this is about to get ugly. "You were seen and followed."

"That Volkswagen . . ." Her voice trails.

"Yeah, that Volkswagen."

"Damn you to hell." Feeling the walls closing in on her, Margaux glares at Wyatt for his incompetency and can tell that a small part of him enjoys watching her shrink, seeing the anguish this is causing her. Seizing Dan's laptop off the desk, she hurls it at him. Wyatt dodges as though he knew it was coming.

Eyeing the broken pieces on the floor, he grinds out the half-smoked cigarette. "I wouldn't have done that."

If only she could take a bat to this place right now. Margaux hovers over his desk, staring him down. "Get me that reporter's phone number and address. I want to know everything about Jules Roth. The name of her fifth-grade teacher. Her favorite ice cream flavor. Every story she has ever worked on. Bring it to the house tonight. No more slipups."

STORMING OUT OF the Maison, Margaux breaks into a run. It's pitch-black outside, but she'd know every inch of the vineyard if she were blindfolded. Weaving in and out of the endless rows of vines with her arms held wide open, she welcomes the sharp branches lashing and cutting her hands. She sprints even faster, inhaling the night air as if it were her last tank of oxygen. The pungent acidic scent wafts deceptively sweet at first, but then the familiar harsh notes of rot rise through her nostrils and cloy at her brain, overtaking her. She can't control this demon. And no matter how fast she runs, she can't outpace it.

That girl—that stupid girl is trying to take away everything that belongs to her—her art, her grandfather's painting, her reputation, Adam. Margaux races until her legs hurt and then pushes herself even harder to experience the exquisite pain fully juiced. She stops running only when she hits her final breath. Leaning over, bloodstained hands to knees, she stares at the dirt path and releases it all, watching with satisfaction as the forceful splash of alcohol and dinner splatters all around her.

When she's done, she steps back and looks up at the gilded

moon embedded in the charcoal sky. How her grandfather used to love the Provençal sky—God's poetry, he used to call it. *Can you feel it, ma petite chérie? There's no more beautiful canvas than Correns at night.* She would nod, smile, and say, Oui, *Grand-papa, I feel it,* but think to herself, *I don't believe in God and I feel nothing.* She knew even then that something was inherently wrong with her, and yet her grandfather saw only the good. So she played along, acting the part of the girl he wanted her to be. But she was a monster inside. After she poisoned the nanny, her parents sent her to a psychologist, who intimated that Margaux possessed psychopathic tendencies. Tendencies—what a joke. How small.

She recalls the epiphany she had as a teenager one particularly miserable Christmas Eve. Her parents were supposed to come home that night to celebrate at the house in Oxford. They told the staff to buy and wrap Margaux's holiday gifts, to wait up with her until they returned home from a party in London. But they never showed up. Margaux waited and waited, sat alone in the Great Room surrounded by gifts, drinking spiked eggnog with the butler and, later, getting high with the housekeeper. She stared blankly at the sparkly panoramic festivities—the silver, the gold, the glitter, the giant red and green bows beneath a lavishly decorated tree. *More lies.*

Happy Christmas, M, the generic card read (your parents are out partying but here's a new YSL leather jacket), *Love, M & S.* Short for Madeline & Sébastien—neither of her parents wanted her to call them Mom or Dad. *I'm just like the wrapping paper,* she told herself. So lovely to admire, but tear away the color, the splendor, the sparkle, and there's nothing there—just a dark, empty box. Except, unfortunately for those around me, I'm far from empty.

When the clock struck midnight, Margaux kicked the gifts

across the room, then, as the butler watched in horror, she demolished each one with the wrought-iron fireplace poker. She knew that one day both "M & S" would pay for their parental crimes. She was determined to put those "tendencies" to work.

A gust of cold wind whips against her face, and Margaux embraces it. She strips down to her panties to feel the impact directly against her skin. She needs to cool down, organize her thoughts. She stands perfectly still until the molten lava beneath her skin simmers and the calm finally sets in. It's always been this way. The intense heat, followed by the insatiable need to hurt someone, to break something apart. She contemplates the young journalist, with her creamy skin, smart eyes, and hair like a Botticelli muse. The girl *will* suffer. Knowing this, Margaux releases an easy, tranquil breath.

THIRTY-EIGHT

CHICAGO

JULES'S PHONE RINGS. She glances across the kitchen table, reaches past her half-eaten sandwich for the phone, and reads Unknown Caller. It must be Bram Bakker again. She answers.

"Hello, Jules . . . This is Margaux de Laurent." Jules freezes at the sound of the woman's voice, the confirmation of her name. "I believe you're looking for me."

Instinctively, Jules grabs her pen and the back of an envelope closest to her to write things down. *Oh my god.* "Ms. de Laurent, this is unexpected," she manages. "May I ask who referred you?" Her heart beats fast. *Who gave you my number?*

"You may ask." Margaux laughs, and the sound is surprisingly dainty. "My old friend Carice van der Pol mentioned she met you in Amsterdam, that you are working on an article about stolen art and told me to contact you."

I gave Carice van der Pol a fake name and number and never told her I was working on a stolen art piece.

Jules's breath catches as she stares at the refrigerator across from her covered with her mother's collection of magnets filled with silly kitchen quotes like "Your opinion is NOT part of the recipe." And Carice—an old friend? Please. That woman was terrified when Jules mentioned Margaux's name and warned her to stay away. Jules struggles to keep her voice steady while trying to think quickly. "I appreciate the call, and . . . yes . . . I'd welcome the opportunity to interview you. Let's arrange a time." She stops. What would Dan do?

Dan is dead. And this woman had something to do with it.

"Perfect," Margaux replies. "Let's do it in person. I happen to be in Chicago on business. That's why I contacted you. I presume that works for you?"

In person. She's here. Jules starts rapidly doodling intersecting circles on the envelope flap. "Great, yes . . . I can meet you at a café." Get basic information. "Where are you staying, and until when?"

"The Four Seasons . . . and unclear how long."

Unclear. Jules swallows hard. Meet her in a public place no matter what. "I can meet you in the hotel's lounge," she offers. Her heartbeat feels like it is bursting out of her chest. "How is tomorrow morning? Does that work?"

"I'm available right now," Margaux says. "Five o'clock today. Two hours. See you then." She hangs up.

Jules's thoughts become a traffic jam in her head. This woman is dangerous. She clearly knows Jules is onto her. Why is she here, and less than one mile away? Jules stands and paces the kitchen, feeling her foot stick to the dried orange juice that she spilled earlier and forgot to clean up. This could go in any direction. She should get backup.

She glances at the kitchen clock. *Two hours . . .* One to put together questions for a fake interview, the other to get out of her sweats, plan, and get to the hotel. *Think, think.* Chills course down her spine as she wipes up the juice. She should call Adam immediately and let him know that Margaux is here. She should warn her mother, who is at work, perhaps even alert Louise, who is still at the paper. Her entire body is sounding off like a pinball machine. No, she will do the interview first and then contact all of them and report what happened. It's a hotel lounge meetup—a public venue—not a dark alley, not a deserted basement or a clandestine meeting under a bridge. The story is so close now . . . Jules can practically touch it. Best not to do anything to blow it.

She quickly jots down notes—interview questions—then crumples up the paper. She doesn't need notes. She knows this subject, this woman, backward and forward. And at this point, she is an expert on stolen art. She's going to wing it.

At 4:20 p.m., she packs up her tote and walks toward the elevator, then stops in her tracks. *Don't be a fool.* She hears her mother's voice in her head: *You need your team.* She leaves a cryptic message on Louise's voice mail: "Big interview with our blond friend today. Will call after." She then calls her mother, but it, too, goes straight to voice mail. She sends her a text.

> Hi—got an important interview for the story at 5 p.m.—
> Four Seasons. Thai for dinner? Love you.

THIRTY-NINE

S ITTING IN THE hotel lounge with her back facing the wall, Margaux scours the room: the upscale, clubby atmosphere, the soft amber lighting, the dozen or so tables filled with mostly business types and Michigan Avenue shoppers with their multiple packages draping their chairs. No one suspicious. She smiles to herself, inhaling the full-bodied jasmine aroma. *Except for me.*

From the corner of her eye, she spots Jules entering the lounge. The girl is fifteen minutes early, as Margaux knew she would be. She'd arrived even earlier so that Jules didn't have time to get settled. The girl sports a black leather jacket and a cream-colored scarf. It is obvious what Adam sees in her. She exudes confidence. Her tight jeans accentuate long legs, and her chestnut hair is tied back loosely in a bouquet of long curls. She is pretty in that natural, no-makeup way. The type who probably has close friends. *Besties.* Margaux sneers.

Girls never liked me, she reflects. They were always jealous or intimidated. They thought she had it all—unfair beauty, the famous family name, and unlimited resources to do whatever the hell she wanted. They were right about that, but no one really knew how truly alone she was; how she was forced to put two drunken, destructive parents to bed, wipe the vomit from their bloated faces, even remove sharp kitchen knives from their hands when they'd threaten each other after myriad infidelities. By the time Margaux turned fifteen, she stopped cleaning up after them and let them lie drunk on the floor. She ignored the vomit, the knives in their hands. She stepped over them until they no longer mattered. They weren't parents—they were roadkill. Until the one day, a week before her seventeenth birthday, when her mother used the knife that she'd intended for her father on herself. *The knife I placed firmly in her hands after a bender and whispered in her ear: Just fucking do it already.* It was the only time her mother ever listened to her. She slit her wrists in the master bedroom wearing only her father's favorite Hermès tie around her neck. It wasn't a good look.

No matter how hard she tried to camouflage her true self, Margaux's peers could smell her otherness from a mile away. They excluded her from their cliques, and by the time she got to college she stopped trying to fit in. Instead, she took pleasure in being an outcast: exacting revenge, sleeping with other girls' boyfriends, stealing clothes and personal items, and playing mean pranks to pit girls against one another. She reveled in her cruelty, taking pride in breaking up so-called happy couples.

And then along came Carice van der Pol, who stopped Margaux, then in her late twenties, in her reckless tracks. She was young, beautiful, intelligent, and aloof, and, like Margaux, art was all that truly mattered to her. Carice's prominent family owned a half dozen important galleries throughout the Netherlands, but she wanted to be free and sell art on her own terms. She moved to Paris, and DLG hired her immediately to help run the gallery. Carice excelled with clients, had a keen eye for spotting new talent, and was gifted at assembling provocative exhibits. None of this was lost on Margaux. More importantly, Carice had a serious Parisian boyfriend, an up-and-coming jazz musician, and that made her impending seduction of the young woman even more enticing.

It was a Tuesday, the gallery was officially closed, and Margaux knew she'd found her moment. It was just the two of them, busy assembling the new collection of prominent Neo-Expressionists. She watched Carice climb the ladder to hang the large Basquiat canvas, her long, smooth legs peeking out of a skimpy wraparound miniskirt. Margaux stood beneath her, pretending to hold the ladder steady, but instead she reached up and lightly ran her fingertips along the backs of the woman's bare thighs. Carice froze, and Margaux pounced. She led her off the ladder, peeled the large canvas from her trembling hands, and pulled her down to the hardwood floor.

Carice didn't resist as Margaux tore open her blouse and buried her face between her breasts. She then hiked up the young woman's skirt, removed her pale blue thong, and went down on her, relishing the woman's cries of ecstasy beneath her expert tongue. When Carice lay spent on the floor, legs spread like butterfly wings, Margaux smiled to herself, knowing that the musician boyfriend never stood a chance.

Looking past Carice, she met the tortured expression of Jean-Michel Basquiat's signature canvas—a huge coup for the gallery. It was an enormous black skull with bared teeth, painted with strokes of pink lipstick. Oddly, a few years later, when she drugged her father and watched him drown off the side of his yacht, his tormented expression reminded her exactly of this very same painting.

No, Margaux thinks as Jules stands before her table, she's never had a real friend.

Margaux can't help but notice the blatant strength in Jules's hazel eyes as she sits across from her. Admirable. Unlike most who have faced her, this girl does not avert her gaze, twitch, or shrink in fear. Margaux nods at the waitress with one eye on Jules. "Cappuccino with soy, right? That's your drink."

Jules's steeled expression instantly falters. *Yes,* Margaux thinks. *Wyatt Ross may be an ass, but when he's good, there's no one better at obtaining the tiny details that make all the difference.*

"Yes," Jules responds, then opens her bag and takes out a yellow pad and pen, then hits her phone recorder and places it on the table—as though they are about to have an actual interview. Margaux practically bursts out laughing at the charade. Up close, Jules's cheeks are naturally rosy, and her full lips are slightly chapped from the outdoors. She pictures her in bed with Adam and is admittedly turned on by the thought.

Taking her time before speaking, Margaux observes Jules over the white ceramic rim of the coffee mug as she slowly sips her espresso. Jules tries to maintain a poker face under Margaux's intense scrutiny but fails. When she's ready, Margaux slams down the cup for impact. "Let's cut to the chase. I'm not here to discuss an article, and neither are you. You are working on an investigation that I'm at the center of—so let's get to the real story at hand, shall we?"

Jules's mouth drops open, and no words emerge, as though the air has left her lungs. Her eyes expand and she blinks rapidly, clearly struggling to calculate her next move. Perhaps Dan Mansfield was right—she is an amateur. This will be so easy. *Too easy.*

"Let me clarify your situation . . ." Margaux reaches across the table, turns off Jules's phone, and hands it back to her. "I want all of your notes, your research—everything you've got on *Woman on Fire*. Everything you have on me. Everything you think you know about Carl Geisler. Everything you worked on with Dan Mansfield, Ellis Baum, Bram Bakker . . . and Adam Chase." She arches a brow. "Yes, I know all about it—you're fucking him and he's painting you."

Jules is about to deny the undeniable—but Margaux holds up her hands. "Don't even try. The good news is you are going to continue your little exposé, but the even better news is that you're going to put your skills to work for me. You're going to write the story that I tell you to write."

Jules leans forward, fists clenched, elbows jammed into the table. "No, that's not happening."

Surprised, Margaux almost wants to applaud the young woman's audacity. She waits as Jules gathers all her materials, then rises. Margaux smiles. It's adorable. "Sit down," she tells her coldly, tapping the table. "And yes, I'm afraid it *is* happening. You will want to hear what I have to say next. Better yet—I will show you." She picks up her own cell phone, taps in a few digits, and turns its face in Jules's direction.

Jules turns chalk white and braces herself against the table. "No!" she screams loudly, covering her mouth. Heads turn. The nearby waitress stops in her tracks.

"Yes, it's true! Congrats!" Margaux exclaims, loud enough for the onlookers to hear. "I know how hard you've worked for this promotion." She points to the picture on the phone, and her voice lowers to a hiss. "Your mother is difficult and stubborn. I can't say that I'm enjoying her company. But I promise you she will remain alive *only* if you do exactly as you're told."

Jules looks as though she might pass out. "Where is she?"

Margaux ignores the question, elated by the girl's fear. *She's upstairs in my hotel room handcuffed to a chair.* "Her whereabouts are irrelevant. What matters are the rules. Can you follow rules? If anyone—the police, Adam, Ellis Baum, Bram Bakker—gets word of our collaboration—your mother . . ." But Margaux doesn't finish the sentence. She loves this part. *The dangle.* Letting the imagination do all the work for her. "And don't be fooled. I can access anything I choose—your phone, computer, home, the newspaper, your mother's law firm—you name it. In fact, I already have." She crosses her arms and sinks back into the cushion of the chair. "And we both know I don't mess around. Just ask Dan Mansfield and Carl Geisler." *Or the forger*, which she doesn't say.

"Did you kill them?" Jules asks.

"Well, they certainly didn't kill themselves." Margaux is enjoying this.

"You're a monster," Jules manages.

"Believe me, I've been told." She signals for the check. "Tell me, Jules, is an old painting worth your mommy?"

"Why is this painting worth so much to you?" Jules's eyes are shooting bullets at her, and if she could, Margaux knows the girl would pick up the small butter knife in front of her and stab her.

"I just want what is rightfully mine, and the other paintings are a bonus for all my hard work." Margaux watches Jules trying to hold back the tears.

"I will do whatever you want me to do, but don't hurt my mother." Her voice, a mix of tremble and bravado, rises. "Do. Not. Hurt. Her."

Margaux is once again inwardly impressed by the young woman's open defiance, while thoroughly savoring the feather ruffling. Maybe not such an amateur after all. She could go on even longer, but why belabor the fait accompli. "Here's how it's going to go. I want everything. Your notes. Your contacts. All your information. Details on your recent travels—Amsterdam, Germany, and New York. You've been very busy. Drop the package of information off at this hotel by nine p.m. You do that, and if I'm satisfied . . . Liz Roth gets to live another day."

"How will I know that she is okay? I want pictures, proof," Jules says, still not backing down.

"You're sexy when you're demanding—has anyone ever told you that? But I call the shots, not you. You get nothing until I decide when."

By the hard slump of her shoulders, Margaux sees Jules's flicker of strength fizzle out. Satisfied, she pays the bill, stands, and smooths down her black jumpsuit—an outfit too fancy for happy hour but perfect for celebrating. She eyes the young couple holding hands at a nearby table with disdain. "Oh, and one more thing. When you drop the package off at the hotel reception desk, leave it for Elizabeth Roth. And remember, think hard before contacting anyone or doing anything to undermine me. I will know immediately." She plasters on a smile. "It's very simple: If I go down, we all go down."

FORTY

JULES BOLTS OUT of the hotel, makes a sharp left onto Michigan Avenue, and keeps running, her tote bag pounding against her leg. She can't think, can't breathe, can't feel her legs as she arrives at her apartment building. Dashing past Owen, toward the elevator, she hears her doorman's voice behind her asking if everything is okay. She freezes. *No, nothing is okay.*

Slowly turning around, she tries to appear calm. "Owen, did you see anything strange when my mom left the building this morning?"

"No, nothing strange." He scrutinizes her. "Is something wrong?"

Jules tries to keep the tremor out of her voice. "No, yes . . . no. One more thing, did anyone ask about me or try to come to the apartment while I was gone? Packages, anything?"

Owen's dark eyes enlarge with concern. "I've been here all day—nothing. Jules—what is it?"

"I've got to go," she manages. "I'll see you later on, okay?"

Unlocking the door to the apartment, her hand shaking, Jules prays it was all just a hoax, that Margaux was bluffing, that her mother is inside curled up on the couch with a good book drinking her post-work glass of Chardonnay. But when she enters the empty apartment, Jules knows it is all too real. Tears stream down her face as she marches straight to her mother's bedroom. She doesn't know what she's looking for but checks everywhere anyway: the drawers, the walk-in closet, the bathroom, under the bed, on the balcony, and then inside her office. Finding nothing, she heads to her own bedroom and falls helplessly to the floor.

I'm so sorry, Mom, she cries out into the emptiness. She should have stopped the investigation after Dan was murdered. She should have told that detective everything she knew. She shouldn't have risked seeing Bram Bakker in an open airport in Amsterdam on her way back from Baden-Baden. Who does she think she is, taking on Margaux de Laurent?

Squeezing her eyes shut, Jules visualizes that photo on Margaux's phone. Her mother's coiffed, highlighted blond bob in disarray, her favorite midnight blue suit wrinkled, the bow of her silky mauve blouse undone. They had breakfast together before she went to her office. Her mother was fine then. Everything was fine. When did Margaux get to her? Did she ever arrive at her office? Jules glances at her phone, about to call the law office to check, and then quickly hangs up, recalling Margaux's warning words not to contact anyone—that she will know. Jules throws her tapped phone down in front of her as though it were contaminated.

An hour passes as she sits on her bedroom floor contemplating her limited options. She eyes the piles of research lining the entire back wall of her bedroom, the rainbow of sticky notes— everything that has led her to this point: Stolen art. Ernst Engel. The painting. Helmuth and Carl Geisler. Bram Bakker. Lucerne. The Dassels. Ellis Baum . . . *That woman wants it all.*

But she can't have my mother. Jules thinks back to Baden-Baden, when the two of them were soaking together in the hotel's mineral-rich bubbly indoor pool after they met with Lilian Dassel. They planned to spend the evening at the casino. Her mother was right. *Why not have some fun while they were there.* It was a perfect moment, until her mother said, "Honey, I think I know why this story means so much to you. It's not just a story. This is about you, isn't it?" She smoothed down Jules's wet hair and played with a few random strands that had already begun to curl up.

"What do you mean?"

"I mean, Dan was a bit of a father figure for you."

"Dan was *not* a father figure—he was my mentor, my friend. Really, Mom? You're going there? I never lacked for anything, okay. You've been the best mom and dad rolled into one. This is about passing a torch, about doing the right thing . . . Dan's story became my story. And yes, I don't want to let him down. He's dead, I get it. But I still hear his voice in my head. Remember, it was you who taught me to fight for the truth, no matter what." She held up her fists. "So, sorry to disappoint, Dr. Freud, but this is not about an AWOL father, it's about fighting the good fight."

Liz Roth, always so quick on the return, was silenced because what Jules said was true, and you can argue with everything, but not the truth—her mother's own words. "Perhaps I forgot to tell you the other thing," her mother countered. "Some truths are best remained buried." She takes Jules's wet hand inside her own. "The trick is knowing what to hold on to tightly and when to let go." Big on having the last word, her mother released her hand and then climbed the few steps out of the pool. She turned back and posed—Liz Roth in full form—giving Jules that superior look of higher rank. "I love you, but you're too much like me, which means be careful."

Jules begins to pray as she gathers up her research for Margaux de Laurent. *I can't lose you, Mom. Please, stay alive.* She makes copies of the most important documents in the home office, then shoves all the paperwork into a small duffel bag. Think hard, she tells herself. Don't allow your emotion to cloud reason. The Rules: *Know thy subject . . . Margaux de Laurent is not about the get, but about the game.* Isn't that what Adam warned them all the first time she met him back at the cabin?

Because of that, Jules decides not to relinquish any information on Lilian Dassel. It is her ace of spades, what that monster wants more than anything. If Jules gives up the prized information now, if that woman wins *too* quickly, then her mother is dead in the water. *Game over.*

Her phone dings. A text from Louise:

Are you okay?

No, Louise, not okay. My mother is being held hostage by the woman who killed Dan and it's all my fault. She types back, just in case her phone is tapped:

Yes, all good.

Jules glances out her opened bedroom door into the empty living room space. Louise's text has reminded her that she still has one more play at her disposal. Inhaling deeply, she gets up off the carpet, walks briskly to the front hallway, and reaches for her tote bag. She checks inside just to be sure and feels a smidgen of hope. As Louise would say, the only way to win this one is to go *old-school.*

FORTY-ONE

"A RE YOU CRAZY, Margaux? You kidnapped the mother?" Wyatt Ross shouts into the phone. "We have enough problems and now this? You should have told me first. I would have made sure—"

"I'm telling you now." Margaux cuts him off as she looks around the hotel lounge, which is practically empty at nine-thirty p.m. Typical boring Midwest. Not like New York, where the action is just getting started. "You're on probation with me, remember? At least the ball is now back in my court, where it belongs. Here's the plan. I have two men who will be picking her up in a few hours and taking her back to Correns. My plane is at Midway Airport, and it's going to leave with her on it and a duffel bag filled with documents from the daughter, Jules Roth. You're going to collect the mother and the documents and send those men and my plane directly back to New York. I will be taking a commercial flight home in the morning."

"Wait—back up. You kidnapped the mother *and* have all of Roth's research—how did you do all this?" *Without me* are his unspoken words.

"Believe me, it was by far the easiest thing I've done all week." Let that sink in. "Now give me an update on the paintings."

There's a long pause. Wyatt clears his throat. "We've earned nearly sixty million dollars paid in Bitcoin so far. That's net—after the mafia and those skinheads took their large cut for fronting the works and keeping us out of it. And that's just from the sale of four paintings. I'm happy to say we didn't have to give them away as I'd originally thought to divert attention from us. And I've also had over seventy inquiries for more paintings on shadow sites. The good news is that these works are moving. There's a demand, but—"

"But what?" Margaux interrupts, taking a long, hard drag on her cigarette.

"According to my contact in Sicily, Bram Bakker has been prying, asking all the right questions about the Geisler stash. My thought is that we've come away from this with major profits and we should lie low, not put any more paintings on the market at least until after Basel. If we continue at this pace—"

"I thought you said we needed to move quickly or the paintings will lose value."

"I did, and they will. But that was before Bakker began sniffing around, getting a little too close for comfort."

Margaux exhales deeply. "Fine, stop everything on that front for now. But on the flip side, Griffin Freund is killing it, placing paintings right and left with his cartel clients. And believe me, those drug dealers couldn't care less if the paintings are hot—in fact, they prefer it—badges of honor. They are outbidding one another, and I don't intend to slow down those sales. Freund sold six in just three days last week. He wants more," she says pointedly. "And you're going to supply him."

"I strongly recommend we hit the pause button across the board," Wyatt emphasizes. "Just think about it, okay?" He takes a dramatic breath. "And another thing . . . as far as Bakker is concerned, your little Chicago busybody met with him in Schiphol Airport on her way back from Baden-Baden with her mother. I've got a photo in my hands of the three of them sitting openly at an airport café. We need to find out exactly what that was about."

"Agreed. I'm on it," Margaux says. "And, Wyatt, I'm about to get my money's worth out of you. *You* will be babysitting Elizabeth Roth until I can get back to Correns." She smiles to herself, picturing his stunned reaction. "Keep her in the cellar, feed her, and find out everything you can." She pauses. "This time, do your fucking job."

MARGAUX FINISHES HER cigarette and her scotch, then heads up to the hotel room on the fifth floor. She finds Jules's mother where she left her several hours ago, sitting on the armchair in the corner of the room, cuffed and gagged. She is in her stockings; her low-heeled black pumps are placed next to the bed, and her boxy suit jacket is laid neatly on top of it. Margaux removes the woman's gag and uncuffs her, then warns her with a gun pressed to her temple not to move or scream. *Or else.*

Margaux then sits on the bed across from the woman, gun pointed. "Enjoying the view?"

Liz grits her teeth as she rubs her wrists. "I've seen better."

Margaux laughs. "I'm sure you have. Just to give you an update . . . in a few hours you're going to take another European vacation—even better than Baden-Baden. Your diligent daughter is now working for me in order to save your life. We cut a deal a few hours ago." She pauses, giving the woman a moment to digest her situation. "Now I'm going to offer you a chance to save Jules right back." She leans forward. "Information will help your cause."

Liz's face turns white. "Why should I believe you?" she challenges. "You killed Dan Mansfield—right? Why would you spare me or my daughter? I demand to know before I give you anything."

"You demand?" Margaux refrains from clapping. *Ballsy, like her daughter.* "I *allegedly* killed Dan Mansfield," she corrects her. "You're a lawyer. Be careful of assumptions before you have all the facts. But this is not about Mansfield; it's about Jules."

The woman's face falls predictably. "What have you done to her?"

"Nothing. To be perfectly frank, it's in my best interest to keep her alive and healthy to do all my legwork. She's quite good at what she does. I get why Dan hired her. Very organized. But there are blanks—missing pieces—that I'm expecting *you* to fill in."

Liz crosses her arms and glares. Margaux imagines she's a killer in the courtroom. "And once you get what you want?" she says.

"Let me put it this way: not once, *when.* I will get exactly what I want from you."

The woman meets Margaux's gaze sharply. "And if I don't comply?"

"Noncompliance is a choice," Margaux tells her. "Is Jules's life worth a painting?"

The woman squints, weighing her very limited options. "I'm not doing or saying anything without hard evidence that my daughter will be okay."

"Like mother, like daughter." Margaux smiles tightly, thinking her own dead, drunken mother would have readily handed her over for a bottle of Cristal and some top-shelf cocaine. "What you need to understand is that Jules is in this way over her head. If I were you, I'd start telling the truth, everything you know, and I give my word that she won't get hurt. Here's the deal . . . I am looking for a painting that is rightfully mine. That's what matters to me. You give me that and I will reward you for the information."

"What matters to you is *you*," Liz counters. "I've prosecuted your type for years."

"My type? You mean psychopaths." This is more fun than Margaux thought it would be. "Good, then I don't have to explain myself. You *know* exactly what you're dealing with here. Let's save ourselves time and energy. We both know I won't stop until I get what I want."

"And you won't stop then either, because it's never enough."

"You seem to *really* know my type," Margaux sneers. "Let's play a game and see where we end up. Why was Adam Chase at your apartment?"

Liz remains mute. Margaux takes a shallow breath. She could hurt her. She could pull every highlighted hair out of the woman's head strand by strand. It would be so damn easy. "Your silence is only going to impact your daughter. But again, your choice."

Margaux stands, hovering over her, and Liz shrinks back. "I have photos in my hand of Adam Chase in your building, sitting on a bench in the lobby—why was he there? What were you *really* doing in Baden-Baden? Why did Jules meet with Bram Bakker in Amsterdam on your way back to Chicago? Why were *you* sniffing around for financial information about my galleries? You *will* answer the questions."

But, determined to hold her ground, the woman keeps her lips sealed tightly. Margaux wants to slap her. "In case I'm not perfectly clear, Counselor, my hacker—whom you will soon meet—has been tapping into your law office computers. So I will know exactly what you've been up to. None of what you or Jules has on me or my galleries is privileged information. You are only alive right now because I need you to fill in the blanks and I don't have time to waste."

"You're going to kill me anyway."

"Maybe, maybe not. And for the record, it won't be me." Margaux hears three quick knocks at her door. *They're early.* She kicks the woman's practical shoes out of her way as she goes to answer it. "I'd advise you to cooperate. Your daughter is going to do everything she can to save your ass. The least you could do is give her the courtesy of *trying* to stay alive."

FORTY-TWO

ART BASEL, MIAMI

MARGAUX GLIDES ACROSS the courtyard of the Versace Mansion. All eyes are glued to her as she strikes a pose, hand to hip, Judith Leiber crystal clutch at her side, soaking up the adulation. She's back with a bang and owes Griffin Freund big-time. Everybody who is anybody showed up to her party, touted as the hottest ticket in town, featuring of-the-moment artist Adam Chase making his Basel comeback. She beams at the well-wishers. *My party, my comeback.*

She eyes Jules from across the room and is pleased. The girl looks spectacular in the one-shouldered bandage dress that she sent her and mandated she wear tonight. Hervé Léger never disappoints. And the rest of it . . . the mane of curls tumbling down the girl's back, the curves, the makeup. She followed Margaux's orders to a T. Jules is now her marionette. That's the beauty of *or else*. It buys unlimited string-pulling power.

She spots Griffin mingling in the distance with a group of collectors, planting the seeds for the latest batch of stolen paintings she's just sent him. That guy knows how to work it. One hand is pressed against a potential client's shoulder, and the other arm is draped loosely around Henri Lamonte, the world-renowned photographer. *Ellis Baum's former lover.* Margaux squeezes her fists. She will deal with that situation right after Basel.

And there's Adam, standing on the far side of the courtyard, in a private corner, being interviewed by *ARTnews*. His paintings are scattered throughout the courtyard and around the opulent pool deck. Each canvas is displayed with gold candles surrounding it like a ritual circle. *Woman, Unplugged*—as the series is now called—is comprised mostly of abstract images of Jules Roth. *As if I don't know.* Margaux smiles wryly. After Basel, she'll deal with him too.

Smoothing down her custom-made Tom Ford tuxedo mini-dress, she turns her attention to the covered masterpiece in the center of the space—the only painting that truly matters tonight. It's waiting for her like a shy girl hiding behind her high school locker. She feels the resentment jolt through her like a lightning rod. *You're a fake!* she yearns to shout at the forged canvas. Holding in her breath, she forcibly wills away the mounting anger. She's promised all the reporters who came out tonight that she will be delivering something spectacular in addition to the highly anticipated Adam Chase resurrection, and she will. Margaux has no doubts that within minutes of the painting's unveiling, it will make headlines around the globe. She manufactures a broad smile, feeling the heat of the cameras flashing around her.

Plucking two flutes of champagne off a roaming server's tray, she walks toward Jules. Up close, the girl is nervous and can't hide it. Margaux brushes her hand over the girl's velvety, exposed shoulder, savoring the revulsion in Jules's eyes. "You look perfect. Take good notes," Margaux whispers. "I promised the *Miami Herald* an exclusive for the Sunday magazine and the international edition. I convinced the editor to let *you* write the story and interview me. You'll be writing it later tonight."

From the corner of her eye, Margaux sees Adam observing their interaction. By the confused look on his face it is clear that he really had no idea that Jules would be here. According to Wyatt, Jules has kept up her end of the deal all week with her sworn silence. Apparently, all her portals have remained squeaky clean as well. She has contacted no one of importance and has stayed off the grid, as instructed. There was that questionable moment earlier in the evening when Adam spotted Jules and tried to talk to her. But Margaux put an immediate stop to the interaction. And Jules played along, knowing any false move would put her mother's life in jeopardy.

Margaux lightly strokes Jules's arm, then lands a kiss on her lips just to mess with her, side glancing at Adam, hoping he catches that too. *See, two can play this game. I just play it better.* From the corner of her eye, she notices that her assistant is signaling her over. Margaux nods back. *It's time.*

Leaving Jules, she makes her way to the makeshift podium, positioning herself next to the painting. Her assistant hands her a microphone, and she waits for the crowd to simmer down. Truthfully, Margaux prefers to stretch out this exquisite moment. She's earned it. Amid the claps, the cheers, and the fanfare, she feels her phone vibrating against her chest nonstop. She ignores it at first, but it won't stop buzzing. She reaches inside the hidden pocket of her tuxedo jacket and quickly hands the phone to her assistant. "Answer it," she orders through her pasted-on smile.

Her assistant leans in. "The man says it's an emergency."

Wyatt Ross. "Tell him I'm busy right now."

The girl looks scared. "He said to tell you, 'Do not let the girl out of your sight . . .'"

Margaux stares across the room at Jules. *What the hell are you up to?* She will personally kill her—dismember her—if she ruins this night for her. "Tell him I've got it covered." Then, lowering her voice, Margaux leans over and whispers instructions into her assistant's ear. The girl smiles elegantly at the onlookers, then scurries off. Margaux clears her throat, adjusts her stance slightly, ensuring that the candlelight glow reflects the sparkle in her eyes for the nearby cameras.

"Good evening. I'm Margaux de Laurent . . ." she begins. Rich, slow, and mesmerizing. She's been told that she has a pitch-perfect voice, and she certainly knows how to work a room. This isn't her first Basel rodeo, but it will be her most memorable. Just look at them, eating out of her hand as she relays the extraordinary tale of the legendary Grand-papa Charles de Laurent and how he made it his life's mission to save modern art during the war, risking everything . . . *God, am I good.*

Margaux slowly lists the famous paintings that her grandfather rescued to rounds of applause, followed by a predictable standing ovation. While speaking, she notes approvingly that the Door Girl, one of her six handpicked hired female security guards, is moving briskly through the crowd, heading toward Jules.

"This painting"—Margaux points behind her at the covered canvas—"created by the incomparable Ernst Engel, founder of the Expressionist movement, once belonged to my grandfather." Her face turns solemn, flawlessly funereal. "It was seized from his gallery in Paris in 1939 by Hitler's art thief, Helmuth Geisler." She pauses for a moment of silence to let that crucial fact sink in.

Everyone in the room knows about the Geisler treasure trove, the murder of his son, and the billion-dollar heist. It is the biggest art story to have hit their community in decades. Margaux goes on to describe the personal meaning of this exquisite painting to her family—especially to her dying grandmother—and how she knew as a young girl that it would be her life's mission to one day find it.

Margaux then shares the exhilarating moment when she heard that an Engel was rumored to be among the stolen art in Geisler's collection. She just knew in her heart that the lost canvas, which meant *everything* to her family, existed. "And then"— she wipes away fake tears from her eyes, fabricates the perfect tremor in her voice—"I heard through a source that it landed in the wrong hands. Yes, my friends . . . as you can all imagine, it has been a grueling experience trying to get it back."

She stops speaking to collect herself. Her assistant, who has since returned to her side, hands her a tissue right on cue. Margaux nods appreciatively, thinking this girl will get a bonus for that one. Cameras click and flash. The optics couldn't be better. "When I'm ready, I promise I will share all the details, everything that went into locating this magnificent painting." She gestures again to the canvas and to her assistant. "Without further ado, I present *Woman on Fire*, Ernst Engel's final work."

The painting is unveiled in one dramatic swoop.

The surround sound of thundering applause is so staggering that Margaux can feel the ground shaking beneath her stilettos. She sees tears in her guests' eyes. Art reporters are scribbling feverishly and making their way over to her. She meets Adam's shocked glare. *Yes, I did just blow this up. Oh, and tell your dying grandfather that the painting is now safe with me.*

The phone that was discreetly placed at the base of the canvas vibrates relentlessly. She looks down. Wyatt Ross. *Again.*

"This better be good," Margaux seethes into the phone as a dozen reporters begin to swarm around her.

"Do not let that girl out of your sight."

"I heard—why?"

"She knows where the real painting is," he shouts. "She fucking knows."

FORTY-THREE

THE DOOR GIRL shoves Jules into the waiting vehicle and hands off her purse to the driver. Before Jules can scream for help, somebody places a bag over her head and cuffs her hands. She can barely breathe. *Where are they taking her?* Her throat constricts, and she feels as though a noose is tightening around her as she leans against the cold leather seat, shivering in her skimpy dress.

As the car accelerates, Jules wills herself to stay calm, to focus on details, to go over the evening's chain of events. *Adam.* She thinks back to the beginning of the night when she walked around the pool deck and first saw his display of paintings—his new series. Only it isn't a series of those women she saw displayed on his inspiration board—*it is her*. The one painting for which she modeled, and others that he must have painted from memory in different angles, various poses. She is the mainstay of his exhibition.

Huge mistake. Why would he do that? As if Margaux doesn't know that it is Jules in the paintings. Squeezing her eyes tightly, she recalls Adam's shock when he saw her enter the party from across the room.

"Why are you here? Why are you dressed like that? And why haven't I heard from you?" he demanded after spotting her and racing over to where she was standing. Jules quickly glanced over at Margaux, who was nearby, locked in a circle of admirers.

"Why did you paint *me*? What happened to the inspiration board?" she managed under her breath as Margaux stopped her conversation and started quickly making her way over to them.

"It was a surprise. I . . . was inspired."

"Jesus, Adam—" Jules knew she had mere seconds to alert him about her mother. "She's got my—"

Before she could utter another word, Margaux quickly intervened, wrapping her arm loosely around Adam. "I see you've met Jules. She's a journalist from Chicago working on a . . . major art story. I invited her here as my guest. Jules"—she pointed behind her to the circle she just left—"that's the editor I told you about. He's waiting to meet you. *Now*." She gently pushed Jules in that direction and gave her a warning look: *Don't even think about it.*

And that was it. Margaux whisked Adam away, looping her arm through his, locking him against her. He glanced back at Jules quizzically. She shook her head, wishing she could scream out the truth. He must have thought that she'd fooled Margaux about the stolen art story and that's why she was here. *She has my mom, Adam. She has her.* But Adam had already turned away, perhaps thinking he was helping Jules by keeping up the charade.

And then later . . . after the painting unveiling, before she knew what was happening to her, before she could contact Adam somehow, the Door Girl grabbed her arm tightly and demanded that she follow her immediately out of the party or her mother would pay the price.

What could she have done? And the painting . . . *How is that even possible? How did Margaux find it?* There's no way she discovered Lilian Dassel's existence that quickly, and no way in hell that Lilian revealed the painting's whereabouts. Unless . . . Jules thinks fearfully, *Unless my mother was forced to tell the story.* Or unless . . . Jules's heart beats rapidly, and her eyes light up with a glimmer of hope, despite her dire situation. Margaux is exhibiting the forgery.

THIRTY MINUTES OR so later, the car stops moving, the automatic locks open, and the bag is removed from Jules's head. She gathers her breath as the driver roughly pulls her out of the car and toward a mammoth Spanish-roofed villa with bougainvillea climbing all over it. The outdoor landscape is lit up in cheesy neon colors. The driver, whose face she now sees clearly, is around thirty with large round eyes, close-cropped red hair, and an anchor beard tracing his jawline. He pushes her forward toward the house and unlocks the front door, and Jules finds herself standing in the entryway next to an enormous floral arrangement filled with fresh calla lilies.

Scanning the sprawling black-and-white marble foyer, she notices the floor-to-ceiling paintings lining the walls and continuing up along the spiral staircase. The man then leads her inside the nearby library, points to the couch, and tells her to sit and not move. He plants himself directly across from her and lays a gun casually across his lap. Staring with those lifeless, globular eyes, he says nothing except, "You don't look like your mother."

Jules's heart sinks. *He's seen my mother. Is she alive?* She yearns to ask him a hundred questions, but he looks like a killer, so she says nothing. There is nowhere to go, nowhere to run. She's a prisoner here. Stilling herself, Jules focuses on the large painting across from her—a Chagall. It's a colorful allegorical dream scene. She's seen it somewhere before. Her face goes slack when she realizes that it was listed as a painting allegedly in Geisler's stolen art collection. It was confiscated from a prominent German Jewish collector during the war. She saw a photograph of the painting while doing her research. *Where am I? Whose house is this?* She inspects the room, searching for clues with just her eyes, keeping her head frozen, afraid of setting off the driver.

A few hours or so later, Margaux walks in. She is no longer wearing her evening attire. She changed into baggy jeans, low boots, and a loose black sweater. She whispers something to the driver. He nods, hands her his gun, and then uncuffs Jules and leaves the room.

Margaux takes his seat, sparks up a cigarette, and points to the painting behind her. "Yes, I know exactly what you're thinking because I now know *how* you think. That piece was in your research—wasn't it? I think you had a pink sticky note over it marked 'stolen.' From my perspective, it's one of the paintings I *rescued*." She takes a long, dramatic drag and blows smoke toward the ceiling like a Hollywood ingenue. "I'm afraid your good friend Bram Bakker, art detective extraordinaire, missed that one."

Margaux slowly crosses her legs as though she has all day, and they are two girlfriends catching up. "In case you're wondering, this is the home of one of our more important clients, who is thrilled to host us for the evening. And, so you know, tonight was a huge success." Her eyes light up. "In just a few minutes, you're going to interview me for the story on stolen art as we planned, the extraordinary tale of how I found the painting that rightfully belongs to my family hidden in a small obscure town in . . . how about Piacenza? I've always loved it there. You're going to make the case as to why I'm the legal heir to this painting. You can throw in a line or two about *forced* sales and the law. I've got all the legal documents to back it up. You know all about forced sales, right? It was there in your research. Under the Washington Conference Principles section—with a yellow sticky note. It was that international meetup calling all European art sold between 1933 and 1945 'suspect' and saying it requires closer inspection." Margaux's mouth quirks upward on one side, and it's frightening. "The way I see it, there is a moral issue at stake here. If I stole from the art robbers—does that make me a villain or a hero?" She cups her chin, as if she were a professor discussing an open-ended philosophical question. Jules remains silent, does not move a muscle.

"After I approve your article," she continues, "we're flying together to see a friend of yours in Baden-Baden—which, to be honest, I'm a bit tired of all the travel this past month. Too much back-and-forth. But this trip seems highly worth my time—wouldn't you say? Apparently, your friend knows where the *real* painting is."

The real *painting*, Jules confirms in her head. The one shown tonight was indeed the fake. But she knows about Lilian. Her mother must have . . . She squeezes her eyes shut briefly. "Is my mother alive?" she manages.

"For now . . ." Margaux's cold gaze never leaves Jules's relieved face. "And yes, that was the forgery I presented tonight. Our little secret. And we're going to keep it that way. The fake, however, will have its use. It will be placed in a museum of my choice, and I will get all the credit for that. The real painting, however, will be coming home with me to the South of France—back where it belongs. And you're going to make sure that it does . . ."

Or else. Jules can't stop the hot tears from rising to the surface. Everything has gone totally wrong, and her mother will surely pay the price.

Margaux hands her a tissue, then reaches inside her large Birkin bag for a micro stick recorder and places it on the coffee table in front of Jules. "You have been chasing me since the day you met Dan Mansfield," she says. "I've decided to celebrate my success by giving you the real story—*all of it*. It's my gift for your hard work. So wipe away your tears and get ready for truth—*answers*. That's what you live . . . and die for, isn't it, Jules?"

Jules is too afraid to speak, to think. She watches Margaux fondle the base of the gun, head cocked, narcissism in full bloom. She knows that look. She's seen it on numerous politicians, myriad celebrities, and those VIPs who believe that without them the world would stop, that they are larger than life. Margaux *wants* to reveal the truth, wants to brag about her depraved escapades. She wants to scare her. But it's more than that . . . This woman craves an audience. What's the point in outsmarting everyone—claiming victory—if you have no one to tell? But if she tells all, Jules thinks, panicking, then she will have to kill me.

"Start!" Margaux orders.

Start? Jules stares at her, not blinking, not quite comprehending.

"Goddamn it, I said, start the interview now!"

Jules kicks into high gear. No notes, no prep. Her mother's life and hers depend on it. This story, this so-called interview, is buying her time. So she begins . . .

"Your name is Margaux de Laurent—where were you born and tell me about your childhood . . ."

Jules keeps going with question after question. Every minute that she fills up is yet another minute that her mother stays alive. But deeper down, in a place that she can't quite access right now, she pushes Margaux for intimate details because no matter how much she despises this woman, Margaux holds the key to this story, carte blanche into a world of art that Jules has only researched but this woman has lived. As the interview progresses, Jules begins to lose herself in the making of Margaux de Laurent, brilliant psychopathic art dealer, mastermind of sinister and destructive behaviors. But beneath it all, she is sad and damaged. Completely alone.

Jules presses her fingers to her temple. "Tell me about the Geisler murder . . . how did you get away with it?"

"I prefer to share a better story that I got away with . . ." Margaux swells with excitement. "The story of my father's death nearly five years ago. The night that Adam Chase murdered him. You know Adam, right? The guy I introduced you to this evening. The artist. Yeah, him." She lightly smacks her lips. "It was a nice act you two presented, considering that you slept in his bed just a few weeks ago. And that he came to Chicago to visit you. And that every painting he showcased tonight was *you*. Do I look stupid?" Margaux gets up, walks toward the bar in the corner, and pours herself some wine. She pours a glass for Jules as well. "I'm going to pair this story with a good Syrah . . . you'll need it."

Margaux never brought anyone to Correns. It was her sanctuary. Her precious memories of her grandfather were all there. Her escape from the rest of the world was there. No one else deserved to see that part of her life, and she fiercely protected it. But Carice van der Pol was different. She was the first woman Margaux had ever felt close to—a real connection. She found herself laughing with Carice, discussing art, and even opening up about her dysfunctional family, because Carice's family was not much different than hers. And when they had sex, Margaux was present and experienced something akin to intimacy. Carice was also her first real friend. If ever she loved anyone other than her grandfather—Carice van der Pol was it. But even then, it was never enough to fill the bottomless void. There was Adam too.

Carice was her lover in Europe and Adam was her lover in the States—a perfect divide. But this one weekend Margaux made the fatal mistake of bringing both worlds together to the only place that ever mattered to her. When Sébastien de Laurent announced to his daughter that for her thirtieth birthday he planned on throwing her a party at the vineyard—her favorite place—and then they would set sail on the yacht together for a few days, Margaux was taken aback. Her father was celebrating *her* for the very first time, wanting to spend time with her for once. She was hesitant to agree, because Sébastien never did anything without an ulterior motive. Ignoring her instinct twice in one day, Margaux said yes to her father, and then she invited both Adam and Carice to join her.

The long weekend was a perfect blend of drugs and sex and food and drink. Sébastien draped his arm around his daughter as they celebrated at the house, on the patio under the twinkle lights. Margaux danced with him, laughed with him, allowed herself to be seduced by her father's wily charms. She finally understood why everyone gravitated to his larger-than-life personality. It was as though she were meeting her father anew, and for once, admittedly, she didn't hate him.

Adam, however, was not doing well. Not only had the heroin become a problem, but also, he could no longer hide his addiction in public. There was a knock much later that night at her bedroom door. She was in there with Carice. It was the butler.

"Mlle Margaux—your friend, the young man. I'm very sorry . . . he's in bad shape. Please come with me."

Margaux ran downstairs and out back by the pool, where she found Adam lying facedown on the patio tile, convulsing. His skin was so pale, he was gasping for air, and his lips were practically purple. She wrapped him in her arms. "Adam—please not now. Not this weekend. Not here. We discussed this . . ."

"I needed it, Margaux . . . Needed it . . ." He started vomiting, choking, and he was delirious. How much did he have? What he really needed was a hospital. But Margaux didn't want the headlines, and more than that, she didn't want this perfect weekend to end. There was a very discreet doctor in town. She called him, begged him to meet her as soon as possible in a private room at the hospital. She had the butler carry Adam out to her car. She left messages for Carice and her father, letting them know what was going on and that she would most likely be spending the night at the hospital, until Adam, who was being administered a heavy dose of Narcan, had stabilized.

As the night wore on, Margaux changed her mind. Her gut told her to get back home.

It was nearly 4:00 a.m. when she climbed up the winding staircase to her bedroom, exhausted and depleted. She walked into her room and froze when she saw the rise of Carice's heart-shaped ass, bouncing up in the air, then a pair of hairy legs strapped around her. *Her father.* She'd seen them dancing together at the party earlier, pressed together, but he danced like that with everyone. She also saw him eyeing Carice at the dinner—but her father eyed everyone that way. What she didn't see was Carice eyeing him right back. Carice was *too* much like her—she enjoyed the game even more than the prize. They didn't see Margaux standing in the doorway. *Good.* They both thought she was still with Adam. Margaux slithered out of the room, letting them fuck, letting them laugh, letting them think they pulled one over on her.

The birthday celebration continued on the yacht the following evening. The champagne flowed, the music played all night, the drugs were top of the line. Her boozy father put his arms around her. "You'll always remember this night, *mon cœur.*"

"Always." She hugged him back.

Margaux bided her time. Later that night, Carice was sleeping on one side of the bed in the main cabin, and Adam, still recuperating, was asleep on the other pillow. They three had shared the bed together earlier. Only she wasn't there, just her body on autopilot, moving in sync with theirs, an erotic entanglement of body parts. But she was gone, disassociated, numbed out as she stared at her two lovers. One a cheat, the other an addict. And when they finally fell asleep, Margaux got up and sat in the armchair facing them, strategizing.

A half hour later, she woke up Adam with a syringe in hand. "You want this, right?" She dangled the needle over his head as he stirred, still weak from the overdose and all that Narcan. She brought her other finger to her lips. "Don't wake up Carice. It's our secret."

"Yes." His glassy eyes were lit as he reached for the syringe. "More than anything."

She pulled it away, out of his reach. "Not yet, but soon. Come with me. You do something for me first, and then I'll do this for you."

Her father, she knew, was out on the deck, practically passed out over a chaise lounge where she'd left him earlier in the night.

She looked at Adam, who hadn't taken his eyes off the drugs in her hands. "My father wants to go for a swim. Help me push him in and you'll get your fix. As much as you want, Adam . . . I promise."

Adam looked conflicted. *He's a good guy*, she thought, shaking her head. A good guy with a very bad habit. "I don't think so, Margaux."

She dangled the needle in front of him, went over to the water, and pretended to drop it into the sea. "Do it now, or else."

Or else . . . Her magic words.

Her bear of a father splayed his fleshy arms as she and Adam lifted him to the edge of the yacht, and then Margaux stood back.

"Now," she ordered Adam. "Push him."

But Adam, in his weakened, hazy state, hesitated. "Do it, you goddamn loser!" she shouted, but he was frozen with his hands on her father. She didn't have time for this. She rushed behind Adam and shoved his hands with all thirty years of built-up rage, loneliness, and abandonment. She then stood back as her father toppled over the ledge. The final push was so clean and swift that Sébastien barely made a splash, like a giant boulder landing in pool of Jell-O. He struggled, the fear filling his eyes, his teeth chattering, as he was struck by the realization that his death warrant had been issued by his own daughter. Margaux felt nothing short of triumphant.

Just as he took his final breath, Margaux turned to see Carice standing behind her in a white T-shirt, nipples erect through the thin cottony material, her mouth dropped open with guilt and realization—*a silent, piercing scream*. She knew this was about her.

"Look at his face, Carice, at those bared teeth," Margaux said in a detached, dead-calm voice. "Doesn't it remind you of that Basquiat painting?"

Jules is horrified when Margaux finishes the story. "And the rest is history." Margaux swipes her hands against her jeans. "Adam Chase, your lover, your painter, can add 'murderer' to his credits. And Carice had her fingerprints all over the drugs my father took before he drowned, I made sure of that. I was also able to pay off the local police to keep it quiet and report Sébastien's death as an accident."

"But none of that is true," Jules argues. "*You* drugged your father. You drugged Adam. You framed Carice. You were behind that push. You're the murderer."

Margaux uses her fingers as a gun. "Get the facts straight. Adam was *not* drugged. Adam *wanted* drugs. He wanted them so badly that he was willing to push my father into the sea for one syringe. And yes, I was there behind him driving that push, but Adam *thinks* he did it. His guilt, not mine. Another truth for you . . . my father would have been dead either way. His drink was loaded with strychnine—a poison meant for rats—a drink that Carice unknowingly handed him earlier in the night. Perfect, right? Carice believes that she inadvertently poisoned my father. So, I bought her silence until you started snooping around. See the beauty in all this, Jules? It's textbook. Seeming and being. Read your Shakespeare." She stands, stares at the bookcase behind her. "Killing someone is not the rush; not even close. It's the before and the after that matters. The planning and the getting away with it." Reveling in her power, she turns to Jules. "Tell me, who has more control, the puppet or the puppeteer? It's that simple."

"Why would you risk revealing all this?" Jules asks Margaux, trying to mask her fear. *There's only one reason.*

"I now know you. The thrill is finding the story, isn't it? The seeking of answers no matter the risk. I'm just taking all the fun out of it for you." Her smirk turns steely. "Now that we finished the interview, you have three hours to write the story that I want the world to read. The driver is bringing you a laptop and a change of clothes, and he'll sit with you while I rest up. And then . . ."

Jules awaits her fate, but Margaux grabs her recorder off the table and gets up to leave, never finishing her sentence.

FORTY-FOUR

BADEN-BADEN, GERMANY

I F LILIAN DASSEL were a good decade younger, she might have enjoyed this, the twist, the intrigue of it all. But now she's tired, older than most, exhausted from a life spent avenging her tragic childhood. As she scrutinizes the two women standing before her, one she's met before and the other a fancy-looking one eyeing her like she's lunch, Lilian understands that the plot has just thickened.

She received the urgent message from the director yesterday. It was from the girl. It read: *Tell Frau Dassel that someone is coming to discuss the painting.* The director asked Lilian if she knew what it was about. She lied and said yes. She lied because she did not intend to die without knowing exactly what would happen to the painting.

The fancy one speaks first. "Lilian, I'm Margaux de Laurent. I'm an art dealer." She extends her hand. "You may have heard of me . . ."

"No, I'm afraid I haven't." Lilian ignores the outstretched

hand and instead observes Jules, who is giving her strange eyes. The girl looks terrified, different from the last time they met, as though trying to cover up something. Or being *forced* to do so. She's seen those eyes too many times—retracted pupils, white and wide open with fear. She lived with that same haunted gaze every single day in Auschwitz, and much later in the wee hours of her nightmares. The girl is hiding something.

"Why are you really here?" Lilian smooths her pouf of white, windblown hair away from her face. She insisted on coming outside even though it is cold, even though there is snow covering the ground. Everyone knows that when Lilian Dassel needs air, it's not air—it's oxygen. Her triggers come without warning, charred memories screaming for breath.

"You have a painting that belongs to me," Margaux says simply.

"Belongs to you. Belongs to YOU!" Lilian roars with laughter. *Who is this woman?* This explains the girl's scared eyes. "That damn painting—is that it? All the lives it has taken with it. Why is it yours, Miss Fancy?" She looks at Jules. "And why not hers? Or why not his?" She points a bony finger at an old man in the distance, bundled up in so many layers that he looks like an igloo. "Tell me, Ms. de Laurent—why do *you* deserve the painting?"

Margaux crosses her arms, clearly not used to being confronted. "Because it belonged to my grandfather, stolen from him during the war. I plan to donate it to a museum to honor it, to honor you."

Lilian's piercing eyes turn to icicles. "A museum? Those scoundrels? That would be the last place I would hang my painting. You don't strike me as a woman who honors honor." She glances at Jules. "Am I right, young lady?" She stares down Margaux.

Margaux shoots Jules a threatening glare that Lilian catches immediately. She knows that look too. "Go ahead, tell her the truth," Margaux tells Jules. "I don't have time for this."

Jules answers carefully. "Frau Dassel, please listen to her . . . She has my mother. Do you remember her? I brought her here to meet you. Please, for me, tell her where the painting is, and then my mother goes free." Jules's eyes become watery, and she wills the tears away, but Lilian is clever. She doesn't miss a beat.

She now sees Margaux in a newer, brighter light, and she doesn't hold back. "I've seen the likes of you in the camps. A *kapo*. You think you're so superior. A bully. Dangling bread for favors. You're a Jew, aren't you? Perhaps a half Jew. I can tell. You grow up during the war—you know these things. You should be ashamed. And I know this because I was once a *kapo* too. I was forced to become one to survive." Lilian's voice is shrill. "I was pretty once too. Prettier than you. But the difference is, I did what I did *only* to make Franz Dassel's privileged life miserable. I spent my life making him pay for killing my family." She points at Jules. "I liked her mother right away. Did you know that she sent me a gift after meeting me, to thank me? And it wasn't just a gift. It meant something. But you wouldn't understand that, would you?" She wags her finger between Margaux's eyes, like a witch about to cast a spell. Margaux flinches, takes a step backward. "I will tell you exactly where the painting is located, but you are going to give this young lady whatever she wants in return. You're going to free that mother. Do you understand me?"

Margaux nods, and Jules knows she is lying. She intends to give Jules exactly what she thinks she deserves.

"It's there . . ." Lilian says, staring off in the distance as though *Woman on Fire* were materializing before her eyes. "In the basement at the house—where the nightmare began. Franz gave it to me when I left him. He begged for me to stay. The only thing that stayed in that godforsaken house was that cursed painting. I hated it, but I couldn't destroy it. It kept my father alive and gave him joy. Franz never knew . . ." She laughs with the deliciousness of a treasured sly memory. "But the painting isn't yours. Don't fool yourself. It's mine. And I decide who gets it."

"It's at the Dassel house?" Margaux raises a brow, not understanding, not knowing the history.

"Ask her." Lilian gestures to Jules. "She gets it. The painting is for her—not you. I didn't like you from the second you walked in." She reaches for Jules's hand and clasps it between her cold, bluish fingers. "The bench . . ." She points to the seat beneath her. "In a world without meaning, I will never forget that."

My mother was right, Jules thinks, with tears in her eyes. *Like always.* Her mother insisted they gift Lilian their winnings from the casino in Baden-Baden. The next day on their way back to the airport, they stopped at the nursing home and spoke to the director. They said that the money should be used for a beautiful bench near Lilian's beloved tree . . . that it would have her name engraved on it and always be known as the Lilian Baum Dassel bench.

Just before they leave her, Jules turns one last time, and her eyes meet Lilian's. But differently this time. They are less scared; more calculating. Lilian, a woman who has lived life distrusting humans, is a reader of eyes. They have always told her the whole story, the truth in a blink. This girl will never go down without a fight. She met her type in the camps too. Usually, that girl didn't survive her defiant nature, but she gave others hope that while the body may be tortured, the human spirit can't be broken. *No matter what.*

FORTY-FIVE

THE GRUNEWALD FOREST, BERLIN

THE FLIGHT FROM Baden-Baden was short—less than two hours to Berlin Brandenburg Airport, followed by a twenty-minute drive to the Grunewald Forest. Jules stares out the car window as they slowly approach the Dassel *Schloss* in the middle of the forest.

Timbered and dense with birch and pine, the three-story monstrosity covered in a thin layer of snow looks like a haunted hunting lodge. Overhead, the sky is a dreary, muted gray, as though someone has taken an eraser to it. No clouds, no sun, just gloom. Dread overwhelms Jules as her breath fogs the window. This is where *Woman on Fire* has been hiding for decades. No wonder it has never been found. Who'd want to come here? Nobody says a word as the car crawls up the long, winding pebbled driveway. Each tire rotation grinds and scrapes through Jules's body. Staring at the backs of her captors' heads, she grips the edge of the leather back seat, clenching her teeth as they park. *I'm going to die here.*

"What a nightmare," Margaux comments to the driver, the

same guy from Miami with the buzz cut and oversized eyes, translucent like a winter's lake. Jules notices a small letter M crudely shaved into the back of his scalp. That wasn't there in Miami. *M for Margaux?* She focuses on the choppy letter—anything to steady her breathing.

"I think it's cozy," he says.

"You would." Margaux turns around and eyes Jules with a grim smile. "Not quite Baden-Baden, is it?"

Jules says nothing. The last thing she wants is to feed the beast and give her the satisfaction.

Margaux refreshes her lipstick in the passenger side mirror then checks her gun. Lipstick—what the hell? "Did you bring me what I asked?" Margaux asks the driver.

"Of course." He hands her a small tool kit and a large flashlight. Lilian told them that the painting is buried inside the basement wall and to use a hidden stairwell along the west side of the house to get inside. Margaux puts the tool kit and flashlight into her large bag, gets out of the car, and signals Jules with a snap-snap of her fingers to do the same.

She sidles up to Jules. "Apparently, no one lives here except the caretakers—a senile husband and wife—and they're at church. I do my homework too."

Clearly, someone is doing the homework for her. Jules watches as Margaux carefully places the gun inside the back of her jeans, then conceals the weapon with her jacket. "If anyone is here or stops us, keep your mouth shut," she says.

Margaux then sticks her head inside the opened car window. "Take the car and go park somewhere where you won't be seen. So many trees—shouldn't be hard. I will call you when I'm ready. Do not come before you get word. Got it, Martin?"

M for Martin. Jules also notes that Margaux says *when I'm ready*, not *when we're ready*.

Her heart beats wildly as she trudges silently alongside Margaux toward the back of the estate on a plowed path between a dense brush of trees and bushes, until they find the hidden stairwell covered in thick ivy and debris. Margaux takes out a Swiss Army knife and hacks her way through it, then easily picks the lock. The door hinges and moans when she opens it. Jules's stomach lurches as they enter the dark, dank basement. Margaux shines the flashlight all around the large cellar. It looks like a molded crypt filled with spiderwebs casing old furniture and boxes. Jules feels sick picturing a young Lilian, who was terrified of spiders, forced to hide here.

"The old lady said the painting was on the far-left side, just past the furnace. Nailed into the wall. Six nails, three in two rows. She was very specific," Margaux says as Jules breathes heavily near her, eyeing the gun now sticking out of her jeans. *One reach and she could grab it.*

"Stop breathing down my back—you're like an animal. Step back." Margaux tugs on a hanging string, and a dim overhead bulb barely lights up the space. She points to the wall across the room. The paneled siding. Six nails, three in two rows. Just as Lilian described. Jules swallows hard as Margaux pushes her forward.

"Take this and pull out the nails." She hands Jules a hammer from the tool kit, removes the gun, and aims it at her. "Do it quickly."

Breathing heavily, like an animal apparently—she can't help it—and shaking too, Jules removes the long, rusty nails one by one with the claws of the hammer, and they go flying. Nail number three catches onto her sweater. Margaux doesn't notice the landing, so Jules quickly shoves the stray nail deep into her waistband

and then immediately begins removing the fourth nail to keep Margaux's attention diverted. Once all the nails are removed, she glances at Margaux, who nods.

"Now the panels."

Jules pulls on the loose panels, so brittle that they break in her hand. She lets the pieces fall to the ground, stands back, and gasps. *Oh my God, it's in there*—rolled tightly, wrapped in a tarp. Jules steps aside for Margaux to see. Her eyes gleam like a jewel thief gazing upon an unguarded diamond. "Take it out carefully and give it to me."

The canvas is large—taller than Jules—and it's stuck, embedded between the soot and cobwebs. Jules coughs. It takes time and effort to remove the canvas. When she's done, she turns with it at her side and faces Margaux.

"Lay it down. Unroll it. I want to see it with my own eyes." She shines the flashlight over the canvas as Jules slowly unrolls it onto the dusty floor.

Woman on Fire reveals herself in all her glory. *Yes, it's me,* the colors proclaim. Despite decades in hibernation, the pigment is even brighter, stronger, and more intense than the fake. Both women look at each other, despising each other but awed by the extraordinary beauty displayed before them. Margaux stands over the painting and shines the light directly onto the barely perceptible signature blended into the bottom right-hand corner. "Ernst Engel. The looped L . . . that's correct. The bar of the T . . . the stroke points to the left." Her eyes become fever-bright and her face splits into a giddy smile. "Indicative of a left-handed signature. This is it. This is fucking it."

It doesn't belong to you. Jules feels light-headed, cold, and yet there's heat stinging at her cheeks. She thinks of Ellis, Dan, and

Adam—the first time they met in the cabin in Montana. *Her team.* Dan died for this painting. And Ellis . . . She hears Margaux pull back the hammer of the pistol. She looks up.

Jules eyes the gun with bated breath. "You're going to take the painting and leave me here to die, aren't you?"

The glow from the flashlight casts a ghostly pallor over Margaux's face. "You've got a better plan?"

Jules's gut wrenches. *It's now or never.* "Actually, I do."

Margaux laughs and the sound bounces off the walls. "I bet you do. But there's no happy ending here. Everything has gone exactly as planned. Your article was published today in the *Miami Herald.* The real painting is now in my hands. The fake will go to a museum, honoring my name." She stretches her arms wide as though prepping for a curtain call. "Villain takes all."

Make it a game. Make her play. "Actually, villain may take nothing," Jules gambles. The silence in the room is deafening.

"What the hell are you talking about?"

Jules's voice shakes, but she tries to control it. *String her along.* She takes a bold step closer, her voice strengthening. "When I was in high school, I worked on a story exposing a nationwide sex trafficking ring. I was used as bait. It was a success. Criminals were brought down, put in jail."

"Why should I give a damn?"

Jules sucks in the musty air. "Because I learned something on that story—something I've never forgotten." She thinks about Rick Janus—the Rick Janus *before* that night. "The lead journalist told me, 'No matter what you do, no matter how big or small a story is, *always* have backup.' Meaning a backup recorder." Jules waits for that to sink in.

Margaux's jaw drops. "What are you talking about? I turned

off your phone at the hotel and took my recorder back in Miami. You're bluffing."

"You did, but you missed my trusty old backup in Chicago." Jules's heart is slamming inside her chest. Her life depends on this. "It was in my bag, in a side pocket, and it recorded everything. Your admission of murder and stealing Geisler's collection. Your words—not mine." Despite the fear spreading like wildfire through her body, Jules sees the color draining from Margaux's face and knows she's gotten to her. A beat of silence drums between them. "Let me put this in terms you can understand. If I go down, we all go down."

"Goddamn bitch." Margaux whacks Jules across the head with the barrel of the gun. Jules falls backward and feels the throbbing pain. But she picks herself up, emboldened, and presses her hand against her bleeding head. *Keep going. You've got her. Buy time.*

"There's more . . ." she continues. "You tapped into everything, right? My phone, my laptop, my home, my mother's office. You cornered me—I give you that. But the one thing you forgot, no surprise—is the human connection. Because you're *not* human."

Her resounding declaration comes from a place deep within, unmoored with nothing left to lose. "The backup recorder is already in the hands of a journalist at my newspaper. But I didn't just leave it at that. I backed up my backup. I also wrote the *real* story by hand—all of it—not the lies published today. Yes, by hand. *Old-school.* If anything happens to me . . . well, you know how it goes. Bad news always makes page one." Jules is bleeding profusely down the side of her face but ignores it. "Picture the headline: 'Margaux de Laurent, murderer and art thief . . .'"

Margaux cocks the trigger.

Jules holds her breath. Every inch of her begins to quake, but she fights through it. "We can strike a deal," she says. "I can stop what I've already put into motion. Your call."

"I don't strike deals." But Margaux hasn't pulled the trigger either.

"Set my mother free. Give this painting to Ellis Baum, and—"

"There's more?" Margaux laughs hard. But she's playing—hooked—still in the game. "Out of curiosity, what do I get in return?"

Jules meets Margaux's hardened gaze. "You keep your reputation. The truth is buried." *For now*, Jules thinks. *Just for now. Cutting a deal with a murderer breaks all the rules. But sometimes there are exceptions, Dan. Sometimes rules need to be broken. If it means surviving. If it means bringing Ellis back his painting . . .*

"The story you want the world to know is already published," Jules tells her. "Here's your chance to do the right thing for once. I don't know if you're afraid of death—but I do know that you are afraid of exposure—and, even more than that, afraid of losing."

Margaux presses the gun to Jules's temple. "I don't lose. Ever. I always win."

And in that moment—the space between—just before Margaux pulls the trigger, Jules plunges the rusty nail deep into the woman's neck with all her might, all her rage, all her pent-up emotion.

Margaux howls as the blood gushes, and her gun goes off. She falls backward to the cement floor. The bullet rips past Jules's shoulder, skimming her shirt and taking off the top layer of skin with it. She feels the razor-sharp burn, but it's a near miss. Margaux tries desperately to pull out the lodged nail, but it seems to have hit an artery. Blood is spurting everywhere. In the dim

light, Jules's eyes blur as she, too, falls to the ground. *Her head.*
Something sharp is ripping at her back, claws digging into her
skin. She reaches around for it, and with what little strength she
has left, she swings it, then plunges the hammer deep into Margaux's thigh before she can reclaim the gun. Using all her weight,
Jules digs the claws into the woman's skin as hard as she can. For
Dan, for Adam, for Ellis, for her mother, for Anonymous Girl.

Margaux, hemorrhaging, cries out in pain. "The deal." Her
breath is shallow, staccato. "My grandfather . . . save his name,
my galleries—and I will give you what you want."

Jules moves toward her with one arm, crawling like a
wounded soldier in a jungle. Her shoulder burns and she can't
stop the bleeding from her head. She wills her voice steady. "Free
my mother now. That's the only deal left."

She grabs the gun from the floor and reaches for Margaux's
bag, pulls out her phone, and takes Margaux's limp hand and
presses her thumbprint into it and unlocks it. She scans the messages but can barely make out the names.

"Wyatt . . . Wyatt." Margaux struggles.

Jules's head is spinning. "Siri—call Wyatt," she yells. *Damn
it, Siri, just do it right for once.* The phone rings, and Jules puts the
phone on speaker and silently prays. *Please, God, let her be okay.*

"Margaux." A man answers on the first ring.

Jules aims the gun. Margaux, her voice weakened, shouts
feebly into the phone. "Let the mother go. Get out now—we're
busted. Caught. Get out of there!"

Jules prays that that was enough to save her mother. Her head
is throbbing unbearably, but she manages, "The other paintings—
where are Geisler's stolen paintings?" *For Dan.* The story.

"My grandfather first . . . promise me." Margaux can't camouflage the beg inside her voice for the only person who ever really cared for her.

"I will protect his name no matter what," Jules vows. "Where are the paintings?"

Margaux is barely breathing now. "Correns. The vault . . . Promise me!" she cries out from a place that isn't human.

"I promise," Jules repeats as Margaux's breath rattles, stalls, then stops completely. Jules heaves a heavy sigh of relief, then the fear creeps in. *She's gone, dead . . . I killed her.*

Reaching for Margaux's phone, pressing the dead woman's thumbprint onto it once again, Jules then taps in 112, the emergency number. *"Emergency!"* she cries into the phone. "Help me!"

Trying desperately to ride out the excruciating pain, Jules glimpses Margaux lying there with the nail sticking out of her bloody neck like a dartboard. She eyes the door on the far side of the room. Miles away. She must get herself and the painting out of here before Martin the driver gets suspicious and decides to check things out and finish the job. She'll hide in the forest until help arrives—if it arrives. There's no other option. Jules struggles to drag her wounded body toward the closest wall and use it as leverage to stand, but her legs won't support her. She leans back against the wall to catch her breath and spots the flashlight on the ground shining across the floor. She follows the path of the long, bright beam . . . to the painting.

She braces herself in disbelief.

Margaux's blood has seeped onto the canvas and bled across the entire bottom half. The deep crimson fluid has fused into the fiery swirls of blue, coral, gold, and scarlet, creating an even richer, more dynamic inferno of color and texture. She glances again at Margaux's body on the cold cement. She was right. She doesn't ever lose. She's had the final word. Her blood, her signature, will be marked on *Woman on Fire* forever. She won.

Dazed and disoriented, Jules slides down the wall to the ground, crawling across it toward the painting just as she hears an ambulance sounding off in the distance and, even closer, the frenetic grind of a car's tires as it makes its getaway.

FORTY-SIX

MANHATTAN

E LLIS HEARS THEM entering his hospital room, Jules whispering to Adam to walk ahead of her, saying that she needs a moment to collect herself before she sees him. *Him*, Ellis thinks, meaning *me*. That's the thing—when one sense falters, another heightens. His sight is now gone, but his hearing has sharpened as though he were a young man again. As if the sounds of the world were still his for the taking.

Jules stands inside the room now, next to the door. Ellis feels her presence. He imagines what she sees. A lump of what was once a man who ruled the world of fashion, who'd walk into a room and have conversations stop. A man with a hidden past. No longer. Now he's this.

Adam came yesterday and read him word for word Jules's front-page story, which made international headlines. All of Ellis's past has been revealed . . . beginning with his mother's murder at the hands of the Nazis, then his coming to this country as a war refugee, the foster homes, his rise to become the world-renowned shoe designer, and, of course, his umbilical connection to Ernst Engel's last known masterwork. Margaux de Laurent's crimes have been exposed—murder, kidnapping, and greed. Even the whereabouts of the Geisler treasure trove have been revealed, and finally, Dan Mansfield's reputation is restored—he is no longer a man who died by his own addictions, but rather a man, a celebrated journalist, who died following a story. And the tiny victory that Ellis secretly relishes: Griffin Freund will be going to jail for peddling Nazi-looted art. *And the painting . . .* His mother is on her way home.

"Jules," he calls out to her. "Is it really true?"

"Yes, Ellis," she laughs, now at the foot of his bed. But it's not a laugh. He's been hearing that same sound all week. It's a laugh designed for a sick, dying person. Forced, trying too hard. "It's true."

Ellis suddenly feels his grandson's strong fingers lace through his. He squeezes Adam's hand tightly. The boy has been here practically every day this week. Everyone he loves has been coming in and out, a revolving door of those paying their last respects, saying goodbye . . . just in case. His wife, his daughters, his granddaughters, his favorite employees, Paul his driver, and yes, even Henri, who told him in vivid detail how he met with the police and gave them all the information he's uncovered about Griffin Freund over the past month. Freund would brag to him about his crooked clients, the stolen art he's sold them. Ellis doesn't want to know the rest, the sordid details swirling inside his head . . . Did Henri sleep with Freund to get that bedside information? *I've missed you,* Henri said when they were alone. *Every single day. And I'm going to miss you every day that you're gone.*

Beautiful Henri. *It is enough.*

"Ellis," Jules says again, interrupting his thoughts. "The painting . . . it's not on its way. It's here. I brought her to you."

This girl. Dan would be so proud. *Don't cry,* he tells himself. *They didn't come to see an old man weep—they came to bring you the joy of reuniting with your mother.* In the distance, he hears the clomp of footsteps approaching the room. And then, a harsher reality sets in. He places his hand on his heart to prevent it from falling out. *My mother is here . . . but I won't be able to see her.*

"Don't worry. Those men are security," Adam reassures him. "We just want to make sure that we will never lose the painting again."

My boy, Ellis thinks, *it's the girl, isn't it? That's why you're filled with life and not brooding about. She has a way about her . . .* He hears the unrolling of the painting near where Jules is standing. He can't hold back any longer. "I won't be able to see her. My mother . . ." he laments as Jules reaches for his hand.

"She's here now, Ellis. That's what matters. Give me your hand. You're going to feel her." Her voice is tender, maternal— just like when she flew back with him from Berlin after that meeting with Stefan Dassel. "What is it that Ernst Engel once said? 'Art is not what you see, but how it makes you feel.'"

As the tears stream silently down Ellis's face, Adam and Jules prop him up so that he faces the painting that he cannot see. The security guards reposition the canvas horizontally across the bed, over Ellis's blanketed legs. Adam takes his grandfather's hand, and together they trace the painting from top to bottom. "It's her hair, Grandfather . . . envision the yellow. Gold like sunshine. Do you remember its scent?"

"Yes, like flowers." Ellis squeezes his eyes, picturing his mother brushing her long blond tresses in the oval vanity mirror.

"Her eyes are blue. Not just any blue, but like the sea at five p.m.," Adam says softly. "Picture it."

"Yes, yes, I see it." And it's true. In Ellis's mind he sees it all right there in front of him—his mother sitting on the bed next to him, stroking his head after he had a bad dream.

Jules takes his other hand and moves it down along the curvature of his mother's torso into the blaze of fire engulfing her. "Can you feel the colors, Ellis? The passion? The flames are crimson, blue, gold, green, orange . . ." Her voice trips, knowing Margaux's dried blood is now mixed in. "Even violet. Ernst Engel captured it all."

"Yes, Jules, yes."

"Ellis," she continues tenderly, "the painting is going to stay here with you. She will watch over you. You can't see her, but you will feel her presence. Until . . ." She stops herself. *Until.*

Ellis's frail hand clutches Jules tightly, like a baby's grip on a parent's finger. "Thank you for bringing her back to me." He visualizes his brave, beautiful mother that very last day . . . a small helpless boy in the window watching her being paraded in the street in her favorite dress and high heels, the walk of death, to the cruel sounds of collective laughter. The soldiers. All those people—many of his neighbors and local shopkeepers—laughing and jeering. And he couldn't save her. He couldn't protect her then.

"She is safe. Finally." Ellis's body quiets, then gradually stills. *And now, I can go.*

EPILOGUE

E VERYONE CAME. ADAM had them all flown in for Ellis's
memorial ceremony at the Anika Baum headquarters in
Midtown. Jules scans the familiar faces, standing together in the
decked-out lobby to honor the extraordinary life of Ellis Baum.
The entire Baum family, Henri, all the Anika Baum employees,
famous designers and celebrities from around the world, Bram
Bakker, her mother, Louise, even Owen her doorman came to
pay homage not only to the unforgettable man but to his story—
and to *his painting*.

Jules's gaze rests on Owen. Her "guardian angel" safeguarded her story that horrific day when she learned her mother
had been kidnapped. She knew that Margaux had access to all her
electronic devices but not to her pad of paper—a reporter's most
basic item. The handwritten sheets of paper that she slipped to
Owen told the whole story—*the truth*. She discreetly passed them
to him in an envelope, careful to avoid the lobby cameras, while
on her way to bring Margaux the research. Inside the envelope

were explicit instructions for Owen to deliver all the information to Louise at the newspaper. She also gave him Bram Bakker's secure line and the name of the investigator on Dan's case, should anything happen to her or her mother. She smiles to herself. The instructions were accompanied by a frenetic rainbow of sticky notes—her specialty. Old-school journalism. Jules knew that Owen, a tough guy from the South Side, would know exactly what to do, and she trusted him implicitly.

Only one person in the room is sitting. Jules reaches down and gently touches the shoulder of perhaps the most important guest who came to pay her respects. Lilian Dassel with her fluffy white cumulous cloud hair, her strong will, and her animated eyes. She came for him, for her illegitimate famous brother and for the painting. Johanna Lutz, the convalescent home director, who accompanied Lilian to New York, told Jules just before the ceremony began that Lilian was determined to make the arduous journey because "The damn painting is finally doing something right. I want to see it with my own eyes." They shared a good laugh.

Adam leans in, his lips lightly grazing Jules's cheek. "It's time."

Nodding, Jules releases her grip on Lilian's shoulder and walks slowly up to the microphone. She stares at the glass-encased painting behind her, which would have its permanent home here as the centerpiece in the Anika Baum building. "Good evening, everyone . . . I'm Jules Roth. I'm a journalist and a friend of Ellis Baum and his family. I'm here because of my mentor, the brilliant Daniel Mansfield, who taught me that seeking the truth is not about instant gratification. It's a process—an ongoing journey—that begins with the first account of an event and builds over time to finding answers. There are rules, and there are no shortcuts." She swallows the lump forming in her throat. "This moment would have meant everything to Dan, who sought to bring this magnificent painting back to his close friend Ellis, but sadly lost his own life while doing so." She pauses and glances upward briefly as tears fill her eyes. "Tonight, I'm going to tell you a story about a painting. A work of art that touched so many lives, with an extraordinary life of its very own . . ."

When Jules finishes, when the claps finally die down, she points to the large gold plaque next to the glass-encased painting and reads it aloud:

WOMAN ON FIRE BY ERNST ENGEL

1938 BERLIN

IN HONOR OF THOSE ARTISTS WHO LOST THEIR LIVES AND THEIR BRUSHES IN NAZI GERMANY

IN LOVING MEMORY OF ANIKA BAUM—MOTHER & MUSE, ELLIS BAUM, ARNO BAUM, AND DANIEL MANSFIELD

IN APPRECIATION OF LILIAN BAUM DASSEL FOR SAFE-GUARDING THIS MASTERPIECE

IN RECOGNITION OF CHARLES DE LAURENT, FOR HIS VALIANT EFFORTS TO SAVE MODERN ART FROM THOSE WHO TRIED TO DESTROY IT.

Only Jules knows that the flames of fire on the canvas are covered in Margaux de Laurent's blood—*her signature*—a secret Jules will take with her to the very end. She knows she is breaking the rules once again but recalls her mother's words in Baden-Baden: *Some truths are best remained buried.*

As Jules slowly descends the podium, Adam comes up to her smiling sheepishly. "You were wonderful. Come with me. I have something for you."

She looks around at the clamoring crowd. "We can't just skip out of here."

"Yes, actually, we can." He gestures to a discreet elevator in the far corner of the large lobby. "Just for a few minutes. No one will notice."

She points to the circle of journalists making their way toward her. "I think pretty much *everyone* will notice."

"Let them. We'll be back." He takes her hand, smiling mysteriously as he leads her past two security guards, who nod back at him. This was obviously prearranged.

"The penthouse suite? Really, Adam?" She blushes as the elevator doors close behind them.

He puts his arms around her and kisses her. "I wish . . . but it's not what you think."

They step out of the elevator into a narrow corridor, which leads directly into Ellis Baum's office. The short hallway is a showcase filled with celebrity and VIP photos—hundreds of red-carpet shots of prominent women in their precious custom-made Anika Baums. But Ellis's office décor is the opposite. No fanfare, no braggadocio, just an understated glimpse into the man himself.

Looking around, Jules feels like she just parachuted into Ellis's personal snow globe. Everything is so white and clean and elegantly Zen. The room is dimly lit, and the only accents of color are his family photos on a corner credenza and samples of his favorite shoes filling one long wall like a mural of shoe art. Behind his massive desk, the entire skyline is encapsulated inside his windows, and Jules can feel the glitter and pulse of the lit-up city. When she turns around, Adam stands before her, holding a box with an oversized golden bow on top.

"This is for you," he says shyly, presenting it. "It was the last thing my grandfather said to me . . . Well, not *the* last." He averts his gaze, as though gathering his nerve. "He told me: 'Give these to Jules, and write down what I have to say, young man' . . . and then his very last words to me were 'Don't let that girl go.'"

Jules feels her skin begin to tingle. "I presume I'm *that* girl." She laughs and takes the gift, her heart skipping a beat as she opens the card:

> For a special young woman, a fighter and truth-seeker who is both practical and dazzling. I will never forget my very first shoes . . . or my last. Thank you, Jules.—Ellis

She looks up at Adam, tears filling her eyes. His last pair of shoes. *For her.*

Adam squeezes her arm gently. "Remember when I told you that they found my grandfather on the floor in the studio of his very first store? Of all his stores, that one was always his favorite. Well, apparently, he was in the middle of designing these shoes in the basement . . ." Adam shakes his head as though picturing his grandfather at work. His voice trembles slightly. "His chief designer finished them just before my grandfather passed. Of course, it's no surprise that he refused to die until he gave his final approval. I'm convinced that waiting for these shoes to be completed is what kept him alive the last few weeks." He gestures to the box. "Open it."

Self-conscious of his gaze on her, Jules slowly opens the box and pulls out Ellis Baum's final creation. The tears now rolling down her cheeks, she holds up the exquisite black stilettos with golden outer soles. Unlike all of Ellis's other designs, these heels are not high and sleek. They are sturdy and stylishly practical. The heels are embedded with a splash of tiny diamonds and one lone microscopic sapphire at its center—her birthstone. She stares at the birthstone. "How did he know . . ."

"He clearly had a crush on you." Adam tenderly pulls back a rogue curl that has fallen over her eyes. "That was my grandfather, an artisan—every detail mattered." He reaches out and grazes his forefinger over the birthstone. "But there's more . . . look inside the shoe."

She holds the shoe up to the light, peers into the lining at the engraved script, copied from Ellis's own handwriting:

The Jules—a woman on fire.

She hugs the shoes tightly to her chest, against her heart, as if the heels were Ellis, embracing both the man and his artistry.

Gently peeling the gift from her hands, Adam places the shoes on his grandfather's empty desk. He then pulls Jules toward him in the same urgent way he did that first night when she returned to Chicago with a stitched shoulder and bruises across her forehead. She and her mother were held together for questioning in the U.S. Embassy in Paris before being released to return home. Adam was waiting at the gate with two police officers when they deplaned at O'Hare Airport.

"By the way . . ." he says. "I know you're going to have a thousand job offers after all this, but don't ever leave like that again, running after a story—no word, no warning." He gives her a long, hard look. "I'm serious."

His words sear through her. She knows exactly what it's like to worry so much that you can barely function. "I can't promise that I'm not going to run after a story . . . but I will work on the *worrying-you* part." She hopes this eases his fears, but they both know she will never stop seeking the truth, getting to the heart of the matter. Reporting is breathing for her. It's not a choice—it's her lifeline.

"I'm very proud of what you do. I just, you know . . ." Adam shuffles his feet against the blond hardwood floor, then looks up at her with those shimmering emerald eyes.

"I know." She lightly touches the scruff along his jaw. *No more cowboy antics*, she warns herself. *There are rules . . .*

A mischievous smile spreads across the horizon of Adam's face as he leans in to kiss her, and Jules remembers seeing him that very first time as he stood in the doorway of his cabin, a handsome loner recovering from a dark past, with his torn jeans, rock band T-shirt, and shy demeanor. She wondered then what he was thinking, and now she knows. He wasn't thinking—he was painting her in his head as she was writing the story in hers—taking in the tiniest of details and saving them all for later.

ACKNOWLEDGMENTS

I T'S EARLY EVENING. No one is home—just me, my laptop, and a tall glass of chardonnay. I'm reflecting on all the wonderful people in my life who helped make this book a reality, who gave me the space to write and embrace my passion once again. My deepest gratitude, as always, goes to my family first, especially to my incredibly supportive, generous, and loving husband, David. My girls, my three beautiful muses, Noa, Maya, Maya, and Izzi (my furry sidekick), you are my greatest loves, the most important chapter of all.

Every author needs her gladiator, the one who slays the dragons and fights the good fight. Stéphanie Abou with Massie & McQuilkin Literary, my badass agent, I'm so grateful for your belief in my work, your expert opinion, and your friendship. I treasure our Friday email/Shabbat connection.

HarperCollins/Harper Perennial has been a spectacular home for my novels, and my editor, Sara Nelson, is probably the best in the biz. Sara, you were right (of course). Those scene changes that you just knew I'd have a hard time letting go of turned out to be exactly what the book needed. So glad I listened. Your instinct is always spot-on and so appreciated. Mary Gaule, thank you for your edits and support. I relish our mutual love of pop culture (hello, Meghan Markle bun on the cover). Much gratitude to my publicist, Kristin Cipolla, and marketing guru, Lisa Erickson. Huge thanks to my production editor, Suzy Lam, who always raises the "Barr" (stet. Hahaha). I'm so grateful for you and your team, Martha Cipolla (copy editor) and Jane Cavolina (proofreader). And the Art Department's Andrea Guinn, I couldn't love this cover more. It gives me serious Nancy Drew vibes, and everybody knows she is my favorite literary character and the reason why I love to write suspense.

Ann-Marie Nieves of Getred PR—*you rock, Mama.* You get me, answer my late-night emails, deal with my type-A concerns, and always find a way to make shit happen. Steve Franzken, my web designer, I appreciate all your beautiful work. Given that I'm an insomniac and you work during the middle of the night, we are quite the team. And to the Current Agency, thank you for guiding this old-school writer (still stuck in her '70s bell-bottoms) into the world of TikTok and Gen Z.

So much gratitude to my large family for their unconditional love and support. My siblings and siblings-in-law are my best friends, my go-to peeps. They ALWAYS show up, always have my back, which makes me the luckiest big sis in the world. And yes, HUGE "Auntie Brag" here—I'm blessed to have the most amazing tribe of nieces and nephews. Special thanks to my parents for their support, and an extra squeeze to my in-laws for always treating me like a daughter and always promoting my work all over town.

My girls, my history: Lisa Eisen, Lisa Newman, Julie Kreamer, Rebecca Fishman, Randi Gideon, Amy Klein, Dina Kaplan, Leslie Kaufman, Bonnie Rochman, Malina Saval, Sharon Feldman, Marjorie Pick, Staci Chase, Lauren Geleerd, Cathie Levitt, Julie Samson, Carla Kim, Melissa Van Pelt, Laurel Hansen, and Ellen Katz. Until the last page, ladies . . . *love you all.*

My book world tribe is filled with incredibly talented authors, bookstagrammers, reviewers, bloggers, podcasters, and librarians. I am so blessed to have a wide network of literary friends who promote and lift one another daily. I always say, "There's room on the shelf for all of us." A special shout-out to Rochelle "YM" Weinstein, Francie Arenson Dickman (my café writing partner in crime), Lauren "Good Book Fairy" Margolin, Andrea Peskind Katz, Elyssa Friedland, Amy Poeppel, Jamie "SCBG" Rosenblit, Jamie Brenner, Sam Bailey, Zibby Owens, Jenna Blum, Courtney Marzilli, Patricia Sands, Sally Koslow, Abby Stern, Renee Rosen, Alison Hammer, Kristy Harvey, Ali Wenzke, Kim Gabriel, Amy Blumenfeld, Jackie Friedland, Kerry Lonsdale, Orit Merlin, Hank Phillippe Ryan, Heather Webb, Hannah Mary McKinnon, Leslie Hooton, and my Women Write pod. And to the "Fab Four"—so grateful for your gorgeous book blurbs igniting *Woman on Fire*'s journey: Mary Kubica, Alyson Richman, Fiona Davis, and Kristin Harmel.

I raise my glass to my beta readers, the talented trio who first glimpsed the manuscript in progress: Bruce Balonick (my lucky charm), Beth Richard (my little sis and forever bestie), and Lisa Eisen (my BFF armed with that evil red pen and huge heart).

To my readers both here and abroad (with a special *todah rabah* to Yaffa Simon-Tov, Hila Shapir, and Yediot Books, Israel), bookstores (particularly my North Shore favorite indies: The Book Stall, Book Bin, Lake Forest Book Store, and Barbara's Bookstore), book clubs, social media book salons, book fests, libraries, and the Jewish Book Council; none of this could have happened without your book love and support.

Woman on Fire begins in Art Basel, Miami, and Alexandra Newman, your insight into the art world is immeasurable. I can't thank you enough for walking me through Art Basel and sharing key details that add so much color to the story. Corey Chase, yes, Adam Chase was named with your blessing. Arthur Brand, the fearless, renowned art detective based in Amsterdam, known as the "Indiana Jones of the art world," inspired my character Bram Bakker. My only regret is that my meeting with Arthur set for March 17, 2020, in Amsterdam was canceled due to COVID-19 travel restrictions. One day, I hope to hear his fascinating stories in person. His work—tracking down stolen art and returning beloved lost works to their legitimate owners—is courageous. Righting the wrongs of history is truly a mitzvah.

Of all the books and documents I pored over during the research stage of this book, I discovered this magnificent, comprehensive must-read: *Rogues' Gallery: The Rise (and Occasional Fall) of Art Dealers, the Hidden Players in the History of Art* by Philip Hook. This nonfiction page-turner is truly in a league of its own; historical and factual but reads like a thriller.

And finally, this writer cannot be without her café, her table in the corner. That Little French Guy in Highland Park, Illinois, with the perfect cappuccino and fresh-baked croissant every morning, keeps my creative engine fueled and fired up. *Merci beaucoup* to the whole crew.

ABOUT THE AUTHOR

Lisa Barr is the author of *Woman on Fire, The Unbreakables,* and the award-winning World War II historical thriller *Fugitive Colors,* which won the 2014 IPPY Gold Medal for Best Literary Fiction and first prize Opus Magnum Discovery Award at the Hollywood Film Festival. In addition, Lisa served as an editor for the *Jerusalem Post,* managing editor of *Today's Chicago Woman* and *Moment* magazine, and as an editor/reporter for the *Chicago Sun-Times.* Among the highlights of her career, Lisa covered the famous handshake at the White House between the late Israeli prime minister Yitzhak Rabin, the late PLO leader Yasser Arafat, and former president Bill Clinton. Lisa has been featured on *Good Morning America* and *Today* for her work as an author, journalist, and blogger. She lives in the Chicago area with her husband and three daughters (aka Drama Central).

WELBECK

PUBLISHING GROUP

Love books? Join the club.

Sign-up and choose your preferred genres to receive tailored news, deals, extracts, author interviews and more about your next favourite read.

From heart-racing thrillers to award-winning historical fiction, through to must-read music tomes, beautiful picture books and delightful gift ideas, Welbeck is proud to publish titles that suit every taste.

bit.ly/welbeckpublishing

WELBECK

ANDRE DEUTSCH

MORTIMER

MORTIMER

WELBECK

WOMAN ON FIRE

ALSO BY LISA BARR

The Unbreakables
Fugitive Colors

WOMAN ON FIRE

LISA BARR

WELBECK

First published in the UK in 2022 by Welbeck Fiction Limited,
an imprint of Welbeck Publishing Group
based in London and Sydney.
www.welbeckpublishing.com

A CIP catalogue record for this book is available from the British Library

Paperback ISBN: 978-1-80279-385-7
Ebook ISBN: 978-1-80279-386-4

Printed and bound by CPI Group (UK) Ltd., Croydon, CR0 4YY

10 9 8 7 6 5 4 3 2 1